HE

S

SWEETHEART

&

UNWRAPPING
HER ITALIAN DOC

BY
CAROL MARINELLI

MILLS
BOON

PLAYING THE PLAYBOY'S SWEETHEART

BY
CAROL MARINELLI

First published in Great Britain 2014
by Mills & Boon, an imprint of Harlequin (UK) Limited,
Eton House, 18-24 Paradise Road, Richmond, Surrey, TW9 1SR

© 2014 Carol Marinelli

ISBN: 978-0-263-90799-5

Dear Reader

I have especially enjoyed writing these two stories, because the first is set in summer and it's rather lovely to watch as Emily's little holiday break becomes rather more complicated—thanks to the very charming, very blond Hugh.

Then I got to take myself straight into winter and a lovely English Christmas, with Louise determined to enjoy it this year. She's rather cheeky, *very* flirty, and absolutely the last thing that brooding, incredibly sexy Anton needs right now.

Ho, ho, ho!

And in the midst of all that along came Alex and Jennifer, tap-dancing across the stage as I tried to write—more about them later!

I love my job!

Happy reading

Carol x

Carol Marinelli recently filled in a form where she was asked for her job title and was thrilled, after all these years, to be able to put down her answer as 'writer'. Then it asked what Carol did for relaxation. After chewing her pen for a moment Carol put down the truth—'writing'. The third question asked: 'What are your hobbies?' Well, not wanting to look obsessed or, worse still, boring, she crossed the fingers on her free hand and answered 'swimming and tennis'. But, given that the chlorine in the pool does terrible things to her highlights, and the closest she's got to a tennis racket in the last couple of years is watching the Australian Open, I'm sure you can guess the real answer!

PROLOGUE

HUGH LINTON CAME with a warning attached.

Emily hadn't even put on her scrubs for her first shift as theatre nurse at The Royal—a busy London hospital—before being told by Louise, one of the other nurses, that the surgical registrar who was operating this Monday morning was, by anyone's standards, a heartbreaker.

'Is Candy very upset?' Louise asked a colleague as she tucked her long blonde hair into her hat.

'What do you think?' came the response. 'I just saw her in the canteen, crying her eyes out with a little crowd gathered!' She smiled at Emily. 'I'm Annie.'

'Hi, Annie,' Emily said, but Annie was already back talking to Louise.

'Mind you,' Annie continued, 'I don't get why she's carrying on so much—surely everyone should know that if you go into any sort of a relationship with Hugh it's going to be fleeting at best, heartbreak at worst.'

'Watch yourself.' Louise winked at Emily.

'No need to,' Emily said, 'because he shan't be breaking mine!' But though she had laughed as she'd said it, in fact she wasn't joking.

Emily loathed anything remotely fleeting and no

one would get close enough to break her heart. She had decided that many, many years ago.

Still, she was somewhat sideswiped by Hugh Linton's exceedingly good looks because when he first walked into the operating theatre Emily found out first-hand what the word 'presence' meant.

He was very tall and his hair was as blond as Emily's was dark. He had the greenest eyes that she had ever seen and his voice was deep and clear, the type who rarely needed to repeat themselves. His smile, as he chatted with Louise and then caught Emily's eye, did make a slight blush spread across Emily's cheeks and confirmed what she already knew—Hugh Linton was *far* from her ideal man!

'Morning, everyone!' Alex, the senior consultant, came in, having just been in to have a last word with the patient before surgery. 'It's going to be a long one,' he warned as he went off to scrub.

The operation was for the removal of an abdominal tumour in a twenty-six-year-old man. It was a complex tumour and before the operation commenced and the patient was brought in, Alex explained why he was doing open surgery as opposed to keyhole, which was his speciality. Then there was time for a little chat.

'I've already heard about your weekend, Hugh,' Alex said, as he was helped into his gown and gloves. 'I've heard about it from several sources, in fact, and so I don't need to hear it again.'

Hugh just grinned.

All joking was cast aside, however, when the patient was opened up and the tumour was found to be worse than Alex had been expecting.

Emily was, this morning, the circulation nurse, a

part of which meant ensuring the operating field was uncontaminated as well as accounting for equipment. Emily loved most roles in Theatre but circulation or scrub nurse were her two favourites and today it was nice to watch how the surgeons worked from a distance, so she could know their nuances when she scrubbed in.

'Not good,' Alex said, once he had opened the patient and taken a good look around. 'We're going to be here for a few hours, Rory,' he said to the anaesthetist.

It was a very long and intricate operation but it went very smoothly, even with a difficult turn of events—though not for the patient. Instead, there was unexpected news for the chief surgeon.

'Alex, Jennifer is on the phone,' Louise said, and Emily watched as Alex paused and frowned.

'Bring the phone over to me.'

Louise held the phone to Alex's ear and Emily glanced over at Hugh, who was looking at his boss as he spoke to his wife—she had clearly asked not to be put through.

'Well, they're under my instructions to put you through if you call,' Alex said, and then listened for a moment. 'I'm here for a couple more hours at least,' Alex said, and then listened some more. 'Okay, darling, please keep me informed. I love you.'

When Louise turned off the phone Alex was quiet for a moment before revealing his news. 'Jennifer's up on the delivery ward.'

'When is she due?' Hugh asked.

'Not for another six weeks.' He carried on working. 'How long do fourth babies take, Louise?' he tossed out to the runner. 'Small ones?'

'Hopefully more than two hours.' Louise answered

his black humour with her own. 'I'm a midwife as well,' she explained to Emily.

Theatre was an intricate and complicated world.

Every swab was counted, every pause noted, every instrument's date of sterilisation checked, not a single blade or needle went unnoted—a seemingly seamless task but it was the black box of surgery and one that required a whole lot of effort from the first to the last in the room.

A small pause in proceedings ensued as Alex and Hugh had a drink of water and then re-gloved then they got back to work and Alex somehow did what he had to and concentrated on the patient.

There was no rushing.

For the young man on the table Alex Hadfield's work was his very best chance at life. Emily watched as Alex explained things to Hugh and carried on as if his wife wasn't in premature labour halfway down the corridor, but close to midday he looked over at Hugh.

'I can take it from here,' Hugh said, as Louise took a phone call.

'I have your wife on the phone,' Louise said, and Alex pulled of his gloves and took the phone and told Jennifer that he was on his way.

'Oi,' called Hugh as Alex walked off. 'Don't we get to know?'

But Alex was gone.

Hugh asked for a swab count before he closed, as was procedure.

Then he asked for another one.

Emily took no offence.

The operation had been interrupted, and she was also new.

Emily took absolutely no offence and counted again all the swabs and the instruments carefully.

It was her job to do so.

'Thanks,' Hugh said as, satisfied nothing was amiss, he started to close.

Lunch was *very* welcome but Emily found herself concentrating on more than her food when Hugh took a seat near her.

He smelt fantastic—somehow crisp even after hours spent operating—and his long outstretched legs were far too easy on the eye.

Oh, he was so far from ideal!

Emily's ideal man came with some very specific prerequisites—looks didn't matter, she would prefer that he was serious and that he didn't make her laugh too much.

Neither must Emily's perfect man imbue in her a sudden desire to get naked.

No, Emily's perfect man was perfectly nice if somewhat staid.

In her ideal world they would have sex on Saturdays, more out of obligation than necessity—occasionally on Tuesday if Emily was on a late shift the next day and there was nothing good on television.

'You're new?' Hugh said.

'Emily has been working here for a year now!' Louise, the nurse who had warned Emily about him in the changing room, quipped. 'How rude that you haven't noticed her before.'

It was just a small exchange, a teeny bit of fun, but Emily felt a slight flutter of unease as his green eyes told her that he certainly had noticed!

'Emily Jackson,' she said.

Hugh certainly had noticed her—from her pale blue

eyes to her creamy skin. He wanted to know if the dark curl that peeked from beneath her theatre hat came from long or short hair and Emily's soft Scottish accent also had him curious.

'How long have you been in London?' Hugh asked. 'It can be a bit daunting at first.' He was about to suggest that he could show her around perhaps when she interrupted him with a slightly wry smile.

'I guess it was at first but I've been living here for years now, so I'm completely undaunted.'

She had meant to shut him down but Hugh had merely smiled. 'Really?'

Let the flirting begin, his eyes said.

Except Emily refused to go there.

Quite simply, *he* daunted her.

Hugh took a phone call and his face broke into a smile. He offered his congratulations and then told everyone the good news. 'It's a little girl and her name is Josie and she's doing very well.'

'How much did she weigh?' Louise asked.

'I forgot to ask,' Hugh admitted, and then stood. 'I'd better go—a hernia repair awaits me.' He turned and smiled at Emily. 'It was nice to meet you.'

'Same,' Emily said, and she smiled but, and Hugh couldn't quite get it, there was something about her smile that he could not put his finger on. It was pleasant, friendly even and yet…he could not find the word.

The afternoon list flew by and Hugh was just about to head up to the wards to check on his postoperative patients when he found out about the hair beneath her theatre cap.

Emily's hair was long, thick, dark and curly. Without

the shapeless theatre scrubs Hugh also noticed a curvy figure dressed in jeans, a heavy jacket and long boots.

'See you,' Hugh said.

'Have a good night.' There was that smile again and Hugh found the word he was looking for.

Sparing.

It was an incredibly cost-effective smile—it did its job but no more than that.

Already he wanted more.

No doubt Emily had been warned about him, Hugh reasoned, because he had felt the coolness of her brush-off. Or perhaps she was already involved with someone?

Still, even with Emily's best efforts to deny that he moved her, the sparks flew between them whenever they were in Theatre together. So much so that at a Christmas work party a few weeks later Emily was relieved when Gina, an anaesthetist, offered her a lift back to her flat from the party, though she warned Emily that she was leaving in fifteen minutes.

With that deadline in mind, knowing she had a legitimate reason to leave soon, when Hugh offered to get Emily a drink she didn't refuse.

'Just a small one,' Emily said, handing him her glass. 'I'm going soon and I don't want to miss my lift.'

Hugh returned with her drink a short while later and an offer too. 'I can give you a lift if you want to stay a bit longer.'

Emily shook her head. 'I have to be up early—I'm going up to Scotland tomorrow.'

'Have you got family there?'

'My mum.' Emily nodded. 'And quite a bit of extended family too.'

'Do you have family here in London?'

Emily nodded again. 'When my parents broke up my dad moved to England...' Emily hesitated; she didn't want to remember that time, moving in with dad's girlfriend Katrina and her daughter Jessica. It actually hurt to recall those events so she hurriedly glossed over them. 'I used to come down a lot to visit.'

'How much?'

'Half the school holidays, but when I left school I moved permanently down here to do nursing.'

'I see.'

'You don't!' Emily rolled her eyes. 'Honestly, we'd be here till next week if I tried to explain it.'

'I'm fine with that.'

There was a sudden plummet in Emily's stomach as they moved deeper into conversation; she looked into very green eyes that, though smiling, for Emily spelt danger.

'So,' Hugh asked, 'will you be in Scotland for Christmas?'

'No.' Emily shook her head. 'I'm working, new girl and all that.'

She chose not to tell him that she preferred to work at Christmas. It was always a painful time. Whether she spent it at her mother's or father's, Emily always felt like a bit of a spare wheel. Her mum and second husband doted on Abby, their daughter together. As for her dad, he was now married to his latest—Donna—and was a father to one-year-old twins.

Yes, it was far too complicated to explain it all to Hugh.

'So what are you doing for Christmas?' Emily asked instead.

'I'll be at my parents',' Hugh said. 'My sister has just

had a baby, first grandchild…' He gave a teeny eye-roll. 'I'm to be on my best behaviour and not upset Kate.'

'Your sister?'

'Yep,' Hugh said.

'You don't get on?'

'We do get on,' Hugh corrected, 'usually.'

He was the easiest person she had ever spoken to and for Hugh it was the same. He had tried to talk to Alex yesterday about his sister Kate and had asked how Jennifer was doing, given that their babies had been born around the same time. Hugh had been told that Jennifer was coping beautifully, despite Josie being her fourth and prem.

Hugh had said nothing then about his concerns for his sister, though he voiced them easily now.

'I think she's got postnatal depression.' Hugh said to Emily what he hadn't to his boss. 'But I have no idea apparently.' Hugh sighed. 'At least, according to my mother, my father, my brother-in-law, oh, and Kate too.'

'It's difficult,' Emily said. 'I remember when Donna had the twins…' She faltered and Hugh noticed.

'Donna?'

'My dad's second wife.'

She had tried so hard not to go there but now that she had she told him a bit more. 'When they were born I had to help out a lot. I was ever so worried.' She thought for a moment about Hugh's situation. 'Can you try talking to her husband again?'

'I might.' Hugh nodded. 'What did your dad do?'

'Not much.' Emily gave a tight smile. She could hardly tell Hugh she had been worried that if things didn't improve, and quickly, that her dad would have been out of the door.

'So, what did you do?'

'I took her to see her GP,' Emily said. 'I rang them and explained my concerns and then made the appointment for her and took her. Things did pick up. It took a while, but they did.'

Yes, things had picked up. Emily had done everything she could to not fall in love with her two half-brothers, but getting up at night, bathing them, feeding them, of course she had.

'How is she now?'

Emily chose not to answer.

'I'd better go.'

'Emily?'

She didn't want to answer, she didn't want to say that, yes, while Donna was fine now, she wasn't so sure that the marriage was.

'Stay for a bit longer,' Hugh pushed.

She didn't want to, though, because she opened up too easily to him.

Fleeting.

She recalled Annie's words.

Heartbreak.

Neither of those did she need.

She wanted her perfect man—one that meant she could hold onto her heart.

Right now that heart was hammering in her chest and very possibly about to be set free if that lovely, sexy mouth moved just a few inches closer, which it was possibly about to do.

'I really do have to go...' Emily chose to play it safe.

'Why?'

'I told you—I don't want to miss my lift.'

'And I told you—I'm very happy to drive you home.'

Hugh had more than noticed Emily and had hoped to get to know her some more tonight.

In the weeks she had been at The Royal she had intrigued him—Emily was friendly yet distant at the same time, and not just with him. Yes, she chatted easily with her colleagues and there was no doubt she was an extremely efficient nurse yet, and Hugh couldn't quite put his finger on it, she held back, really revealing nothing.

Until tonight.

That small sliver of information about her parents had Hugh wanting to know more about Emily.

She was a curious girl, Hugh thought.

Something told him there was a lot more going on in that sensible head of hers and her cool exterior told Hugh that the full force of his charm would not be welcomed just yet.

Yes, his intention had been to take things very slowly until Gina called Emily's name.

'Emily!'

Hugh watched as she turned to the sound of her name but this time it was Hugh's stomach that plummeted as he realised that it was Gina who would be driving Emily home.

Just yesterday Hugh had voiced his concerns about Gina to Alex and then Mr Eccleston, the head of anaesthetics. The decision as to whether or not to speak with Gina's boss had been eating at him for weeks. Hugh had been through medical school with Gina—they were good friends and he had always looked out for her.

But he had to look out for the patients first.

He could not turn his back so had voiced his concerns and the truth was tonight he wasn't sure that Gina hadn't been drinking, or even if she was on something else.

All he knew now was that he could not let Emily get into a car with Gina and, given the delicate nature of his complaint, neither could he share his concerns with Emily. He instead chose to act on the undeniable sexual tension between them.

'*I'm* taking you home.'

His words were very decisive and Emily looked back at him. An alarm was ringing in her head, warning her to just walk away now, except there was something else signalling louder.

Instinct.

She had never been more aware of it. Simply, her instinct told her to accept the kiss that was nearing.

'Emily!' They could both hear Gina calling her name again, but this time it seemed to be coming from a very long way off.

She caught the fresh tang of him, a scent that had remained trapped in her senses since the first day they had met. Oh, where was her perfect man when she needed him? The one that didn't move her so.

Hugh lowered his head and his mouth brushed hers. Soft and warm, it made her own lips want to part like the Red Sea but she somehow held them closed. Except that meant she inhaled his scent, and the scent of Hugh was possibly more potent so she borrowed the wall behind her to lean on. His lips were more insistent now, nudging hers as his hands held her face, and finally their mouths commenced their first dance—a gentle dance at first to accustom themselves, then a playful dance that began to tease, but when their tongues met it was like an accelerant.

Hugh actually felt the shift. One minute they were

kissing and the next their mouths belonged to each other. The party disappeared, the only noise was them—cool to his words she was hot to his mouth, Hugh felt as if he'd tripped and found a portal as he held the passion that burned in his arms. His hands left her face and moved to her hips without thought and were made very welcome for her bottom left the wall and the press of her body was as suggestive as his.

He pulled back but only because to continue would have them on the edge of indecent. Emily could taste his breath, see his lips wet from hers and she wanted to be back there now, yet she resisted the call of her body and moved her hips away from him.

Oh, it wasn't that Hugh was bad that terrified her, it was that he was so, so good.

'I really do have to go.'

She moved to the side and slipped past, and Hugh watched as she walked off, both trying to get his breath back and trying to ignore the fact he had been dismissed. Then he smothered the smile that came to his lips when Louise told Emily that Gina had just gone. 'She said you looked busy.'

There was a flush on Emily's cheeks but it wasn't from embarrassment, it was from arousal by the man who was now by her side.

'Let's go.'

It could have been an awkward ride home except Emily knew that she was possibly approaching the ride of her life.

Never, in all her twenty-three years had a man detonated her the way Hugh had.

His hand was on her thigh as they drove and she took

no offence for hers was on his and it was suggestive down to her fingernails in a way she had never been before. The relief when he turned off the engine at the same time as he pulled up the handbrake had her snap off her seat belt in haste to return to his mouth.

'Emily…' His hand was up her skirt like two out-of-control teenagers and the spinning wheels in her head slowed as he halted. 'Not here.'

She was going to ask him in.

Sex.

Brilliant, sex and, and…

Emily pulled back her head and denied instinct.

'I'm going in…'

'Sure.' Hugh would, of course, rather she asked him in too but, well, this would be so worth the wait.

She watched his mouth move and offer dinner, a catch-up next week, though his hand between her thighs told her it would definitely end in bed and it was time to bring things to a halt.

'Hugh.' She let out a breath. 'I don't know…' She changed tack. 'It's just…' How could she deny the want that thrummed between them? For Emily there was but one thing left to do so she came up with a rapid lie. 'I'm seeing someone.'

'Oh.'

'Gregory.'

'It's fine, I get it…' Though he didn't. Poor Gregory, Hugh thought as he reclaimed his hand, because five minutes from now he'd have had her knickers off.

'He's in Scotland, so we don't see each other as much as—'

'You really don't need to explain.'

And so the phantom Gregory was born.

* * *

When her father and Donna broke up in the New Year it was to Gregory she turned, rather than Hugh, though they did touch on it once, because Hugh came into the staffroom when Emily was on the phone.

'Donna, I get it that you have issues with my father but I don't understand what that has to do with me. If you don't want to see me that's fine but can I just take the twins to the park or for an ice cream every now and then…?' She turned in her chair and saw that Hugh had come in just as Donna told her that, no, she'd prefer Emily didn't have extra contact with the twins—she could see them when her father bothered to.

'Is she not letting you see the twins?' Hugh asked when she came off the phone.

'I can see them when they're with my dad, which isn't very often. I asked if I could take them out at the weekend but it unsettles them apparently.'

'Can she do that?'

'Of course she can.' Emily stood and went to walk past but Hugh caught her arm.

'Emily?'

'What?'

'Do you want…?' Hugh didn't really know what he was offering.

Emily did.

Yes, she did want.

She wanted to burst into tears, she wanted him to take her out and not cheer her up, just share…

She wanted to share with him.

Emily looked down at the fingers that still held her wrist.

Oh, he could hurt her, Emily thought, and then looked up to his eyes. He could really, really hurt her.

'I'll sort it out,' Emily said. 'Gregory is going to try and speak with her.'

At the mention of Gregory his hand disengaged from her arm.

For the next three months, every time Emily went to visit her mother Hugh was brought up to speed through vague conversations. However, just as he was starting to wonder about the fact that Gregory never seemed to come down to London, Emily actually found her perfect guy for real, so Gregory was swiftly dumped.

Marcus *was* perfect.

Dark haired, terribly serious, he was a social worker at the hospital and liked to hike at weekends. Sex happened on Saturdays, occasional Tuesdays, and Emily developed solid calf muscles from trips up hillsides.

It was perfect for close to two years when the breaking news arrow shot across the hospital grapevine that Marcus had been found in a compromising position in the X-ray department with Heidi, the Swedish radiographer.

Hugh, now a senior registrar and going out with Olivia by then, expected tears in the staffroom, blushes and drama—the usual type of thing that happened with a very public break-up. With Emily that didn't happen, though...

Oh, she was a curious thing.

Emily just shrugged it off and got on with work.

The very next Monday they stood in Theatre and Emily glanced up as the alarm went off on the cardiac monitor when the anaesthetised patient kicked off a few ectopic heartbeats.

'All fine,' Rory, the anaesthetist, called as the patient's heart steadied back into a regular rhythm.

There were no flashing lights, no drama—it was hardly an event really.

And that was just how Emily liked things.

It was how she kept control.

CHAPTER ONE

'I DON'T WANT to work there.'

It was, for Emily, as simple as that.

She and Hugh had been working together for close to three years now and often caught up on a Monday. Now, in their lunch break, they sat in the staffroom at their favourite table, putting the world to rights.

'I think you'd be very good in Accident and Emergency,' Hugh said. 'Anyway, it's only for three months.'

'Well, why don't you go and work in Labour and Delivery for three months and then get back to me with that statement.'

'Fair point,' Hugh conceded.

'I'm going to speak to Miriam today and see if there's any way I can get out of doing it.'

Miriam, the head of Critical Nursing, had, last year, decided to rotate the staff on the units. Emily had reluctantly done a three-month stint in ICU and had thought that would be the end of it, but Miriam had decided to press on with internally rotating the staff. Emily had been told that in June she would be commencing a term in Accident and Emergency.

Theatre was Emily's stomping ground. The thought of working in Emergency was unsettling—the drama of it, the emotion, the constant loaning out of your heart if you chose to empathise, or the burn-out that left you a tough bitch. Emily couldn't decide what was worse. She had no intention of revealing to Hugh the real reasons she was so opposed to the idea, so instead she changed the subject.

'So, is it true?' Hugh didn't reply to her question but Emily pushed on. 'Have you and Olivia broken up?'

'Yep.'

'I thought you two were happy.'

'We were,' Hugh said. 'When we were together.'

'What do you mean?'

It was Hugh who sat silent for a moment now. He and Olivia had been happy. Everyone had said how suited they were and, yes, their relationship had ticked most boxes.

Two boxes had been missing, though.

Olivia's jealousy and trust issues were one and as for the other…

He looked across the table to where Emily was peeling open her croissant and sprinkling more black pepper onto the cheese and tomato that filled it. She loved black pepper—there were always a couple of sachets in the pocket of her scrubs.

He knew a lot more about her than he had three years ago.

Just not enough.

'I don't know how to explain it, Em,' Hugh admitted. 'I don't know why Olivia felt that every time I was late home or out on a work do that there had to be more to it…'

'You do have a reputation,' Emily pointed out. As much as she liked catching up with Hugh, she loathed hearing about his life, his girlfriends, the wild parties and frequent holidays and weekends away.

Mondays were sometimes torture.

In fact, sometimes Emily dreaded them.

'Perhaps I do have a reputation around the hospital but I've never cheated when I'm seeing someone...' Hugh chose to go back a few years and watched a dull blush spread on her neck. 'If I am then I wouldn't so much as kiss another person.'

'Well...' Emily flustered a little. It was far too late, all these years on, to tell him there had never been a Gregory. It was far safer not to—that little black mark against her name was one she would happily wear if it kept her at a distance from Hugh. 'So what brought it to a head?'

'There's a conference coming up in a couple of months that Hadfield wants me to go on. I only mentioned it in passing but... The thing is, if I'm going to stand any chance of getting the consultancy then I really ought to go and concentrate—but Olivia seemed to think it was a good chance to have a couple of days' holiday, then she couldn't fathom why I might not want her to go with me...' His green eyes met Emily's. 'If I do get the consultancy position, things are only going to get busier for me. Call me selfish but I want to focus on my career and that means I can't be checking in every five minutes and reassuring someone that I'm behaving...' Hugh shook his head. 'Am I unreasonable?'

'No.' Emily fully agreed and she genuinely meant her words. She had long ago learnt from her parents that a million phone calls and texts meant little. 'If someone's going to cheat, they will.'

Hugh rolled his eyes. 'The point is, Em, I don't cheat.

More to the point right now, Alex is pretty angry that I've broken up with Olivia and I want that promotion.' Hugh brooded for a moment. 'I got turned down last year.'

'Ouch,' Emily said.

'I get it that I perhaps wasn't ready then but I am ready now.'

'He can't judge whether or not you get the role on that.'

'I'm sure he wouldn't admit to it, but he's of the opinion that behind every great surgeon is a stable home life…' Hugh rolled his eyes and Emily laughed. 'I want that role,' Hugh said. Alex was a professor now and a consultancy position had officially opened up and Hugh could think of no one that he wanted to work alongside more. Alex was an amazing mentor. His technique and studies into laparoscopic surgery were right at the front of the game and every hour of every day Alex taught him something new.

'Behave for a few months, then!' Emily said. 'It really isn't that difficult.'

'Oh, but it is when you find yourself suddenly single.' Hugh drained his cup and then headed back to work. Emily sat alone for a while, pondering a suddenly single Hugh.

It was the time she loathed him most.

Or rather the time she loathed most.

Hugh worked hard and partied the same way. If she didn't have to hear it on Monday in Theatre then it was all over bloody Facebook.

She had the next hour at the computer to work on the off-duty roster then she was down to scrub for Alex, but instead of heading to tackle the roster Emily looked over at Miriam, who was just heading out of the staffroom.

Instead of rinsing her cup and plate, Emily put them in the sink and caught up with her. 'Miriam, I wondered if I could have a word.'

'Now?' Miriam checked, and Emily nodded.

This needed to be done.

They stepped into Miriam's office and Emily took a seat as Miriam gave her a thin smile. 'I can guess what this is about. I know that you're not keen to go to A and E.'

'Because I'm happy here,' Emily said.

'Emily, rotating the critical care staff has proved a success. Handovers are smoother, we're all more aware of the other departments' procedures...'

'I understand that,' Emily said, 'but I chose to be a theatre nurse.'

'And you're a very good one,' Miriam said. 'One who I hope will go far...' She left the rest unsaid but to Emily it was clear that if she wanted to go further in her career here, which she did, then she would have to comply. 'It's a couple of months away,' Miriam added. 'There's plenty of time to get used to the idea.'

Emily didn't want to get used to the idea, she liked being used to *here*!

'Any luck with Miriam?' Hugh asked at the end of the day as Emily came out of the changing room dressed for the outside world. Hugh was looking pretty drained—he'd been operating since eight a.m. and now would be heading up to the wards to check on his post-operative patients.

'Nope.' Emily's jaw tensed and she let out a tense breath. 'If I want to get on—'

'Ha,' Hugh interrupted. 'Don't complain about that to me—at least you don't have Alex as your boss. I need a wife if I want to get on.'

'When we're in charge we'll change the world,' Emily said as they walked together. Hugh was heading up to ICU, Emily for home, and it felt like a long time till next Monday for Hugh.

Hugh was possibly the one person who *did* like Mondays. Sure, he and Emily caught up during the week at various times but Monday was Alex's rostered operating day and on the days that Emily wasn't there he missed her.

Yes, Hugh wanted to finally move things on between them and give this *almost* romance its wings. He wanted a nice table between them and a waiter whose arm would probably drop off as he cracked enough pepper to satisfy Emily.

Okay, Hugh decided as they walked down the long corridor, whatever happened, he would not let it affect their friendship.

'You do realise,' Hugh said as they reached the swing doors that would take them out of Theatre and to their separate destinations, 'that this is the first time in three years that we've both been single at the same time.'

Nice opening! Hugh was just silently congratulating himself when Emily delivered her response.

'Well, I don't know about you but I'm staying that way,' Emily said, shutting down the conversation as firmly as the black doors swung closed behind them. ''Night, Hugh, it was nice working with you today.'

Was he missing something?

Hugh just watched as she walked off.

Did he have body odour that only Emily could smell?

They liked each other!

They fancied each other!

He could taste it.

If only she'd let him.

'Problem?' Alex asked, as he came out and saw his junior standing with a puzzled frown on his face.

'More a mystery,' Hugh said. 'One I intend to work out.'

He couldn't, though.

It would seem Emily was serious about staying single and for two whole months she did just that.

Till Hugh decided they might need a little helping hand.

CHAPTER TWO

'ARE YOU COMING to Emily's leaving do on Friday?' Louise asked Hugh, and Emily rather hoped the answer would be no—a meal at Imelda's and a few drinks afterwards would probably be a bit tame for Hugh.

'Can we do the swab count before I start to close?' Hugh said, instead of answering.

Nothing distracted him, Emily noted.

It was the mark of a brilliant surgeon.

Hugh chatted and joked but when it mattered he concentrated totally. As boring as the swab count and equipment check might be, it was necessary to ensure that nothing was left inside the patient before the surgeon closed, and Hugh took it seriously.

The counts all tallied.

'It isn't Emily's leaving do,' Hugh said, as he started to close the incision. 'She's only going to be working in A and E for three months but, yes, I'll be there. Actually, Alex and his wife are coming too, if they can get a babysitter.'

'It's just a few drinks…' Emily frowned because why the hell was Alex coming, let alone his wife? 'As you said, it's not even a leaving do.'

Except, unbeknown to anyone but Emily, it very possibly was her leaving do.

Emily hadn't yet handed in her notice but next Wednesday she was going to Cornwall for a week and had decided if, after a break, she still felt the same way about working in A and E, then that was what she would do.

'You're going to be missed,' Hugh said. Emily saw his lovely green eyes over the mask and, yes, he was speaking the truth both personally and professionally. Emily was efficient, incredibly efficient, some might say pedantic and others set in her ways, but Theatre worked well with pedantic nurses. 'Mondays won't be the same.'

'Actually, they shall, for a little while at least,' Emily said. 'I'm back working here on Monday as an extra shift—they haven't found my replacement yet. The nurse who was coming here from A and E resigned.'

'When do you go on holiday?' Louise asked.

'Next Wednesday,' Emily answered. 'A whole week of doing nothing but walking and reading. I can't wait.'

'There's some nice weather predicted…' Louise smiled.

'Which means it will rain!' Hugh's comment was dry.

'I don't care,' Emily said. 'I just want to read and walk on the beach and relax.'

'Well, you'll need it before you go to A and E,' Louise said.

'How are we doing, Rory?' Hugh glanced over at the anaesthetist as a couple of alarms started to sound.

'All good. How much longer?'

'Done,' Hugh said.

Yes, it was a very small world in Theatre. Emily headed to the large staffroom. She was the first there but everyone would soon come in. Rarely did anyone go to the canteen—it was too much trouble to change shoes and things. She turned and gave a brief smile as Hugh came in and she got out her lunch from the fridge but, as they sat down, instead of their usual catch-up Hugh got paged to go up to a ward.

'Damn,' Hugh said. 'I wanted to talk to you.'

'I'm sure it will keep.'

Hugh thought for a moment as he answered his page. Emily was right, it would keep and what he had to ask her would probably go better with wine!

'Can I borrow you for ten minutes on Friday night?'

'Borrow me?'

'Well, I know you'll be busy but there's something that I want to ask you away from everyone else.'

'Like what?'

'Not here.'

'Have you got another rash?' Emily smirked.

'Ha-ha.'

They both smiled as they remembered the day when Hugh, for once, had struggled to focus. Emily had been scrub nurse and had frowned as a usually together Hugh had breathed loudly beside her, sweat beading on his forehead as he kept moving from one foot to the other. The second the operation had been over he had fled and, walking past the male changing rooms on the way to the staffroom, Emily had seen his frantic face peer out.

'Emily…' he'd hissed. 'I need some antihistamine.'

'What?'

'Now. IM…'

'An injection?'

Hugh let the towel slip a fraction and Emily's eyes widened at the sight of the angry red welts and urticarial rash spreading down his buttocks.

'Believe me, Emily, that's not the worst of it…'

'I don't want to see the rest.'

Oh, my!

Emily had returned with the injection and some hydrocortisone cream for Hugh to put on *himself* and had happily stabbed him.

'Maybe it was the shaving cream…'

She didn't want to know that he'd shaved, or that *she*, whoever *she* was this week, had shaved him. Emily was tired of the glimpses into his love life.

'Have you changed your washing powder?' Emily asked instead.

'No.' Hugh shook his head and thought for a moment. 'Though I did buy the liquid one.'

As it turned out, he had bought the triple-strength liquid one!

Happily, his reaction had calmed and the theatre list had gone ahead, Emily trying and failing not to dwell on the fact that he was naked and bald beneath his scrubs.

'What will I do without you?' Hugh asked, still smiling as he recalled that day.

'Inject your own antihistamine!'

'That was a long time ago, Emily.'

Yet she remembered it like it was yesterday.

The hurt, the jealousy, the itch of her own that she simply refused to scratch.

'If I don't catch up with you properly,' Hugh said, 'then I'll see you Friday.'

'Okay.'

* * *

Friday found her in the staff changing room, getting ready to go to Imelda's, a nice casual bar that did amazing food and, on weekends, had a band.

Emily was tired before the night had even started but, given it was her leaving do, she did her best not to show it.

Louise and she changed at work. Emily into a tube skirt and top, Louise into the tightest red dress and high heels. They were close friends now.

Louise looked stunning, especially when she topped it off with dark red lipstick.

'Tart,' Emily said.

'A happy tart, though.' Louise smiled.

'Are you?' Emily checked. Louise was coming out of a terrible break up and had been very subdued but finally she seemed to be finding herself again.

'I'm getting there,' Louise said. 'Come on.'

They walked out of Theatre and down the corridor and there, coming towards them, was Anton, the new Italian obstetrician who had hearts thumping everywhere.

'Hi, Anton.' Louise smiled.

'Evening.'

'We're heading over to Imelda's—there will be quite a few of us.' Louise gave a smile that could be described as sweet were it not for the wanton red lips, but it was barely returned.

'I'm working,' Anton said, and strode off.

'You're subtle,' Emily commented.

'He's fresh off the plane,' Louise said. 'I was just doing my social duty. God, don't you want to just grab him by the stethoscope and climb up it?'

'No.' Emily laughed. 'Not in the least, he's far too moody for me.'

They had booked a room at the back of the restaurant and it was actually really nice to be among friends and colleagues. Hugh hadn't arrived but that was possibly a good thing as Emily didn't really want to meet whomever it was that he was dating now.

Surely he was seeing someone.

Two months single for Hugh would be a record.

Or maybe he was just enjoying the off-season and sleeping around, though, for once, Emily had heard nothing on the grapevine about him.

Emily sat between Louise and Alex's wife Jennifer and, as it turned out, Louise had news of her own.

'It will be my leaving do next,' Louise said.

'You've just done your internal rotation.' Emily frowned.

'No, mine will be for real.' Louise's blue eyes were shining. 'I'm going to work in Maternity.'

'When did you decide that?'

'It's been brewing for a while,' Louise admitted. 'I can't wait to get back there.'

'It wouldn't have anything to do with Anton?' Emily teased.

'God, no! I'm not that shallow,' Louise said, because despite walking a little on the wild side she took her work seriously. 'I'm just ready for a change. I love the Caesareans we have in Theatre and lately it's just not been enough for me. I want to be more involved with the mothers and babies.' She smiled at Emily. 'You like the cool of Theatre, don't you?'

'I do,' Emily said.

'I just want back out there…' Louise admitted.

'Have you told Miriam?'

'Not yet.' Louise winced at the very thought. 'I haven't actually applied for a position yet, I'm just putting out feelers, but I don't think Miriam will be very pleased—a lot of staff have left recently.'

'Well, she should have thought of that before she moved the goalposts for getting a promotion,' Emily said, but as Louise went to open her mouth to respond she stopped her. 'If another person tells me I'll be great and that it will fly by, I won't be responsible for my response.'

'I'll say nothing, then.' Louise smiled. 'I'll get you a drink instead.'

Hugh arrived just as dessert was being served. Emily was sitting chatting to Alex and Jennifer when Hugh came over. He gave her a kiss on the cheek, which was a bit uncalled for, but, yes, at the time Emily put it down to the fact that it was her leaving do.

'Sorry, I tried to get here earlier…' Hugh said.

'It's fine.'

'I got stuck up on ICU…'

'Really, Hugh, it's fine,' Emily said. She had no idea why he was making such a fuss about not getting here on time—a lot of her colleagues were only dropping in for a drink after all.

'I'll get you a drink,' Hugh offered.

'I don't want one…' Emily said, only Hugh wasn't listening. He headed off to the bar and returned with something very icy and bubbly and so not what Emily wanted. She'd had a bit too much icy and bubbly and she wasn't a big drinker at the best of times but everyone seemed determined to buy her one tonight.

'You'll be dancing on the tables in a few weeks,'

Hugh said, squeezing a chair into the tiny gap between herself and Louise.

'Why?'

'I'm here tomorrow night with the emergency mob for Gina's thirtieth—believe me, the theatre staff's nights outs are very civilised in comparison to that lot.'

Emily went over to speak with Connor, another theatre nurse, but Hugh was like an annoying wasp and hanging around her like some lovesick teenager. Frankly, he was starting to really annoy her.

'What?' Emily snapped, when still Hugh hovered. 'What's going on, Hugh?'

'Can I have that ten minutes now?'

'Fine,' Emily sighed, and turned to him.

'Outside.'

'Hugh, it's my leaving do, I'm not going to—'

'Ten minutes.'

Emily headed outside.

'I want to ask you something. You know what I said about us still being single—do you want to give us a try?'

Emily was taken aback by his directness.

'No.'

'Can I ask why?'

'I don't need to give a reason.' She went to head back but Hugh caught her arm.

'I've still got nine minutes of your time left.'

'Use them wisely, then,' Emily said.

'Okay.' Hugh took a breath. 'Second question. Would you consider pretending to go out with me?'

'Pretend?'

'I want the consultancy. Alex likes you…'

'That's the most ridiculous idea I've ever heard. He'd soon find out you were lying.'

'Not if we're clever about it.'

'No.'

'Give me one good reason why not,' Hugh said.

She looked at Hugh, his hair flopping over his eyes, his green eyes smiling, and he was just so cocky and assured, so utterly at ease with himself that Emily could tell he was a touch taken back that she hadn't jumped at the chance to be his fake girlfriend.

'You know what Alex is like,' Hugh persisted. 'He hasn't come right out and said it but the writing's on the wall—he wants to know that my party days are over before he'll give me the consultancy.'

'But they're not over,' Emily pointed out.

'They could be for the next couple of months.'

'I'm not handing over two months of my life to be your fake girlfriend—'

'No,' Hugh interrupted. 'I'm not asking for two months, I'm asking for a couple of Saturday nights and the occasional wedding. I could come down to Cornwall at the weekend and kick things off with a few photos. You're not seeing anyone and surely...' He hesitated.

'Go on.'

'It will be exciting.'

'Really!' Emily was having trouble keeping an incredulous smile from her lips. 'Tell me how.'

'Well...' Hugh actually had the decency to look a touch uncomfortable. 'You said that your holiday was going to be a bit boring...'

'No, I didn't,' Emily corrected him. 'I said my holiday was going to be very quiet, which, somewhere between here...' she tapped her lips '...and there...' she tapped his forehead '…you translated as boring. A week in a cottage, doing nothing, isn't boring, Hugh.'

'It certainly wouldn't be if I came along.' Hugh grinned.

'Would I have to sleep with you?' Emily asked. 'In this little charade of yours, would sex be on the books?'

'If you want to,' Hugh said, mildly surprised that Emily had so readily brought it up. 'If you're saddled with being my girlfriend, there would have to be perks…'

'Your ego knows no bounds.'

'Think about it,' Hugh said.

'I have,' Emily said, and started to walk back inside, 'and the answer's no.'

'Come on, Emily…'

'Was that the reason for the kisses and the "Sorry I couldn't get here earlier" and following me about?'

'Yep.'

'I tell you one thing,' Emily said, 'if we were going out then we wouldn't be for long if you followed me about like that.'

'I know.' Hugh laughed. 'I was just trying to get Alex used to the possibility that we were on with each other…I was actually starting to annoy myself.'

Had he left it at that, all would have been okay.

If a glass of champagne hadn't been thrust into her hand by Louise then possibly things wouldn't have unravelled but, unknown to anyone, she was battling tears.

His fake girlfriend.

Bloody cheek, Emily thought.

She wanted to be his real one.

So why hadn't she simply said yes when he'd asked

to give them a try? Or had that been just a ruse for Alex's benefit too?

Damn you, Hugh!

Emily knew she was being contrary, she knew that over the years Hugh must at times have felt like some baffled semaphore signaller as she'd flirted and waved red flags while her mouth had done its best to refute what her body said.

After the break-up with Marcus it had been relatively easy to move on, but getting over Hugh… Emily tried to imagine working alongside him when she had been relegated to being his ex and—fake girlfriend or real one—she knew that one day the inevitable would happen.

But if she wasn't working there…

Stop it, Emily told herself, determined not to go there. It was a relief when people started to leave and Emily could go and retrieve her bag. Hugh's strange offer had left her all unsettled and quite simply she wanted home.

Only Hugh had other ideas.

As she stepped out onto the street she heard him call her name.

'Emily…' Hugh caught her arm. 'Have you thought about it?'

'Sorry?'

'You know…' Hugh said, moving her into the shadows, 'what we were talking about before.'

'I've already given you my answer.'

'Oh, come on, Emily, it would be fun.'

'How?'

Emily stood there. A taxi was approaching and her

friends were calling for her to join them and there was Alex and his wife Jennifer leaving.

She knew that because Hugh chose his moment and started kissing her neck.

'Foreshadowing,' Hugh said, in between kisses.

'Or just adding to your reputation,' Emily said, trying to ignore the sensations his lips were delivering, trying not to be moved by the feel of Hugh's hands on her waist.

Little butterfly kisses were being delivered to her cheeks and her lips were starting to thrum hungrily in anticipation as, three years on, the master picked up the lead and offered a decadent walk. And just as she had when last they'd kissed, Emily had to come up with a rapid reason why it wouldn't work.

Before lips met she had to come up with a reason or she'd be dragging him by the hair to the taxi and up the stairs to her bed.

Or would she let him drag her.

Oh, my!

She was again starting to consider the possibilities, just tossing all warnings aside and going along with his ridiculous plan. It was the feeling of suddenly wavering that had Emily pull back.

'I can't do it.'

'I'm waiting for the reason.'

'I can't do it because…' Come on, think, Emily, she told herself, come up with one very good reason why it would be an impossible idea. And then her champagne- and Hugh-befuddled brain found a solution. 'Because I don't like you,' Emily said. Hugh just grinned.

'No, I mean it, I don't really enjoy your company so…' Shut up, Emily, her mind said, but she simply couldn't stop. Emily could actually see the frown between his eyes as the words hit. 'I put up with you at work, of course, it's part of my job, but…'

'Okay.' He stepped back.

'You asked why not,' Emily said. 'You asked for one good reason…'

'I get the message,' Hugh said. 'Finally.'

Emily closed her eyes, very aware that she had handled that terribly, then she forced them open and took a breath, knowing that she had to apologise.

But how?

How could she explain that she didn't like his company at times because it ate her up inside? How could she explain when he was inches from her mouth that her feelings for him terrified her?

'Hugh…'

'Let's just leave it.'

They walked over to the line of taxis and Hugh opened the door of one for her.

'Hugh…' Emily said as she got in.

''Night, Emily.' He closed the door.

All the way home Emily kicked herself. She couldn't have handled that more badly if she had tried but the near kiss had actually caused her to panic.

Get over yourself.

Maybe it was time to, Emily thought. Perhaps she could apologise properly on Monday.

Maybe even explain how she felt?

That she was actually terrified to get close to anyone.

She paid the taxi driver and headed to her home, and for the first time her resolution wavered, the cloak of self-preservation almost slid off, for she wanted the feelings Hugh triggered and yet she knew, from his undeniable track record, that soon they'd be done.

Time to take a risk, Emily.

In fact, it was long overdue that she did.

She was just pulling him up on her computer, just trying to convince herself to wait till tomorrow to attempt contact because she'd made enough of a mess of things tonight already.

Then she saw that she had a message.

From her dad.

Emily, I tried to call.
I've got some good news, two bits of good news actually.

Emily read the message, her eyes filling with tears as she heard that her dad was marrying again and soon, because—guess what—Cathy was pregnant!

A little brother or sister for you, her dad tossed in, and she was very glad she'd missed his call because she felt like screaming.

Would it be like it had been with the twins all over again?

She actually ached to see them but it wasn't just the blood relations that hurt. There had been so many girl-friends and along with them their children, and it was much the same with her mum.

'I don't want to go to your wedding.' Emily said it out loud as she stared at the screen, though she knew she'd do the right thing and be there, more in the hope of seeing the twins, though.

If Donna let them attend.

That was why she was like this, Emily reminded herself. That was why she let no one in.

She checked her reminders. It was her half-sister Abby's birthday tomorrow and though she had sent a gift in the post Emily posted a message on her mum's timeline.

She flicked through some images; saw Abby smiling with her own dad's children from a previous relationship.

There wasn't enough wood in a forest to map Emily's family tree.

It was always *the one*, her parents told her when they met the latest love of their life.

This time they were sure.

Until it was over.

Emily allowed herself one look at the smiling image of Hugh on her screen and then clicked off.

Hugh was a sure-fire recipe for disaster.

She was right to refuse herself a taste.

CHAPTER THREE

FOR ONCE HUGH wasn't looking forward to Monday.

And it wasn't just Emily's revelation that had soured the weekend!

The accident and emergency do *had* been a little wild and Hugh had again had to put out an increasingly regular fire named Gina.

He'd gone round yesterday to speak to her and she'd done her best to convince him it had just been a one-off, that she hadn't been the only one who'd had too much to drink.

True.

And, yes, it had been her thirtieth birthday after all.

Yet Hugh wasn't so sure it was just the drinking that was the problem.

Three years ago when he'd voiced his concerns first to Alex and then to Mr Eccleston, the head of Anaesthetics, he had been taken seriously. Gina had actually cried on him about the unknown person who had threatened her career.

It had all come to nothing and it had eaten Hugh up since then that possibly he had jumped the gun because Gina really was an amazing doctor and she had proved it over and over.

Just lately, though, Hugh felt that things were sliding again.

Driving to work, he took a call from his sister. 'Is everything okay?' Hugh instantly checked.

'Of course. Why wouldn't it be?' Kate answered.

'It's not even seven a.m.'

'Well, I knew you'd be on your way to work and I don't like to trouble you there.'

'You can call me any time, Kate.'

'Hugh, can you take your social-worker voice off? Just because I've had a baby it doesn't mean that there has to be a problem.'

Easy for you to say, Hugh thought, pulling up at traffic lights. Three years ago Hugh had taken Emily's advice and practically frogmarched Kate to her doctor, and still, all these years on, what had happened in Kate's dark teenage years ate at him.

'So, what are you calling for?' Hugh asked instead.

'We've booked Billy's christening,' Kate said, 'for the end of June.' Hugh grimaced when she gave him the date. He was quite sure he was on take that weekend and he'd already swapped his roster once to accommodate an upcoming wedding that he wouldn't miss for the world.

He'd actually given Kate a list of his available dates when she had started to talk about making plans for the christening.

Let it go, Hugh, he told himself as the lights changed.

Yet he always let it go around Kate.

'The thing is, I'm actually—' Hugh attempted, but Kate cut in.

'We want you to be godfather.'

'Oh!' Hugh didn't know what to say at first and then he said the right thing. 'I'd be delighted to.'

So there was no getting out of it, then.

Damn.

Hugh loved his sister and nephews very, very much; it was just the timing of things that was a serious issue. How the hell could he ask for another Sunday off?

'Will you be bringing someone?' Kate asked.

'Probably not.'

'I'll need to know for the restaurant.'

'No, then.'

'Hugh?' Kate checked, because there was a terse edge to his voice.

'It's just a bit of a sore point at the moment.'

'I thought you and Olivia were well over and done with.'

'We are,' Hugh said, 'well, I am.'

'Is she still calling?'

'Now and then.'

'So what's the sore point?'

'I've got to go, Kate,' Hugh said. 'I'll give you a call in the week. Thanks for asking me to be godfather, it means a lot.'

It did.

Hugh pulled into the work car park and saw the rare sight of Emily's car. Usually she took public transport but occasionally she brought the bomb in.

There was the sore point.

He didn't buy it that Emily didn't like him.

He knew that she did.

And he liked her.

He had from the first day they had met. Hugh liked

strong women, strong, independent women, and Emily was all of that.

Oh, not the shaved-head, unshaved-leg kind, it was her independence along with her femininity that continued to draw him in. With Emily he was himself, without qualification, without having to apologise if something he had said or done might have caused offence.

'Hugh!' He turned at the sound of Alex's voice and waited while he caught up with him.

'Hi, Alex, good weekend?'

'A very good weekend,' Alex said, as the men walked through the car park. 'Jennifer's mother came for a visit and has agreed to stay with us for the summer.'

'That's good news, is it?' Hugh smiled because wasn't your mother-in-law coming for an extended visit most husbands' idea of hell?

'It is.' Alex nodded. 'With all my work and studying I've let things slide a bit, I feel, but we've had a talk and with Jennifer's mum here for a few months we can make a bit more of my days off. Jennifer needs a break.'

Hugh glanced over. He had nothing but admiration for the man—from toddlers to teenagers, Alex dealt with it all, as well as study and research and holding down such a demanding position. Hugh wanted that consultancy position. There wasn't a day that went by that he didn't learn something from Alex, and not just in the operating theatre.

'You have to work at anything if you want it to be successful, Hugh,' Alex said, 'and I'm not just talking about the salaried stuff.'

Hugh wasn't sure if that was a small dig about his and Olivia's break-up but, then again, he was surprised that Alex was talking about bumpy times at home to him. 'Well, I hope you both have a great summer.'

'We shall,' Alex said. 'Right now I'm off to breakfast with Clem. I'll see you in theatre.'

Emily hadn't been looking forward to Monday either.

She walked into the staffroom and there was Hugh sitting in his usual spot. After making a coffee, Emily went and joined him, just as she usually did. 'About what I said the other night—' Emily started.

'Your shift doesn't start for another ten minutes,' Hugh interrupted, 'so you don't have to talk to me yet.'

'Hugh, it came out all wrong.'

'I think you made yourself very clear.'

'I do like you,' Emily said, her cheeks going red, 'just not in that way.'

'Okay.'

'And if we did suddenly start going out…' She just gave a shake of her head and tried to explain how it could never work. 'I've got my dad's wedding next month. Do you really want to go to that circus? Because he'd know about us too.'

'How?'

'Because he follows me on Facebook,' Emily said. 'It's pretty much how we communicate and Mum follows me too. It would just all get too complicated.'

'Fine.' He looked at her and she could see the hurt in his eyes. 'I shan't keep you. I'll see you in Theatre.'

'Hugh,' Emily called him before he could walk off. 'I'm not in Theatre today, I'm rostered for Anaesthetics.'

'You don't have to run your schedule by me.'

'I'm just explaining that I'm not avoiding you, I'm filling in this morning so I didn't get to do the placements…'

Hugh didn't answer, he just walked off.

What a mess, Emily thought as she made her way to the anaesthetic room. It was a small annexe that led to two of the theatres. Here the patient would be anaesthetised and intubated before being taken into the operating theatre. She was in for a busy morning. First was Ernest Bailey and though his was a long case, before Hugh's next one there were two epidurals scheduled for two planned Caesareans.

Emily smiled when she saw that it was Rory who was on. He was pulling up medication so that everything would be ready, well out of sight of the patient, and they chatted for a moment as they set up. 'I thought I was down to work with Gina,' Emily said.

'And I thought I had Monday off,' Rory responded, and then explained that he'd been called in the early hours to come in. 'She called in sick—I think she had a bit too much Hugh on Saturday night.'

Emily simply rolled her eyes—maybe Hugh had been busy trying to persuade Gina to pull the wool over Alex's eyes for a few weeks.

Maybe the two of them had got it on.

Emily bit her lip as she looked at the theatre list. That burn of jealousy was low in her chest and reminded her how much getting too close to Hugh could only inevitably hurt.

He *was* a friend, though, despite what she had said the other night, and that was something she didn't want to lose.

Rory was explaining to Emily that Ernest would be going to ICU after his surgery when Hugh came in.

'He's not here yet,' Emily said, because usually the

patient would be here by now and waiting for a brief word with the surgeon before going under.

'I know,' Hugh said. 'He's taking his time to say goodbye to his wife. Poor old boy doesn't really want the surgery but his wife has told him she wants him there for their golden wedding anniversary...' He paused as Ernest was wheeled in. 'Good morning, Mr Bailey.' Hugh was lovely to the man. 'How's Hannah?'

'Fussing,' Ernest said.

'And how are you feeling?'

'Thirsty!' came another one-word answer as Hugh checked again the markings he had made on Ernest's stomach. 'When can I get a cup of tea?'

'That's a bit of a way off for you,' Hugh said. 'I'll come and see you in Recovery after the operation and then later again on ICU.'

Ernest rolled his eyes. All he wanted to know was when his next drink would be, but soon he was under and Emily moved him through to the theatre and then came back to prepare the room for the next patient.

'Morning,' Emily said, as Anton and Declan, another anaesthetist, came in just as Emily had finished setting up for the epidural.

'Change of plan.' Declan smiled, unlike Anton, who just got straight down to business.

'We're going attempt a vaginal delivery in Theatre,' Anton said. 'Then we will do the planned cases.'

He went into Theatre to get ready and Emily rolled her eyes at Declan. 'Nice of the labour ward to let us know,' she said, just as the phone rang with that very news.

It was just a busy morning, punctuated by the sound of a woman grunting and screaming. Louise was in her element, Emily was wincing and Rory laughed when Hugh came in once Ernest's surgery was over.

'Lovely background noise,' Hugh said. 'I'm just going to speak to Ernest's wife and then I'll have a quick drink. I've sent down for the next one.'

'Mr Bailey didn't take long,' Emily commented.

'It went better than expected,' Hugh said. 'I didn't end up doing a colostomy, he'll be pleased about that.'

As an ear-splitting scream filled the morning. Rory came in and laughed when he saw Emily's reaction. 'Is that with an epidural?' Emily asked him.

'Apparently she doesn't want any drugs.' Rory peered through the window into Theatre. 'Declan's just gone in, so maybe she's changed her mind. No, it looks like Anton's going to use forceps.'

'Oh, my,' Emily said.

'Is childbirth not for you, lovely Emily?' Rory asked, because Emily was the opposite of Louise and avoided that side of Theatre whenever possible.

'Not even with drugs,' Emily said. 'God, listen to Anton!'

It sounded like a football match was taking place, with the woman screaming, Anton urging her on and even Louise was cheering. Then there was a long stretch of silence, followed by lusty screams.

'Phew,' Emily said. 'I can uncross my legs now!' But Hugh didn't laugh at her joke, as he usually would have, and Emily remembered that they weren't talking.

'The next one up is very nervous,' Hugh said to Rory. 'I'll come and have a word with her before she goes under.'

'I ordered her a strong pre-op,' Rory commented, 'though I think it's the mother who needs it.'

Emily chose not to grab a coffee and spend another uncomfortable ten minutes with Hugh. Instead she opted for a cola from the vending machine before setting up for the next patient—Jessica O'Farrell, an eighteen-year-old in for an exploratory laparoscopy.

'Mum wants to come in while she goes under.' Connor put his head through the doors and gave Rory a wry smile. 'I've said no but she's asked me to double-check!'

Rory shook his head. 'I've already spoken to Jessica about this. Mum's more stressed than her.'

Hugh was soon back from his quick coffee break and asked where the patient was as he was ahead of schedule and hoping to fit another patient onto the end of the list.

'Connor is just bringing her in now,' Emily answered, but as the trolley was wheeled in, for a second Emily froze.

She had been Jessica Albert when Emily had known her but of course her name might have changed all these years on.

'Emily!' Jessica's tears halted and the surprise in her voice had Hugh look at Emily for her reaction, but she just stood there as Jessica's tears actually stopped in mid-stream. 'It *is* you.'

'Jessica!' Hugh watched as Emily pushed out a smile but though it was a wide one, Hugh could see the shock in Emily's eyes and that her smile was guarded.

In all Emily's years of nursing it had never happened. Well, once an uncle had had a hip replacement, but she'd been expecting to see him.

This, though, was completely unexpected and Jessica wasn't even a relation.

She had once felt like one, though.

Today, had she been scrubbing in, as was her usual,

Emily might not have even know that the patient was the Jessica she had known all those years ago. Thirteen years was a long time and with the different name and with her eyes closed, as they would have been in Theatre, Emily might not have even recognised her.

Emily pushed back the wave of emotion that threatened to knock her off course and walked over to the young woman. 'How are you?' Emily said, and then gave a little laugh. 'Well, that's a silly question, given that you're about to have surgery.'

'I've been dreading it,' Jessica said. 'I'm so scared of having an anaesthetic.'

'A lot of people are.' Emily squeezed her hand. 'Rory's on today and he's amazing, he'll take such good care of you. Have you met him?'

'He came and saw me this morning.' Jessica looked over at Rory and then back at Emily. 'Will you be there?'

'I'll be with you while you're put to sleep,' Emily said, and then bit her bottom lip as Jessica looked at Hugh.

'Emily and I were sisters…'

Hugh smiled back, though of course he didn't really understand. He was pleased to see his patient looking a lot more relaxed but right now he was more concerned about the nurse because Emily's face was chalk white and he watched as Jessica turned back to Emily. 'I've looked you up a few times,' Jessica admitted. 'I was going to friend you on Facebook but I didn't know if I'd be welcome…'

'I've tried to look you up too,' Emily said, 'though no wonder I didn't get very far, as that your surname's changed.'

'Mum married again and I took Mike's surname.'

Emily hesitated. She didn't really want to know how Katrina was doing and yet there was a small part of her that did. 'How is your mum?'

'She's good,' Emily said. 'She's happy. Well, I think she is.'

Does she ever mention me? Emily wanted to ask. And does she ever give me so much as a passing thought?

Tears were starting to sting at the back of Emily's eyes and she quickly turned away and busied herself with the medicines she had already pulled up—she certainly didn't want to add to Jessica's difficult morning with her own gush of emotion.

Thankfully Hugh seemed to realise that Emily was struggling and he started chatting away to Jessica, telling her that it wouldn't be a long procedure and he'd see her again when she woke up.

Hugh went to go. Rory had administered a stronger sedative, but the emotion in Jessica's voice in the moment before she went under had Hugh pause at the door. 'I missed you so much.'

Emily stared into her eyes and was honest in her response. 'I missed you too.'

Oh, how she had.

They had been weekend and holiday sisters and losing Jessica and even Katrina had been a hurt that had gone unacknowledged by all. And there had been many more losses since then.

Emily held Jessica's hand as she slid under and then helped wheel her through to the theatre and onto the operating table.

She glanced over to Hugh, who was scrubbing up, and he gave a small nod that said he'd take good care.

He always did.

Hugh worked on smaller procedures himself yet more and more he was honing his skills and was ready for that next step.

As he performed the procedure, an investigative laparoscopy for recurrent abdominal pain, Emily was the furthest thing from his mind.

He carefully checked the abdominal cavity and organs. Jessica had undergone many investigations and all had come back as normal.

As was this.

With the procedure over and Jessica being moved to Recovery, Hugh headed over there to check on Ernest.

'He looks terrible…' Hannah, his wife, was by the trolley, being comforted by their daughter, Laura.

'He's just had surgery, Mum, he was never going to be looking his best.' Laura tried to reassure her mother but her eyes were anxious when they met Hugh's. 'I know you warned us about the tubes and things but Mum didn't realise just how many there would be.'

'I should never had made him go through with it,' Hannah fretted. 'He didn't want the operation…'

'He's actually doing very well,' Hugh said, checking through the observations. 'I know it was a big decision but you both made it,' Hugh said gently. 'From what I've seen of your husband, he wouldn't be talked into anything he didn't want to do.'

He spent a few minutes reassuring Hannah but, glancing at Jessica, whose mother was being let in, his mind returned to Emily.

It was none of his business, Hugh told himself. Emily had made it very clear that she wanted no more than the relationship they had at work. Even so, he couldn't help listening to the conversation that was taking place.

'Emily's here…' They were the first words Jessica said as she struggled to sit up and take off her oxygen as a nurse gently kept her lying down.

'Emily?' Katrina said. Hugh wasn't just idly listening, he was watching and not even attempting to hide that he was.

'Emily,' Jessica said again. 'She's a nurse here. Maybe you could see her, say hello…'

Katrina shook her head. 'There's no need for that. How are you?'

'But Emily's here!' Groggy from anaesthetic, Jessica had no reserves and started pulling her oxygen mask off. 'Why wouldn't you want to see her?'

'Go back to sleep.' Katrina smiled, replacing the mask. 'You're a bit confused from all the medicine.'

Nice get-out, Mum, Hugh thought, but then he got back to business and headed over to let Jessica's mother know how the procedure had gone.

Yes, he should be cross with Emily, Hugh thought a little while later, or at the very least sulk and take his lunch elsewhere, but he could see her sitting, pretending to read a magazine, and Hugh knew she'd been crying.

'How was your morning?' Hugh asked, taking his usual seat.

'Busy,' Emily said. 'You've got a big afternoon coming up,' she added, because he and Alex were doing an aneurism repair, but Hugh shook his head.

'Not any more. Rory wasn't happy with his blood work, but maybe tonight…' Hugh yawned and then looked at her swollen eyes. 'You know, if I was a friend, instead of someone you tolerated because you're paid to, you could talk to me about this morning.'

Emily didn't want to talk about that morning but she was glad of the chance to address Friday night. 'Hugh, I really am sorry about that. It came out all wrong. I just don't want to mess up our friendship…'

'You nearly did!' Hugh said, his voice serious, and Emily nodded. 'So what was this morning about? I know that it's hard when a relative comes in.'

'She's not a relative, though,' Emily said, with more than a dash of bitterness, and then decided it couldn't hurt to explain. 'When my parents' marriage broke up my dad moved down here and moved in with Katrina, Jessica's mum. I used to come down once a month, half the holidays…'

'How old were you?'

'Twelve,' Emily said. 'I didn't like Katrina at first but I was always nice to her and my dad made sure to let me know she'd be my stepmum once the divorce was through and that this was my new family. I loved Jessica from the start, though. When I was there we shared a room. She was only little but we used to have such a laugh and then one weekend I came down to stay and found out that Katrina and my dad had split up.'

'Did you not see them after that?'

'Nope.' Emily shook her head. 'I asked where they were, but it didn't matter apparently, and clearly I didn't matter enough to Katrina to stay in touch…' Emily closed her eyes as she recalled how easily people that she had been told to love, to treat as family, to care for had been removed from her life. 'It was just the start of it. After Katrina, Dad met someone else and then someone else, then it was Donna and the twins…' She gave a tight smile, as she recalled that Hugh knew about that. 'You get the drift.' She didn't want to go on but Hugh persisted.

'Your dad's getting married again?'

Emily nodded.

'Do you see the twins?'

'Not really. I send them presents and things and they might be there at the wedding but Donna has majority access and...' She shook her head. 'I'm over talking about it.' Emily looked around the staffroom that was emptying as everyone headed back. 'I'd better go...'

It was very possibly her last shift—Emily didn't know if she'd be coming back and if she did she wasn't sure if her notice would be served out here or in Theatre.

It was very possibly the last time she would sit chatting to Hugh.

'I really am sorry for what I said on Friday night...'

'If you'd just told me the truth then it would have been fine.'

'Yeah, well, don't buy me champagne and then demand common sense.'

The opportunity to ask her out was there again.

He could ask her, they both knew it, except Hugh didn't go for a second try. Instead he gave her a thin smile and Emily walked off.

What was it with Emily that had Hugh pondering calling her back and asking her out again?

In that moment he took a very honest inventory of himself and maybe Olivia had been right to be concerned. No, he'd never have cheated but there was something about his feelings for Emily that sat in a place marked unresolved.

There were many women he fancied and he had many women who were friends.

Sometimes the boundaries merged but never more so than they did with Emily. Hugh considered her a friend, though Emily had kept it pretty much at colleague level, yet there was no one he spoke more readily with, no one who got what he was saying even before the sentence had finished...

As for attraction.

Always.

Absolutely.

Yes.

He saw the tension in Emily's shoulders as she headed out of the staffroom and, no, he wasn't going to call her back and make an idiot of himself again.

Emily knew that too.

She'd left things on such a bad note that she'd probably lost her friend anyway if she quit working here, Emily realised. It was a terrible way to end three years of working together, but Hugh would be a very silly reason to stay.

Tears were starting again as she walked back to work but at the last minute she turned around, about to make her way back to the staffroom, but then she saw Alex walking in.

Yes, she did like Hugh in every way.

Maybe this way, maybe if they followed Hugh's way, she could get the best of both worlds—time with the man who made her heart flutter, safe in the knowledge it would end soon. Maybe it would be easier to get a little bit more involved knowing from the start that they had a use-by date on the box.

She could handle that, surely?

As for sex?

There was an unfamiliar shiver in her stomach as she thought of it. No, it would be a terrible idea and yet…

Emily wasn't completely closed to it either.

No.

If she was going to do this then sex had to stay off the agenda. She was doing this to cement her friendship with Hugh out of work.

A structured timeframe, company at her father's wedding, a few Saturdays shared and then a very neat ending.

And it would be neat because, after today, she might not be back at the hospital.

Yes, it might be nice to have some time with Hugh and then a more natural break-up away from prying eyes, because she doubted she would be working here by then.

She could do that, Emily decided.

She would do that.

Emily walked into the staffroom, out of the corner of her eye she could see Alex at the urn, making a drink, and it would be very easy for Emily to think she had Hugh in the staffroom alone and so she took a deep breath and just made herself say it.

'Hugh, did you manage to speak to Alex?'

She watched as Hugh frowned. 'Speak to Alex about what?'

'Don't tell me you've forgotten! Hugh, you said that you would try—'

It was Alex who interrupted. 'Talk to Alex about what?' Alex said, and Emily jumped as if she hadn't known that he was in the staffroom.

'Oh, sorry.' Emily pretended to fluster. 'I didn't know you were here.'

'What did you want Hugh to ask me about?' Alex persisted, and Emily didn't have to fake being embarrassed as a blush started to spread over her cheeks as she spoke.

'Hugh was going to ask if he could possibly take Friday off and join me for a part of my holiday. I've rented a cottage in Cornwall and I was hoping that Hugh might be able to come for a couple of days.' She turned to Hugh, who was still frowning. 'I'm sorry, Hugh, I know that you didn't want anyone at work to know about us.'

'Are you two…' A huge grin was spreading over Alex's face. So that was the reason for Emily's swollen eyes that morning and Hugh's dark mood, Alex reasoned. Yes, Alex had also heard the rumour through the grapevine about Gina and Hugh getting off with each other over the weekend. 'I didn't realise!'

Neither had Hugh.

In fact, it took a moment for him to work out just what Emily was doing but when it dawned he cleared his throat before answering Alex. 'We were going to try and keep things well away from work at least until Emily started in Accident and Emergency.' Hugh looked at Emily, a wry smile turning the edges of his lips. Well, well, his green eyes said, and Emily returned a small smile.

'That's lovely news,' Alex said. 'And Cornwall is a beautiful part of the world—Jennifer and I have often spoken about buying a holiday house there. I don't see any problem with taking Friday off—we're not on take at the weekend. I'm sure I can manage one day without you. Enjoy yourselves!'

'You're sure?' Hugh checked.

'Absolutely!' Alex nodded. 'I can't wait to see the photos.'

Hugh dragged Emily to one side the very second that he got the chance. 'You do realise I *am* going to have to come and visit you. Alex's son, Jonathan, follows me on Facebook. That's what Alex meant about seeing the photos.'

'Come and visit on one of the days, then.' Emily shrugged, unperturbed, because she'd already thought about that. 'We can take a few selfies and post them. If we change clothes a few times and take pictures of meals and things, we can spread the posts out and pretend that you were there for the whole weekend.'

'We could,' Hugh said, 'but Cornwall's a pretty big day trip from here.'

'Then you'll have to get up very early.' Emily smiled because she knew what he was getting at. 'You *shall* be driving home.'

'So, what made you change your mind?' Hugh asked.

'Guilt about Friday night.' Emily admitted a small part of her reasoning and then she was serious. 'I don't want to lose a friend.'

'You're not going to lose a friend,' Hugh said, and then he looked into her blue eyes and tried to fathom the mystery there. 'I'll never work you out, Emily.'

'No, you won't,' Emily said. 'Anyway, working me out isn't a part of our deal.'

Emily headed back to work, glad that she had their friendship back and very determined to keep it at just that!

CHAPTER FOUR

IN A MINUTE she would get up and get dressed and tidy up a bit before Hugh got here, Emily thought, enjoying the warm sun on her skin.

The weather was blissfully warm and after a long walk on the beach Emily had returned to the small cottage she was renting. She made herself a big glass of iced water filled with slices of cucumber and lemon and headed out to the sundeck to enjoy her latest book, along with the sound of the sea in the background.

Emily lay on her stomach and undid her bikini top to avoid strap marks and settled in to read the morning away. Hugh had just texted to say that he expected to get there at about one and that he was bringing not just lunch but afternoon tea and dessert. The plan was to take loads of photos inside and out and change clothes and things and then Hugh would head off for the night and tomorrow Emily could get on with doing precisely nothing.

She was looking forward to seeing him, though, but was just a little bit nervous too because their friendship had mainly been in the safe confines of theatre walls. It was outside Theatre that things tended to get a little out of hand.

Still, she was nicely nervous at the thought of Hugh joining her and Emily put down her book and allowed herself to indulge in one tiny daydream, or rather one tiny memory, Emily corrected herself as she returned to their near kiss the other night.

Ah, but the next night he'd got off with Gina, Emily reminded herself.

They would be friends with *no* benefits, Emily told herself firmly, and then closed her eyes and got back to thinking about a problem that wasn't named Hugh.

Did she really want to leave her job?

She should be dwelling on that, instead of remembering the feel of his lips on her face, but thinking about work was too complicated for eleven in the morning and she was here to relax after all, so she didn't fight it when her mind slipped to a kiss that had taken place all those years ago…

For Hugh, it had been a long and difficult week. He'd had to take Ernest back to Theatre and was very worried about the elderly man, but he was also concerned about Gina. She had been off sick all week and it had not gone unnoticed by Hugh.

The thought of spending a day with Emily, even if it involved a ten-hour round trip, had been a very pleasant distraction during a trying week. His rare quiet times had been taken up with the question that if he *were* going to join Emily for two nights of sizzling sex and two days of the same, what supplies would he bring?

Instead of stopping at the supermarket for a quiche and a few tomatoes, as well as some champagne, which was Hugh's best attempt at a picnic, he took Alex's advice and rang Fortnum & Mason and ordered their best picnic hamper, filled with delicious treats. As well as that, while picking it up he bought a few extras in the food hall and so, with a gorgeous scent filling the car, by the time he arrived, just a little behind schedule, Hugh was starving.

He had found the cottage easily but there was no smiling Emily opening the door.

It would seem that there was no Emily home.

Maybe she had gone for a walk, Hugh thought, calling out her name as he headed around the side of the cottage to the back garden, and then he saw an Emily he never had before.

There she lay on her back, and her large breasts were, to his discredit, the first thing that Hugh noticed.

They were very pink, as was her stomach.

For a moment there he did consider waking her up by pouring the remains of her jug of water over her but he knew that Emily would loathe that she had been caught in an unguarded moment and she was doing him a huge favour after all. So Hugh resisted a more fun awakening for Emily and headed back to the front of the house and knocked more loudly on the door while calling out her name, and it was that that Emily woke up to.

God!

Emily pulled off that bikini top that had travelled up around her neck and quickly put on a loose T-shirt before opening the door. 'Sorry!' She gave Hugh a wide smile. 'I was on the phone.'

Liar, Hugh thought. 'For a moment there I thought that I had the wrong place, or that maybe you'd decided it was all too much trouble.'

'It's no trouble, if that's what I think it is!' Emily said, her eyes widening when she saw the picnic hamper and then widening more as Hugh unloaded the rest of the car with some very nice treats. 'How much food have you brought?'

'Three days' worth!' Hugh said, putting the basket down on the kitchen table. 'Nothing is too much trouble for you, my love,' he teased. 'We're the talk of the hospital, you know!'

'I do know!'

Since they had announced on Facebook that they were in a relationship the hospital grapevine had gone a little bit wild, but the main comments had been What took the two of you so long? Or About time.

'We'll be old news soon,' Hugh said.

They unloaded the shopping into the kitchen and Emily gave him a little tour of downstairs but halted him as he went to head upstairs.

'Where are you going?'

'Nature's calling.'

'There's a loo downstairs,' Emily said, because she hadn't even made the bed upstairs and she had knickers and bras all over the bathroom.

Why the hell had she fallen asleep?

'How many bedrooms does it have?' Hugh asked. 'Seriously, Emily, that was a very long drive.'

'Two,' Emily said, but didn't offer him the use of the spare one. She had, till he'd arrived, felt a bit guilty about making him drive all the way back tonight, but now she was rather relieved that she had been so firm about it.

He looked tired but there was a certain energy to him, a side to him she didn't really see at work. Usually Hugh wore dark blue scrubs, sometimes she saw him in a suit, but it was the outside-work Hugh that tended to get them into trouble, and now she was starting to see why.

Jeans were just jeans until Hugh decided to wear them. She couldn't help but notice his bum as he put some food, champagne and wine in the fridge. His top was gunmetal grey and possibly, possibly a bit too tight, or rather too tight for Emily's liking because she could see the stretch of lean muscles and when he turned around it confirmed his stomach was deliciously flat.

No, it was the fridge contents that were delicious, Emily told herself as her face burnt under his gaze.

'You're sunburnt,' Hugh said, misreading her flaming cheeks.

'Just a bit.'

'More than just a bit,' Hugh said. 'You're going to be in absolute agony tonight.'

'I shan't, and anyway,' Emily added, deciding to deal with the spare-room issue he had raised, here and now, 'if I am in agony you won't be here to witness it.'

'Then we'd better get started,' Hugh said, regretting her choice but for now accepting it. 'Right, let's kick things off.'

He sat at the kitchen table and pulled out his phone. 'Come and sit on my knee and we'll take a photo of the two of us.'

'Stop it!' Emily started to laugh. 'There's no way that I'm sitting on your knee. Why don't I just take a photo of you and then put it up and you can do the same of me?'

'We're supposed to be a couple,' Hugh pointed out. 'Come on, don't be shy now...' he teased.

It wasn't shyness that was the issue! Emily perched on his knee and tried to deny just how gorgeous he felt to her naked thigh.

'I'm not some pervy uncle,' Hugh said, pulling her higher up his lap, but when his hand met her suntanned, oiled thigh and Emily wriggled to get a little bit more comfortable for the picture, he amended that statement. 'Whoops, maybe I am!'

That made Emily laugh, just enough that a very nice photo was taken and Emily remained on his knee as they examined the image and then Hugh updated his status.

Emily has sunburn in June. he typed, and then, before posting he thought for a moment. 'Should I make a joke about you being a Scottish rose or something?'

'No, because then Alex really would know that we were faking it,' Emily said. 'Just leave it at that.'

Hugh posted his status and very soon a couple of his friends had 'liked' the image.

'We should do a few like that,' Hugh said, but Emily would prefer that they didn't. She was still on his knee and it felt very nice to be there. She could feel the heat of his palm on her thigh and the solidness between his legs and was actually grateful for the excuse of being sunburnt, because her body felt as if it were on fire.

She smelt of summer—suntan oil, combined with the crisp scent of her T-shirt and an elusive fragrance that seem to be designed just for him, because in that moment both were turned on.

She could feel his eyes burning into the back of her neck and worried she might leave a damp patch on his jeans as his hand pressed a little into her thigh. She was so turned on.

'What's for lunch?' Emily asked, but with the air so thick and lust-laden even that sounded suggestive because had he said *This* and then pulled her a fraction back further onto his lap, offended was the very last thing Emily would have been.

Or had he said *This* and then planted his lips where the pulse in her neck was jumping, Emily might have found herself turning around and so, rather quickly, Emily jumped from his lap.

Her T-shirt felt like a blanket. There it was again— the sudden urge to shed her clothing that occurred when he was around. Emily opened the fridge and was rather tempted to climb into it, just so that she could have a cool place to hide.

'What do you want for lunch?' Emily said, but her words were very stilted because she was choosing them very carefully.

'I would like,' Hugh answered, equally carefully, because he was as turned on as she was, 'whatever you would like.'

Emily pulled out a bottle of wine.

'That's what got us here in the first place,' Hugh pointed out.

'I'm on holiday,' Emily said, and poured two glasses.

'I've got a very long drive tonight, so I'd better not.'

'It's just for the photos,' Emily said, putting a glass on the table beside him.

'That's very cruel,' Hugh said.

It actually was—he wanted a glass of wine, he wanted to stay here a while, he wanted her to raise her arms so that he could simply strip off her T-shirt.

Sex was in the air and he didn't get how Emily consistently denied it.

Hugh watched as she added a few cubes to her wine. 'That's so wrong!'

'Ah, but it's so nice,' Emily said, taking a sip.

'Get changed,' Hugh said.

'Changed?'

'For *tomorrow's* picnic.'

'Of course.'

Emily ran upstairs and selected denim shorts and a black halterneck, put on some large silver loops and some lipstick then pulled her hair out of her ponytail.

'Wow!' Hugh said, as she came down the stairs. 'I wish I *was* here tomorrow to see you!'

He had changed too but only into a different T-shirt, which was now white and only served to make his eyes more green.

Help!

'Aren't you wearing shorts on your holiday?' Emily teased, as they headed out to the back garden.

'I don't want you getting too excited, Em.'

He was joking, of course, teasing her too, yet, Emily conceded, he was also telling a bit of the truth. Yes, perhaps the less of Hugh's skin on show the better, Emily thought as she spread a blanket under the shade of a tree.

Hugh was thinking the same because her rather ample breasts were still without a bra and when she bent over, her ample bottom actually had him look away.

'Oh, my,' Emily said, opening the hamper. 'I don't know where to start.'

'I do,' Hugh said, taking out a Scotch egg, 'these taste nothing like you remember them.'

'Have you had one already?' Her eyes accused him of cheating.

'One, when I was collecting the order.'

'Anything else?'

'No.'

She squeezed lemon over wild Scottish salmon and Hugh got straight into the potted lobster, but there was just too much to choose from. From pepper and jalapeno-stuffed olives, to gorgeous cheeses and quince paste, and they chatted and laughed and smacked hands away when someone pounced on a delicacy the other wanted.

They did everything but feed each other and in the end, for safety's sake, Emily lay on her back rather than face him.

'I never want to stop eating,' Emily said.

'Nor me.'

'But I have to,' Emily said, closing her eyes under the lovely weight of feeling full. 'Though the pastries are calling me.'

'We'll have dessert later,' Hugh said, and she thought of the tiny blueberry and lemon-curd tarts and wanted an empty stomach to devour them. 'It will be good for the photos to spread them out a bit...' Hugh's voice trailed off as realisation hit.

'Oh!' Emily's eyes snapped open and met Hugh's.

They hadn't taken a single photo.

Which was the whole point of him being here!

'Okay,' Hugh said, and dealt with it immediately. 'Just stay there.' He pulled out his phone and took a photo of Emily half-asleep, surrounded by empty containers. 'I'll put it up tomorrow.'

'And if you write "Feeding time at the zoo is over",' Emily warned, 'we'll be over before we start.'

'I was going to write exactly that.' Hugh smiled but for a second it wavered, not that she'd notice. Emily's eyes were still closed, but because they knew each other so well, shared the same kind of humour, they got all excited over the blood orange no-peel marmalade he'd bought her. The fact that they *got* each other bemused him at times.

Why wouldn't she give them a try?

It was late afternoon and idyllic and more tempting than dessert was Emily's breasts falling a little to the side, her nipples beckoning him, and he moved his gaze to her mouth and wondered what would happen if he simply leant over and kissed her.

She'd kiss him right back.

Emily was very glad that her eyes were closed because she was wondering if sex in a garden was illegal.

Maybe he could stay one night after all?

It would be mean to send him off and there was that lovely champagne he'd bought.

Emily's mind was turning like a carousel as she lay there, wrestling with common sense, telling herself that sex she could handle, it was the emotional part, the inevitable bitter ending that she was attempting to shield herself from.

She knew that his eyes were on her, could almost feel his gaze as a caress, and if she opened her own eyes…

She did and there was his gaze waiting, but when his phone rang Hugh let out a small cuss as Emily let out a sigh of relief. She sat up, glad the moment of madness had been broken before any harm had been done, and started to collect together the picnic things.

'Oh, Alex, hi.' Hugh rolled his eyes as Alex checked in on him. 'Yes, the weather's being very kind. Emily is already sunburnt.'

He glanced over to smile but Emily wasn't looking

at him. Instead, she was torturing him with her cleavage as she gathered together the plates.

But then, as Alex told him the reason for his phone call, Hugh stopped thinking rude thoughts and wondered just what the hell he was supposed to do and how on earth he could tell Emily.

'I'll just check if Emily has any plans...' He grimaced as Emily looked up and frowned at him. 'Emily, Alex and Jennifer are heading up this way tomorrow to look at houses and they wondered if they might join us for dinner?'

'That would be lovely!' Emily said, though the smile on her face was black.

'Great,' Hugh said to Alex. 'About six?' Then he gave another wince and ignored her shaking head as he continued. 'Of course you don't need to book anywhere, there's a spare room here.'

'Oh, no!' Emily said the second Hugh ended the call. 'What the hell did you invite them to stay for?'

'I didn't invite them,' Hugh protested. 'Alex practically invited himself. I don't doubt that he's checking up on us. What was I supposed to say?'

Emily picked up the basket and headed back to the house, and when Hugh followed her in she got straight to the point. 'I'm not sharing a bed with you tomorrow night,' she said, because she was having enough trouble keeping them apart with the kitchen table between them.

'Fine. I'll sleep on the floor.' He went to the fridge and finally poured the glass of wine that he'd wanted since Emily had first poured hers.

'You're driving!' Emily reminded him.

'Emily, you surely don't expect me to drive back

tonight and then come here again tomorrow.' Before she could answer that, yes, as unreasonable as it was, she expected just that, Hugh spoke over her. 'If I do that then you'll complain that I left shopping and all the meal preparation to you.' When still she said nothing Hugh let out a sigh. 'All right, I'll see if I can get a bed and breakfast for tonight.'

With a martyred sigh he went back to his phone and started looking for accommodation.

'Did you suggest this to Alex?' Emily asked.

'I swear that I didn't. Alex was actually saying the other day that he was going to make a bit more effort with his marriage.'

'Are they having problems?'

'Why do you jump straight to they must be having problems?' Hugh asked.

'Because isn't that what it usually means?'

'Not in their case. As far as I know, they are very happy, and not by accident.' Hugh added, 'You know how Alex always has a project on the go and he's decided it's time to make it about Jennifer.' Hugh carried on looking through his phone. 'Right, there's a bed and breakfast two doors down from here with a vacancy.' He carried on reading. 'I get a full breakfast served by a very friendly host, which is more than I'll probably get here.' He gave her a wicked smile. 'But I'm taking back the marmalade.'

'No, you're not,' Emily said, and as he went to book his reservation, she gave in. 'Okay, you can have the spare room tonight just so long as you change the sheets and get it ready for Jennifer and Alex tomorrow.'

'Change the sheets?' Hugh frowned. 'I'm only going to be sleeping in it for one night, I don't have the lurgy.' Then he saw her expression. 'Fine, I'll change the sheets.'

Emily did her very best to sulk for the rest of the afternoon but it proved impossible.

It started to rain and so they went shopping in the village for tomorrow's dinner and planned the menu as they went along.

'There's a slow cooker at the cottage,' Emily said as they looked at the meat. 'We could do Greek-style slow-cooked lamb on a nice salad, or is that too easy?'

'Easy sounds good.' Hugh nodded but shook his head as Emily went to add tzatziki to the trolley. 'I'll make it.'

They got all the usual things for breakfast as well as some amazing bread but Emily was adamant about one thing. 'They're not having my marmalade at breakfast.'

'We'll hide it,' Hugh agreed.

They decided on strawberries soaked in Cointreau and cream for dessert and, yay, they'd found the easiest dinner to prepare in the world.

'We'll have plenty of time to relax,' Hugh said.

'Oh, I intend to,' Emily said, 'but what do I wear?' It was the age-old problem but a real one this late afternoon. 'I packed shorts and shorts and shorts.'

'It's fine,' Hugh said, but when they passed a little boutique Emily wandered in and after a quick look found a dress that might just calm the sunburn that by tomorrow would be raging—it was pale blue and loose and the fabric was so sheer it felt like a sheet of ice as she slipped it over her head in the changing room.

It was gorgeous.

Too gorgeous perhaps for Hugh.

'Emily?' he called from behind the curtain. 'Let's have a look.'

'Oh, you have to approve, do you?' Emily said, slipping it off and pulling on her shorts and top and then stepping out.

'No,' Hugh said, 'I just wanted to see.'

'You'll see tomorrow.'

'I'll get it,' Hugh said.

'No!' Emily said, and then smiled. 'Actually, if I'm playing the part of your tart then I *should* have a clothing allowance.'

It was fun, just fun, no matter how much she tried to sulk.

The shower passed and the sun came back out for its final gasps before it set. They refilled the picnic basket and headed to the beach, and there was no choice but to briefly hold hands as he helped her down the steep cliff path, slippery from the rain, and to their oasis.

The beach was practically empty, a huge stretch of sand, and the most magnificent sunset was theirs to enjoy.

Yes, it was very difficult to sulk with a mouthful of lemon curd and Hugh making her laugh as they took another photo of the two of them.

'Ooh, that's a good one,' Emily said, taking his phone and looking at Hugh in the image before herself.

'Very good,' Hugh said, looking at the image of Emily instead of himself.

'Send it to my phone and I'll post it.'

'Why don't I just put it up?' Hugh asked.

'Our relationship's starting to look a little one-sided in cyberland.'

'It's pretty one-sided in real life,' Hugh said, but without a trace of bitterness. In fact, he was smiling as he sent the image to her phone and then looked her straight in the eye. 'Or is it?'

Emily didn't appreciate the question—the lust between them was as relentless as the waves and she left his question unanswered as they headed back up the cliff. Hugh, at eye level with her bottom as they made their way up, resisted making a comment about the amazing view.

In fact, he resisted full stop.

The ball had been placed in Emily's court.

Back in the cottage he stretched out on one of the sofas as Emily cracked the champagne. 'God, it's been so good to get away,' Hugh admitted, as Emily lay on the sofa opposite. 'And even better not to have to drive back.' Hugh yawned. 'I've had a shocking week at work. I'm worried about…' He hesitated. His concerns about Gina must remain in his head, but for a second there he'd forgotten that they were pretending. So nice had the day been, he had completely forgotten that Emily didn't actually want him there so there was no way he could tell her about his issues with Gina.

'Worried about what?' Emily pushed.

'Just a patient who isn't doing very well.'

They could have gone to the pub but it was Emily's holiday and all she wanted to do was lounge on the sofa and watch a film.

Unfortunately, the only film that was on turned out to be incredibly sexy and, given that she had already declared there was no way she was watching sport, Emily and Hugh had to suffer their way through it.

'Great choice, Emily,' Hugh groaned during one very steamy scene.

It was torture.

And no less of a torture for Emily to lie in bed a little while later, knowing that he was across the hallway.

Her sunburn *was* agony.

At midnight all she wanted to do was cross the hall and fill the bathroom sink with cold water and drop her breasts into it, except Hugh's bedroom was next to the bathroom and she had the wretched thought of sinking her breasts in his face.

''Night, Emily,' he called out at one in the morning as she returned from getting a drink.

''Night, Hugh.'

It had been an almost perfect day except for one thing. One thing between her legs that ached perhaps as much as his.

If he made a move, if he called her again…

Just sleep with him, Emily!

But she was truly scared to now.

Today had been amazing and a relationship with Hugh would be very different from the one she'd had with Marcus.

She and Marcus had been more like friends, which was what she was with Hugh, but with Marcus her stomach hadn't had a butterfly house in permanent residence in her stomach whenever he'd been around, and though she'd cared about Marcus she hadn't cared in the dangerous sense.

Emily closed her eyes in the hope sleep would arrive yet as she lay there she thought about the break-up with her ex—the so-called public shaming when he'd got off with Heidi.

How could she explain that she'd actually been happy

for him in the end, happy that Marcus had had the guts to go after the love of his life.

Tears slid from closed eyes to the pillow as she acknowledged to herself that possibly Hugh was that for her.

Emily gave up trying to sleep and took her phone from the bedside table and stared at the picture they'd taken that evening. They looked happy and carefree, which was how she actually felt when he was around.

When he was around, but how would she feel when he was gone?

After her break-up with Marcus, Emily had boxed up his stuff to return to him with much the same emotions as when she took the Christmas tree down. A little sad that it was over but ready to start afresh.

With Hugh it would be agonising and looking at her phone, staring into his green eyes, seeing her smiling face beside his, Emily finally understood the meaning behind a well-known saying.

Don't start what you can't finish.

It would kill her to be finished with Hugh and that was the reason she chose to stay alone tonight.

CHAPTER FIVE

EMILY WOKE THE next morning to the sound of a knock on her door, and Hugh scored no points for good behaviour even though he brought her in a mug of tea.

'Why did you wake me up?' Emily asked.

'It's ten o'clock.'

'But I wanted to lie in.'

'Which is why I waited till ten o'clock. How long do you usually lie in for?'

'I don't have to answer that,' Emily said, taking a sip of tea and wishing he wouldn't sit on the bed.

'The lamb is in the slow cooker and I've made the tzatziki,' Hugh said.

'Did you make any toast with that blood orange no-peel marmalade on it while you were down there?' From beneath the sheet Emily kicked his thigh with her foot.

'Will all my sins be forgiven if I make toast?'

'Nearly all of them.'

He made some for himself too and brought up his own mug of tea. Yesterday they had been too busy avoiding their attraction to each other to spend time working out the nuts and bolts of their charade but agreed to do it now so they wouldn't get things wrong at their little dinner party.

'How long have we been seeing each other?' Hugh asked, as they munched through the nicest toast in the world.

'Well, I said to Louise that we'd been on and off for a couple of months.'

'Okay.' Hugh nodded but then he gave a small wince. 'Have you heard the rumours…?'

'Yes, yes,' Emily dismissed. 'I know that you got off with Gina after the emergency do.'

'But I didn't get off with her. Gina and I are just friends.'

'Friends who just can't keep their hands off each other in the car park.' Emily smirked.

'Emily, there really is nothing between Gina and I. There never has been.' Hugh hesitated. Again he wanted to tell Emily what was on his mind but in fairness to Gina he couldn't. 'It is going to make things a bit awkward, though. People are going to think that I cheated on you…'

'I'm sure I'll survive.' Emily laughed and Hugh frowned.

'It doesn't bother you?'

'If we actually were an item then, yes, I might want to know the details, but we're not an item and anyway…' Emily started, but then changed her mind. She really didn't want to reveal to Hugh that she was thinking of leaving her job and so people talking about them wasn't going to be an issue for her. 'Don't worry about work for now,' Emily said instead. 'Let's just sort out what we're going to say tonight.'

'Well, I'm guessing that Jennifer might talk about

Rima and Matthew's wedding, which is in July. Do you know Rima?'

Emily shook her head.

'I think she got sick just before you started at The Royal. Okay, Rima and I went to med school together, along with Gina. Matthew's a dentist,' Hugh said as Emily yawned. 'Pay attention, Emily, they're good friends of mine and if we are going out then Alex and Jennifer would expect you to be going to the wedding with me and to at least know a little about them.' He had a sudden thought. 'When is your dad's wedding?'

'The last week of June, but you don't have to come to that.'

'It will look a bit odd if I don't,' Hugh said, as he went through his diary on his phone. 'You'd actually be doing me a favour, Emily. My nephew is getting christened that Sunday and I'm godfather. I think Alex might be a bit more accommodating about me swapping my weekend for your father getting married than my nephew's christening.'

'Alex has got four children of his own,' Emily pointed out. 'I'm sure he'd understand.'

'Ah, but Alex's wife is Jennifer,' Hugh said. 'Keeper of his diary. If it was her nephew, I'd swear that she'd say no, that they couldn't attend unless they swapped weekends…'

'Really?'

'Yep.'

'You can't tell your sister the same?'

'Nope. I actually wrote down all the weekends I was available when she started talking about the christening. She told me she had enough on her own calendar without taking into consideration mine, which is fair enough, I guess, but every couple I know seems to be getting married this summer...' He let out a breath of frustration because his sister was such hard work at times. 'I'm thrilled I'm the baby's godfather, even if I don't know that I'll make a brilliant one, but, hell, one weekend in three I'm on take and Kate thinks it's as easy as swapping a shift as a trainee in a burger bar.'

'Hey, I worked in a burger bar for three years and it's not so easy to change a shift.' She smiled and then frowned. 'Can't you just explain to her—not about the christening, I guess it's too late for that, but for the future?'

'Kate has very sensitive toes,' Hugh sighed, 'and we're not allowed to step on them.'

'Or?' Emily asked.

'Who knows?' Hugh said, and she looked at him because his voice was suddenly serious, but he quickly made it lighter. 'It's no big deal but if you could slip in that your father's getting married, I'd love you for ever—' his smile was genuine then '—which isn't what you want either.'

Even Emily laughed. 'I don't think you're capable of loving anyone for ever.'

There was a conversation to be had but she refused to go there and Hugh said nothing.

He didn't know about for ever, he lived for now. He wanted a chance for them but he refused to beg.

'Am I the reason that you and Olivia broke up?' Emily asked, as they tried to get their stories straight.

Hugh looked at her. She was very possibly the reason all his relationships had broken up.

'Yes.'

'What else would I know about you that I don't know now, if we'd been going out for two months?' Emily asked.

'Not much,' Hugh said after a moment's thought. 'I think we know each other pretty well, or at least you know me. What would I know about you if we had been going out with each other for two months?'

'Nothing that I'd want you to discuss at the dinner table.' Emily smiled. 'I think we're good to go.'

The afternoon flew by. Hugh had, of course, lied about changing the sheets and Emily outed him.

'How can you tell?' he asked, because he thought he'd made the bed really well.

'You just can,' Emily said. 'Don't you love getting in a freshly made bed with clean sheets?' Emily started to blush as that naked thought reared its head again but thankfully Hugh halted himself from suggesting he find out. After all, he didn't want to have to make the bed again.

But *it* was there.

It was there in the kitchen as she whipped the cream for the strawberries that were soaking in Cointreau and Hugh dipped his finger into it and she wanted to be the one to suck that cream off.

It was there in the bathroom as he walked in on Emily putting on her make-up and he got a first glimpse of her pale blue dress, or rather her bare shoulders, and with a quick 'Sorry' Hugh turned and walked out with so much haste he might just as well have walked in on Emily sitting on the toilet.

It was just there.

Which meant that by the time Alex and Jennifer

arrived Emily was doing her level best to avoid any physical contact with Hugh and nearly jumped out of her skin when their hands met over the pistachio nuts as they discussed Emily's father's wedding.

'Do you like her?' Jennifer asked. 'Your future step-mother?'

Emily blinked. 'Well, I wouldn't call her my step-mother,' she admitted, 'given she's not much older than me and...'

Hugh watched as her voice trailed off and Emily changed whatever she was about to say. 'Cathy seems very nice, though I've only met her once. I wasn't ex-pecting Dad to marry again so quickly—he's not one for giving much notice,' Emily said, and then glanced at Hugh. 'Though neither is your sister.'

He was very grateful for the opening. 'Yes, I'm sup-posed to be godfather to my nephew and it's his chris-tening that weekend but I've already told Kate that I'm working.'

'No, no,' Alex said, 'you should be there for Emily's father's wedding. We can sort something out.'

Hugh followed her into the kitchen and gave a de-lighted grin. 'How easy was that?'

'I know!' Emily said.

'Though bit more affection wouldn't go amiss,' Hugh said. 'It's a bit strained in there.'

'They might think we've just had a row,' Emily said.

'We're supposed to be dating, not married,' Hugh said. 'You handed me my drink in the same way you pass a scalpel.'

'I don't like public displays of affection,' Emily said, and then pulled a face and changed her voice to a whis-per. 'Unlike those two.'

'I know!' Hugh laughed. 'They're all over each other.'

'Tell you what,' Hugh said, as the sound of conversation from the other room stopped, 'Jennifer will come and offer a hand in a moment so if she catches us kissing, your frigid nature at the dining table can be excused.'

'No!'

'Just once,' Hugh said, his hands on her hips. 'Relax, Em, we've done this before.'

His mouth came down on hers and unlike Emily's lips, which were rigid, his were very relaxed and attempting to knead hers into a response.

'I'm not your hairy aunt either,' Hugh said, pulling back, and that moved her mouth into a smile and he kissed her some more.

Sure that any moment now they'd be disturbed, Emily relaxed into it.

She had tried so hard to forget how nice kissing Hugh was.

Now a night and a day of holding back was washed away by the stroke of his tongue.

Come on, Jennifer, Emily thought as his kiss deepened, because she was kissing him back in the way she wanted to.

Any minute now, Jennifer, her mind begged as Hugh pressed her into the bench with his groin and her hands, on instinct, slid down his jeans to the curve of his bum. He could feel the consent in her fingers and then the wrestle as she moved her head back and terminated their kiss, yet their bodies still caressed and thrummed.

He looked at her flushed face and glittering eyes and could not fathom her constant denial of want.

'I don't think we're going to get our audience,' Emily said.

'Do you care?'

Not really.

She wanted more of Hugh. Her reasons for resistance were falling like dominoes and Emily desperately wanted them back.

'We'd better take dinner through.' Emily picked up two plates and Hugh did the same and quickly found out the reason for the silence in the other room.

No, Alex and Jennifer really couldn't keep their hands off each other!

It really was a lovely evening but Emily found it increasingly hard to concentrate on the conversation given that tonight she would be sharing a room with Hugh.

But not a bed.

Emily simply did not want to know just how good they could be.

CHAPTER SIX

'WHERE ARE YOU going?' Hugh asked as Emily, sleep-wear in hand, went to head out of the bedroom.

'To get changed in the bathroom.'

'Well, that won't look odd!' he said, with more than a hint of sarcasm. 'Just get changed here. I promise not to look.'

They could hear Jennifer and Alex laughing and talking as they got ready for bed and Emily knew that Hugh was right—it would look odd, her creeping in and out of the bathroom with her clothes, and so Emily started to undress as Hugh lay on the makeshift bed on the floor.

He turned on his side and read through his emails but it was a futile effort because all he could see was the image of Emily yesterday, when he had caught her sunbathing with her top off.

'How's the sunburn?'

'Better,' Emily said, pulling on a pair of pyjama shorts and strappy top and then climbing into bed.

'Do you think they believe us?' Hugh asked, and Emily turned and looked down to where he lay on the floor.

'I don't know,' she admitted in a harsh whisper as she recalled the evening. 'It was a bit strained at times.'

'How could you not know how old I am or when my birthday is?' Hugh asked, referring to a small sticking point in the conversation when Jennifer had said something about it being his birthday next month. 'You came out for drinks on my thirtieth birthday.'

'I did,' Emily said, 'but it's not etched in my memory.'

Actually, Emily had done her level best to forget his thirtieth birthday last year because Hugh had just started seeing Olivia.

Horrible person that she was at times, Emily had loathed seeing him so happy and had been quite convinced that night that Hugh had finally found *the one*. 'Oh, and you didn't tell me the wedding was going to be in the Lake District...'

'Ah, so that was what that dirty look was for,' he said, as Emily turned out the light. 'It will be fun,' Hugh said, 'though hopefully that room at least has a sofa I can sleep on, rather than a stone floor.'

She said nothing.

'Emily?' Hugh said to the darkness a few tense moments later.

'What?'

'I am so uncomfortable.'

'Tough.'

'We could sleep with a pillow between us just in case you can't resist me.'

Emily didn't answer. She actually didn't trust herself to answer because the truth was she probably couldn't resist.

Why was she like this?

Emily stared at the ceiling. She knew why, she did all she could to avoid getting hurt.

'You haven't even worked there for one shift and already you've got all hard,' Hugh moaned.

'Sorry?' Emily said. She hadn't really been paying attention to his words.

'In Accident and Emergency—they breed them tough there.'

Still Emily said nothing.

'Are you looking forward to it, even a little bit?' Hugh asked, because he knew that she had tried to get out of working there.

'I'm not going to be working there.' There was a long stretch of silence as Emily willed herself to open up to him. 'I'm handing in my notice.'

'Emily?'

'I am.' Her voice was thick with suppressed tears because it had been a very difficult decision to make, but the right one, she was sure.

Possibly by consent, Hugh moved from the hard floor and into the bed beside her.

'Why?' he asked, but she didn't answer. 'Emily, it's for three months, it will be over before you know it.'

'Please don't try to talk me out of it.'

'I bloody well will. Accident and Emergency really isn't that bad,' Hugh said. 'Most of it will be bandages and plaster...'

'Hugh.' She turned and faced him. 'They're going to have me in Resus.'

'I don't get what you're so worried about.'

'I'm not worried,' Emily said, 'because I'm not going to be doing it.'

'You'd be great.'

'I'm great already,' Emily said.

'I just don't get it.' Hugh was genuinely bemused,

but then Emily often bemused him. 'I thought that you loved your job.'

'I do.'

'And if you want to get on, which I think you do, surely it's worth doing the occasional rotation. From my position it works better—the transition for the patient—'

'I don't want to hear it, Hugh,' Emily said, because she didn't. Miriam was right, Hugh was right—it was better for the patients, and the new system was working well. It was for her own private reasons that she was digging her heels in and she chose then to tell Hugh a little of why.

'You know that sign in Theatre that says no relatives beyond this point?'

'Yes.'

'That's the part of Theatre I like.'

'You prefer your patients unconscious?' Hugh tried to make a joke but was taken aback by her response.

'Yes,' Emily admitted. 'I don't like all the drama of relatives and I actually prefer being in Theatre. I can focus on the patient, I can do my very best for them even if they don't know it.'

'Emily—'

'I don't want to talk about it any more.'

They lay in mutual silence till Hugh broke it.

'Maybe if they heard us at it…'

'Ha-ha,' Emily said.

'Just a few moans would suffice.'

'No.'

'Go on,' Hugh said, and made a low moaning noise.

'Was that it?' Emily said. 'You were very quick!'

Hugh laughed and they lay again in silence and

Emily was just about to drift off when another moan came from Hugh, a very different kind.

'Please, no!' Hugh said, and Emily opened her eyes and smothered her laughter with her hand as she realised what Hugh was referring to, because there was a certain regular noise coming from the room across the hall.

'Oh, God!' Hugh said, appalled. 'It's like finding out that your parents do it!'

'Stop it.' Emily was nearly crying from laughter.

'I wish they would.'

It seemed to go on for ever but finally, *finally* the house was quiet and Emily lay there strangely resigned to her fate, because even though they weren't touching she could almost feel his thigh next to hers and if he made a move now, she knew what would happen, knew because she actually ached from resistance.

''Night, Emily.'

A light kiss to her forehead surprised her.

So too did Hugh, rolling to his side so that his back was to her.

And so too, a short while later, did the sound of his breathing surprise her for it told her that he was asleep.

Damn you, Hugh, for behaving!

He did behave.

In fact, Hugh fell asleep with a slightly triumphant smile because he could feel her tension.

Deny it all you like, Emily, he thought as, just before dawn, with its mistress finally sleeping, her body broke from its self-imposed chains and rolled into his and Hugh lay on his back, wondering what the hell went on in that head of hers.

Wondering too what was going on in his own because outside his career Hugh rarely thought in the long term.

He was thinking of it now.

Emily woke just after dawn to the nicest place she had ever been. Warm and relaxed, their limbs were knotted together like the necklaces in her jewellery box...

And she couldn't be bothered to untangle them either.

Neither could she be bothered to untangle her thoughts, because sex was just sex, Emily convinced herself in the rosy pink light of dawn, it didn't mean she was handing over her heart.

A one-morning stand for good behaviour and it had been so hard to be so good.

'They just did it again,' Hugh whispered, as he felt her stir in his arms. 'I don't think I'm going to be able to look at him at breakfast. I'm traumatised.'

He wasn't, especially when Emily opened her eyes and pulled back her head and then smiled.

It was a smile he had never seen and one Emily had never given to anyone before, for it was neither guarded nor sparing.

'Did you sleep?' Hugh asked.

'Not much. How about you?'

'Like a log.'

They were both smiling and she could feel the goosebumps rise on her arm as his fingers dusted the top of it and her head went back to his chest and her hand that was on his stomach moved down a little, brushing his flat stomach with her fingers and feeling his breathing halt for a few seconds as she worked her way deliberately down more.

'Not too traumatised,' Emily said, dusting the thick length of his erection.

It could not have been better for Hugh, for he did not want a kiss that got out of hand, he did not want regret, and so her bold decision suited him, as did the fingers slipping in to his hipsters.

Emily lifted her mouth to his and kissed him as she had always wanted to. Deep and intimate, it was a long, silent kiss that had her burn and ache for more of his skin.

'I want this off,' Hugh said, his fingers at her top, 'but I don't want to move your hand.'

'Can't have both,' Emily said, and her hands slid down his hipsters and Hugh sorted out her shorts, both kicking off their bottom halves as Hugh rapidly dealt with her top.

He pulled it and Emily closed her eyes in bliss as he took one hot, burnt nipple and cooled it with his mouth till she whimpered for him to do the same with the other.

'God, Em...' Hugh said, between breasts. He'd known they would be fantastic, they had enthralled him with the way they danced beneath her theatre top and the occasional glimpse of lacy bra, but Hugh was in second heaven and so too was she.

Hugh's fingers were working magic and hers were doing the same to him.

He was back to her mouth but as their lips met again, stupid, stupid necessities attempted to beckon and Hugh tried to remember where he'd taken off his jeans, which held his wallet...

'I'm on the Pill.' She answered his brief distraction and got back to his mouth, but now she had her own thoughts to contend with as she tried to remember if she'd taken it this lazy morning.

Sex, though, was proving a very powerful distraction from bothersome thoughts.

Who cared?

Not they.

'Quietly,' Emily warned.

Face on, he slid inside her and both were just about coming in relief because it had been a very long twenty-four hours, but as they started to move the bed creaked like a rusty gate.

'Shh…' Emily said, but they couldn't stop the noise.

'They won't care…' Hugh said.

'I care!' Emily responded, and a frantic decision was made to head for the floor.

His makeshift bed was actually very comfortable now, because this was no whoops-we-went-too-far sex. Emily was on top and the view really was fantastic now.

Emily didn't do Sunday morning sex. Well, once on Marcus's birthday, poor guy, but she was loving this lazy morning. The feel of cool air on her warm body, the feel of his hands roaming her hips and the dance of her breasts had never found her more free.

His finger on her clitoris had her face redden with imminent pleasure. She almost wanted to slap his hand for it should come with the discretionary warning of flashing lights, so much so that she lost her rhythm but Hugh gave it back to her.

Emily pressed her lips together when she wanted to moan, a hum building in her throat, and Hugh prised open her lips and slipped in his fingers to warn her back to quiet. She sucked on them like a birth aid and then released them, scared she might bite as she started to come. Hugh held her chin up with his free hand, an erotic head support that tightened as his orgasm extended hers, and then he released her. Emily collapsed to his mouth, slowly riding the final waves that brought them both in to a very different shore.

He kissed her for what felt like for ever and then, while they lay there, Hugh pulled the covers down from the bed and covered them.

It was too early to get up and there was no point going back up to the bed, for as they lay in their little fortress, their bodies better acquainted, they both knew from their kisses they were going again.

CHAPTER SEVEN

TWICE?

Emily stood in the shower and let the water run over her.

And she had a feeling Hugh would be more than happy to go for a third time the second Jennifer and Alex left.

He'd said he wanted to hear her moan.

She blew out a breath of laughter as she imagined some version of the *Benny Hill Show* taking place in the cottage as they chased each other around, but her laughter strangled because she wanted to get back to her safe haven.

This time she *had* brought her clothes into the bathroom and would emerge fully dressed and with her make-up on and then get breakfast ready for her guests.

And then see them all off, and she wasn't just thinking about Alex and Jennifer.

Hugh might think, given what had taken place this morning, that the rules had changed, but to Emily it just made her more certain that a relationship with Hugh would be a very foolish thing.

She *was* crazy about him.

Emily massaged conditioner into her hair and she

loathed where she was—crazy about someone, that il-logical place she'd avoided for more than half of her life.

Oh, it was different, of course, from the other loves in her life.

Dangerously different—for this had the potential for even more hurt.

Back to friends, back to business, Emily told herself as she dried herself off and got dressed.

She tied her hair back and then headed downstairs, where Hugh was making breakfast as he chatted to Alex and Jennifer.

'We've got two places we're hoping to see today,' Jennifer said.

'Three,' Alex said, 'though we'll only be driving past the third one, it hasn't yet come on the market.' He turned and smiled as Emily came in. 'Good morning.'

'Morning,' Emily said. Hugh handed her a mug of tea and she took a seat at the kitchen table.

No, she didn't offer to help Hugh, though she did no-tice when she went to put marmalade on her toast that he *hadn't* put out her favourite one.

Hugh gave her a wink as she looked up and she gave him a smile but inside she wavered, because it would be so easy to give in, to just fall a bit further into the man who spoke the same language without words.

And then she felt mean.

Hugh laughed when she got up and got out the very, very nice marmalade.

'The things I do to further your career,' Emily said, when Alex and Jennifer had gone and she put the lid on a nearly empty jar.

'I'll buy you a box of them,' Hugh said. 'You should have seen your face when they went for their fourth slices.'

'Scavengers,' Emily said. 'No wonder they were so hungry!' It was all too nice and too easy to be nice and easy with Hugh so she made herself say it. 'What time are you heading off?'

She saw the slight rise of his eyebrows and knew her message had just been delivered—she wanted him gone, she wanted to get back to her holiday, and what had happened upstairs, well, there it would remain.

'After I've talked some sense into you about work.'

'I wish I hadn't said anything about it.'

'Because you know what you're proposing to do makes no sense. Why don't you at least wait until you've got another job before you hand in your notice? You've got another week before you start to look around. If Accident and Emergency is so bad then you will at least have another job to go to.'

Emily closed her eyes.

'It might take a while to find a job that suits you,' Hugh continued. 'A lot of hospitals rotate their critical care staff. Perhaps you could do some agency work, though you might find yourself pushed out of your comfort zone every shift…'

'Is that what you think? That I don't want to be pushed out of my comfort zone?'

'That's exactly what I think.'

'Well, thanks for the little pep talk.'

'You can't just blow up your career…'

'I'm not,' Emily said, 'I'm just standing my ground. Hugh…' She didn't know how best to explain it. 'I hated

A and E when I did my training. I mean, I seriously hated it. I like routine, I like procedure, I don't like all the drama of A and E. I can't stand seeing people so raw and then you're supposed to just…' she didn't know how to explain it '…loan yourself to them.'

'Loan yourself?' Hugh asked. 'What the hell does that mean?'

'I don't know how better—'

'Can I ask?' Hugh interrupted and in his very own way got straight to the point. 'Why did you do nursing, then? If you don't want to see people at their most raw, if you don't want to *loan yourself,* as you call it, why would you do this job?' Emily didn't answer and he looked at her tense lips and knew he was on the right track. 'Or did you always want to be a theatre nurse? Did Emily scrub in for her dolls?' Still she didn't answer. 'I mean, it's a pretty specific goal.'

'I always wanted to be a nurse,' Emily said.

'Then surely—'

'I didn't want to let my parents mess another part of me up,' Emily almost shouted. And she never shouted, she never rowed, yet Hugh seemed to take her to the edge in all areas. 'Hugh, I know myself. I know what I want and what I don't. Don't try and change me.'

'I'm not trying to change you, Emily—I'm trying to understand you.'

'You don't have to understand me.' She didn't want him close enough to understand her and so she asked her question again. 'What time are you heading off?'

'You…you want me gone, don't you?'

'You were supposed to be here for a few hours and it's been two nights.'

Hugh was very unused to being dismissed and given

what had taken place that morning he hadn't expected to be so quickly shown the door.

'What about this morning?' Hugh said.

'What about it?' Emily frowned. 'It doesn't change anything.'

'It did for me.' Hugh just looked at the stranger who stood in Emily's shoes, a complete different person from the one who had woken up in his arms. 'Do you know why I didn't try anything last night?' Hugh said, and when Emily didn't answer, he did. 'Because I didn't want you regretting it in the morning.'

'I don't regret it,' Emily said, 'but neither do I want to repeat it. We had sex, Hugh. As you said, being your fake girlfriend comes with the occasional perk.'

'Why does it have to be fake?'

Emily couldn't actually tell him that without breaking down so she gave a brief shrug, and it incensed him enough not to even attempt to argue.

Instead, he gathered his things.

'I'll let you get on with your holiday, then.'

The peace she craved had finally been delivered yet it wasn't so pleasant any more.

She wanted to text him, to ask him to turn the car around and come back. To continue where they'd left off earlier that morning. And then what? A few weeks or months as partners?

The best few weeks and months of her adult life, no doubt.

But then what?

She didn't want to have to get over him. She didn't want to pay the price of love—the potential for pain.

She wasn't scared of the sparks that she and Hugh ignited. She was more scared of the wildfire it would create and the charred remains when it inevitably burnt out.

He had been spot on about her career, though.

Moneywise it would be foolish at best to hand in her notice without securing another job first and he had been right about working for an agency.

A few phone calls to various agencies told Emily that she couldn't be guaranteed full-time work in Theatre but there was a big demand for ICU nurses and, with her skills, she could also work in Emergency.

Hugh was right, she didn't want to move out of her comfort zone.

She really didn't have a choice and so just over a week later Emily found herself working in Emergency.

'You'll soon get used to it,' Lydia, the charge nurse, said as she showed her around.

Emily didn't want to get used to it. She remembered A nd E well from her training and even though it was a different hospital the pace of it hadn't changed.

And the staff still gossiped like crazy.

'So, how long have you been seeing Hugh?' Gerry, one of the head nurses asked, as Emily wrote Gina's name on the board.

'A couple of months on and off,' Emily said, and could feel the smirks behind her because they'd all heard the rumour that he'd got off with Gina.

Oh, they were like witches around the cauldron, waiting for the show to begin, and at the end of her first week in the dreaded accident and emergency, they got what they wanted.

Gina and Emily face to face.

'Hannah Bailey.' The paramedics rushed in an

elderly lady who had collapsed with chest pain. The other staff were working on a cyclist who had been hit by a car and Emily knew that this patient was hers.

Hannah was gravely ill and Emily took the handover as she connected the chest and ECG leads and Duncan, a resident, came over and examined her.

'Let's get her something for her pain,' Duncan said as he read the ECG, and ordered morphine, which Emily quickly drew up.

'You'll be much more comfortable soon,' Emily said to the elderly lady, and for a little while she was.

'My husband…' Hannah said. 'He'll be worried.'

'We'll take care of that,' Emily said. 'I'll go and speak to your daughter soon. The paramedics said she came in with you…'

Hannah nodded but even before the monitor started alarming, Duncan told Emily to call for the crash team and just as they started to arrive Hannah went into cardiac arrest.

'What do we have?' Gina came straight to the head of the bed and Emily didn't even look up to acknowledge her as she was busy setting up for Gina to intubate her. As Duncan delivered cardiac massage he gave Gina his findings.

Gina and Emily had worked together for years and, more importantly, worked well together so there was little need for conversation. Emily opened up an endotracheal tube as Gina suctioned the airway and then handed it to her, and in less than a moment the tube was in.

Cardiology had arrived and were reading the ECG that Emily had run off before Hannah had gone into cardiac arrest, and Lydia had come in and taken over from Duncan and was giving chest compressions.

'Did she have any family with her?' Lydia asked.

'A daughter,' Emily said, relaying what the paramedics had told her. 'She's in the interview room.'

'Could you go and speak to her, please, Emily? Let her know that things don't look good at all.'

'Sure,' Emily said, though she would far rather be delivering chest compressions than going in to speak with relatives.

Emily introduced herself to the woman and found out her name was Laura and asked what had happened.

'We were actually on our way here,' Laura explained. 'I'd gone to pick up Mum to take her to visit my dad—he's a patient on ICU. Mum's been so worried about him. We were just ten minutes away from the hospital when suddenly she said she had a pain in her chest. I didn't know whether to just keep on driving or pull over but she started to be sick so I stopped and called an ambulance.'

'You did the right thing,' Emily said, and then took a breath. 'Your mum's condition deteriorated rapidly when she arrived,' Emily explained. 'She went into cardiac arrest. The doctors are with her now and she's been intubated and they're working on getting her heart started again.'

'What am I going to tell my dad? They were just moving him to a general ward today, she's been so worried about him.' Laura started to cry. 'This is going to kill Dad.'

'What's your father's first name?' Emily asked.

'Ernest.'

'Did he have surgery for bowel cancer?' Emily

asked, because she wanted to be sure she had the right patient in mind, and she was sure that she did when Laura nodded.

'He didn't even want to have the operation, he just did it for Mum.'

'I remember your dad,' Emily said. 'I was working in Theatre when he had his operation. He was very keen to know when he'd get a cup of tea.'

Laura actually gave a small laugh. 'That's my dad.' Then she started to cry again. 'I don't know how to tell him. I don't know if he's well enough to come down and see her but he'll want to.'

'Okay.' Emily thought for a moment. 'Let me go and see what's happening with your mum and I'll come back to you soon.'

Hannah's heart was beating again but she was unconscious and the cardiologist was about to go in and speak to the daughter and explain that she didn't have very long to live and that Gina was going to extubate her and let things take their natural course.

'Her husband is a patient on ICU,' Emily explained. 'Apparently he's being moved to a general ward today. Laura, the daughter, thinks he would want to see her.'

Lydia suggested that Emily telephone ICU and explain the situation, and Emily went and did just that.

Though she didn't like to admit it, Emily was actually grateful for the time she'd spent on ICU because she did understand better how they would deal with this.

Emily spoke to Patrick, the head nurse in ICU. 'Ernest will be shattered,' Patrick said. 'He's already starting to fret that she's not here. Hannah has been here every morning at nine.' There was a small pause. 'Hold on a moment, Emily, I'll just let Hugh know what's happening. He's actually with him now.'

Emily waited for a few moments but instead of Patrick it was Hugh who came to the phone. Apart from a couple of texts and confirmation that they'd both attend Emily's father's wedding and his nephew's christening, they had barely spoken since Cornwall but certainly the state of, or rather their lack of, relationship wasn't the issue now. 'Hi, Emily, it's Hugh. Could I speak to Ernest's daughter?'

'Sure.'

'What's her name?'

'Laura.'

Emily took the phone to Laura and waited with her as Hugh spoke to her and then the phone was handed back to Emily.

'I'm going to tell Ernest now what's happening,' Hugh said. 'I'm assuming he'll want to see her and if so I'll bring him down, along with one of the ICU nurses to watch him. Is there enough space?'

'Not in Resus but I'll sort out a cubicle for them.'

'Thanks.'

Hugh rang off and Emily took Laura in to see her mother and left her with Lydia as she went to sort out a cubicle and organise it as best she could.

She took out the trolleys that wouldn't be needed and then wheeled Hannah over.

'Dad's coming to see you,' Laura said to her mum, and squeezed her hand. Emily just wanted to cry. Of course death happened in Theatre but Emily did her best to avoid the relative part. Here she couldn't pass it on to anyone.

She looked up when Hugh put his head in the cubicle. 'Is it okay to bring Ernest in?'

'Yes.' Emily nodded and Ernest's trolley was wheeled in. It was heart-breaking because Ernest didn't break down, he just kept holding his wife's hand and kissing her face and telling her how much he loved her and what a wonderful life they'd had together.

'How is she?' Gina came in.

'Comfortable,' Emily said. 'Though her breathing's very rattly.'

'I just want to have a listen to her chest,' Gina said, and she gave Ernest a smile as she gently examined his wife. 'I'll get Hannah something to help make her breathing a little more comfortable.'

Beth, the ICU nurse, said she'd watch both patients and as Emily went to get the drug Gina came over and wrote Hannah up for some more morphine if needed.

To the surprise of a few onlookers Emily gave Gina a smile. 'You've been off sick for a while.'

'I've had the worst flu,' Gina said.

It must have been bad because Gina had lost an awful lot of weight.

'How come you're in A and E?' Gina asked.

'Internal rotation.'

'Oh, that sounds painful,' Gina said, and to the ire of the onlookers Emily laughed.

Then she stopped laughing as Ernest finally broke down and the sound of his tears came from the cubicle.

Hannah had gone.

How, Emily wondered, did everyone but her seem to deal with these things? Beth was all calm and present and had her arm around Laura, Hugh was there with Ernest and Emily just felt like a spare wheel.

A spare wheel with tight lips and tears in her eyes.

'I'm going to miss you so much,' Ernest said, and Beth's arm tightened around Laura as she started to break down. 'I don't want to go home without you being there,' Ernest sobbed.

'I'll take care of you, Dad, you know that.'

And Emily stood there, wondering how everyone did it.

'Ernest,' Hugh finally said when his pager went off, 'I have to go back to ICU but you stay here with Hannah as long as you need, or as long as you're well enough.' He glanced at Beth, who nodded.

'I'll stay with them,' Beth said, to Emily's relief, and Emily headed out at the same time as Hugh.

'That was awful,' she admitted, and Hugh looked at her.

'It was nice,' Hugh said. 'Sad but nice that they were together.' He glanced up as Gina joined them. 'Hey,' Hugh said. 'It's good to see you back. How are you?'

'Better, though I don't recommend flu as a way to diet,' she added. 'Are you going up to ICU?' Gina asked Hugh, and he nodded. 'I'll walk with you.'

Hugh turned to Emily. 'Thanks for all your help this morning. It was nice that they had some time together.'

It was normal.

As normal as it would have been two weeks ago.

It just didn't feel normal now.

But then Hugh turned around.

'Hey, Emily…' he walked over '…page me when you take a lunch break. If I'm free…'

And, had they been going out, that was exactly what he'd have done.

Emily was about to make an excuse, she really didn't

want lunch with Hugh, but he spoke over her when she tried to voice one.

'There's something I'd like to say.'

He *was* free at lunchtime and they found themselves for the first time together in the hospital canteen.

'How are you finding it?' Hugh asked.

'Just as I expected,' Emily said.

'You did really well this morning.'

'I don't know about that.' Emily shrugged. 'Ernest has gone back up to the ward now.'

'Yep, I'm going to check in on him this afternoon.' Hugh got to the reason he had asked her for lunch. 'Look, I never realised how awkward it would be for you and I just wanted to say I'm sorry. I've heard all the rumours flying around about Gina and I and that Saturday night.'

'I'd heard the rumours before I offered,' Emily said. 'They're having a bit of a field day with it in Emergency but I was expecting that. I think they were hoping I'd scratch Gina's eyes out.' She gave Hugh a smile, because when they were together she so easily did. 'It's fun in a way.'

It was far from fun for Hugh but he was glad to see that Emily didn't seem upset about the gossip. 'The thing is…' Hugh stopped and Emily frowned because the usually laid-back Hugh for once looked tense.

'Are you okay?' Emily checked.

'I've got some things on my mind,' Hugh admitted. 'Can you accept that there are some things I can't tell you?'

'Yep.'

And that short answer was the reason he persisted

with Emily. Hugh could think of few women who would not ask for more information, few who would not press him to reveal when he'd said that he couldn't.

God, they could be so good.

He watched as she gave a small wave when someone called her name and Hugh glanced over and saw Marcus, Emily's ex, who was lunching with Heidi, who was now his wife.

'How can you be so friendly with your ex?' Hugh asked. 'Olivia ducks into doorways if she sees me and then rings me up crying the same night.'

'Is she still calling you?' Emily said.

'Now and then.'

'Good God!'

'Haven't you ever got upset and rung an ex and begged to give it another go?' He watched as she laughed at the very idea and a small smile played on his lips as another piece of the Emily jigsaw slotted into place.

'Seriously, Em, when Marcus got off with Heidi, weren't you upset?'

'A bit at first,' Emily admitted, 'but then I thought about it and if Marcus was so taken with Heidi that he'd go off for a quickie in the radiology department then clearly he wasn't the guy for me.'

'What if Marcus had wanted a quickie with you in the radiology department?'

Emily laughed again at the very thought. 'Then I'd be the very wrong girl for him.'

Hugh picked up a random piece of the jigsaw and decided to try and see if it fitted, if his theory about Emily was possibly correct. 'I don't believe you.'

'You can believe whatever you want, Hugh.'

There was the Emily who looked him right in the eye and denied them and then there was the Emily he was sure was there beneath.

'Why don't we go to the on-call room now? I've got the key.'

'Not a chance.'

'Come on, Em…' He had never spoken like this to her, but the burn on her cheeks made him push on. 'I am so turned on…'

'Then you've got a problem.' Emily smiled.

'Em…' He took her hand and she went to pull back but then she remembered that to the rest of the canteen they were supposed to be more than friends. Even so, she was the least touchy-feely person she knew!

'I don't hold hands.' Emily went to pull hers back but his grip on her fingers tightened. 'Hugh.' She just looked at him. 'What are you doing? Even if we were together, there is no way I'd…' The ridiculous thing was that his thumb in the palm of her hand seemed to have a direct route to the top of her thighs and she kept having images of being taken against the wall in the on-call room.

This was what he did to her and this was why she didn't want to pursue things.

'I need to get back.'

Hugh just dropped her hand and smiled at a suddenly flustered Emily. 'I'll walk with you.'

She'd have preferred that he didn't but he had a patient in Emergency to see.

'So, we're on for your dad's wedding tomorrow.'

'Yes, I've said that I'm bringing you. Thankfully it's just a small one this time, I was a bridesmaid at the last one.' Emily was actually glad that Hugh was coming with her. She found these things excruciating and at least Hugh always made her laugh and he was doing so now as they passed the on-call room and he nudged her.

'Last chance,' Hugh said.

'No chance!' Emily laughed.

They walked back into A and E and Emily rolled her eyes. 'Back to it.'

Finally he got her words, finally the jigsaw was starting to take shape.

That morning with Emily she had only been on loan to him.

CHAPTER EIGHT

'THIRD TIME LUCKY.'

Hugh turned and looked at Emily as her father delivered the opening line of his wedding speech.

She didn't smile or laugh, as the rest of the room did.

Yes, third time lucky perhaps, Hugh thought, but at what cost?

Cathy, his bride, was around Emily's age and Hugh watched a little while later as Emily smiled and congratulated her father's new wife.

'So when are you due?' Emily asked, when Cathy said how excited she was to be having a baby.

'Christmas!' Cathy beamed and Emily duly smiled back.

He knew that smile well, for it had been used regularly on him.

It was a smile that didn't quite meet her eyes, a smile that, to the untrained in Emily, might look wide, rather than guarded.

He wanted the smile of that morning in the holiday cottage, yet it was gone for now.

'Are you happy for your dad?' Hugh asked, as they danced.

'I don't know,' Emily said. 'I got off that roller-coaster a long time ago.'

'They look happy and it was a really nice service,' Hugh said. 'You really don't cry at weddings, do you?'

'Nope, I save it for the decree nisi.'

'Ah, so cynical, Emily.'

'It means nothing,' Emily said, 'it's just an excuse for a party…'

Hugh shook his head. 'Marriage means a lot to a lot of people.'

'Well, it means nothing to me.'

Emily looked as the twins, her half-brothers, chased each other around the room. Donna hadn't come, of course—apparently she would collect them later. And, of course, her father was too busy to keep a proper eye on them.

She'd cried so many tears over the twins.

There were parts of her heart scattered all across the dance floor and parts of her heart that were absent today too.

She thought about Jessica and, as she did so, Hugh actually felt the tension rip through her body.

'It's my family tomorrow,' Hugh said.

'I bet they're pretty tame compared to my lot.'

'Every family has its things. My sister is the perfect wife and mum but you should have seen her as a teenager!' Hugh rolled his eyes. 'Now she's all butter wouldn't melt in her mouth.'

'How old's the baby?'

'Five months,' Hugh said. 'He freaks me out a bit, he's the absolute image of me…'

'A mini-Hugh.' Emily smiled.

'The twins look like you.'

'I know,' Emily said. 'Come on, let's go and say hello properly, I didn't get a chance to at the registry office.'

They were very cute, very naughty, and Hugh actually winced for Emily when it was clear that they had no idea who she was.

'Can you watch them?' her dad said to Emily when they ran off as she tried to pick one up. 'They're getting into everything.'

Hugh could happily have knocked the groom out for his insensitivity but instead they did their best to police the twins until late in the evening when Donna texted her ex-husband to say that she was in the car outside.

Yes, it was Hugh and Emily who took the terrible two out to the car to where Donna was waiting.

'I was wondering,' Emily attempted, after Donna had strapped them into their seats and was about to get into the car. 'Now that they're a bit older, do you think maybe I could see the twins now and then?'

'Oh, I'm sure you'll see them again,' Donna said with malice that should have been aimed at their father. 'At his *next* wedding.'

As Donna drove off, Emily stood there. She actually felt like an ATM machine, though not for money.

An ATM machine that had just run out.

'I'm going to say goodbye to Dad and go home.'

'Fair enough,' Hugh said, silently appalled at the way she was treated but knowing it could only make it worse if he pointed it out.

'Or should I stay for a bit longer?' It was the first time he had heard her sound unsure.

'Do what's right for you.'

Home.

Hugh pulled up outside her place and for once he didn't know what to do or say. She was close to tears, he knew, and he guessed, rightly, that she just wanted to get inside.

He'd have loved to be invited in, not just her home but her mind.

'I'll see you tomorrow,' Emily said.

'I'll be here at ten,' Hugh said. 'Emily…' His hand went to her cheek. 'I'm sorry tonight was tough on you.'

'Thanks.' She moved her cheek from his hand. 'I'm going to go in. I'll post some of the wedding photos onto Facebook tomorrow, I'm too tired tonight.'

I get the message, Em, Hugh thought as she walked up the path.

Why couldn't he accept it, though?

Emily let herself into the home that was her haven.

Flat shares had felt as chaotic as her childhood and though the rent was at times a struggle, from the second she had moved in here it had been bliss to have her own space, one room, one wardrobe.

It felt lonely tonight, though.

By her own choosing.

Emily kicked off her shoes and lay on the sofa—tonight had been far better for having Hugh there.

Maybe she should give them a chance?

Just one chance and if it didn't work out she'd survive.

Tomorrow, after the christening of mini-Hugh…

Emily smiled at their conversation, remembering the bliss of dancing and talking with him before the debacle with the twins.

Then she suddenly stopped smiling as she thought of mini-Hughs and tried to do the maths as to when her last period had been.

No.

She was on the Pill.

Lackadaisically, though, Emily thought as she remembered lying in bed, eating toast and sorting out the upcoming weeks, when usually she'd have been up.

Surely one lie-in wasn't going to change both their lives.

CHAPTER NINE

HUGH ARRIVED FIFTEEN minutes early but he held up two coffees so was forgiven.

Emily smiled as she let him in.

'I'm just finishing my make-up.'

'Sure.'

'I've put the photos up on Facebook,' Emily called, as she headed upstairs. 'Have a look and then put a couple of them on yours.'

Hugh didn't peek at her friends or anything, he'd done all that before. He 'shared' a couple of photos but did startle a bit when a friend request from Donna came in.

He was very tempted to decline the witch on Emily's behalf but he breathed his way through it and smiled when Emily came down, her hair worn down, and dressed in suitable Sunday best. 'You look lovely.'

'So do you.' Emily came and looked over his shoulder and rolled her eyes at the picture of Hugh and herself standing next to the bride and groom. 'Surely Alex must believe us now.'

'You'd think so.'

'Do you think you're going to get the job?'

'I hope so,' Hugh said, 'because if I don't then I'll be resigning.'

'Hugh?'

'Come on, Emily, we've worked together for years, it would be a pretty big vote of no-confidence if he doesn't give it to me.' Hugh realised then he had lost his audience because Emily had seen her message.

'What does she want?' Emily said, then corrected herself. 'Sorry…'

'It's fine. It's just come in. I was wondering the same. Are you going to respond?'

'Why wouldn't I?'

'Er, the way she spoke to you last night, for starters,' Hugh pointed out.

Emily said, 'Hugh, I can't stand Donna, not that she'll ever know it. I'll be friendly and polite if it means I get to see my brothers and I'll be the same with Cathy.' Emily let out a tense breath and then clicked off the computer. 'Yes, I'll friend her but not now. I don't want to think about last night.'

She didn't want to think about any part of last night, especially about the realisation of her late period.

Surely not, Emily told herself on the drive to the church.

Why so sure? the sensible part of her checked.

'Are you okay?' Hugh asked as they pulled up.

'I'm fine.'

'It won't be a long day.'

Billy really was a mini-Hugh!

Blond, long-limbed, he looked as ridiculous in a dress as Hugh would, and Emily smothered a laugh as he nearly head-butted the vicar, while Edward ran amok in the pews.

Hugh did all his godfather duties and he did them well, but as they headed out of the church he let out a breath. 'Remind me not to have children for the next decade.'

Then keep your condoms within arm's reach, Emily was tempted to say, but she knew it wasn't his fault.

The christening party headed to a gorgeous restaurant, where she met his far more normal family and they were all very friendly.

After the meal they cut the cake and Emily watched as Hugh posed for the photos. It was all very low key and casual and over with by three. As they drove home, Emily truly didn't get why Kate couldn't have accommodated Hugh's schedule and they discussed it a bit on the car ride home.

'Is it hard to get a booking at the church?'

'Maybe,' Hugh said. 'Anyway, it's done now, without anyone getting upset.'

'Upset?'

'If I'd not been able to make it or had asked her to move the date.'

'It looks like the two of you get on.'

'We do,' Hugh said. 'Or I think we do…' He knew he wasn't making much sense. 'When I started at medical school I got a phone call to come home.' Hugh carried on driving as he spoke. 'Kate had broken up with her boyfriend and had made an attempt on her life. Thankfully she'd told a friend how she was feeling and she'd gone to check on her. Otherwise…'

'How awful.'

'Do you know the awful part, for me anyway?' Hugh

said. 'I always thought we were close. I honestly thought if she was having problems she could talk to me. Thank God she had a friend looking out for her.'

He fell silent. Part of the reason that he looked out for Gina so much and worried so much for her was because of the friend who had saved his sister's life.

'You still worry about her?'

'Not as much now,' Hugh admitted. 'She went very dark after she had Edward but she's done well with Billy and, look, I just have to hope that if there are issues she has someone she can talk to.'

'And maybe learn to say no to her a few times,' Emily nudged.

'Yep, that too.' He turned and gave Emily a brief smile. 'Thanks for being there today.'

'No problem.'

'Well, you've got a week off from pretending about us now as I've got my conference tomorrow, so just the Lake District next weekend,' Hugh said as they pulled up at her home. ''Do you want to drive up Friday night?'

'I'm on a late shift.' Emily shook her head. 'Saturday morning would be better.'

Hugh gave a tight smile, because he knew she'd do anything to avoid two nights with him. 'Then, after that, it's my interview with Alex.'

'Are you serious about quitting if you don't get the role?'

'I am,' Hugh said. 'I've already started looking about. There's a position in York that I've applied for. I've got an interview in a fortnight.'

'York?' Emily's heart started to beat faster, not just at the thought of Hugh so far away but if, *if* she was pregnant…

Oh, God.

'If I get another no, I'm gone.' Hugh turned and looked at her then and she was sure he was talking about them.

He was.

'I'll see you on Saturday bright and early,' Hugh said.

'You shall.'

He didn't make a move so Emily let herself out of the car, her heart pounding.

No, he'd said not a word but Emily knew, she simply knew, that Saturday was going to be her very last chance with him.

CHAPTER TEN

AH, DENIAL—SUCH a fleeting friend.

It stayed by Emily's side for the week and encouraged her to buy tampons every time she went shopping till she had quite a stockpile, a sort of build it and it will come, in her bathroom.

It didn't come, though.

And her new friend, Denial, also had a yen for salty peanut butter eaten straight from the jar, which was probably, Denial said, the reason Emily felt sick.

Of course she didn't have to worry, it was the worry that was causing her period to be so late. And don't be ridiculous, Denial said as she climbed on a ladder and stacked shelves on the Friday before the wedding in the Lake District, of course she didn't have to tell Hugh.

There was nothing to tell him anyway.

So why was she hiding in a large cupboard because Hugh had unexpectedly arrived in the department to speak to Alex?

Why was she staring at the pregnancy testing kits and wondering if she should just swipe one and put herself out of her misery?

'Em.' She jumped at the sound of her name, or rather

the sound of Hugh saying her name. 'Are you avoiding me?'

'Why would I be avoiding you?' Emily said. 'We're in *lurve*, remember?' She carried on tidying the shelf. 'I thought you had your conference?'

'It finished at lunchtime—I just came by to discuss something with Alex, but he's talking to some relatives.'

'Oh.'

'How was your week?' Hugh asked.

Emily gave a tight smile and wondered how he'd react if she told him it had been mainly spent on period watch. 'It was good,' she answered instead. 'I have a new *friend* called Donna.'

'What did she want?'

'To apologise for what she said on Saturday night.'

'What did you say?' Hugh asked, genuinely impressed that she hadn't told her to get lost but he could feel her volatile mood as she moved pack after pack when there was surely no need. 'Can you get down from that ladder before you answer?'

Emily did so, just to show she was capable of standing without jumping into his arms, but she wanted to so badly. It had been five days since she'd seen him after all. 'I thanked her for her apology and I said that I understood she might be cautious about letting me into the twins' lives but that this particular apple did fall far from the tree and that I'm not going to forget about them.'

'Any response?'

'A lukewarm one but I'll keep chipping away,' Emily said, and went back up her ladder.

Hugh wouldn't.

There would be no more chipping away. She drove him insane, an obsessive insanity that was going to come to a head tomorrow.

Yes, tomorrow.

He had it all worked out because the contrary Emily was going to be told just how he felt, but not now, not here.

'You're sure you don't want to drive up tonight?'

'I'm sure.'

'Well, be ready at five,' Hugh said, because Emily had refused to make a weekend of it so they were leaving at the crack of dawn. 'I'll pick you up...'

'Actually, I want to drive, my car needs a good run,' Emily said.

'Sure,' Hugh said, and then thought of the bomb she drove. 'Have you got roadside assistance? I don't want to be stuck on the edge of a motorway with you in this mood.'

Hugh watched as she actually laughed.

He'd known she would.

She got him.

Yet she didn't want him?

'Don't be late,' Hugh said, and headed off and left her alone with Denial.

'Go, have a drink, have fun,' Denial said. 'Let Hugh drive.'

But if she was pregnant...

She wanted the excuse of a long drive the next day so she didn't have any champagne because it wouldn't be good for the baby.

If there was a baby.

Emily slipped a pregnancy test card in her pocket.

You don't need it, Denial warned, you'll be caught, Security might be watching you now on the cameras and then the whole hospital might find out that you're *pregnant*.

Finally it was just Emily.

Sitting on the loo as Accident and Emergency carried on doing its thing while she did hers.

She couldn't wait a single second longer and, really, she already knew the answer.

Whose stupid idea had it been to invent a pregnancy indicator with a smiley face if it came back positive?

Emily certainly wasn't smiling.

She wrapped the indicator in a hand towel to hide it and then threw it in a big yellow bin and headed back out there.

'Hey, Emily…' Hugh was checking an X-ray with Alex and *Daddy* was in patient mode. 'Alex is taking him straight up to Theatre. Could you start getting him ready?'

'I'm just going off duty now, but I'll pass it on.'

'Thanks.'

'Hey, Hugh…' She wasn't going to tell him here, but as two thousand conflicting thoughts circled in her head she did consider that perhaps he should come over tonight but then she immediately changed her mind.

Emily didn't know how she felt herself yet, let alone share the news with Hugh, so she went to the bottom of her list and shared the very last thing that was on her mind. 'Make sure you set your alarm.'

CHAPTER ELEVEN

'WE'RE NOT GOING to get there,' Emily said, glancing at the dashboard. She had picked Hugh up bang on five but roadworks and traffic lights had conspired against them.

Emily hadn't slept much.

Instead, she had lain in bed tossing and turning and trying to somehow get her head around the fact that she was pregnant. Then she had looked at the clock and seen that it was after one in the morning and had lain worried that she'd oversleep.

In the end she had given up even trying to sleep and had just lain there, worried about the future.

Terrified, in fact.

A baby was so far off her agenda that it wasn't even pencilled in at some future stage to consider.

Emily didn't want to be in love with anyone, or anything, didn't want the potential for hurt, and, oh my, a baby was a huge potential for just that.

Of course she had fallen asleep in the end but it felt as if it was ten seconds later that her alarm had gone off, and when she'd arrived at Hugh's he'd come straight out looking so dazzling and ready to go that he might just as well have been on a health farm for a week.

Hugh had taken one look at her and declared that

he'd drive, and she'd happily handed over her keys and had dozed most of the way.

Now, though, it was after twelve and the wedding was at one and they needed to get petrol, oh, and tights for her.

'We're not going to have time to check into the hotel,' Hugh said, 'so let's stop at the next service station and get ready and we'll just park at the church.'

It sounded like a plan.

He pulled in and they both got out. 'I'll get petrol and park over there.' Hugh pointed. 'Don't take your time!'

Emily grabbed her dress, shoes and toiletry bag and made a dash for the ladies.

Her long brown hair she pinned up and then attempted to add some colour to her pale face. Then there was a quick change into her dress.

It was lilac and summery and had fitted perfectly when she had bought it in a sale a couple of weeks ago, but her breasts seemed to have grown an inch on both sides and Emily stared down at the canyon of cleavage.

Oh, well.

She dashed out to the car but then remembered that she needed to buy tights. Out of the corner of her eye she could see Hugh by the car but she pretended she hadn't and raced into the shop.

There wasn't much of a selection and she could just imagine Hugh tapping his fingers.

He was.

'I just need to…' Emily pointed back to the ladies as she came out of the shop, but Hugh shook his head and gestured for her to come on.

Bloody men, Emily thought, because five minutes

was all it took for them to look gorgeous. He was in a
dark grey suit and his tie was actually lilac.

'We match!' Hugh said, referring to her dress and
his tie, and when she climbed into the passenger seat
and put on her belt he glanced at her cleavage. 'Somewhere to put your phone?'

'Ha-ha,' Emily said, as he gunned the car in the hope
of getting them to the church on time.

'If we'd driven up last night, as I suggested,' Hugh
said, 'this could all have been avoided.'

'Careful,' Emily said, wrestling her legs into tights,
'we're starting to sound like a real couple.'

Hugh gave a half-laugh and then turned and gave
her a brief wide-eyed look as she pulled up her tights
over her bottom.

'Can I make a suggestion,' Hugh said, 'from someone who knows little about women's fashion? I don't
think orange stockings go with what you're wearing.'

'Can I make a suggestion?' Emily responded. 'Just
say I look nice and leave it at that.'

Hugh turned and smiled. 'You look nice.'

'So do you,' Emily said.

He did.

Oh God, he looked so, so nice and smelt so, so brilliant and she didn't need rouge now to bring some
colour to her cheeks. Instead, she fiddled with the air-
conditioner and then looked out the window as they got
off the motorway.

'We're going to make it,' Emily said.

'Absolutely,' came Hugh's response. 'There's no way
I'd miss this wedding.'

Emily's conscience prickled just a touch because,
thanks to her refusal to drive up last night, they almost

had. Weddings meant very little to Emily, she had been to many after all. Attending her father's had been more out of duty, and it had been a very long time, if ever, that she had looked forward to a wedding in the way Hugh was.

'We can't park here,' Emily said. 'It's double yellow lines.'

'The bride's already getting out of the car!' Hugh said, deciding he'd just pay the fine for their rather illegal parking, and soon they were in the church and there was just time for a quick flurry of hellos before the ceremony commenced.

'Talk about cutting it fine,' Gina hissed. 'Jennifer and Alex aren't here either.'

'Yes, we are,' Alex said, making his way along the pew. 'Sorry, sorry, running late.'

'I thought you came up last night.' Hugh frowned, because they seemed as flushed and as rushed as he and Emily.

'We did,' Jennifer said. 'We just...'

She didn't elaborate and Emily actually let out a little laugh as Hugh rolled his eyes skywards at her.

'They're like rabbits,' Hugh said into her ear as they all turned round to smile for the bride.

It was, as weddings went, a particularly lovely one.

Rima, Hugh had explained to Emily on the drive up there, had been at medical school with him but had been diagnosed with cancer just two weeks after she and Matthew had started going out. They'd been through the sickness part already and there was much more to come. Gina teared up as the vows were read out.

So too did Jennifer.

Hugh looked over at Emily, who had that vague smile

on that might just as well mean she was watching the Japanese news.

Hugh let out a breath of actual nervousness.

In half an hour or so his secret would be out and he no idea how Emily would react. He had never been able to fully read her. There she sat, under her little pyramid of indifference that only he could see, and he wanted it off, he wanted it gone.

No, he couldn't read her, because Emily was attempting to keep her emotions in check. That was the reason for her blank look, she was doing everything she could to zone out, because never before had a wedding moved her so much.

Confused her even.

She looked at the groom and saw the undeniable love in his eyes, and Rima too, who, despite poor health, seemed to be glowing.

It wasn't just the happy couple, though, that had the rusted cogs in Emily's brain starting to turn. She glanced at Jennifer and Alex, who might as well be confirming their vows, they simply couldn't keep their eyes from each other. Four children on and their love was so real, and she thought too of Ernest and Hannah.

Yes, Hugh was nervous because he cussed when he saw the parking ticket and was unusually tense as they checked in.

There was half an hour or so to kill before the wedding breakfast and possibly a friendship to kill too.

He hoped not.

Hugh really hoped not.

'Do you want to go to the bar?' Gina asked, but Jennifer and Alex declined.

'Jennifer's got a bit of a headache,' Alex explained.

'We haven't taken our bags up yet,' Hugh said, and then wavered.

He did not want Gina at the bar but he wasn't there to police her and, anyway, Hugh had something rather more important on his mind.

They shared the lift up with Alex and Jennifer and made polite small talk, though the lift was fit to burst with sexual tension, and it didn't come from the younger two!

'I'm going to dump these bags and dash out,' Emily said, 'and try and find some stockings that aren't orange!'

'It is so nice to have a weekend without the children,' Jennifer said. 'Nice to be able to have a lie-down.'

When Hugh and Emily stepped out and the lift doors were safely closed, Emily let out a laugh.

'I think Jennifer's use of a headache is different from every other woman's.'

'Do you feign headaches, Em?'

'God, yes,' Emily said, as Hugh opened the door to their hotel room. 'Marcus actually asked me the other week if my migraines had settled down.' She gave Hugh a smirk. 'I don't even get them!'

Yes, Hugh almost punched the air, as his theory was surely proved right.

The more boring the better for Emily.

'Oh!' Emily stared at the champagne and flowers.

'Aren't I romantic?' Hugh said.

'Did you order this?'

'I ordered the one-night escape package.' Hugh took out the receipt from checking in. 'Whoops, I booked the one-night romantic escape package.'

'Well, it's wasted on us,' Emily said. 'Maybe we should swap with Jennifer and Alex...'

Hugh was just about to say it, to admit he hadn't booked the room by mistake, when...and neither would ever know how it happened, but it did. The tension in the lift must have just raced down the corridor behind them and pushed its way under the closed door but she smiled that smile and so did Hugh.

'Oh, Alex, we've got a whole eighteen minutes,' Emily said, and she went for his tie.

'Jennifer,' Hugh said, 'your stockings are making me go blind.'

'Get them off me, Alex!' Emily begged.

It was fun, it was like lovers who had been lovers for ages, just so locked in their new game, getting the other, wanting the other and forgetting about everything else.

God, for the first time since the pregnancy thought had hit, her mind was empty of anything but Hugh.

His kiss was searing, her mouth urgent. It was go straight to bed kissing and Emily had never known feelings like it, never allowed feelings like it.

For Hugh it was like the woman he knew was in there was finally out.

She was on the bed with Hugh standing tearing at her stockings as she wrestled his belt with a 'get out of that suit and into my vagina' feeling but then he spoiled it.

'I booked the room deliberately.'

'Hugh!' *Don't* was the word her voice said.

'I'm crazy about you Emily, and I don't want to fake it.'

'I don't think you could be accused of faking it,' Emily said, trying to make a joke as she went for his erection, but he would not let her sex her way out of it.

He undressed and the rapid sex she had suddenly hoped for slipped away at the same time as her dress.

'I only came up with that idea to give us a chance.'

He was over her, kissing her from her neck to her stomach and then down, ever down. 'We've got fifteen minutes, Hugh,' Emily warned.

'We'll be late,' he mumbled into her sex, and she could, if she could just relax, really get to like that, Emily thought as his tongue explored her.

'Hugh, please…' She didn't know if she wanted to pull him up by his hair or push him further into her. Whetted by him, on the edge because of him, she almost sobbed in frustration as that lovely mouth stopped.

'Next time,' Hugh said, because there would be a next time and she'd relax enough to enjoy it, but for now he slid in between still parted legs.

He made love to her slowly and she tried to hold in her moans, even if she didn't have to now, but it was the way he unfurled her that had her clinging onto his shoulders and trying to deny that her body craved this.

'We'll take it slowly,' Hugh said into her ear.

'No longer an option,' Emily said, because she was about to come and from the building thrusts in Hugh, so too was he.

'I meant us,' Hugh said, but he didn't really have time to explain because her mouth was hot on his neck and her nails were digging deep into his back as Emily gave up fighting.

She *was* crazy about him, head over heels with him, every thrust drove her deeper in love and locked her there as he released into her. And all Emily knew was that she wanted this, more of this, as his weight came down on her and for a few breathless moments they lay there.

'We'll take it slowly,' Hugh said. 'I know you've got some trust issues…'

Emily closed her eyes. No, she didn't have trust issues, she had head over heels in love issues.

'We'd better go down.'

Hugh chose not to press for now. After all, they still had tonight.

Did they have to be such good speeches?

Emily sat and listened as she heard about the hard times the couple had already endured and the challenges they had faced.

And had there not been a positive pregnancy test, had they been able to take things slowly, as Hugh had suggested, maybe she could get used to the possibility of a future, a proper one, with Hugh.

Emily closed her eyes for a second, imagining the very free and very sociable Hugh, who wanted to concentrate on his career, suddenly a father.

And she, who didn't even want a baby, suddenly a mum and, no, it wasn't the same challenges as the happy couple that they faced but to Emily it felt unsurmountable.

As they danced she remembered his little dig in the church about not having children for another decade.

Oh, it had been a joke but he was right. Children were hard work at the best of times, and at the worst?

'Do you want a drink?' Hugh offered, as they made their way back to their table but Emily shook her head. She was already sick of sparkling water.

'Have you seen Gina?' Jennifer asked Hugh, as they sat down.

'Maybe she's gone to the loo,' Hugh said.

'She's been gone for ages,' Jennifer said. 'I'll go and check.'

'I'll go,' Hugh said, and Emily frowned.

'To the ladies?'

'She might be outside. She was pretty teary in the service, she and Rima are close...'

Jennifer returned a few minutes later and said that Hugh was outside talking to Gina. Emily didn't really give it much thought, she was too busy thinking about the baby inside her and the one relationship that might have worked had it not got off to the most difficult start.

She imagined herself up there at her own wedding, six months pregnant, Hugh giving a strained speech and everyone knowing they were marrying because Emily had been bloody late taking her Pill. Or perhaps it would be more a case of slamming car doors, like Donna had on an access visit.

Or Hugh in York and the long, lonely train rides for her child that she herself had endured.

She wanted it over, she wanted away from Hugh, just so she could think.

She wanted to end it and to tell him, if she told him, from the safe distance of cool disdain, and she knew how to end it right now.

Emily knew Hugh's buttons, they had been friends for a very long time after all, and so she took out her phone and pushed one of his buttons now.

Where are you?

I'll explain in a bit... was Hugh's response.

Do you like making a complete fool of me?

For God's sake, Em, I'll explain tonight.

Emily typed back.

Screw you. You've made me a laughing stock once. You shan't again. Have a nice train ride home.

Poor Hugh.

He delivered an off-her-face Gina to her hotel room and then went to his, where an off-her-head Emily was angrily packing.

'You're not serious?'

'What the hell were you two talking about that took so long?'

'Emily!' Tonight Hugh might have told her about Gina, tonight he probably would have, but it would be absolutely impossible to now.

He simply did not recognise her.

Was this what Emily was like in a relationship, a real one? he asked himself.

No.

He didn't buy it.

'You're being utterly ridiculous and you know it. You can't drive home tonight.'

'Tell them *I've* got a headache and *I'm* having a lie-down—no one turned a hair when it was Jennifer!'

'I'm not telling them anything. I don't have to explain things to them and I shouldn't have to explain myself to you.' Hugh dragged in a breath and told himself to calm down, to try and see things from the irrational side. 'I told you there is nothing going on between Gina and I.'

'So what happened at the emergency do?' Emily pushed.

Hugh just stood there. Yes, he could explain his way out of it but was that how it would be?

Explaining himself every five minutes?

'I thought more of you than that, Em. I thought more of us than that.'

'There never *was* us!' Emily said, and then she couldn't stand to see the hurt in his usually smiling eyes so she zipped her bag closed. 'I'm going.'

'You can have this room. I'll book another.'

'I said I'm going.'

'Maybe check into somewhere else…'

'I'm not your problem, Hugh.'

He gave in then and nodded. 'Will you at least text me when you're home?'

'Sure.'

It was a long, lonely drive back, going over an entirely manufactured row, but at least she had space now and time to think about what she was going to do.

Home, Emily texted just after dawn.

Thanks, came his rapid but brief reply.

Way to go, Emily.

CHAPTER TWELVE

'I'M FINE.' GINA came out of the bathroom and sat on the bed and put her head in her hands as Hugh opened the curtains to the morning.

'You are so far from fine it's not funny.'

'Hugh, I just had too much to drink.'

'Bull!' Hugh was struggling to hold onto his temper. 'I've been through your case and you had a whole lot more than alcohol on board.'

Round in circles they went, Gina denying it, Hugh growing angrier by the minute, though trying to stay calm.

'I can get you into somewhere today.'

'I don't need to go anywhere,' Gina said.

'Gina, talk to me,' Hugh begged. 'I can't help you if you don't talk to me.' It was his sister all over again and Hugh was actually petrified for her.

'I don't need your help,' Gina said. 'I'm going to get dressed for breakfast…' She pulled her clothes out of her case and her toiletry bag too, and Hugh sat there as she went to the bathroom and then after a few minutes later of frantic searching came out.

'You bastard.'

'Yep.' Hugh stood. 'I'm going to go and pack and then I'll drive you home.'

'What about Emily?'

Hugh said nothing and headed out and walked straight into Lydia, who had a mouth like the Mersey Tunnel.

Great.

Worse, though, was the disappointment in Alex's eyes as Hugh checked out, with Gina sitting in the foyer, waiting for him.

York, here I come, thought Hugh as they waited for the car to be brought around.

Gina slept most of the way and Hugh just drove, his mind in about twenty places.

Yes, maybe Emily deserved an explanation but she'd not even given him a chance.

He was in two minds whether to go round there once he'd dropped Gina home and explain, as best he could, what had happened before the rumour mill set to work.

Maybe he should but he had been up since five a.m. yesterday and knew he probably wouldn't deliver the best of speeches.

He was still cross with her.

'Will you think about what I've said?' Hugh asked Gina as they pulled up at her house.

'Just leave it, Hugh,' Gina said, slamming the boot closed and marching angrily down her path.

He couldn't, though.

Emily had a new friend.

Hypochondria.

She had got home and fallen asleep straight away,

awaking hours later to the sound of her doorbell and a horrible wave of nausea.

It was Hugh, Emily was sure, but there was no way she was letting him see her like this.

Instead, she hunched over the toilet. Nausea she was starting to get used to but there was also a pain in her stomach.

Stress, Emily said.

It could be an ectopic pregnancy, Hypochondria said.

Er, no, it was in the centre of her stomach.

Appendix, Hypochondria offered, because it can start there and then shift to the right.

Emily ignored the doorbell and went back to bed.

When you were involved with someone you worked with and it broke up, especially as spectacularly as Saturday night, it spread like wildfire.

No one could meet Emily's eyes when she started her shift the next morning and every time she walked into a room or approached a huddle, it either fell silent or they started discussing the weather.

Emily truly could not care less. There were other things to worry about.

Like her ectopic pregnancy.

It was really starting to hurt and maybe she ought to go and speak to Lydia and get herself seen, or go home and see her own GP.

Candy, one of the nurses was pulling some antibiotics up for a patient and checking it with Emily. Candy was sweet and embarrassed and started rambling on about the lovely long summer that they were having.

'I need a hand!' Raymond, the porter, called, and hearing the urgency in his voice Candy nodded to Emily.

'Go.'

Emily raced out to the foyer.

'My wife's bleeding…' a young, very stressed man was shouting, and Emily pulled some gloves from her pocket and went to the car as Raymond came over with a trolley. 'She's pregnant…'

She was very pregnant and also losing a lot of blood.

'What's her name?' Emily asked.

'Sasha.'

'How far along is she?'

'Thirty-eight weeks.'

'Okay…'

Sometimes patients didn't get as far as Maternity, and with the amount of blood Sasha was losing it was an emergency.

Candy was fantastic and even as they were wheeling her in she paged the obstetrician.

'Anton is on his way down.'

'He might want to do a Caesarean here,' Lydia said, rushing in and starting to bring over some theatre packs. 'Emily, go and get the blood warmer.'

Emily retrieved it from the storeroom and met Anton on the way back. 'Why the hell did the paramedics bring her here?' Anton barked as they ran.

'Her husband brought her in.'

All animosity stopped the second he was beside the patient and he could not have been more lovely to her.

'I am going to look after you and your baby,' he said as he examined her. It looked as if they might do an emergency Caesarean here in Emergency but with Sasha on her left side and oxygen on, the baby seemed to be settling and Anton made his call. 'Let's get her straight up to Theatre. Let them know and page the anaesthetist and blood bank for me.'

'Who's the anaesthetist?' Lydia called.

'Gina,' someone responded, but Anton refuted that.

'She's off this morning. Just page the first on,' he snapped in his less-than-charming way.

They set up the trolley very quickly and Emily did her best to ignore the nausea that would not abate.

She actually felt terrible and as they raced upstairs she did her best to ignore the pain in her stomach, but as soon as Sasha had been safely handed over Emily decided that she was going to sign herself off duty and go home.

'You're in the right place,' Emily said to Sasha. 'You're going to be very well looked after here.'

'I'm so scared...'

'Of course you are,' Emily said, as Rory came in and started setting up. He was her favourite anaesthetist and though she could leave now, Emily chose not to. Instead, she helped Rory as Miriam gave grateful thanks and headed into the theatre to help prepare for the delivery.

Maybe Miriam was right because it was all a lot more seamless for Sasha—she had the same nurse helping her from the moment she had hit A and E till the moment her body shuddered as she went under and Miriam had been freed up to get things ready for the baby, who would be born minutes from now.

Emily should really head back down and tell them that she was going home but the birth was imminent and it felt nice to be back in Theatre. Even in an emergency it was all so controlled and Emily stood, looking through the glass window, as Anton came in and was helped into his gown.

He gloved up and Emily watched as Sasha's stomach was swabbed and Anton rapidly set to work.

There was so much that could go wrong, Emily thought, terrified to be at the beginning of this journey.

There were just so, so many things that could go wrong.

But sometimes, even at the direst of times, everything went right.

The baby was kicking and screaming even as it was handed over to Louise and still Emily stood, looking through the glass, watching as the baby was given the once-over by the paediatrician and then Louise wheeled her out to where Emily stood.

'Isn't she gorgeous?' Louise said, as she wrapped the baby, chatting away. 'I am going to take you out to your daddy very soon!'

'Anton got her out quickly.'

'He's brilliant,' Louise said, then rolled her eyes. 'But I swear he's the most arrogant person to work with.'

'You've changed your tune.'

'Oh, yes,' Louise said, and then looked at Emily. 'Are you okay?'

'You've heard, then.'

'Everyone's heard. God, we all know Hugh fools around, I just never thought he would on you. If it's any consolation, Alex Hadfield's furious with him,' Louise said. 'I mean, he's seriously angry. Hugh is snapping at everyone. Gina's off sick again, which is possibly wise as I don't think she's anyone's favourite person today.'

'I maybe overreacted. I should maybe have—'

'Emily,' Louise interrupted, 'you weren't overreacting. Hugh was seen coming out of her hotel room in the morning.'

And in that moment Emily knew just how much she loved him.

She knew because she didn't panic, or think, *lying bastard*. Instead, her very first thought, her absolute first thought was that there was something wrong with Gina.

He had her love and he had her trust, which was terrifying in itself, but it was the scariest thing in the world to know that she had blown it.

'Are you okay, Emily?' Louise frowned as they walked out with the teeny new life. 'You look awful.' Then she smiled. 'Stupid question, given the weekend you had...' Her voice trailed off as Hugh came out of the staffroom.

Emily would never forget the look he gave her—hurt, disappointed, angry—and she knew that she deserved all three.

He came straight over and Louise left them to it.

'I don't know what time I'll finish here but I'm going to come over tonight and try and address some rumours that are flying around.'

'There's no need.'

'Oh, don't try and fob me off,' Hugh said. 'I *shall* be coming around but don't worry, Emily, it's only to talk. No need to pretend you're tired or have got a headache. We're done.' He gave a shallow, mirthless laugh. 'Well, we never were on, were we? I'll text you when I'm leaving here.'

Her stomach was hurting and her head was all confused and as Emily walked down the corridor those last thirty steps to Emergency looked a very long way off.

'Emily?' It was Raymond who caught her.

'I don't want to be seen here,' Emily said, as she was wheeled into Emergency.

And then she simply didn't care any more. Her stomach hurt so much and there was no relief from being sick.

'It's okay...' Sarah, the registrar, had been called, and she was very, very kind and gentle as Emily kept crying in her confusion.

'I'm pregnant,' Emily explained, 'about four weeks.' Then she remembered that you added two weeks. 'Six weeks,' Emily amended, and started to cry. 'It's ectopic, isn't it?'

'Emily, just lie still and let me examine you.'

It was the most horrible day of her life but Hugh wasn't having much fun either.

He was just checking on a patient in Recovery and his head was pounding.

It had been one helluva weekend, followed by a black Monday.

He'd finally done it.

In writing this time he had put his misgivings about Gina yet there was no sense of relief at doing the right thing whatsoever.

He got a glimmer of that relief, though, just a few minutes later.

'Hugh.' Alex was grim. 'I need to speak to you.'

'Can we discuss the disaster of my weekend well away from this lot?' Hugh said, loudly enough for all the wagging ears to shuffle off.

'It's not about that.' Alex pulled him aside. 'I'm heading down to A and E and you are *not* to join me or follow me down.' Hugh frowned as Alex spoke on. 'I've got a twenty-six-year-old acute abdomen, query ectopic, query appendicitis.' There weren't many other ways to break it and he'd be hearing it on the grapevine soon, Alex knew. Hugh was already sweating before he had said the name. 'It's Emily.'

'Is she definitely pregnant?'

'I'll know more soon. You're to stay here.'

Fat chance of that, Alex thought as he made his way down.

'Emily!' Alex gave her his most professional smile. It didn't work.

'It's okay,' Alex said, looking at her bloodwork.

'It's not,' Emily said, because it would never be okay. 'I'll never be able to look at you again,' Emily said a little while later, with his finger up her bum.

Then Alex rolled her over and gave her a smile. 'You're looking at me now.'

'Hardly.'

He did a very gentle PV exam and felt her tubes and uterus.

'It looks like appendicitis,' he said. 'I'm going to do a quick ultrasound.'

'What about the baby?'

'The baby is very protected and,' he said, 'we'll take very good care, but the last thing we want is your appendix to perforate.' He asked her another question, only this time it wasn't as a doctor. 'Had you told Hugh?'

Emily shook her head. 'I was trying to work out how to.' Then she frowned. 'Does he know?'

'I told him what little I knew because I didn't want him hearing it from someone else. I've told him to wait up in Theatre.' He gave a thin smile at the sound of Hugh's footsteps.

'I don't think Hugh followed my explicit orders!' Alex said to Emily, but for Hugh's benefit too.

'I don't want to see him.'

'Tough,' came a voice from the other side of the curtain.

'So much for patient privacy,' Emily called back.

'I'll get rid of him for you,' Alex said, but Emily shook her head.

'It's fine. I might as well get it over with.' She gave a thin smile as he stepped into the cubicle. 'At least I'll be unconscious soon.'

Alex ignored Hugh when he came in and spoke to Emily instead. 'I'll get you some analgesia and we'll give you some more IV fluids and then we'll get you up to Theatre.' He went through the consent and asked about next of kin.

'I rang my dad but he wasn't there. I've left a message. I don't think he'll come, but if he does, can we not tell him about the pregnancy if at all possible?'

She glanced at Hugh, who met her stare but said nothing.

'What about your mum?' Alex said, and Emily gave a weary nod.

'I'll call her.'

Finally Alex left them to it. Hugh went outside as Emily called her mum but was sent straight to voice-mail again.

'I've left a message for her,' Emily said.

'Do you want me to have your phone?' Hugh offered. 'They'll be worried when they get the message.'

Emily handed it over to him.

'How long have you known?' Hugh said.

'Friday night,' Emily said. 'Well, I'd been worried for a week or so before that.'

'And you didn't think to tell me?'

'Of course I thought about telling you,' Emily snapped, and then she was quiet as Lydia came and gave her IV pain control.

Hugh watched as her pupils went to pinpoints and he put on some nasal prongs as Emily, thanks to some decent pain control, lost her control and told him exactly what she'd been thinking!

'On Friday evening I decided on an abortion; on Friday night I thought I might ring you. On Saturday I had this strange vision of us pushing a baby on a swing, but I had this vision of joint access, and then I decided to just tell you at the wedding, then I decided to move to Scotland and have it and never tell you...'

'Okay, Em,' Hugh said, 'I'm not cross with you for not telling me. I get you were working it out.'

'Are you cross with me, though?' Emily asked, with her own eyes crossed as she tried to focus on him. God, he looked fantastic, he looked amazing. 'Do you think I tried to trap you?'

'Grow up,' Hugh said, but not unkindly. 'Actually, I'm the one who needs to grow up. It does take two.'

'Yeah.'

She wasn't worried about that now. His eyes were the nicest shade of green in the world.

'I'll probably lose it now anyway,' Emily said.

'Probably not,' came Anton's voice, and then Emily

knew she really must be pregnant because for once Anton wasn't scowling. In fact, he gave her a nice smile.

'I was just speaking with Alex about your surgery. I'll come and see you afterwards. Do you have any questions?'

'No.'

Hugh did, and he went outside and spoke to Anton for a couple of moments before coming back to Emily.

'We're going to get her ready now,' Lydia said, and Hugh stepped back as they checked her ID and allergies and all the million things they had to before she went under anaesthetic.

And it was then, in that moment, that he got the glimmer he had done the right thing about Gina.

Even if he was wrong, he just couldn't turn a blind eye any more.

And he'd just have to wear it if he was loathed for reporting her.

He could not live with himself if anything happened to a patient.

He looked at Emily and knew it should have been Gina on this morning.

Yes, it sucked big time, but he'd done the right thing.

'Can I have two minutes?' Hugh asked, as Raymond and Lydia arrived to take her up, and he didn't wait for an answer, just shooed everyone out.

'Emily.' He snapped her out of her stupor. 'We'll sort this out.'

'Yeah.'

'I mean it, you're not to worry.'

'I'm not worried…' She put a hand up to his lovely, lovely face and stared into his gorgeous green eyes. 'Give me a kiss for luck.'

'You lush…' Hugh said.

'Please.'

'No,' Hugh said, 'because then you'll accuse me later of taking advantage.' But he kissed his fingers and pressed them to her mouth. 'You'll be fine.'

She would be, Hugh told himself as the hordes then descended.

For Emily it all passed in a bit of a blur. She stared up at the ceiling of a very familiar room. It looked different from this angle.

'We meet again.' Rory smiled. 'I'm fantastic, remember, so you have nothing to worry about.'

'I never said you were fantastic. I tell the patients you're amazing,' Emily said, and then Miriam's face came into focus.

'I'm resigning,' Emily said, as her boss smiled down at her. 'I was going to resign anyway because I hate Accident and Emergency but there's no way I'm going back there now.'

'We'll talk soon.' Miriam continued to smile as a very drugged Emily started to tell her exactly what she thought of internal rotation.

'You'll feel better soon, Emily,' Miriam said, and Emily fought to get across her point.

'You don't…'

Emily didn't finish; she was out for the count.

'Not a happy camper,' Rory said to Miriam.

'It would seem that way.'

A perk of the job was that he was there when she came round in recovery.

'Dad!' Emily was very surprised to see him. She didn't have a clue where she was.

'Mum's on her way,' came a voice, and she could see Alex talking to Hugh.

That's right, she'd had an operation.

Oh, God, she was pregnant.

Maybe.

'We've made sure you get your own room.' Louise drifted into focus as Emily was wheeled down to the ward. 'Give you some privacy.'

There was no such thing as privacy when you worked here, though.

Her mum flew straight down from Scotland and though she was touched that they'd both come it was a terrible strain having both Mum and Dad in the same room, and a huge relief when at eight that night they left.

'Not now,' Emily said a little while later, when Hugh walked in.

'I know,' Hugh said. 'I'm heading home. I just wanted to see that you were okay.'

'Well, I am.'

'Emily—'

'I don't want to talk about it.'

'Fair enough,' Hugh said. 'Here's your phone.'

Hugh walked out and past the cool stares of the ward staff and then to the on-call room, where he'd decided to stay for the night. He knew she'd be okay, he just wanted to be sure.

In a way it was a relief that she didn't want to speak just yet because, though worried, Hugh was still prickling from her accusations the other night.

Then his phone went off and Hugh took a breath before answering it.

Oh, he needed that breath as a stream of expletives met his ear.

'It was you, wasn't it?'

'Gina.' Hugh tried to interrupt and was told again what a louse he was, how he'd damaged her career, that she'd trusted him.

'Do you know what, Gina?' Hugh said. 'You call me when you want to talk properly, but right now I'm in no mood for your lies. Sort yourself out, or not, it's entirely up to you. Just do it well away from patients.'

CHAPTER THIRTEEN

'I HEAR YOU'RE still vomiting?'

Hugh stood at the door on day three post-op.

'They're keeping me in again tonight.' Emily nodded.
She wanted to go home and away from all the eyes and
just curl up in a ball and heal, but every couple of hours
she started retching and they weren't sure if it was the
anaesthetic or morning sickness. So the drip stayed in
and apart from a shuffle to the loo and shower she was
pretty much still in bed.

'You've lost weight,' Hugh said.

'I was going to say the same thing about you.' He
looked haggard and a bit thinner and very, very trou-
bled, even if he was trying to sound upbeat.

'I know it's a shock…'

'Emily…' Hugh tried to keep his patience. 'I've got
a lot on my mind at the moment, but can you please get
it into your head that I am not cross about the baby, I
am not running screaming for the hills…'

'You're not upset?'

'God…' He let out an exasperated sigh. 'I'm pleased.'
She blinked when he said it. 'I'm actually pleased that
you're pregnant because now, like it or not, we have
to talk.'

'So what are you looking so worried about?'

'You,' Hugh said. 'Surgery at six weeks gestation...'

But she knew there was more. 'Hugh?'

'Stuff,' Hugh said. 'I've just got a lot going on. You don't need to hear it.'

'Is Alex angry?'

'Yeah, there's that too.' He turned from the window. 'I'm not exactly his favourite person at the moment.' He came and sat by her bed. 'Your HCG is still rising,' he said, and watched her face to see if the fact her HCG level was still rising, indicating the pregnancy was progressing, might bring a smile to her eyes, but she just stared back at him.

'I asked Alex if I could have an ultrasound,' Emily said. 'It's booked in for nine tomorrow. Maybe when I see for myself...' Emily closed her eyes. It was all numbers at the moment and she could barely remember the brief ultrasound that had been done in Emergency.

'Do you want to come?' she offered.

Hugh nodded. 'When will you be well enough for that row?'

'Are we going to have a row?'

'I assume so,' Hugh said. 'You weren't exactly holding back on Saturday night.'

'Well, it would seem you didn't either,' Emily said. 'I heard you left her room on Sunday morning.'

'I didn't sleep with her.'

'La-la-la-la-la,' Emily said.

'Grow up,' Hugh said, only this time not quite so kindly. 'I'm crazy about you, Emily, and I have been for a very long time, and if you think I slept with Gina after our row, then there's really not much point.' He stood. 'I'm going to go or I'll say something I regret and then I really will be the bastard everyone thinks I am.'

'Hugh—'

'Nope.' He shook his head. 'I can't do this now. I want you to rest and to get better. I'll be here at nine.' Then he changed his mind and revealed a little of what was on his mind. 'Do you know why I respect Alex so much?' he asked. Emily just looked at him. 'Do you remember when Jennifer went into labour and he must have been as worried as hell but he did not miss a beat, he just kept on operating? He knew that Jennifer would be okay without him there. She might not like it, but that was part of their deal…she trusted him. And you don't trust me.'

He looked down at her.

'I am going through some stuff right now that I cannot share with you, especially given the extremely tenuous nature of our relationship, but I will tell you this much. I will do my best to be here tomorrow and at any future appointments, and I take full responsibility for this baby and, whether you like it or not, I will be in this baby's life.'

'From York!' Emily called to his departing back.

'I've already pulled the application.' Hugh turned around. 'Get used to me, Emily, because I won't be keeping in touch with my child via Facebook. Don't ever compare me to *him*.'

Emily lay there after he had gone.

And lay there.

'No vomiting,' the night nurse said. 'That's good.'

Was it, though?

What if the morning sickness had faded because she wasn't pregnant any more?

It was the first time her brain was quiet.

She just stared at the ceiling through a very long night and looked back on the years she had known Hugh.

And then looked ahead to the years possibly with him.

CHAPTER FOURTEEN

HUGH SLEPT FOR about two and half hours and was up at five and at work by seven.

It was the day of his interview but no way was he going to sit through a formality just to be told he was way too immature for such a senior role.

Immature?

He felt about a hundred years old this morning.

There was an email from the head of anaesthetics, asking him to meet at ten, and Hugh wondered if Gina would be present.

Oh, God, he hoped not.

First, though, there was the ultrasound and he was most nervous about that, because for all the HCG was rising, it was a fragile time and again Hugh wondered if he had come down too hard on Emily last night.

Maybe he could put up with it?

Given all she went through with her family, maybe some jealousy and suspicion were to be expected.

'Morning.' Alex was less than effusive in his greeting. 'I want to go up to ICU and check on Mr Hill before we start rounds.'

'Sure,' Hugh said. 'Is it okay if I slip off at nine? Emily's having—'

'I know,' Alex clipped. 'Fine.'

'And at ten I have to meet Mr Eccleston...'

'Mr Eccleston.' Alex frowned, and Hugh debated whether or not to tell him but, no, not just yet. He decided to see how things were panning out before sharing the burden with Alex.

Mr Hill was extremely unstable when they arrived and they were actually considering taking him back to Theatre when Alex glanced at the clock.

'Go,' he said. 'I've got this.'

'Thanks.'

Okay, Hugh thought, making his way down to the surgical unit. Daddy face on? Happy face on? Worried face on?

He stopped at the vending machine at the entrance to the ward and was just buying a bottle of water when he heard his name.

'Hugh?'

Hugh swung around and saw Gina. He was momentarily sideswiped, wondering if she was going to beg him to withdraw his accusations, or plead with him that she was getting help, or just scream at him again. Then he watched her crumple.

'Help me...' She was in his arms and he actually thought in that moment that if he let her go he might never see her again. In fact, he didn't think, he knew. 'I need help, Hugh, now, now, now...'

He pulled her into the patients' lounge and asked an elderly man to please excuse them.

'Help me, don't leave me...' Gina begged.

'I'm not going to leave you.'

'I'm scared.'

'I know.'

'I'm scared what I'm going to do...'

'I'm not leaving you,' Hugh said, and he looked out of the glass window at the frowning man, who thankfully took his cue and walked away. 'We're going to get you some help.'

He unscrewed the cap of the bottle of water and gave it to Gina then fired off a very quick text. But then saw the water spilling over her face.

'Have you taken anything?'

'No.'

He checked her pulse and her pupils and, no, it would seem she hadn't.

'Help me.'

'I've told you already that I will,' Hugh said. 'Talk to me,' he said, and finally Gina did.

CHAPTER FIFTEEN

JUST AFTER NINE her phone bleeped, indicating a text had come in, and Emily saw that it was from Hugh.

Held up, sorry, I will get there ASAP, let me know.

Hugh wouldn't choose to miss this, Emily knew. He must be stuck with something pretty serious if he couldn't get away for the ultrasound.

She smiled in surprise when Anton came in because she'd been expecting the radiographer, but he gave her a very nice smile back and wished her good morning.

'You're much nicer to your patients than you are to your colleagues,' Emily observed.

'Of course I am.'

She lay back and tried not to let on just how petrified she was.

Emily wanted this baby.

Accident or not, mistake or carelessness, the possibility she might have already lost it before she truly loved it was terrifying.

'You've had lots to drink?'

'Lots,' Emily said.

'So you have,' Anton said as he lifted her gown,

because her bladder was full to bursting, which helped get a better image.

Some jelly was squeezed on her abdomen and then came the interminable wait. The screen was visible but Emily just closed her eyes but then she opened them and looked and saw a little flicker on the screen.

'Is that its heartbeat…?'

'It is, and it is all looking good,' Anton said. 'Six weeks…' He peeled off a tissue and handed it to Emily as she started to cry.

'Sorry,' Emily said. 'I didn't realise how scared I was.'

'It is fine to cry.' Anton smiled. 'I'm so pleased it's good news.'

'I didn't even know if I wanted to be pregnant.'

'Well, you know now,' Anton said, and Emily nodded because she did want this baby very much. 'It is normal,' Anton continued, 'especially when the pregnancy is unexpected, to take a while to get used to the idea. How are things with Hugh?'

She was terribly grateful that Anton didn't pretend he hadn't heard all the horrible gossip and she answered him honestly. 'It's a big shock to him too, I guess, but he seems okay about the baby, though *we're* not so okay right now.' She looked at Anton, knew there was nothing he could really say.

Except she didn't know Anton.

Yes, he had heard all the rumours—in fact, he'd just walked past the patients' lounge and had seen Hugh and Gina sitting holding hands in deep conversation.

Anton, more than anyone, knew what was going on.

'I'm going to tell you something.' He actually took

Emily's hand. 'I am not friendly with staff, for my own reasons. I loathe gossip and I avoid it as if it were poison.'

'I don't care about gossip,' Emily said.

'Good.' He gave her hand a squeeze. 'Keep your own counsel.'

'I shall.'

'Then you shan't go wrong.' He gave her a smile that had Emily wanting to reach for her phone and text Louise to climb right up that stethoscope, but she restrained herself and decided to put it down to hormones as Anton spoke on. 'Right, from this side of things I can discharge you. Your nausea has gone, the ultrasound is fine. But because of your surgery you shall see me for your antenatal care from now on. Normally it is two weeks off work after an appendectomy but I would like you to take three, perhaps more, and then I want you to come and see me before you go back to work. Have some quality time off and relax.'

'Sounds good.'

Anton left and she was just about to text Hugh *or* go to the loo when the domestic breezed in.

'It's fine,' Emily said, putting on her dressing gown, deciding she'd use the loo on the ward instead of the one in her room.

And then she'd text Hugh.

Nature was seriously calling.

So much so that when she walked past the patients' lounge she barely halted as she saw Hugh. She just stood there for a second as she found out the reason Hugh couldn't be at the ultrasound.

He was deep in conversation with Gina.

And very possibly it wasn't work they were discussing because he was holding her hands.

He glanced up and she could have confirmed the row they'd had on Saturday by sticking up her fingers or huffing off.

She could have ended it then but she kept her own counsel and instead let him into her heart with a small brief smile and then went to the loo.

Back in her room she sent a text.

All looks good, nice heartbeat. Em

She got back three smiley faces and a row of kisses.

And then she got morning tea.

And then lunch.

Then a brief visit from Alex, who examined her abdomen and saw her temperature was on the edge of normal and said he would like her to stay for one more night and that she could go home in the morning if all her observations were within normal ranges.

And there was still no word from Hugh, though it didn't bother her. The less she was told the more important Emily knew it was.

'Em...' She opened her eyes to the sight of Hugh. He wasn't smiling, just looked haggard. 'I'm so sorry I couldn't get there... I'm so pleased the ultrasound went well.'

'Is Gina okay?' Emily asked.

'No.' Hugh shook his head. 'She's very ill indeed.'

Emily watched the haze of tears rise higher in his eyes and heard him quickly try to grab them back with a sniff.

It didn't work.

'She's in a very dark place,' Hugh admitted, 'but she's finally admitted that there's a problem and she's in the right place to get the help she needs.'

'How long has she been ill?'

'It's been on and off,' Hugh said. 'You remember the first night we got off with each other? I didn't want you to get into the car with Gina.'

'Did you think she'd been drinking?'

'No, I thought she might be on something, or that she'd been drinking. I'd reported her to her boss the previous day. I just couldn't let you get into the car with her and I couldn't properly tell you why. As it turned out, I was wrong. I even had Gina crying on me a week or so later about some bastard who had made terrible accusations. I've just told her today that that bastard was me.'

'Oh, Hugh.'

'It's been a very long day. If I could have been here I would have but Gina broke down and told me some things that have been going on and how depressed she was and that she needs help…' He looked at Emily. 'You don't leave a seriously depressed anaesthetist alone—can you understand that?'

'I can.'

'I've been worried for weeks. I didn't know whether to speak to Alex, given I'd reported her once and nothing had come of it. I went to Mr Eccleston and, as it turns out, I wasn't the only one. Anton's voiced his concerns rather loudly.'

'Anton!'

Hugh nodded. 'Nothing's happened at work, I believe Gina when she says that, but out of work…' Hugh closed his eyes. 'The lines were starting to blur. Apparently she turned up in the car park the worse for wear on Monday and Anton just took her car keys from her and drove her home and then went and reported her.'

No wonder Anton had been in a filthy mood on Monday, Emily thought.

'How's Gina now?'

'She's been admitted, though not here,' Hugh replied, 'but she's getting the help she needs now. Nothing has ever happened between Gina and I,' Hugh said. 'The world thinks we have an on-off thing, but I'm a very good judge of people and I had her pegged from the first week we started as med students. I love Gina, but not in that way. I care for her and, as I told her today, I will always be her friend, but she has to help herself.'

'God…' Emily lay back on the pillow. He had been so honest. Ought she be? He stopped speaking and looked up as Alex and Jennifer came in.

'Jennifer.' Hugh stood up and smiled at Emily's visitors. 'Alex, nice of you to come by.'

'Ooh, lovely,' Emily said, taking a huge bunch of flowers.

'I just brought Alex in some afternoon tea and he told me some of what's been happening. How are things?' Jennifer said.

'Very well.' Emily smiled.

'Could I have a word, please, Hugh?' Alex asked.

Hugh was stony-faced as they headed out into the corridor. 'I've heard about Gina.' Alex's expression was equally grim. 'You didn't think to discuss it with me?'

'I did think of it,' Hugh said, 'but at the end of the day these are serious accusations and I decided to make the call. I was hoping it would all be a bit more discreet and maybe it would have been if Gina hadn't had her meltdown here.'

'I apologise for jumping to conclusions,' Alex said.

'You weren't the only one…'

It was that Emily had jumped to them that hurt most.

Emily glanced out of the window to where Hugh and Alex were talking, and loathed the mess she'd made of things.

'He got the job.' Jennifer broke into her thoughts.

'Really?'

'It must have been a hard time for him, deciding whether to report her or not. I've known Gina for years. She's the loveliest woman, I don't know where it all went wrong.'

'I guess she's working it out.'

It was an afternoon for visitors and Emily smiled when Miriam came in. 'How are you feeling?'

'Sore but much better,' Emily said, and then she frowned and then she started cringing as vague, hazy memories fought to return. 'Oh, my…did I…?'

'You did,' Miriam said. 'I'm sorry you're so unhappy. I certainly don't want you working somewhere while you're pregnant where you feel miserable. Maybe we can look at you doing a stint in A and E when you come back from maternity leave, or…'

'Miriam.' It was Emily who knew what she wanted now. 'I want to go back to A and E. If I put it off now, it will never happen and I really do want to get on. Also, it's actually not that bad.'

'You're sure?'

Emily nodded. 'It's certainly better for the patients and…' She thought for a moment. 'In many ways I do enjoy it. I never expected to.'

'Well, you've got a couple of weeks off to think about it.'

More than a couple of weeks. This pregnancy was suddenly vital to Emily and after a rocky start she wanted to give it every chance.

'Anton said to take some time off, so I was wondering if I could tag some annual leave onto sick leave.'

'Of course,' Miriam said. 'Take what you need. Then you've got another eight weeks in Emergency and then...' Miriam gave her a lovely smile '...we'll talk about that Clinical Nurse Specialist position that's coming up.'

When Alex and Jennifer had gone, she thought she might get a smile from Hugh and that he would share the news that he'd got the job but instead he wanted to speak about them.

'Emily, maybe I came on too hard. You know I have a thing about women who question my every move, but I can get that maybe you're going to have trust issues. A bit rich, though, given you got off with me when you were seeing Gregory.'

She looked at him and her instincts had been right, they had been that very night they'd first kissed. She simply hadn't followed them.

So she followed them now.

'There was no Greg. I made him up.'

'Sorry?'

'To keep you away.' She took a deep breath and said it. 'I don't have trust issues,' Emily said. 'I manufactured that row on Saturday.'

'You manufactured it?'

'I knew there had to be a reason you were outside, speaking to Gina. I knew you wouldn't do that to me.'

'Why the hell would you make up a row?'

'Because I wanted space away from you to think. I don't want to fall in love so hard it hurts. I don't want to be crazy about someone…'

'You don't want to feel?' Hugh just smiled. 'Oh, dear, Emily, like it or not, you're going to. You can lock yourself away with boring boyfriends and unconscious patients but about eight months from now you're going to have your heart held hostage for ever by this little one.'

'I know,' Emily said, 'it already is.'

'You do have trust issues…'

'I don't.'

'Yes, you do, because you don't trust me not to try and make it work, but I shall.' He thought about his boss who had taught him so much and the effort he was putting into his own marriage. 'At the first sign of trouble your parents just walk away. Well, that's them and this is me—I'm a very hard worker, Emily, and not just in my career…'

A couple of hours later, her obs done, his pager handed in for the day, it was just the two of them, lying on the bed, watching the news on TV.

'Do you think we'll be like that?' Hugh suddenly asked.

'Like what?'

'Alex and Jennifer. Will you be popping in for some afternoon delight?'

'She was bringing him something to eat.'

'Please,' Hugh scoffed. 'It really affected me that night. I think I'm damaged.' Emily smiled to herself as she turned to Hugh because he still hadn't told her that he'd got the job.

'What did Alex want?'

'A very quick formal interview and then he told me I've got the job.'

'Hugh, that's fantastic. I'm so pleased.'

'I haven't accepted it yet,' Hugh said. 'I said I needed to speak to you first.'

'Speak to me?'

'I don't know if you'd prefer a fresh start,' Hugh said. 'We do have a bit of history scattered around the hospital.'

'Er, I have one bit of history,' Emily said, referring to Marcus.

'Exactly,' Hugh said. 'And I get it if you want to make a go of things well away from my past.'

'There's no need,' Emily said.

'You're sure?'

'Absolutely.' She turned to him. 'I'm sorry. I don't know how you put up with me...'

'I have asked myself that a few times,' Hugh admitted.

'But you did?'

'Yep, I told you—I work at things.'

'But—'

'I love you,' Hugh said, as if it was the least complicated emotion in the world, and maybe sometimes it was because it was right here in the room. 'Whenever you're ready, Emily,' he nudged.

'Iloveyoutoo.' She said it very quickly, more as one word, but Hugh just smiled.

'Progress!'

Emily reached for her phone. 'I'd better call Dad and

let him know I'll definitely be home tomorrow. He and my new stepmum are going to come over and then Mum will come down…'

'You really don't get this partnership lark, do you?' Hugh said. 'Ring your father and tell him there's no need to worry. I've got five days' carer's leave.'

'Oh!'

'Alex told me. Well, so long as we're living together…' He gave her a very nice smile. 'Your place or mine?' Hugh said.

'Mine,' Emily said, because she wanted to recover among her own things, wanted her own bed, her own bathroom. And then she looked at Hugh and amended all that, because more than that she wanted him. 'To pick up a few things.'

'Good choice,' Hugh said, 'because I have a cleaner who comes in every other day.'

'Ooh!' Emily smiled. 'How lovely.'

The future suddenly was.

CHAPTER SIXTEEN

EMILY DID PICK up a few things and on her second trip Hugh asked that she pick up a few more things, namely her birth certificate.

Which she did.

But staring at the mountain of paperwork, just thinking of the impossibility of it all, Emily baulked at the final moment.

'I don't want to get married, Hugh.'

'It will be tiny,' Hugh said. They'd *almost* decided to get married in Scotland at her old church but just the thought of her mum and her dad and half-brothers and -sisters and even Jessica, who was now a Facebook friend, tiny was something it could never be.

'I don't want to,' Emily said. 'You said we could take things slowly.'

'That was before I knew you were pregnant,' Hugh said, but then dropped it.

'Will you be all right tomorrow?' Hugh checked, because after a weekend off and five days' leave he was back at work and on call for the entire weekend. 'Your mum said she'd come down and Kate's going to drop in.'

'Hugh, I don't need anyone. I'm not even sore now.'
Just tired.

Kate did drop in and so too did her dad, and he brought the twins, who were on a weekend access. And then Jessica sent her a message and asked if she could drop by, which she did.

'These are for you,' Jessica said, handing over some DVDs. It was the entire series of a show Emily had said in passing during their chats that she'd never watched. 'Well, when I say they're for you I want them back, but I watched them back to back after I had my operation.'

It was funny but after all these years apart they slipped back so easily and Jessica set up the DVD in Hugh's bedroom and they watched the first episode to-gether and then the second.

'One more,' Emily said, only pausing it to take a call from her mum, who felt a little put out that Emily hadn't needed her to come down.

'Mum's coming next week with Abby,' Emily said as she concluded the call. 'It's exhausting, being sick.'

It was nice, though.

Not the surgery part but finally, after all these years, Emily knew she had a family. As complicated as it was, as scattered as they were, the news about her operation had somehow reminded people about the relative that they'd tended to forget, and finally Emily knew she was loved. The twins now knew who she was and Emily was determined that it would remain that way.

Best of all, though, was knowing she had Hugh and also knowing that he had her.

'What happened to the bedroom?' Hugh asked, when he came home a little grey around the gills after a long weekend on call, but he had stopped for two coffees on the way and handed her one as he looked around the room. The television was at the foot of the bed and it looked like there had been a little party and there sat Emily in bed, having pressed the pause button on her show at the sound of his car.

It was very nice to come home to.

'Jessica set up the room,' Emily said, taking a long drink of coffee. 'Is that okay?'

'Of course,' Hugh said. 'I should have thought to bring the television down.'

'I'm fine,' Emily said. 'I was just being a sloth. It was so good. How was work?'

'Busy,' Hugh said, 'but good. At least till this morning.' He pulled a face. 'Ernest Bailey died in the small hours.'

'I'm sorry,' Emily said. 'Was it expected?'

'Nope.' Hugh shook his head and told her what had happened as he got undressed. 'He was supposed to be discharged home this morning. He was going to live with his daughter.' Hugh had a quick shower and then, damp and lovely, he climbed into bed. 'He didn't really want to go and live with his daughter. He was a very proud man. He couldn't have lived alone, though.' Hugh lay and thought for a moment. 'I spoke with Laura for a long time and she said it's how he would have wanted it.'

'Did he get his cup of tea?'

'Many of them. Laura brought a Thermos in for him to have by his bed every night.' Hugh was quiet for a moment. 'I had a little cry but then I knew she was right—it would have been their golden wedding anniversary tomorrow, so it's nice that they're together.'

She looked at Hugh and he looked back and smiled. 'I didn't boo-hoo.'

'I know.'

'I've got to go to sleep.'

'So do I,' Emily said. 'I'm on Hugh time. I've been up all night. One more episode to go.'

'Watch it now.'

'No, no, I'll save it for tonight.'

'Just watch it. You know you want to.'

Did life get better than this? Emily wondered as her back-to-back DVD marathon concluded. Hugh was half-asleep beside her and the last sip of coffee was still warm as she flicked off the television.

'Was it good?' Hugh asked, pulling her down beside him.

'So good,' Emily said. 'I've never done that before— watched a whole series back to back.'

'It's the best way,' Hugh mumbled. 'I've been thinking…' He had. Hugh had been lying there thinking of Ernest and Hannah and all the things that mattered most. 'After you see Anton for your check-up I've got a long weekend. Do you want to go to the Lake District? Maybe take a few days before you go back to work?'

'I'd love to.'

'We never did get full use of that room.'

'It would be lovely,' Emily said. 'Go to sleep.'

They had a kiss and she felt his hair in her hands still damp from the shower and she revelled in his sleepy kiss. Emily changed her mind—about sleeping, that was—because her other hand moved down his torso, their kiss moving seamlessly from tender to passionate by the swirl of her tongue. She loved the quickening of his breath and how he gathered her closer into him. There was no need to ask if it was too soon, or if she was ready, her body just was. Warm and relaxed and turned on in his arms, the icing appeared on the cake as Hugh kissed her till she lay beneath him and he took all his weight on his elbows. 'I missed you,' Hugh said.

She had missed him too but was just a little nervous as he entered her, scared that something might tear, but he took it really slowly and gave her time to get accustomed to the stretch of him inside her, and then slowly, as he moved inside her, her abdomen learned how first to relax and then it started to tense, but in pleasure now.

Emily's hands met behind his neck, loving the sight of his concentrated effort and the pleasure that was moving through her, the delicious friction combined with tenderness, and this risky thing called love that came with benefits galore.

She could feel his restraint and it turned her on, could feel him holding back from driving in deep, and as his arm slipped under her back and lifted her higher into him, it possibly hurt a bit but she'd take it for the pleasure as her orgasm started to home in and, yes, she was ready, more than ready as Hugh started to thrust faster while holding back on going very deep. One final swell of Hugh and then the bliss of his release gave him two gifts—a liberating shout of pleasure from Emily, combined with a very intense orgasm. They both welcomed the rewards of his restraint.

'I'll sleep now,' Hugh said, smiling down at her. 'Can we pretend you've just had surgery quite often?'

'We can.' Emily smiled.

'Depending on your migraines, of course.'

'I don't get migraines any more.' It was lovely to smile at their history, to lie and fall asleep in each other's arms and know they were the person the other wanted beside them in everything yet to come.

Yes, Emily thought as she drifted off to sleep, life could not get better than this.

She was wrong.

CHAPTER SEVENTEEN

'I CAN COME with you if Hugh can't make it,' Louise offered.

Emily had just seen Alex for her post-operative check-up and was having a coffee up in Theatre before her antenatal appointment with Anton.

'I'll be fine.' Emily smiled. 'And you were right, he is lovely to his patients.'

'Told you,' Louise said. 'Shame he's so miserable with all the staff. Honestly, I am so tired of him checking and re-checking everything. I wonder what he's like with the staff on Maternity.'

'You'll find out soon,' Emily said, because Louise was starting there next week. 'I'm sorry I can't make your leaving do. Hugh had already booked for us to go to the Lake District before I knew the date.'

'It's fine,' Louise said. 'I'm sure there'll be other nights out. You'd better head down for your appointment. You don't want to keep Anton waiting.'

Emily walked from Theatre down to Maternity Outpatients and tried to tell herself that it was natural to be nervous.

It didn't worry her that Hugh hadn't made it, but then

she saw him walking briskly toward her and it was very, very nice that he had.

Emily gave her name at Reception and then they took their seats to wait their turn to see Anton.

'Why don't we drive tomorrow?' Emily said, but Hugh shook his head.

'I'm going to have a sleep when we get in and then we can head off at midnight. I've only got four days off.'

And Hugh wanted to squeeze everything in.

'Are you nervous?'

'Yes,' Emily admitted. 'You?'

'Yes,' Hugh said, though he actually wasn't too nervous about the appointment. He had an awful lot else to be nervous about, though he daren't tell Emily just yet.

'Good to see they keep doctors waiting too,' Hugh said, and she pulled a face.

'I'm a nurse and this is my appointment.'

It was Hugh who smiled now. They knew just how to wind the other up, just how to make the other smile. Living together was a journey of both discovery and also a kind familiarity. They had been friends for way longer than they should have been after all.

'Well, if I was pregnant,' Hugh said, 'I'd expect to be seen on time.'

'If you were pregnant, you'd be seen on time by every doctor and medical student in the place.'

It was a very long wait and Hugh tapped his feet with impatience and read all the sex tips in all the magazines, along with the problem pages, as Emily read her book and tried to tell herself it would all be fine.

'Emily Jackson.'

Finally they were called in.

'Get used to waiting.' Anton smiled by way of greeting. 'One day it might be you two keeping the waiting room waiting.'

'Might be?' Emily checked, as he took her blood pressure.

'Planned Caesareans, for me, are a very beautiful thing.' Anton smiled again and Emily blushed. Louise was right, he was gorgeous. Oh, God, she was going to be one of those women who had a crush on their obstetrician. How embarrassing!

They went through all the usual questions and he asked if she had any plans for her delivery.

'None,' Emily said.

'Are you still getting used to the idea that you're pregnant?'

'I'm used to it being in there now,' Emily said. 'I've just not thought as far as getting it out.'

'Well, you're not due till the twenty fourth of February so you have plenty of time to work out your birth plan.'

'Lots of drugs,' Emily said, recalling the screams that had come from Theatre. 'Actually, that planned Caesarean is starting to sound very beautiful to me too.'

Anton continued smiling. 'Let's see how things progress. Usually I don't do an ultrasound at this stage,' Anton said, 'but I would like to just check and I'm sure you want to see for yourself that it is all okay, and then we can leave things till the nineteen-week scan.'

Hugh hadn't been there for her ultrasound and he saw their baby for the very first time. There was a lot more to see four weeks later and it moved and wriggled and Hugh could barely take in the evidence of what had happened that morning.

'Meant to be,' Hugh said.

It was.

As they headed off for a mountain of blood tests, she realised again that Hugh knew her very well indeed. 'You fancy him, don't you?'

'Stop it.' Emily was appalled that he could tell. 'Maybe it's hormones.'

'Or that Italian accent,' Hugh nudged, and then stopped teasing. 'I'm sure he's very used to his patients being a little in love with him. Apparently he's got a very good success rate for IVF. He was a top fertility specialist in Milan. It would seem you're in very good hands.'

Emily had her bloods done and then booked in for her nineteen-week ultrasound. 'We're not finding out what we're having,' Emily said, because Hugh wanted to and she didn't.

'Fine.'

'And if you can tell from the ultrasound then please don't tell me.'

'I'm not going to,' Hugh said, and then gave her a warning of how it would be. 'No matter how many times you ask me.'

Emily smiled. There was a lot to smile about, but not when Hugh woke her up at midnight and said that it was time to head off.

'Can't we drive in the morning?'

'No,' Hugh said. 'I want to be there by morning.'

It was actually nice, driving through the darkness and chatting away, and Emily asked if he'd heard any more about Gina.

'I'll go and visit next week,' Hugh said, 'but Mr Eccleston went and saw her yesterday and she's doing very well apparently. Her family hasn't exactly rallied around her though. She wants to get out of anaesthetics.' He glanced at her. 'Why don't you go to sleep?'

'Isn't the passenger supposed to talk to keep the driver awake?'

'You've never bothered before,' Hugh pointed out. 'Have a sleep. I'm fine, I had a few hours when we got home.'

Emily dozed off just before dawn, thinking about Gina and all the decisions she had to make but so glad she was getting help and support. She awoke a couple of hours later, frowning when she saw the road signs for Carlisle and trying to orientate herself for they'd passed the exit for the Lake District.

'We've passed it.'

'I know.'

'Shouldn't we—?'

'We're not going to the Lake District,' Hugh said. 'We're eloping.'

'Sorry?'

'We're going to Gretna Green. Remember those forms you signed…'

'And remember that I then changed my mind,' Emily reminded him. 'Hugh, I told you, it doesn't mean anything.'

'Well, it does to me. Even if your parents don't take their vows seriously, I will, and I believe you will too. I'm not going to force you but, honestly, if it really means nothing to you, do it for me.' Emily sat there. 'I don't want to hear them call out Ms Jackson. I don't want our baby to be called Jackson-Linton or Linton-Jackson. Boring as I am, I want us all to have the same surname. Now, if marriage does mean something to you and you don't think I'm the man you want to marry then it's a different story…'

'You are the one.' She did want to be married, she was just scared. 'I just swore I never would.'

'If this marriage doesn't work,' Hugh said, 'I won't be doing it again. I'm not going to have our child walking up the aisle behind one of its parents over and over… We'll do it once,' Hugh said. 'That can be our vow.'

'What if—?'

'Widow and widowers excepted.' Hugh smiled. 'I'll leave you rich enough to be a very wicked widow.' Then he was serious. 'Marry me, Emily.'

She nodded.

'Is that a yes?'

'Yes, but so many people are going to be upset…' Emily stopped there and then. She didn't care if her marriage offended some people, for their efforts had offended her deeply after all, but then she thought of something. 'Won't your parents be upset?'

'They were a bit at first.'

'You've already told them?'

'Yes.' Hugh nodded. 'Then Kate came up with a plan that they'd all book into a hotel and if you said yes…' Hugh shook his head. 'No way!'

'You said no to her.'

'We had a row actually,' Hugh said, 'and, God, it felt good. I said that I didn't even know if you were going to say yes. I didn't want complete public humiliation.'

'Oh, Hugh.' She couldn't believe all he'd been through just to get her to this point and, no, she couldn't say no to him.

'I'd love to marry you,' Emily said. 'And, for the record, it means everything to me.'

'We get married at three,' Hugh said, as the signs came up for Gretna Green.

'What about—?'

'I've covered everything.' He gave her a very nice smile. 'Don't panic, I have very good taste and once Kate had got over her hissy fit she actually helped me with a lot of the arrangements.'

They stopped thirty minutes from Gretna Green to pick up the rings that Hugh had chosen—Emily's a diamond and platinum ring stamped with an image of the anvil. It could not have been a better choice. And Hugh's ring was the same, just minus the diamonds.

'So you don't say I cheated you out of an engagement ring,' Hugh explained.

Emily's nerves were really fluttering as they pulled up at a small hotel and Hugh told her he'd booked her in for hair and make-up, which was all very lovely but there was nothing in her case for such a big day.

'God, what do I wear?'

He *had* thought of everything.

Hugh opened his suitcase and there, wrapped in tissue paper, was an ivory dress.

'You know your favourite black dress, the one you said ages ago that you wish you'd bought it in every size, because it was perfect for you?'

That conversation had been close to two years ago and that he'd remembered, that he knew it was still her favourite dress touched Emily deeply. 'I had it made up…'

'You've really planned this.'

'Oh, yes,' Hugh said. 'Now, are you sure you don't want to ring your parents? We can delay it.'

'No.'

'Do you want Louise or—?'

'I just want you, Hugh.' Now she could more easily admit it. 'I always have.'

'Then let's make it official.'

It was the only way Emily could have ever married, or rather the best way for Emily to marry, and it was the most beautiful day, apart from her feet, because a half-size up would have been better but she chose not to say anything.

It was near the end of summer and the beginning of their new lives.

A piper walked Emily to the wedding room and Hugh was wrong about one thing.

She did cry at weddings.

But only her own.

Emily looked down as he slid a ring on her finger and they said their vows and both meant every word.

Then the anvil was struck and they were husband and wife yet the fun had only just started.

Yes, it had all been planned.

A photographer was waiting and photos were taken outside the old blacksmith's and by the sign that said 'Gretna Green'. A little while later the first images came to Hugh's phone as they sat holding hands and trying to eat at the same time, with Emily's shoes on the floor beside her feet.

'Time to update our statuses,' Hugh said. 'Or do you want to ring your parents first?'

'Do it this way.'

Guess where we are?

He posted the image of them dressed for their wedding, kissing beside the Gretna Green sign, and not even a minute later her mum was on the phone.

Then her dad.
And then the 'likes' started and the comments.

What took you so long?

About time.

Congratulations.

We're all having a champagne for you both!

And a picture of colleagues and friends toasting them
was posted from Louise's leaving do.

A cyber wedding party was happening and it was
possibly the only way Emily's complicated family could
all be together to share in the celebration.

Her mum joined in, as did her dad and Cathy.

Donna got off the animosity horse and said she was
thrilled and that the twins were really excited and would
love to see them both soon.

'Wow!' Emily blinked.

Jonathan had clearly told Jennifer because she sent
a long message saying she was ringing Alex with the
happy news now.

Then came a message from Jessica.

Wonderful news. Mum says to say she is pleased for
you. xx

It was very nice to know that Katrina perhaps had
cared after all.

'I thought she'd forgotten me,' Emily admitted.

'No.' Hugh told her he had seen her in the recovery ward and how awkward Katrina had been. 'Some-times people don't like to look at their mistakes. She was angry with your father, it was never about you.'

'I know.'

It was just nice to have it confirmed.

Yes, it was the best wedding, but just as Hugh went to switch off his phone and get back to the two of them, Emily took out hers and posted a little teaser of her own.

More good news to come.

There was.

Emily knew it and so did Hugh.

Finally she was safe in love.

* * * * *

UNWRAPPING
HER ITALIAN DOC

BY
CAROL MARINELLI

MILLS
BOON

First published in Great Britain 2014
by Mills & Boon, an imprint of Harlequin (UK) Limited,
Eton House, 18-24 Paradise Road, Richmond, Surrey, TW9 1SR

© 2014 Carol Marinelli

ISBN: 978-0-263-90799-5

Printed and bound in Spain
by Blackprint CPI, Barcelona

CHAPTER ONE

'ANTON, WOULD YOU do me a favour?'

Anton Rossi's long, brisk stride was broken by the sound of Louise's voice.

He had tried very hard not to notice her as he had stepped into the maternity unit of The Royal in London, though, of course, he had.

Louise was up a stepladder and putting up Christmas decorations. Her skinny frame was more apparent this morning as she was dressed in very loose, navy scrubs with a long-sleeved, pale pink top worn underneath. Her blonde hair was tied in a high ponytail and she had layer after layer of tinsel around her neck.

She was also, Anton noted, by far too pale.

Yes, whether he had wanted to or not, he had noticed her.

He tended to notice Louise Carter a lot.

'What is it that you want?' Anton asked, as he reluctantly turned around.

'In that box, over there…' Louise raised a slender arm and pointed it towards the nurses' station '…there's some gold tinsel.'

He just stood there and Louise wondered if possibly he didn't understand what she was asking for.

'Tin-sel...' she said slowly, in the strange attempt at an Italian accent that Louise did now and then when she was trying to explain a word to him. Anton watched in concealed amusement as she jiggled the pieces around her neck. 'Tin-sel, go-o-old.'

'And?'

Louise gave up on her accent. 'Could you just get it for me? I've run out of gold.'

'I'm here to check on Hannah Evans.'

'It will only take you a second,' Louise pointed out. 'Look, if I get down now I'll have to start again.' Her hand was holding one piece of gaudy green tinsel to the tired maternity wall. 'I'm trying to make a pattern.'

'You are *trying*, full stop,' Anton said, and walked off.

'Bah, humbug,' Louise called to his departing shoulders.

Anton, had moved to London from Milan and, having never spent a Christmas in England, would have to find out later what that translated as but he certainly got the gist.

Yes, he wasn't exactly in the festive spirit. For the last few years Anton had, in fact, dreaded Christmas.

Unfortunately there was no escaping it at The Royal—December had today hit and there were invites galore for Christmas lunches, dinners and parties piling into his inbox that he really ought to attend. Walking into work this morning, he had seen a huge Christmas tree being erected in the hospital foyer and now Louise had got in on the act. She seemed to be attempting to singlehandedly turn the maternity ward into Santa's grotto.

Reluctantly, *very* reluctantly, he headed over to the

box, retrieved a long piece of gold tinsel and returned to Louise, who gave him a sweet smile as she took it.

Actually, no, Anton decided, it was far from a sweet smile—it was a slightly sarcastic, rather triumphant smile.

'Thank you very much,' Louise said.

'You're more than welcome,' Anton responded, and walked off.

Anton knew, just knew that if he turned around it would be to the sight of Louise poking her tongue out at him.

Keep going, he told himself.

Do not turn around, for it would just serve to encourage her and he was doing everything in his power to discourage Louise. She was the most skilled flirt he had ever come across. At first he has assumed Louise was like that with everyone—it had come as a disconcerting, if somewhat pleasant surprise to realise that the blatant flirting seemed to be saved solely for him.

Little known to Louise, he enjoyed their encounters, not that he would ever let on.

Ignore her, Anton told himself.

Yet he could not.

Anton turned to the sight of Louise on the stepladder, tongue out, fingers up and well and truly caught!

Louise actually froze for a second, which was very unfortunate, given the gesture she was making, but then she unfroze as Anton turned and walked back towards her. A shriek of nervous laughter started to pour from Louise because, from the way that Anton was walking, it felt as if he might be about to haul her from the ladder and over his shoulder. Wouldn't that be nice? both simultaneously thought, but instead he came right up to her, his face level with her groin, and looked up into china-blue eyes as she looked down at the sexiest, most aloof, impossibly arrogant man to have ever graced The Royal.

'I got you your tinsel.' Anton pointed at her and his voice was stern but, Louise noted, that sulky mouth of his was doing its level best not to smile.

'Yes, Anton, you did,' Louise said, wondering if he could feel the blast of heat coming from her loins. God knew, he was miserable and moody but her body responded to him as if someone had just thrown another log on the fire whenever he was around.

On many levels he annoyed her—Anton checked and re-checked everything that she did, as if she was someone who had just wandered in from the street and offered to help out for the day, rather than a qualified midwife. Yet, aside from their professional differences, he was as sexy as hell and the sparks just flew off the two of them, no matter how Anton might deny that they did.

'So why this?' Anton asked, and pulled a face and poked his tongue out at her, and Louise smiled at the sight of his tongue and screwed-up features as he mimicked her gestures. He was still gorgeous—olive-skinned, his black hair was glossy and straight and so well cut that Louise constantly had to resist running her hands through it just to see it messed up. His eyes were a very dark blue and she ached to see them smile, yet, possibly for the first time, while aimed at her, now they were.

Oh, his expression was cross but, Louise could just see, those eyes were finally smiling and so she took the opportunity to let him know a few home truths.

'It's the way that you do things, Anton.' Louise attempted to explain. 'Why couldn't you just say, "Sure, Louise," and go and get the tinsel?'

'Because, as I've told you, I am on my way to see a patient.'

'Okay, why didn't you smile when you walked into the unit and saw the decorations that I've spent the last two hours putting up and say, "Ooh, that looks nice"?'

'Truth?' Anton said.

'Truth.' Louise nodded.

'I happen to think that you have too many decorations...' He watched her eyes narrow at his criticism. 'You asked why I didn't tell you how nice they looked.'

'I did,' Louise responded. 'Okay, then, third question, why didn't you say hello to me when you walked past?'

For Anton, that was the trickiest to answer. 'Because I didn't see you.'

'Please!' Louise rolled her eyes. 'You saw me—you just chose to ignore me, as I'm going to choose to ignore your slight about my decorations. You can never have too much tinsel.'

'Oh, believe me Louise, you can,' Anton said, looking around. The corridor was a riot of red, gold and green tinsel stars. He looked up to where silver foil balloons hung from the ceilings. Then he looked down to plastic snowmen dancing along the bottom of the walls. Half of the windows to the patients' rooms had been sprayed with fake snow. Louise had clearly been busy. 'Nothing matches.' Anton couldn't help but smile and he *really* tried to help but smile! 'You don't have a theme.'

'The theme is Christmas, Anton,' Louise said in response. 'I had a very tinsel-starved Christmas last year and I intend to make up for it this one. I'm doing the nativity scene this afternoon.'

'Good for you,' Anton said, and walked off.

Louise didn't poke out her tongue again and even if she had Anton wouldn't have seen it because this time he very deliberately didn't turn around.

He didn't want to engage in conversation with Louise. He didn't want to find out why she'd had a tinsel-starved Christmas the previous year.

Or rather he *did* want to find out.

Louise was flaky, funny, sexy and everything Anton did not need to distract him at work. He wasn't here to make friends—his social life was conducted well away from the hospital walls. Anton did his level best to keep his distance from everyone at work except his patients.

'Hannah.' He smiled as he stepped into the four-bedded ward but Hannah didn't smile back and Anton pulled the curtains around her bed before asking his patient any questions. 'Are you okay?' Anton checked.

'I'm so worried.'

'Tell me,' Anton offered.

'I'm probably being stupid, I know, but Brenda came in this morning and I said the baby had moved and I'm sure that it did, but it hasn't since then.'

'So you're lying here, imagining the worst?'

'Yes,' Hannah admitted. 'It's taken so long to get here that I'm scared something's going to go wrong now.'

'I know how hard your journey has been,' Anton said. Hannah had conceived by IVF and near the end of a tricky pregnancy she had been brought in for bed rest as her blood pressure was high and the baby's amniotic fluid was a little on the low side. Anton specialised in high-risk pregnancies and so he was very comfortable listening to Hannah's concerns.

'Let me have a feel,' Anton said. 'It is probably asleep.'

For all he was miserable with the staff and kept himself to himself, Anton was completely lovely and open with his patients. He had a feel of Hannah's stomach and then took out a Doppler machine and had a listen, locating the heartbeat straight away. 'Beautiful,' Anton said, and they listened for a moment. 'Have you had breakfast?' Anton asked, because if Hannah had low blood sugar, that could slow movements down.

'I have.'

'How many movements are you getting?'

'I felt one now,' Hanna said.

'That's because I just nudged your baby awake when I was feeling your stomach.'

He sat going through her charts. Hannah's blood pressure was at the higher limits of normal and Anton wondered for a long moment how best to proceed. While the uterus was usually the best incubator, there were times when the baby was safest out. He had more than a vested interested in this pregnancy and he told Hannah that. 'Do you know you will be the first patient that I have ever helped both to conceive through IVF *and* deliver their baby?'

'No.' Hannah frowned. 'I thought in your line of work that that would happen to you all the time.'

'No.' Anton shook his head. 'Remember how upset you were when I first saw you because the doctor you had been expecting was sick on the day of your egg retrieval?'

Hannah nodded and actually blushed. 'I was very rude to you.'

'Because you didn't want a locum to be taking over your care.' Anton smiled. 'And that is fair enough. In Italy I used to do obstetrics but then I moved into reproductive endocrinology and specialised there. In my opinion you can't do both simultaneously, they are completely different specialties—you have to always be available for either. I only helped out that week because Richard was sick. I still cover very occasionally to help out and also because I like to keep up to date but in truth I cannot do both.'

'So how come you moved back to obstetrics?'

'I missed it,' Anton admitted. 'I do like the fertility side of things and I do see patients where that is their issue but if they need IVF then I refer them. Obstetrics is where I prefer to be.'

The movements were slowing down. Anton could see that and with her low level of amniotic fluid, Hannah would be more aware than most of any movement. 'I think your baby might be just about cooked,' Anton said, and then headed out of the ward and asked Brenda to come in. 'I'm just going to examine Hannah,' Anton said, and spoke to both women as he did so. 'Your cervix is thinning and you're already three centimetres dilated.' He looked at Brenda. 'Kicks are down from yesterday.'

Anton had considered delivering Hannah last night and now, with the news that the kicks were down combined with Hannah's distress, he decided to go ahead this morning.

'I think we'll get things started,' Anton said.

'Now?'

'Yes.' Anton nodded and he explained to Hannah his reasoning. 'We've discussed how your placenta is coming to the end of its use-by date. Sometimes the baby does better on the outside than in and I think we've just reached that time.' He let it sink in for a moment. 'I'll start a drip, though we'll just give you a low dose to help move things along.'

Hannah called her husband and Anton spoke with Brenda at the nurses' station, then Hannah was taken around to the delivery ward.

All births were special and precious but Anton had been concerned about Hannah for a couple of weeks as the baby was a little on the small side. Anton would actually be very relieved once this baby was out.

By the time he had set up the drip and Hannah was attached to the baby monitor, with Luke, her husband, by her side, Anton was ready for a coffee break. He checked on another lady who would soon deliver and then he checked on his other patients on the ward.

Stephanie, another obstetrician, had been on last night and had handed over to him but, though Anton respected Stephanie, he had learnt never to rely on handovers. Anton liked to see for himself where his patients were and though he knew it infuriated some of the staff it was the way he now worked and he wasn't about to change that.

Satisfied that all was well, he was just about to take himself to the staffroom when he saw Louise, still up that ladder, but she offered no snarky comment this time, neither were there any requests for assistance. Instead, she was pressing her fingers into her eyes and clearly felt dizzy.

Not my problem, Anton decided.

But, of course, it was.

CHAPTER TWO

'LOUISE…' HE WALKED over and saw her already pale features were now white, right down to her lips. 'Louise, you need to get down from the ladder.'

The sound of his voice created a small chasm between the stars dancing in her eyes and Louise opened her eyes to the sight of Anton walking towards her. And she would get down if only she could remember how her legs worked.

'Come on,' Anton said. This time he *did* take her down from the ladder, though not over his shoulder, as they had both briefly considered before. Instead, he held his hand out and she took it and shakily stepped down. Anton put a hand around her waist and led her to the staffroom, where he sat her down and then went to the fridge and got out some orange juice.

'Here,' he said, handing the glass to her.

Louise took a grateful gulp and then another and blew out a breath. 'I'm so sorry about that. I just got a bit dizzy.'

'Did you have breakfast this morning?'

'I did.' Louise nodded but he gave her a look that said he didn't believe a word. Anton then huffed off, leaving her sitting in the staffroom while he went to the kitchen. Louise could hear him feeding bread into the toaster.

God, Louise thought, rolling her eyes, here comes the lecture.

Anton returned a moment later with two slices of toast smothered in butter and honey.

'I just told you that I'd already had breakfast,' Louise said.

'I think you should eat this.'

'If I eat that I'll be sick. I just need to lie down for a few minutes.'

'Do you have a photo shoot coming up?' Anton asked, and Louise sighed. 'Answer me,' Anton said.

'Yes, I have a big photo shoot taking place on Christmas Eve but that has no part in my nearly fainting.'

Louise was a part-time lingerie model. She completely loved her side job and took it seriously. Everyone thought that it was hilarious, everyone, that was, except Anton. Mind, he didn't find anything very funny these days.

'You're too thin.' Anton was blunt and though Louise knew it was out of concern, there was no reason for him to be. She knew only too well the reason for the little episode on the ladder.

'Actually, I'm not too thin, I'm in the healthy weight range,' Louise said. 'Look, I just got dizzy. Please don't peg me as having an eating disorder just because I model part time.'

'My sister is a model in Milan,' Anton said, and Louise could possibly have guessed that, had Anton had a sister, then a model she might be because Anton really was seriously beautiful.

Louise lay down on the sofa because she could still

see stars and she didn't want Anton to know that. In fact, she just wanted him gone. And she knew how to get rid of him! A little flirt would have him running off.

'Are my hips not childbearing enough for you, Anton?' Louise teased, and Anton glanced down and it wasn't a baby he was thinking about between those legs! No way!

Louise had used to work in Theatre—in fact, she had been the nurse who had scrubbed in on his first emergency Caesarean here at The Royal. It had been the first emergency Caesarean section he had performed since losing Alberto. Of course, Louise hadn't known just how nervous Anton had been that day and she could not possibly have guessed how her presence had both helped and unsettled him.

During surgery Anton had been grateful for a very efficient scrub nurse and one who had immediately worked well with him.

After surgery, when he'd gone to check in on the infant, Louise had been there, smiling and cooing at the baby. She had turned around and congratulated him on getting the baby out in time, and he had actually forgotten to thank her for her help in Theatre.

Possibly he had snapped an order instead—anything rather than like her.

Except he did.

A few months ago Louise had decided to more fully utilise her midwifery training and had come to work on Maternity, which was, of course, Anton's stomping ground.

Seeing her most days, resisting her on each and every one of them, was quietly driving him insane.

She was very direct, a bit off the wall and terribly

beautiful too, and if she hadn't worked here Anton would not hesitate.

Mind you, if she hadn't worked here he wouldn't know just how clever and funny she was.

Anton looked down where she lay, eyes closed on the sofa, and saw there was a touch of colour coming back to her cheeks and her breathing was nice and regular now. Then Anton pulled his eyes up from the rise and fall of her chest and instead of leaving the room he met her very blue eyes.

Louise could see the concern was still there. 'Honestly, Anton, I didn't get dizzy because I have an eating disorder,' Louise said, and, because this was the maternity ward and such things were easily discussed, especially if your name was Louise, she told him what the real problem was. 'I've got the worst period in the history of the world, if you must know.'

'Okay.' He looked at her very pale face and her hand that moved low onto her stomach and decided she was telling the truth.

'Do you need some painkillers?'

'I've had some,' Louise said, closing her eyes. 'They didn't do a thing.'

'Do you need to go home?' Anton asked.

'Are you going to write me a note, Doctor?'

He watched her lips turn up in a smile as she teased but then shook her head. 'No, I'll be fine soon, though I might just stay lying down here for a few minutes.'

'Do you want me to let Brenda know?'

'Please.' Louise nodded.

'You're sure I can't get you anything?' Anton checked.

'A heat pack would be lovely,' Louise said, glad that

her eyes were closed because she could imagine his expression at being asked to fetch a heat pack, when surely that was a nurse's job. 'It needs two minutes in the microwave,' she called, as he walked out.

It took five minutes for Anton to locate the heat packs and so he returned seven minutes later to where she lay, knees up with her eyes closed, and he placed the heat pack gently over her uterus.

'You make a lovely midwife,' Louise said, feeling the weight and the warmth.

'I've told Brenda,' Anton said, 'and she said that you are to take your time and come back when you're ready.' He went to go but she still concerned him and Anton walked over and sat down by her waist on the sofa where she lay.

Louise felt him sit down beside her and then he picked up her hand. She knew that he was checking her nails for signs of anaemia and she was about to make a little tease about her not knowing he cared, except Anton this close made talking impossible. She opened her eyes and he pulled down her lower lids and she wished, oh, how she wished, those fingers were on her face for very different reasons.

'You're anaemic,' Anton said.

'I'm on iron and folic acid…'

'You're seeing someone?'

'Yes, but I…' Louise had started to let a few close friends know what was going on in her personal life but she wasn't quite ready to tell the world just yet. She ached to discuss it with Anton, not on a personal level but a professional one, yet was a little shy to. 'I've spoken to my GP.' His pager went off and though he read it he still sat there, but the moment had gone and Louise decided not to tell him her plans and what was going on.

'He's told you that you don't have to struggle like this. There is the Pill and there is also an IUD that can give you a break from menstr—'

'Anton,' Louise interrupted. 'My GP is a she, and I *am* a midwife, which means, oh, about ten times a day I give contraceptive advice, so I do know these things.'

'Then you should know that you don't have to put up with this.'

'I do. Thanks for your help,' Louise said, and then, aware of her snappy tone, she halted. After all, he was just trying to help. He simply didn't know what was going on in her world. 'I owe you one.' She gave him a smile. 'I'll buy you a drink tonight.'

'Tonight?' Anton frowned.

'It's the theatre Christmas do,' Louise said, and Anton inwardly groaned, because another non-work version of Louise seared into his brain he truly did not need! Anton had seen Louise dressed to the nines a few times since he had started here and it was a very appealing sight. He had braced himself for the maternity do in a couple of weeks—in fact, he had a date lined up for that night—but it had never entered his head that Louise would be at the theatre do tonight.

'So you will be going tonight?' Anton checked. 'Even though you're not feeling well?'

'Of course I'm going,' Louise said. 'I worked there for five years.' She opened her eyes and gave him a very nice smile, though their interlude was over. Concerned Anton had gone and he was back to bah, humbug as he stood. 'I'll see you tonight, Anton.'

Stop the drip! Anton wanted to say as he went in to

check on Hannah, for he would dearly love a reason to be stuck at the hospital tonight.

Of course, he didn't stop the drip and instead Hannah progressed beautifully.

'Louise, would you be able to go and work in Delivery after lunch?' Brenda came over as Louise added the finishing touches to her nativity scene during her lunch break. She'd taken her chicken and avocado salad out with her and was eating it as she arranged all the pieces. 'Angie called in sick and we're trying to get an agency nurse.'

Louise had to stop herself from rolling her eyes. While she loved being in Delivery for an entire shift, she loathed being sent in for a couple of hours. Louise liked to be there for her patient for the entire shift.

'Sure,' Louise said instead.

'They're a bit short now,' Brenda pushed, and Louise decided not to point out that she'd only had fifteen minutes' break, given the half-hour she'd taken earlier that morning. So, instead, she popped the cutest Baby Jesus ever into the crib, covered him in a little rug and headed off to Delivery.

She took the handover, read through Hannah's birth plan then went in and said hello to Hannah and Luke. Hannah had been a patient on the ward for a couple of weeks now so introductions had long since been done.

Hannah was lying on her side and clearly felt uncomfortable.

'It really hurts.'

'I know that it does,' Louise said, showing Luke a nice spot to rub on the bottom of Hannah's back, but Hannah kept pushing his hand away.

'Do you want to have a little walk?' Louise offered, and at first Hannah shook her head but then agreed. Louise sorted out the drip and got her up off the delivery bed and they shuffled up and down the corridor, sometimes silent between contractions, when Hannah leant against the wall, other times talking.

'I still can't believe we'll have a baby for Christmas,' Hannah said.

'How exciting.' Louise smiled. 'Have you shopped for the baby?'

'Not yet!' Hannah shook her head. 'Didn't want the bad luck.' She leant against the wall and gave a very low moan and then another one.

'Let's get you back,' Louise said, guiding the drip as Luke helped his wife.

Hannah didn't like the idea of sitting on a birthing ball—in fact, she climbed back onto the delivery bed and went back to lying on her side as Louise checked the baby's heart, which was fine.

'You're doing wonderfully, Hannah,' Louise said.

'I can't believe we're going to get our baby,' Hannah said. 'We tried for ages.'

'I know that you did,' Louise said.

'I'm so lucky to have Anton,' Hannah said. 'He got me pregnant!'

Louise looked over at Luke and they shared a smile because at this stage of labour women said the strangest things at times, only Louise's smile turned into a slight frown as Luke explained what she'd meant. 'Anton was the one who put back the embryo...'

'Oh!' Louise said, more than a little surprised, because that was something she hadn't known—yes, of course he would deal with infertility to a point, but it was a very specific specialty and for Anton to have performed the embryo transfer confused Louise.

'He was a reproductive specialist in Milan, one of the top ones,' Luke explained further, when he saw Louise's frown. 'We thought we were getting a fill-in doctor when Richard, the specialist overseeing Hannah's treatment, got sick, but it turned out we were getting one of the best.' He looked up as Anton came in. 'I was just telling Louise that you were the one who got Hannah pregnant.'

Anton gave a small smile of acknowledgement of the conversation then he turned to Louise. 'How is she?'

'Very well.'

Anton gave another brief nod and went to examine Hannah.

Hannah was doing very well because things soon started to get busy and by four o'clock, just when Louise should be heading home to get ready for tonight, she was cheering Hannah on.

'Are you okay, Louise?' Brenda popped her head in to see if Louise wanted one of the late staff to come in and take over but instead Louise smiled and nodded. 'I'm fine, Brenda,' Louise said. 'We're nearly there.'

She would never leave so close to the end of a birth, Anton knew that, and she was enthusiastic at every birth, even if the mother was in Theatre, unconscious.

'How much longer?' Hannah begged.

'Not long,' Louise said. 'Don't push, just hold it now.' Louise was holding Hannah's leg and watched as the head came out and Anton carefully looped a rather thin and straggly umbilical cord from around the baby's neck.

She and Anton actually worked well in this part. Anton liked how Louise got into it and encouraged the woman no end, urging her on when required, helping him to slow things down too, if that was the course of action needed. This was the case here, because the baby was only thirty-five weeks and also rather small for dates.

'Oh, Hannah!' Louise was ecstatic as the shoulders were delivered and Anton placed the slippery bundle on Hannah's stomach and Louise rubbed the baby's back. They all watched as he took his first breath and finally Hannah and Luke had their wish come true.

'He's beautiful,' Hannah said, examining her son in awe, holding his tiny hand, scarcely able to believe she had a son.

He was small, even for thirty-five weeks, and, having delivered the placenta, Anton could well see why. The baby had certainly been delivered at the right time and could now get the nourishment he needed from his mother to fatten up.

Anton came and looked at the baby. The paediatrician was finishing up checking him over as Louise watched.

'He looks good,' Anton said.

'So good,' Louise agreed, and then smiled at the baby's worried-looking face. He was wearing the concerned expression that a lot of small-for-dates babies had. 'And so hungry!'

The paediatrician went to have a word with the parents to explain their baby's care as Louise wrapped him up in a tight parcel and popped a little hat on him.

'How does it feel,' Louise asked Anton, 'to have been there at conception and delivery?' She started to laugh at her own question. 'That sounds rude! You know what I mean.'

'I was just saying to Hannah this morning that it has never happened to me before. So this little one is a bit more special,' Anton admitted. 'I'm going to go and write my notes. I'll be back to check on Hannah in a while.'

'Well, I'll be going home soon,' Louise said, 'but I'll pass it all on.' She picked up the baby. 'Come on, little man, let's get you back to your mum.'

She didn't rush home then either, though. Louise helped with the baby's first feed, though he quickly tired and would need gavage top-ups. Having put him under a warmer beside his parents, she then went and made Hannah a massive mug of tea. Anton, who was getting a cup of tea of his own, watched as she went into her pocket and took out a teabag.

'Why do you keep teabags in your pocket?'

'Would you want that…' she sneered at the hospital teabags on the bench '…if you'd just pushed a baby out?'

'No.'

'There's your answer, then. I make sure my mums get one nice cup of tea after they've given birth and then they wonder their entire stay in hospital why the rest of them taste so terrible after that,' Louise said. 'It's my service to women.' She went back into her pocket and gave him a teabag and Anton took it because the hospital tea really was that bad. 'Here, but that's *not* the drink I owe you for this morning. You'll get that later.'

He actually smiled at someone who wasn't a patient. 'I'll see you tonight,' Louise said, and their eyes met, just for a second but Anton was the one who looked away, and with good reason.

Yes, Anton thought, she would see him tonight but here endeth the flirting.

CHAPTER THREE

LOUISE LIVED FAIRLY close to the hospital and arrived at her small terraced home just after five to a ringing phone.

She did consider not answering it because she was already running late but, seeing that it was her mum, Louise picked up.

'I can't talk for long,' Louise warned, and then spent half an hour chatting about plans for Christmas Day.

'Mum!' Louise said, for the twentieth time. 'I'm on days off after Christmas Eve all the way till after New Year. I've told you that I'll be there for Christmas Day.'

'You said you'd be there last year,' Susan pointed out.

'Can we not go through that again,' Louise said, regretting the hurt she had caused last year by not telling her parents the truth about what had been going on in her life. 'I was just trying to—'

'Well, don't ever do that again,' Susan said. 'I can't bear that you chose to spend Christmas miserable and alone in some hotel rather than coming home to your family.'

'You know why I did, Mum,' Louise said, and then conceded, 'But I know now that I should have just come home.' She flicked the lights of her Christmas tree to

on, smiling as she did so. 'Mum, I honestly can't wait
for Christmas.'

'Neither can I. I've ordered the turkey,' Susan said,
'and I'm going to try something extra-special for Boxing Day—kedgeree…'

'Is that the thing with fish and eggs?' Louise checked.

'And curry powder,' Susan agreed.

'That's great, Mum,' Louise said, pulling a face because her mother was the worst cook in the world. The
trouble was, though, that Susan considered herself an
amazing cook! Louise ached for her dad sometimes, he
was the kindest, most patient man, only that had proved
part of the problem—the compliments he'd first given
had gone straight to Susan's head and, in the kitchen,
she thought she could do no wrong. 'Mum, I'd love to
chat more but I have to go now and get ready, it's the
theatre Christmas night out. I'll call you soon.'

'Well, enjoy.'

'I shall.'

'Oh, one other thing before you go,' Susan said. 'Did
you get the referral for the specialist?'

'Not yet,' Louise sighed. 'She says she wants me
to have a full six months off the Pill before she refers
me…' Louise thought for a moment. She really wasn't
happy with her GP. 'I know I said that I didn't want to
go to The Royal for this but it might be the best place.'

'I think you're right,' Susan said. 'I didn't like to
say so at the time but I don't think she took you very
seriously.'

Louise nodded then glanced at the clock. So much
for a quick chat!

'I have to get ready, Mum.'

'Well, if you do go to The Royal, let me know when and I'll come with you...'

'I will,' Louise said, and then there were all the *I love you*s and *Do you want a quick word with Dad?*

Louise smiled as she put down the phone because, apart from her cooking, Louise knew that she had the best mum and possibly the best family in the world.

Her dad was the most patient person and Louise's two younger sisters were amazing young women who rang Louise often, and they all got on very well.

This was part of the reason why she hadn't wanted to spoil Christmas for everyone last year and had pretended that something had happened at work. At the time it had seemed kinder to say that they were short-staffed rather than arrive home in such a fragile state on Christmas morning and ruin everyone's day.

Her sisters looked up to her and often asked her opinion on guys; it had been hard, admitting how badly she had judged Wesley. Even a part of the truth had hurt them and her dad would just about die if he knew even half of what had really gone on.

Louise lay on her bed while her bath was running, thinking back to that terrible time. Not just the break-up with Wesley but the horrible lonely time before it.

Louise's wings had been clipped during their relationship. *Seriously* clipped, to the point that she had given up her modelling side job, which she loved. Somehow, she wasn't quite sure how it had happened, her hems had got lower, her hair darker until her sparkle had almost been extinguished.

At a work function Wesley had loathed that she had chatted with Rory, an anaesthetist who was also ex-boyfriend of Louise's from way back.

She and Rory had remained very good friends up to that point.

Louise had given Wesley the benefit of the doubt after that first toxic row. Yes, she'd decided, it wasn't unreasonable for him to be jealous that she was so friendly with her ex. She had severed things with Rory, which had been hard to do and had caused considerable hurt when she had.

It hadn't stopped there, though.

Wesley hadn't liked Emily, Louise's close friend, either. He hadn't liked their odd nights out or their phone calls and texting and gradually that had all tapered off too.

Finally, realising that she had been constantly walking on eggshells and that she'd barely recognised herself any more, Louise had known she had to end things. It had been far easier said than done, though, knowing, with Wesley's building temper, that the ending would be terrible.

It had been.

On Christmas Eve, when Wesley had decided that her family didn't like him and perhaps it should be just the two of them for Christmas, Louise had known she had to get the hell out. An argument had ensued and the gentle, happy Louise had finally lost her temper.

No, he hadn't taken it well.

It would soon be a year to the very day since it had happened, and in the year that had followed Louise had found herself again—the woman she had been before Wesley, the happy person she had once been, though it had taken a while.

Louise's confidence had been severely shaken around men but her dad, her uncles, Rory, Emily's now-

husband, Hugh, all the people Wesley had been so jealous of had been such huge support—insisting that Wesley wasn't in the regular mould men were cast from.
Finally convincing her that she should simply be her
sparkling, annoying, once irrepressible self.

Without her family and friends, Louise did not know
how she'd have survived emotionally.

She'd never turn her back on them again.

Anton had appeared at The Royal around March and
the jolt of attraction had been so intense Louise had felt
her mojo dash back. Possibly because he was so aloof
and just so unobtainable that it had felt safe to test her
flirting wings on him.

Anton never really responded, yet he never stopped
her either. He simply let her be, which was nice.

It was all for fun, a little confidence boost as she
slowly returned to her old self, yet in the ensuing
months it had gathered steam.

Nope!

Louise got of the bed and looked around her room.
It was a sexy boudoir indeed, thanks to a few freebies
from a couple of photo shoots. There was a velvet red
chair that went with the velvet bedspread, and it made
Louise smile every time she sat in it. She smiled even
more at the thought of Anton in here but she pushed
that thought aside.

In the flirting department he was divine but his ar-
rogance, the way he double-checked everything Louise
did at work, rendered him far from relationship mate-
rial.

Not that she knew if he even liked her.

To Louise, Anton was a very confusing man.

Still, flirting was fun!

Not that she felt particularly sparkly tonight.

After her bath, Louise did her make-up carefully, topped it off with loads of red lipstick and then started to dry her hair.

It still fell to the right, even after nearly a year of parting it to fall to the left.

Louise examined the shiny red scar on her scalp for a moment. She could still see the needle marks. Thanks to her delay in getting sutured, the stitches had had to stay in for ten days. Unable to deal with the memory, she quickly moved on and tonged her hair into wild ringlets. She put on the Christmas holly underwear that she'd modelled a couple of months ago, along with the stockings from the same range, which were a very sheer red with green sprigs of holly and little red dots for berries.

They were fabulous!

As were the red dress and high-heeled shoes.

Hearing Emily blast the horn outside, Louise pushed out a smile, determined to enjoy all the celebrations that took place at her very favourite time of the year, however unwell she felt.

'God help Anton!' Hugh said, as Louise stepped out of her house and waved to him and Emily.

'Why haven't they got it on?' Emily asked, as Louise dashed back in the house to check that she'd turned off her curling tongs.

'I don't know,' Hugh mused. 'Though I thought that Louise had sworn off men.'

'She's sworn off relationships,' Emily said, 'not joined a nunnery.'

Hugh laughed. No, he could not imagine Louise in a nunnery.

'Is Anton seeing anyone?' Emily asked, but Hugh shook his head.

'I don't think so—mind you, Anton's not exactly friendly and chatty.'

'He is to me.'

'Because you're six months pregnant and his patient,' Hugh pointed out, as Louise came down her path for the second time. 'Maybe you could ask him if he's seeing someone next time you see him.'

'That's a good idea.' Emily smiled. 'I'll just slip that question in while he examines me, shall I?'

She turned and smiled as Louise got into the back of the car.

'Hi, Emily. You make a lovely taxi driver—thank you for this,' Louise said. 'Hi, Hugh, how lucky you are to have a pregnant wife over Christmas!'

'Very lucky,' Hugh agreed, as Emily drove off.

'You look gorgeous, Louise,' Emily said.

'Thank you, but I feel like crap,' Louise happily admitted. 'I've got the worst period and I can only have one eggnog as I'm working in the morning.'

Hugh arched his neck at Louise's openness and Emily smiled.

They both loved her.

As they arrived at the rather nice venue, Louise got her first full-length look at Emily.

'You look gorgeous and I want one…' she said, referring to Emily's six–months-pregnant belly, which was tonight dressed in black and looking amazing.

'You will soon,' Emily said, because Louise had shared with her her plans to get pregnant next year.

'I hope so.'

Louise's eyes scanned the room. It had been very

tastefully decorated—there were pale pinkish gold twigs in vases on the tables and pale pinkish gold decorations and lights that twinkled, and there was Anton, talking to Alex, who was Hugh's boss, and Rory was with them as well.

Perfect, Louise thought as the trio made their way over and all the hellos began.

'Aren't the decorations gorgeous?' Emily said, but Louise pulled a face.

'Some colour would be nice. Who would choose pink for Christmas decorations?' As a waiter passed with a tray, she took a mini pale pink chocolate that the waiter called a frosted snowball but even the coconut was pink. 'They have a *theme*,' she said, and smiled at Anton, but it went to the wall because he wasn't looking at her.

'No Jennifer?' Hugh checked with Alex, because normally his wife Jennifer accompanied him on nights such as this.

'No, Josie's got a fever.' Alex explained things a little better for Anton. 'Josie's our youngest child. You haven't yet met my wife Jennifer, have you?'

'Your wife?' Anton said. 'I have heard a lot of nice things.'

Perhaps because Louise was close to PhD level in Anton's facial features, Anton's accent, Anton's words, oh, just everything Anton, she frowned just a little at his slightly vague response. Still, she didn't dwell on it for long because he simply looked fantastic in an evening suit. Her eyes swept his body, taking in his long legs, his very long black leather shoes and then, when her mind darted to rude places, she looked up. His olive complexion was accentuated by the white of his shirt and he was just so austere that it made her want to jump onto his lap and whisper in his ear all the things she wanted him to do to her for Christmas.

Oh, a relationship might not be on the agenda but so pointed was his dismissal of her tonight that they were clearly both thinking sex.

'Is that holly on your stockings?' Rory asked, and everyone looked down to examine Louise's long legs.

Everyone, that was, but Anton.

'Yes, I got them free after that shoot I did a couple of months ago,' Louise said. 'I've been dying to wear them ever since. Got to get into the Christmas spirit. Speaking of which, does anyone want a drink?'

'No, thank you,' Alex said.

'I'll have a tomato juice,' Emily sighed. 'A virgin bloody Mary.'

'Hugh?' Louise asked.

'I'd love an eggnog.'

'Yay!' Louise said. 'Anton?'

'No, thank you.'

'Are you sure?' Louise said. 'I thought I owed you one.'

'I'm fine,' he responded, barely looking at her. 'I think Saffarella is getting me a drink. Here she is...'

Here she was, indeed!

Rippling black hair, chocolate-brown eyes, a figure to die for, and she was so seriously stunning that she actually made Louise feel drab, especially when her thick Italian accent purred around every name as introductions were made.

'Em-il-ee, Loo-ease.'

On sight the two women bristled.

It was like two cats meeting in the back yard and

Louise almost felt her tail bush up as they both smiled and nodded.

'Sorry, I didn't catch your name,' Louise said.

Saffarella was already getting on her nerves.

'Saffarella,' she repeated in her beautiful, treacle voice, and then was kind enough to give Louise a further explanation. 'Like Cinderella.'

With a staph infection attached, Louise thought, but thankfully Rory knew Louise's humour and decided to move her on quickly!

'I'll come and help you with the drinks.' Rory took Louise's arm and they both walked over to the bar.

'Good God!' Louise said the second they were out of earshot.

'No wonder you've got nowhere with him.' Rory laughed. 'She's stunning.'

'Oh!' Louise was seriously rattled, she was far too used to being the best-looking woman in the room. 'What sort of name is Saffarella? Well, there goes my fun for the night. I thought I'd at least get a dance with him. I don't have anyone to fancy any more,' Louise sighed. 'And I'm going to look like a wallflower.'

'Don't worry, Louise.' Rory smiled. 'I'll dance with you.'

'You have to now,' Louise said. 'I'm not having him seeing me sitting on my own. I was so positive that he liked me.'

Louise returned with Emily's virgin bloody Mary but then she caught sight of Connor and Miriam and excused herself and headed over for a good old catch up with ex-colleagues. It was actually a good, if not brilliant night—Rory was as good as his word and midway through proceedings he did dance with her.

Rory was lovely, possibly one of the nicest men that a woman could know.

In fact, Rory was the last really nice boyfriend that Louise had had.

There was absolutely nothing going on between them. Their parting, three years ago, had been an amicable one. Though most people lied when they said that, in Rory and Louise's case it had been true. Just a few weeks into their relationship Louise had, while undergoing what she'd thought were basic investigations for her erratic menstrual cycle, received the confronting news that, when the time came, she might not fall pregnant very easily.

It hadn't been a complete bombshell, Louise had known things hadn't been right, but when it had finally dropped Louise had been inconsolable. Rory had put his hands up in the end and had said that, as much as he liked her, there wasn't enough there to be talking baby, baby, baby every day of the week.

They were far better as exes than as a couple.

'How's Christmas behaving?' Rory asked, as they danced.

'Much better this time.'

'You look so much happier.'

'I'm sorry we stopped being friends,' Louise said.

'We never stopped being friends,' Rory said. 'Well, I didn't. I was so worried when you were with him.'

'I know,' Louise said. 'Thanks for being there for me.' She gave him a smile. 'I might have some happy news soon.'

'What are you up to, Louise?'

'I'm going to be trying for a baby,' Louise admitted, 'by myself.'

'How did I not guess that?' Rory smiled.

'Please don't ask me if I've thought about it.'

'I wouldn't. I know that it's all you think about.'

'It's got worse since I've gone back to midwifery,' Louise said. 'My fallopian tubes want to reach out and steal all the little babies.'

'It might end any chance of things between you and Anton,' Rory said gently, but Louise just shrugged.

'He's the last person I'd go out with, he's way too controlling and moody for my taste. I just wanted a loan of that body for a night or two.' Louise smiled. 'Nope...' She had made up her mind. In the three years since she and Rory had broken up she had made some poor choices when it came to men. The news that she might have issues getting pregnant had seriously rocked Louise's world, leaving her a touch vulnerable and exposed. She was so much stronger now, though her desire to become a mother had not diminished an inch. 'I want a baby far more than I want another failed relationship.'

'Fair enough.'

They danced on, Louise with her mind on Anton. She was seriously annoyed at the sight of them laughing and talking as they danced and the way Saffarella ran her hands through his hair and over his bum had Louise burn with jealousy. Worse, though, was the way Anton laughed a deep laugh at something she must have said.

'I don't think I've ever seen him laugh till now, and I know that I'm funnier than her,' Louise grumbled. 'God, why does she have to be so, so beautiful? What did he introduce her as?'

'Saffarella.'

'Did he say girlfriend when he introduced her?' Louise pushed. 'Or my wife...?' She was clutching at straws as she remembered that his sister was a model. 'It's not his sister, is it?'

'If it's his sister then we should consider calling the police!' Rory said. 'Sorry, Louise, they're on together.'

But then a little while later came the good news!

She and Rory were enjoying another dance, imagining things that could never happen to John Lennon's 'Imagine'. Louise was thinking of Anton while Rory was thinking of a woman who couldn't be here tonight. He glanced up and saw that Anton was watching them, and then Anton looked over again.

'Anton keeps looking over,' Rory whispered in Louise's ear.

'Really?'

'He does,' Rory said. 'I don't think he likes me any more—in fact, I'd say from the look I just got he wants to take me out the back and knock my lights out.'

'Seriously?' Louise was delighted at the turn of events.

'Well, not quite that much, but I think you may be be right, Louise, Anton does like you.'

'I told you that he did. Is he still looking?'

'He's trying not to.'

'You have to kiss me,' Louise said.

'No.'

'Please.' Louise was insistent. 'Just one long one—it will serve him bloody right for trying to make me jealous. Come on, Rory,' she said when, instead of kissing her, he still shook his head. 'It's not like we never have before and I do it all the time when I'm modelling. It doesn't mean anything.'

'No,' Rory said.

'I got off with you a couple of years ago when Gina

got drunk and was making a play for you!' Louise reminded him.

Gina was an anaesthetist who had had a drink and drug problem and had gone into treatment a few months ago. A couple of years back Rory had been trying to avoid Gina at a Christmas party. Gina had tended to make blatant plays for him when drunk, so he and Louise had had a kiss and pretended to leave together.

'Come on, Rory.'

'No,' he said, and then he rolled his eyes and reluctantly admitted the reason why not. 'I like someone.'

'Who?' Louise's curiosity was instant.

'Just someone.'

'Is she here?'

'No,' Rory said. 'But I don't want it getting back to her that I got off with my ex.'

'Do I know her?'

'Leave it, Louise,' Rory said. 'Please.'

It really was turning out to be the most frustrating night! First Anton and Saffarella, now Rory with his secret.

Hugh and Emily watched the action from the safety of the tables, trying to work out just what was going on.

'Anton is holding Saffarella like a police riot shield,' Hugh observed, but Emily laughed just a little too late.

'Are you okay?' Hugh checked, looking at his wife, who, all of a sudden, was unusually quiet.

'I'm a bit tired,' Emily admitted.

'Do you want to go home?' Hugh checked, and Emily nodded. 'But I promised Louise a lift.'

'She'll be fine,' Hugh said, standing as Louise and Rory made their way over from the dance floor. 'We're going to go,' Hugh said. 'Emily's a bit tired.'

'Emily?' Louise frowned as she looked at her friend. 'Are you okay?'

'Can I not just be tired?' Emily snapped, and then corrected herself. 'Sorry, Louise. Look, I know that I said I'd give you a lift—'

'Don't be daft,' Louise interrupted. 'Go home to bed.'

'I'll see Louise home,' Rory said, and Hugh gave a nod of thanks.

They said their goodnights but as Hugh and Emily walked off, Rory could see the concern on Louise's face.

'Louise!' Rory knew what she was thinking and dismissed it. 'Emily's fine. It isn't any wonder that she's feeling tired. She's six months pregnant and working. Theatre was really busy today...'

'I guess, but...' Louise didn't know what to say. Rory didn't really get her intuition where pregnant women were concerned. She wasn't about to explain it to him again but he'd already guessed what she was thinking.

'Not your witch thing again?' Rory sighed.

'Midwives know.' Louise nodded. 'I'm honestly worried.'

'Come on, I'll get you a drink,' Rory said. 'You can have two eggnogs.' But Louise shook her head. 'I just want to go home,' she admitted. 'You stay, I can get a taxi.'

'Don't be daft,' Rory said, and, not thinking, he put his arm around her and they headed out, followed by the very disapproving eyes of Anton.

Rory dropped her home and, though tired, Louise couldn't sleep. She looked at the crib, still wrapped in Cellophane, that she had hidden in her room, in case Emily dropped round. It was a present Louise had bought. It was stunning and better still it had been on sale. Louise had chosen not to say anything to Emily, knowing how superstitious first-time mums were about not getting anything in advance.

Emily had already been through an appendectomy at six weeks' gestation, as well as marrying Hugh and sorting out stuff with her difficult family. She was due to finish working in the New Year and finally relax and enjoy the last few weeks of pregnancy.

Louise lay there fretting, trying to tell herself that this time she was wrong.

It was very hard to understand let alone explain it but Emily had had that *look* that Louise knew too well.

Please, no!

It really was too soon.

CHAPTER FOUR

ANTON WAS RARELY uncomfortable with women.

Even the most beautiful ones.

He and Saffarella went back a long way, in a very loose way. They had met through his sister a couple of years ago and saw each other now and then. He had known that she would be in London over Christmas and Saffarella had, in fact, been the date he had planned to take to the maternity Christmas evening.

'Where are we going?' Saffarella frowned, because she clearly thought they were going back to his apartment but instead they had turned the opposite way.

'I thought I might take you back to the hotel,' Anton said.

'And are you coming in?' Saffarella asked, and gave a slightly derisive snort at Anton's lack of response. 'I guess that means, no, you're not.'

'It's been a long day...' Anton attempted, but Saffarella knew very well the terms of their friendship and it was *this* part of the night that she had been most looking forward to and she argued her case in loud Italian.

'Don't give me that, Anton. Since when have you ever been too tired? I saw you looking at that blonde tart...'

'Hey!' Anton warned, but his instant defence of Louise, combined with the fact that they both knew just who he was referring to, confirmed that Anton's mind had been elsewhere tonight. Saffarella chose to twist the knife as they pulled into the hotel. 'I doubt that she's being dropped off home by that Rory. They couldn't even wait for the night to finish to get out of the place.' When the doorman opened the door for her Saffarella got out of the car. 'Don't you ever do that to me again.' She didn't wait for the doorman, instead slamming the door closed.

Anton copped it because he knew that he deserved it.

His intention had never been to use Saffarella, they were actually good together. Or had been. Occasionally.

Anton had never, till now, properly considered just how attracted he really was to Louise. Oh, she was the reason he had called Saffarella and asked if she was free tonight, and Saffarella had certainly used him in the same way at times.

But it wasn't just the ache of his physical attraction to Louise that was the problem. He liked her. A lot. He liked her humour, her flirting, the way she just openly declared whatever was on her mind, not that he'd ever tell her that.

But knowing she was on with Rory, knowing he had taken her home, meant that Anton just wanted to be alone tonight to sulk.

It's your own fault, Anton, he said to himself as he drove home.

He should have asked Louise out months ago but then he reminded himself of the reason he hadn't, couldn't, wouldn't be getting involved with anyone from work ever again.

Approaching four years ago, Christmas Day had suddenly turned into a living nightmare. Telling parents on Christmas Day that their newborn baby was going to die was hell at the best of times.

But at the worst of times, telling parents, while knowing that the death could have been avoided, was a hell which Anton could not yet escape from and he returned to the nightmare time and again.

The shouts and the accusations from Alberto's father, Anton could still hear some nights before going to sleep.

The coroner's report had pointed to a string of communication errors but found that it had been no one person's fault in particular. Anton could recite it off by heart, because he had gone over and over and over it, trying to see what he could have done differently.

But the year in the between the death and the coroner's report had been one Anton could rarely stand to recall.

He took his foot off the brake as he realised he was speeding and pulled over for a moment because he could not safely think about that time and drive.

His relationship hadn't survived either. Dahnya, his girlfriend at the time, had been one of the midwives on duty that Christmas morning and when she hadn't called him, the continual excuses she had made instead of accepting her part in the matter, had proved far too much for them.

Friends and colleagues had all been injected with the poison of gossip. Everyone had raced to cover their backs by stabbing others in theirs and the once close, supportive unit he had been a part of had turned into a war zone.

Anton had been angry too.

Furious.

He had raged when he had seen that information had not been passed on to him. Information that would have meant he would have come to see and then got the labouring mother into Theatre far sooner than he had.

The magic had gone from obstetrics and even before the coroner's findings had been in, Anton had moved into reproductive endocrinology, immersing himself in it, honing his skills, concentrating on the maths and co-nundrum of infertility. It had absorbed him and he had enjoyed it, especially the good times—when a woman who had thought she never would get pregnant finally did, and yet more and more he had missed obstetrics.

To go back to it, Anton had known he would need a completely fresh start, for he no longer trusted his old colleagues. He had come to London and really had done his best to put things behind him.

It was not so easy, though, and he was aware that he tended to take over. He sat there and thought about his first emergency Caesarean at The Royal. Louise just so brisk and efficient and completely in sync with him as they'd fought to get the deteriorating baby out.

He had slept more easily that night.

That hurdle he had passed and perhaps things would have got better. Perhaps he might have started to hand over the reins to skilled hands a touch further had Gina not rear-ended him in the hospital car park.

Anton had got out, taken one look at her, parked her car, pocketed the keys and then driven her home.

Twenty minutes later he'd reported her to the chief of Anaesthetics and Anton had been hyper-vigilant ever since then.

Anton looked down the street at the Christmas lights but they offered no reprieve; instead, they made it worse. He loathed Christmas. Alberto, the baby, had missed out on far too many.

Yep, Anton reminded himself as he drove home and then walked into his apartment, which had not a single shred of tinsel or a decoration on display, there was a very good reason not to get involved with Louise or anyone at work.

He took out his work phone and called the ward to check on a couple of patients, glad to hear that all was quiet tonight.

Anton poured a drink and pulled out his other phone, read an angry text from Saffarella, telling him he should find someone else for the maternity night out, followed by a few insults that Anton knew she expected a response to.

He was too tired for a row and too disengaged for an exchange of texts that might end up in bed.

Instead, he picked up his work phone and scrolled through some texts. All the staff knew they could contact him and with texting often it was easy just to send some obs through or say you were on your way.

He scrolled through and looked at a couple of Louise's messages.

BP 140/60—and yes, Santa, before you ask, I've read your list and I've checked it twice—it's still 140/60. From your little helper

He'd had no idea what that little gem had meant until he'd been in a department store, with annoying music grating in his ears, and a song had come on and he'd burst out laughing there and then.

He had realised then how lame his response at the time had been.

Call me if it goes up again.

Her response:

Bah, humbug!

Followed by another text.

Yes, Anton, I do know.

He must, Anton thought, find out what 'bah, humbug' meant.

Then he read another text from a couple of months ago that made him smile. But not at her humour, more at how spot-on she had been.

I know it is your weekend off, sorry, but you did say to text with any concerns with any of your patients. Can you happen to be passing by?

Anton had *happened* to be passing by half an hour later and had found Louise sitting on the bed, chatting with the usually sombre Mrs Calini, who was in an unusually elated mood.

'Oh, here's Anton.' Louise had beamed as he had stopped by the bed for a *chat*.

'Anton!' Mrs Calini had started talking in rapid Italian, saying how gorgeous her baby was, just how very, very beautiful he was. Yes, there was nothing specific but Anton had been on this journey with his patient and Louise was right, this was most irregular.

Twelve hours and a lot of investigations later, Mrs Calini had moved from elation to paranoia—loudly declaring that all the other mothers were jealous and likely to steal her beautiful baby. She had been taken up to the psych ward and her infant had remained on Maternity.

Two weeks later the baby had been reunited with Mrs Calini on the psychiatric mother and baby unit and just a month ago they had gone home well.

Anton looked up 'bah, humbug' and soon found out she wasn't talking about odd-looking black and white mints when she used that term.

He read a little bit about Scrooge and how he despised Christmas and started to smile.

Oh, Louise.

God, but he was tempted to text her now, by accident, of course. In his contacts Louise was there next to 'Labour Ward' after all.

He loathed that she was with Rory but, then again, she had every right to be happy. He'd had his chances over the months and had declined them. So Anton decided against an accidental text to Louise, surprised that he had even considered sending one.

He wasn't usually into games.

He just didn't like that the games had now ended with Louise.

Louise checked her phone the second she awoke, just in case Emily had called or texted her and she'd missed it, but, no, there was nothing.

It had been a very restless night's sleep and it wasn't

even five. Louise lay in the dark, wishing she could go back to sleep while knowing it was hopeless.

Instead, she got up and made a big mug of tea and took that back to bed.

Bloody Anton, Louise thought, a little embarrassed at her blatant flirting when she now knew he had the stunning Saffarella to go home to.

Had it all been one-sided?

Louise didn't think so but she gave up torturing herself with it. Anton had always been unavailable to her, even if just emotionally.

After a quick shower Louise blasted her hair with the hairdryer, and as a public service to everyone put some rouge on very pale cheeks then wiped it off because it made her look like a clown.

She took her vitamins and iron and then decided to cheer herself up by wearing the *best* underwear in the world to work today. She had been saving it for the maternity Christmas party but instead she decided to debut it today. It was from the Mistletoe range, the lace dotted with leaves of green and embroidered silk cream berries topped with a pretty red bow—and that was just the panties. The bra was empress line and almost gave her a cleavage, and she loved the little red bow in the middle.

It was far too glamorous for work but, then, Louise's underwear was always far too glamorous for work.

Instead of having another cup of tea and watching the news, Louise decided to simply go in early and hopefully put her mind at rest by not finding Emily there.

She lived close enough to walk to work. It was very cold so she draped on scarves and walked through the dark and damp morning. It was lovely to step into the maternity unit, which was always nice and warm.

There was Anton sitting sulking at the desk, writing up notes amidst the Naughty Baby Club—comprising all the little ones that had been brought up to the desk to hopefully give their mothers a couple of hours' sleep.

Louise read through the admission board, checking for Emily's name and letting out a breath of relief when she saw that it wasn't there.

'How come you're in early?' she asked Anton, wondering if he was waiting for Emily.

'I couldn't sleep,' Anton said, 'so I thought I'd catch up on some notes.'

They were both sulking, both jealous that the other had had a better night than they'd had.

'I'm going to make some tea,' Louise said. 'Would you like some?'

'Please.' Anton nodded.

'Evie?' Louise asked, and got a shake of the head from the night nurse. 'Tara?'

'No, thanks, we've just had one.'

Louise changed into her scrubs then headed to the kitchen and made herself a nice one, and this time Anton got a hospital teabag.

He knew he was in her bad books with one sip of his tea.

Well, she was in his bad books too.

'You and Rory left very suddenly,' Anton commented. 'I didn't realise that the two of you…'

'We're not on together,' Louise said. 'Well, we were three years ago but we broke up after a few weeks. We're just good friends now.'

'Oh.'

'Rory took me home early last night because I'm worried about Emily,' Louise admitted. She was too concerned about her friend to play games. 'She hasn't called you, has she? You're not here, waiting for her to come in?'

'No.' Anton frowned. 'Why are you worried? She seemed fine last night.'

'She was at first but then she was suddenly tired and went home. Rory said that she'd had a big day at work but...'

'Tell me.'

'She snapped at me and she had that look,' Louise said. 'You know the one...'

'Yep,' Anton said, because, unlike Rory, he did know what Louise meant and he took her concerns about Emily seriously.

'How many weeks is she now?'

'Twenty-seven,' Louise said.

'And how many days...?' Anton asked, pulling Emily's notes up on his computer. 'No, she's twenty-eight weeks today.' Anton read through his notes. 'I saw her last week and all was fine. The pregnancy has progressed normally, just the appendectomy at six weeks.'

'Could that cause problems now?' Louise asked.

'I would have expected any problems from surgery to surface much earlier than this,' Anton said, and he gave Louise a thin smile. 'Maybe she *was* just tired...'

'I'll ring Theatre later and find out what shift she's on,' Louise said. 'In fact, I'll do it now.'

She got put through and was told that Emily was on a late shift today.

'Maybe I am just worrying about nothing,' Louise said.

'Let us hope so.'

A baby was waking up and Tara, a night nurse, was just dashing off to do the morning obs.

'I'll get him.'

Louise picked up the little one and snuggled him in. 'God, I love that smell,' Louise said, inhaling the scent of the baby's hair, then she looked over at Anton.

'Did Saffron have a good night?'

She watched his lips move into a wry smile.

'Not really,' Anton said, and then added, 'And her name is Saffarella.'

'Oh, sorry,' Louise said. 'I got mixed up. Saffron's the one you put in your rice to make it go yellow, isn't it?' Louise corrected herself. 'Expensive stuff, costs a fortune and you only get a tiny—'

'Louise,' Anton warned, 'I don't know quite where you're going there but, please, don't be a bitch.'

'I can't help myself, Anton,' Louise swiftly retorted. 'If you get off with another woman in front of me then you'll see my bitchy side.'

Anton actually grinned; she was so open that she fancied him, so relentless, so *aaagggh*, he thought as he sat there.

'I didn't *get off*, as you say, with Saffarella. We danced.'

'Please,' Louise scoffed.

Maybe he wanted to share the relief he had felt when he had just heard that she and Rory were only friends but, for whatever reason, he put her out of her misery too.

'I took Saffarella back to the hotel she is staying at last night.'

He gave her an inch and, yep, Louise took a mile.

'Really!' Louise gave a delighted grin and covered the baby's ears. 'So you didn't—'

'Louise!'

'The baby can't hear, I've covered his ears. So you and she didn't...?'

'No, we didn't.'

'Did she sulk?' Louise asked with glee, and he grimaced a touch at the memory of the car door slamming.

'Yes.'

'Oh, poor Saffron, I mean Saffarella—now that I know you and she didn't do anything, I can like her.'

They both smiled, though it was with a touch of regret because last night could have been such a nicer night.

'Thanks so much,' Tara said, coming over and looking at the baby. 'He's asleep now, Louise. You can put him back in his isolette.'

'But I don't want to,' Louise said, looking down at the sleeping baby. He was all curled up in her arms, his knees were up and his ankles crossed as if he were still in the womb. His little feet were poking out of the baby blanket and Louise was stroking them.

'They're like kittens' paws,' Louise said, watching his teeny toes curl.

'You are so seriously clucky,' Tara said.

'Oh, I'm more than clucky,' Louise admitted. 'I keep going over to the nativity scene just to pick up Baby Jesus. I have to have one.'

'It will ruin your lingerie career,' Tara warned, but Louise just laughed.

'I'm sure pregnant women can and do wear fabulously sexy underwear—in fact, my agent's going to speak to a couple of companies to see what sort of work they might have for me if I get pregnant.'

'Surely you're missing something if you want a baby…' Tara said, referring to Louise's lack of a love life, but now she had told her mum, now she'd told Rory and Emily knew too, Louise had decided it was time to start to let the world know.

'No, I'm not missing anything.' Louise smiled. 'In fact, I might have to pay a visit to Anton.'

She was referring to the fact she'd found out he was a reproductive specialist too and he gave a wry smile at the ease of her double entendre.

'I have an excellent record,' Anton said.

'So I've heard.' Louise smirked.

Then Anton stopped the joking around and went to get back to his notes. 'You don't need to be rushing. How old are you?'

'Thirty next year!' Louise sighed.

'Plenty of time. You don't have to be thinking about it yet,' Anton said, but it turned out that the ditzy Louise ran deep.

'I think about it a lot,' she admitted. 'In all seriousness, Anton,' she continued, as Tara headed off to do more obs, 'I'm actually confused by the whole thing. I recently saw my GP but she just told me to come off the Pill for a few months.'

Anton frowned, fighting the urge to step in while not wanting to get involved with this aspect of Louise, so he was a little brusque in response. 'The fertility centre at this hospital runs an information night for single women,' Anton offered. 'Your questions would be best answered there.'

'I know they do,' Louise said. 'I've booked in for the next one but it's not till February. That's ages away.'

'It will be here before you know it. As I said, there's no rush.'

'There might be, though,' Louise said, and told him the truth. 'A few years ago I found out I'd probably have problems getting pregnant. That's why I'm off the Pill and trying to sort out my cycle. I know quite a bit but even I'm confused.'

'You need a specialist. Perhaps see an ob/gyn and have him answer your questions, but I would think, from the little you've told me, that you would be referred to a fertility specialist. Certainly, if you are considering pregnancy, you need to get some base bloods down and an ultrasound.'

'Can I come and see you?' Louise was completely serious now. 'Make an appointment, I mean, and then if I did get pregnant…'

'There is a long wait to see me.'

'Even for colleagues?' Louise cheekily checked.

'Especially for colleagues,' Anton said, *really* not liking the way this conversation was going.

'What about privately?' Louise asked, and she was serious about that because all her money from modelling was going into her baby fund.

'Louise.' Anton was even brusquer now. 'Why would you want to be a single mother?'

'I'm sure that's not the first thing you ask your patients when they come to see you,' Louise scolded. 'I don't think that's very PC.'

'But you're not my patient,' Anton pointed out, 'so I don't have to watch what I say. Why would you want to be a single mother?'

'How do you know I'm not in a relationship?' Louise said.

'You just told me that you and Rory were only friends.'

'Hah, but I could have an infertile partner at home.'

'Do you?'

'Lorenzo,' Louise teased, kicking him gently with her foot. 'And he's very upset that he can't give me babies.'

He knew she was joking, though he refused to smile, and he wanted to capture her foot as she prattled on.

'Or,' Louise continued, 'I might be a lesbian in a very happy relationship and we've decided that we want to have a baby together.' She loved how his lips twitched as she continued. 'I'm the girly one!'

'You're not a very good lesbian,' Anton said, 'given the way that you flirt with me.'

'Ha-ha.' Louise laughed. 'Seriously, Anton—' and she was '—about seeing you privately. You're right, I need to get an ultrasound and some bloods done. I'm going in circles on my own—fertility drugs, artificial insemination or IVF. I'm worried about twins or triplets or even more...' Louise truly was. 'I want someone who knows what they are doing.'

'Of course you do,' Anton agreed. 'If you want, I can recommend someone to you. Richard here is excellent, I can speak with him and give you a referral and get you seen quickly—' Anton started, but Louise interrupted him.

'Why would I see someone else when we both know you're the best?' she pushed. 'Look, I know we mess around...'

'*You* mess around,' Anton corrected.

'Only at work.'

Louise *was* serious, Anton realised. She had that look in her eyes that Anton recognised on women who came to his office. It was a look that said she was determined to get pregnant, so he had no real choice now but to be honest.

No, this conversation wasn't going well for him at all.

'It would be unethical for me to see you,' Anton said, and stood.

'Unethical?' Louise frowned. 'What, because we work together?'

'Professionally unethical,' Anton said, and rolled his eyes as a delighted smile spread across her face. 'I can't say it any clearer than that.'

Ooooh!

She hugged the baby as Anton walked off.

'He *has* got the hots for me,' Louise whispered to the baby, and then let out a loud wolf whistle to Anton's departing back.

No, Anton did not turn around but he did smile.

CHAPTER FIVE

'I NEED SOMEONE to buddy this,' Beth called, and Louise went over to the nurses' station to look at the CTG tracing of one of Beth's patients.

The policy at The Royal was that only two experienced midwives could sign off on a tracing and so a buddy system was in place.

It was way more than a cursory look Louise gave to the tracing. They discussed it for a few moments, going over the recordings of the contractions and foetal heart rate before Louise signed off.

It was a busy morning and it sped by. At lunchtime, as Anton walked into the staffroom, had he had sunglasses then he would have put them on. There was a silver Christmas tree by the television and it was dressed in silver balls. There were silver stars hanging from the ceiling—really, there was silver everything hanging from every available space.

'Have you been at the tinsel again?' Anton said to Louise, who was eating a tuna salad.

'I have. I just can't help myself. I might have to go and speak with someone about my little tinsel problem—though I took up your suggestion and went with a theme in here!'

'I cannot guess what it was.'

Anton chose to sit well away from her and, for something to do, rather than listen to all the incessant gossip, he picked up a magazine.

Oh, no!

There she was and Louise was right—the underwear was divine.

'Christmas Holly' said the title and there a stunning Louise was in the stockings she'd had on last night but now he got the full effect—bra, stockings and suspenders. Anton turned the page to the Mistletoe range, and the shots, though very lovely and very tasteful, were so sexy that Anton felt his body responding, like some sad old man reading a porn magazine, and he hastily turned to the problem page, just not in time.

Oh, God, he was thinking about swiping the magazine, especially when he glimpsed the Holly and the Ivy shots.

'Ooooh.' Louise looked over and saw what he was reading. 'I'm in that one.' She plucked it from his hands and knelt at the coffee table and turned to the section in the magazine as a little crowd gathered around.

She was so unabashed by it, just totally at ease with her body and its functions in a way that sort of fascinated Anton.

'You've got a cleavage,' Beth said, admiring the shot.

'I know,' Louise said. 'Gorgeous, isn't it?'

'But how?'

Anton closed his eyes. These were women who spent most of their days dealing with breasts and vaginas and they chatted with absolute ease about such things, an ease Anton usually had too, just not when Miss Louise was around.

'Well,' Louise said as Anton stared at the news, 'they take what little I have and sort of squeeze it together and then tape it—there's a lot of scaffolding under that bra,' Louise explained. 'Then they pad the empty part and then they edit out my nipples.'

'Wow!'

'I wish they *were* real,' Louise sighed.

'Would you ever get them done?' Beth asked.

'No,' Louise said, as Anton intently watched the weather report. 'I did think about it one time but, no, I'll stick with what I've been given, which admittedly isn't much. Hopefully they'll be *massive* when I get pregnant and then breastfeed.'

'Anton!' Brenda popped her head in to save the day. 'I've got the husband of one of your patients on the phone. Twenty-eight weeks, back pain...'

'Who?'

'Emily Linton.'

'Merda.' Anton cursed under his breath and then took the phone while trying to ignore Louise, who was now standing over him as Hugh brought him up to speed.

'Okay,' Anton said, as Louise hopped on the spot. 'I'll come down now and meet you at the maternity entrance.'

'Back pain, some contractions,' Anton said. 'Her waters are intact...' As Louise went to follow him out Anton shook his head. 'Maybe Emily needs someone who is not close to her,' Anton said.

'Maybe she needs someone who *is* close to her,' Louise retorted. 'You're not getting rid of me.'

Anton nodded.

'Brenda, can you let the paediatricians know?'

'Of course.'

They stood waiting for the car and Anton looked over. Louise was shivering in the weak winter sun and her teeth were chattering. 'Emily isn't the most straight-forward person,' Louise said. 'She acts like she doesn't care when, really, she does.'

Anton nodded and watched as, even though she was terrified for her friend, Louise's lips spread into a wide smile as the car pulled up.

'Come on, trouble,' Louise said, helping her friend into a wheelchair.

'I'm sure it's nothing,' Emily said, as Louise gave directions.

'Hugh, go and park the car and meet us there.'

Once Hugh was out of earshot, Emily let out a little of her fear. 'It's way too soon,' Emily said. Her expression was grim but there were no tears.

'Let's just see where we are,' Anton said.

Though Anton would do his level best to make sure that the pregnancy remained intact, Emily was taken straight through to the delivery ward, just in case.

'I had a bit of a backache last night,' Emily admitted. 'At first I thought it was from standing for so long yesterday. Then, late this morning, I thought I was getting Braxton-Hicks…'

Louise was putting on a foetal monitor as Anton put in an IV line and took some bloods, and then, as Hugh arrived, Anton looked at the tracing. 'The baby is looking very content,' Anton said, and then he put a hand on Emily's stomach as the monitor showed another contraction starting.

'I'm only getting them occasionally,' Emily said.

But sometimes you only needed a few with a baby this small.

'Emily,' Anton said when the contraction had passed, 'I am going to examine you and see where we are.'

But Emily kept panicking, possibly because she didn't *want* to know where they were, and nothing Hugh or Anton might say would reassure her.

'I need you to try and relax,' Anton said.

'Oh, it's so easy for them to say that when they come at you with a gloved hand!' Louise chimed in, and Anton conceded Louise was right to be there because Emily let out a little laugh and she did relax just a touch.

'How long are you here for?' Emily asked Louise, because even though Louise had yesterday told her she was on an early today, clearly such conversations were the last thing on Emily's mind at the moment and it was obvious that she wanted her friend to be here.

'I've just come on duty,' Louise lied, 'so I'm afraid that you're stuck with me for hours yet.'

Anton examined Emily and Louise passed him a sterile speculum and he took some swabs to check for amniotic fluid and also some swabs to check for any infection.

'You are in pre-term labour,' Anton said. 'You have some funnelling,' Anton explained further. 'Your cervix is a little dilated but if you think of a funnel…' he showed the shape with his hands '…your cervix is opening from the top but we are going to give you medication that will hopefully be able to, if not halt things, at least delay them.' He gave his orders to Louise and she started to prepare the drugs Anton had chosen. 'This should taper off the contractions,' he said as he hooked up the IV, 'and these steroids will help the baby's lungs mature in case it decides to be born. You shall get another dose of these in twenty-four hours.'

Louise did everything she could to keep the atmosphere nice and calm but it was all very busy. The paediatricians came down and spoke with Anton. NICU was notified that there might be an imminent admission. Anton did an ultrasound and everything on there looked fine. Though the contractions were occasionally still coming, they started to weaken, though Emily had a lot of pain in her back, which was a considerable concern.

'Content,' Anton said again, but this time to the screen. 'Stay in there, little one.'

'And if it doesn't?' Emily asked.

'Then we have everything on hand to deal with that if your baby is born,' Anton said. 'But for now things are settling and what I need for you to do is to lie there and rest.'

'I will,' Emily said. 'First, though, I need a wee.'

'I'll get you a bedpan!' Louise said.

'Please no.'

'I'm afraid so.' Louise smiled. 'Anton's rules.'

Anton smiled as he explained his rules. 'Many say that it makes no difference. If the baby is going to be born then it shall be. Call me old-fashioned but I still prefer that you have complete bed rest, perhaps the occasional shower…'

'Fine.' Emily nodded, perhaps for the first time realising that she was going to be there for a while.

Hugh and Anton waited outside as much laughter came from the room, mainly from Louise, but Emily actually joined in too as they attempted to get a sterile specimen and also to check for a urinary tract infection.

Bedpans were not the easiest things to sit on.

But then Emily stopped laughing. 'Louise, I'm scared if I wee it will come out.'

'You have to wee, Emily,' Louise said, and gave her friend a cuddle. 'And you have to poo and do all those things, but I'm right here.'

It helped to hear that.

'I've got such a bad feeling,' Emily admitted, and Hugh gave a grim smile to Anton as outside they listened to Emily expressing her fears out loud. 'I really do.'

'Okay.' Louise was practical. 'How many women at twenty-eight weeks sit on that bed you're on, having contractions, and say, "I've got a really good feeling"? How many?' Louise asked.

'None.'

'I had a bad feeling last night,' Louise admitted. 'You can ask Anton, you can ask Rory, because I left five minutes after you and I came in early just to look at the board to see if you had been admitted, but I don't have a bad feeling now.'

'Honest?'

'Promise,' Louise said. 'So have a wee.'

'I'm going to give her a sedative,' Anton said to Hugh.

'Won't that relax her uterus?' Hugh checked, and then stopped himself because he trusted Anton.

'I want her to sleep and I want to give her the best chance for those medications to really take hold,' Anton said. 'You saw that her blood pressure was high?'

Hugh nodded—Emily's raised blood pressure could simply be down to anxiety but could also be a sign that she had pre-eclampsia.

'We'll see if there's any protein in her urine,' Anton said. If she did that would be another unwelcome sign that things were not going well.

Louise came out with the bedpan and urine sample, which would be sent to the lab.

'Can you check for protein?' Anton asked.

Louise rolled her eyes at Hugh. 'He thinks that because I'm blonde I'm thick,' she said to a very blond Hugh, who smiled back. 'Of course I'm going to check for protein!'

'He's blondist,' Hugh joked, but then breathed out in relief when Louise called from the pan room.

'No protein, no blood, no glucose—all normal, just some ketones.'

'She hasn't eaten since last night,' Hugh said, which explained the ketones.

'I've put dextrose up but right now the best thing she can do is to rest.'

It was a very long afternoon and evening.

Louise stayed close by Emily, while Anton delivered two babies but in between checked in on Emily.

At eight, Louise sat and wrote up her notes. It felt strange to be writing about Emily and her baby. She peeled off the latest CTG recording and headed out.

'Can you buddy this?' Louise asked Siobhan, a nurse on labour and delivery this evening.

'Sure.'

They went through the tracing thoroughly, both taking their time and offering opinions before the two midwives signed off.

'It's looking a lot better than before,' Siobhan said. 'Let's hope she keeps improving.'

Around nine-thirty p.m. Anton walked into the womb-like atmosphere Louise had created. The curtains were closed and the room was in darkness and there was just the noise of the baby's heartbeat from the CTG. Emily was asleep and so too was Hugh. Louise sat in a rocking chair, her feet up on a stool, reading a magazine with a clip-on light attached to it that she carried in her pocket for such times, while holding Emily's hand. She let go of the magazine to give a thumb's-up to Anton, and then she put her finger to her lips and shushed him as he walked over to look at the monitors—Louise loathed noisy doctors.

All looked good.

Anton nudged his head towards the corridor and Louise stepped outside and they went into the small kitchenette where all the flower vases were stored and spoke for a while.

'She's still got back pain,' Louise said, and Anton nodded.

'We'll keep her in Delivery tonight but, hopefully, if things continue to improve we can get her onto the ward tomorrow morning.'

'Good.'

'You were right,' Anton said. 'There *was* something going on with her last night.' He saw the sparkle of tears in Louise's eyes because, despite positive appearances, Anton knew she was very worried for her friend.

'I'd love to have been wrong.'

'I know.'

'Anton…' Louise spilled what was on her mind. 'I bought a crib for the baby a few days ago.'

'Okay.'

'It was in a sale and I couldn't resist it. I didn't tell Emily in case she thought it bad luck…'

'Louise!' Anton's firm use of her name told her to let that thought go.

She took a breath.

'Louise,' he said again, and she met his eye. 'That's crazy. I've got Mrs Adams in room two, who's forty-one weeks. She's done everything, the nursery is ready...'

'I know, I know.'

'Just put that out of your mind.'

Louise did. She blew it away then but a tear did sneak out because Louise cared so much about Emily and she was also pretty exhausted. 'Why did it have to be now?' she asked.

'I would love to know that answer,' Anton said, and Louise gave a small smile as he continued. 'It would save me many sleepless nights.'

'I wasn't asking a medical question.'

'I know you weren't.'

Anton stood in the small annexe and looked at Louise. Today she had been amazing, though it wasn't just because she was Emily's friend. Every mother got Louise's full attention. It was wrong of him to compare her to Dahnya, Anton realised. It was futile to keep going back to that terrible day.

Louise was too worried about Emily to notice his silence and she rattled on with her fears.

'I know twenty-eight weeks isn't tiny tiny but...'

'It is far too soon,' Anton agreed. 'She's *just* into her third trimester but we'll do all we can to prolong it. It looks like we've just bought her another day and those steroids are in. The night staff have arrived, Evie is on and she is very good.'

Louise nodded. 'I know she is but I'm going to sleep here tonight.'

'Go home,' Anton said, because Louise really did

look pale, but she shook her head at his suggestion. 'Louise, you have been here since six.'

'And so have you,' Louise pointed out. 'I didn't think you were on call tonight, Anton, so what's your excuse for being here?'

'I'll be a lot happier by morning. I just want to be close if something occurs.'

'Well, I'm the same. If something happens tonight then I want to be here with Emily.'

'I get that but—Louise, I never thought I'd say this to you, but you look awful.'

It was a rather backhanded compliment but it did make her smile. 'I'll go and lie down soon,' Louise said, and looked over as Hugh came out.

'Is she awake?'

'Yes, they're just doing her obs. Thanks for today,' Hugh said to them both. 'I'm going to text and ring five thousand people now. Emily told her mum and, honestly, it's spread like wildfire…'

'I get it,' Louise said, because she knew about Emily's very complex family and the last thing she needed now was the hordes arriving. 'I've put her down as no visitors.'

'Thanks for that,' Hugh said. 'I'm going to ring for pizza—do you want some?'

'No, thanks.' Louise shook her head and yawned. 'I'm going to go and sleep.'

'Anton?'

'Sounds good.'

Louise handed over to Evie, the night nurse who would be taking care of Emily. 'Promise, promise, promise that you'll come and get me if anything happens.'

'Promise.'

'I'm going to take a pager,' Louise said, 'just in case you're too busy, so if you page him…' she nodded to Anton '…page me too.'

Louise went to the hotbox and took out one of the warm blankets that they covered newly delivered mums in. Brenda would freak if she knew the damage that Louise singlehandedly did to the laundry budget but she was too cold and tired to care about that right now.

'I'll be in the store cupboard if anything happens.'

'Store cupboard?' Anton said.

'Where all the night nurses sleep.' Louise nodded to the end of the corridor. ''Night, guys. 'Night, Hugh. I'll just go and say night to Emily if she's awake.'

She popped in and there was Emily half-awake as Evie fiddled with her IV.

'You've done so well today.' Louise smiled, standing wrapped in her blanket. 'I'm just going to get some shut-eye but I'm just down the hall, though I have a feeling I shan't be needed.'

'Thanks so much for staying,' Emily said.

'Please.' Louise gave her a kiss goodnight on her forehead. 'Hopefully we'll move you to a room tomorrow. I'm going to have a jiggle with the beds in the morning and give you one of the nice ones.' She spoke then in a loud whisper. 'One of the private ones!'

'You're such a bad girl.' Evie smiled.

'I know.' Louise grinned. 'Sleep!' Louise said to Emily and then stroked her stomach. 'And you, little one, stay in there.'

'Do you know what I'm having?' Emily asked, and Louise just smiled as Emily spoke on. 'Hugh knows and when I said that I didn't want to find out, he said that he wouldn't tell me even if I begged him.'

'Do you want to know?' Louise asked.

'No, yes, no,' Emily admitted. 'But I want to know if you know.'

'I do,' Louise said, and then burst into Abba. '"I do, I do, I do, I do, I do,"' Louise sang, just as Anton and Hugh walked in. 'But I'm not telling. If you want to know you can speak to Anton.'

'She's mad,' Emily said, when Louise had gone but she said it in the nicest way.

'Completely mad,' Anton agreed. 'How are you feeling now?'

'A bit better.'

'Any questions?' Anton checked, but Emily shook her head.

'I think you've answered them all. Presumably you know what I'm having?'

'Of course I do,' Anton said. 'You know you are allowed to change your mind and find out if you want to.'

'I want it to be a surprise.'

'Then a surprise it will be.'

'Are you going home now?' Emily asked, because she had been told he was only here till six and she felt both guilty and relieved when Anton shook his head.

'Stephanie is the on-call obstetrician tonight and she will be keeping an eye on you so that I can get some rest as I am working tomorrow. I am staying here tonight, though, and if anything changes, I have asked her to discuss it with me.'

'Thank you.'

The store cupboard was actually an empty four-bedded ward at the front of the unit and was used to store beds, trolleys, stirrups, birth balls and all that sort of stuff.

Louise curled up on one of the beds and lay there with her eyes closed, hoping that they would stay that way till morning.

She was exhausted, she'd barely had any sleep last night, but now that she finally could sleep, Louise simply could not relax. There was that knot of worry about Emily and another knot between her legs when she thought about Anton and the fact that he actually liked her.

In *that* way!

After half an hour spent growing more awake by the minute Louise padded out with her blanket around her.

Anton gave her a smile and she couldn't really remember him smiling like that, unless to a patient. In fact, he didn't smile like *that* to the patients.

'Food should be here soon,' Anton said.

Louise shook her head and instead of waiting for the pizza to arrive she had a bowl of cornflakes in the kitchen. Anton looked up as she returned with a bottle of sparkling water and a heat pack for her cramping stomach and then took two painkillers.

She tossed her now cold blanket into the linen skip and took out a newly warm one.

'If Brenda knew...' Anton warned, because the cost of laundering a blanket was posted on many walls, warning staff to use them sparingly.

'I like to be warm at night,' Louise said, and, no, she hadn't meant it to be provocative but from the look that burnt between them it was.

She headed back to the storeroom but sleep still would not come.

Then she heard the slam of the door. Louise climbed

out of the bed to tell whoever it was off for doing that but then a delicious scent reached her nose.

Pizza.

OMG.

She could almost taste the pepperoni.

Louise hadn't said no to Anton because of some diet, she had said no because...

Well.

Because.

No, she did not want to be huddled up at the desk with him—she might, the way she was feeling this moment, very possibly end up licking his face.

God, he was hot.

Her stomach was growling, though, and it was the scent of pizza that was at fault, not her, Louise decided as she smiled and pulled out her phone.

Anton had two phones and one of the numbers she was privy to. It was his work phone and she'd call him on it at times if one of his patients weren't well while he was off duty, or she might text him sometimes for advice.

She wondered if he'd tell her off for using it for something so trivial.

Or if he'd ignore her request, perhaps?

Anton sat eating pizza as Hugh fired off texts to family to let them know that Emily was doing well.

When his work phone buzzed, indicating a text, Anton read it and decided it might be best to ignore it.

For months he had done his best to ignore her yet since he'd see her up that stepladder it had been a futile effort at best.

He did try to ignore it. In fact, he said goodnight to

Hugh and then went into the on-call room, grimly determined to sleep.

Then he read her text again and gave up fighting. He went back to the desk, picked up two slices of pizza and headed off to where perhaps he shouldn't.

CHAPTER SIX

'PIZZA MAN!' ANTON said, as he came into the dark room.

'Oh, my, and an authentic Italian one too!' Louise smiled in the dark and sat up and then took out her light from her pocket and shone it up at him. 'And so good looking.'

'You changed your mind about the pizza?'

'I did,' Louise said. 'A bowl of cornflakes wasn't going to cut it tonight.'

'I could have told you that half an hour ago—you need to eat more.'

'I do eat.'

Anton shook his head very slowly. 'With my sister's line of work I know all the tricks, *all* of them,' Anton said. 'Tell me the truth.'

'Okay, I do watch my weight,' Louise admitted, 'a lot! But I am not anorexic.'

'I can see that you're not anorexic but you do seem to live off salad.'

'Ah, so you notice what I eat, Anton, how sweet!' Louise teased, and then she answered him properly. 'I love my modelling work,' Louise said. 'I mean I *love* it and it is my job to present at a certain weight but I don't do the dangerously thin stuff. Yes, for the most part I have to watch what I eat but, in saying that, I eat very well. I'm nearly thirty. I can't believe I'm still working…'

'I can.' Anton smiled.

'Anyway, I've got a huge photo shoot on Christmas Eve,' Louise explained, as she ate warm pizza. 'It's for Valentine's Day and I'm going to pay a small fortune to get dressed up to the nines and have my hair and make-up done so, yes, I'm being careful.' Her slice of pizza was finished and he handed her the other one. 'I'm just not being very careful tonight.'

'If you are looking at trying for a baby…'

'I would never jeopardise that for work, Anton. I'm just eating healthily. What happened this morning is unrelated to that.'

'Good to know.'

He glanced at the stirrups over the bed. 'You really sleep here?'

'Of course,' Louise said, and then she looked to where his gaze fell. 'Do you want me in stirrups, Anton?'

He actually laughed. 'No. It is that I *don't* want you in stirrups that means you can't be my patient.' He explained as best he could. 'Louise, I know I have given mixed messages. Yes, I like you but I never wanted to get involved with someone at work.'

'We're not at work.' Louise smiled a provocative smile. 'Officially we're both off duty.'

'Louise, the thing is—'

'Please, please, don't,' Louise said. 'Please spare me the lecture, because, guess what, I'm the same. The last thing I want now is a full-on relationship, particularly with you.'

Anton frowned in slight surprise. He'd come in having finally given in and deciding that they should perhaps give it a go, only to find out that a relationship with him was far from her mind.

'Why *particularly* not with me?'

'Okay, I think you're as sexy as hell and occasionally funny but I think you'd be very controlling, and that's fine in the bedroom perhaps—'

'I am not controlling,' Anton immediately interrupted. 'Well, I know that I am at work but not when I'm in a relationship.'

'Oh, they all say that.' Louise put on an Italian accent. 'I do not want my woman posing in her underwear…'

'That is the worst Italian accent ever.' He frowned at her opinion of him. 'I happen to think your work is very beautiful.'

'Really?'

'Of course it is.' He was still frowning. 'Have you had trouble in the past—?'

'I have,' Louise said quickly, hurrying over that part of her life, 'and so I keep things on my terms. The only thing I want to focus on right now is myself and becoming a mum. I'm not on a husband shop.'

A flirt, some fun, was all she was prepared to give to a man right now.

Though she had fancied Anton for ages.

Ages.

Pizza done, Louise went into her pocket, peeled off some baby wipes from a small packet she carried and wiped her hands. Then she went into her pockets again and pulled out a breath spray.

'What the hell have you got in those pockets?'

'Many, many things—basically my pockets are designed so that I don't have to get up if I'm comfy.' Louise smiled and settled back on the pillow. 'The breath spay is so that I don't submit a labouring woman to my pizza breath, and,' she added, 'it's also terribly convenient if you want to kiss me goodnight.'

'Louise,' Anton warned. 'We're not going to be skulking around in the shadows.'

'I know,' Louise sighed regretfully. 'How come you left fertility?' She yawned, but was pleased when Anton sat on the edge of the bed.

'I missed obstetrics,' Anton admitted, though he too chose to avoid the dark stuff.

'Is it nice to be back doing it?'

'Some days,' Anton said, 'like yesterday with Hannah's son—that was a really good day. Today…' He thought for a moment. 'Yes, it is still good. Thanks for your help today, you were right to stay—it is good for Emily to have you nearby.'

'You're making me nervous, Anton—you're being too nice.'

Anton smiled and watched as she put her hand under the blanket and turned the hot pack on her stomach.

'Still hurt?'

'Yep.'

He wanted his hand there.

Louise wanted the same thing.

She wanted him to lean forward and Anton actually felt as if her hand were at the back of his head, dragging him down, but it wasn't her hand that was pressuring him, it was want.

'I'm going to go,' Anton said. 'I just wanted to clear the air.'

'It doesn't feel very clear,' Louise said, because it was thick with sexual tension, a tension that had come to a head last night but had had no outlet for either of them.

'You're right, it doesn't,' Anton agreed. 'You are such a flirt, Louise,' he said, his mouth approaching hers.

'I know.' She smiled then asked a question as his lovely mouth approached. 'If you were intending to just pop in to clear the air, why did you brush your teeth before you came in?'

'I was *hoping* to clear the air but you have worn me down.'

They were far from worn down as their mouths finally met. It was supposed to break the tension but instead it upped it as, in the dark, Louise found out how lovely that sulky mouth could be.

The mixture of soft lips and rough stubble had her break on contact.

Anton had decided on one small kiss to chase away a wretched day but small was relative, Anton told himself as he slipped in his tongue and met the caress of hers, for it was still a small kiss if he compared it to the one he really wanted to give.

For Louise, it was bliss. She could not remember a kiss that had been nicer, and her hands moved up to his head and their kiss deepened from intimate to provocative. As he moved to remove her hands and halt things he changed his mind as his thumb grazed her breast. Anton heard the purr and the nudge of her body into his palm, like a cat demanding attention, and so he stroked her through the fabric, until for both of them he had to feel her.

Anton went to lift her top, just to get to her breast, but the heat pack slipped off and she willed his hand to change direction, her tongue urging him on as Anton obliged.

He could feel the ball of tension of her uterus as his hand slipped down instead of up, stroking her tense stomach as he kissed her more deeply.

Louise lifted her knees to the bliss and the sensation but then she peeled her mouth from his.

'Anton...'

'I know that you do,' he said, not caring a bit. 'What colour underwear?' he asked, as he toyed with the lace.

'Cream and green, with a red bow—it's from the Mistletoe collection.'

She loved his moan in her mouth and the feel of his fingers creeping lower. His warm palm massaged low on her stomach as his finger hit the spot and Louise felt her face become red and hot as she kissed now his neck then his ears. One of his hands was behind her head, supporting it, while beneath the other she succumbed.

The tension hit and his mouth suckled hers as he stroked her through the deepest come of her life and then she felt the bliss abate as her stomach lay soft beneath his palm. Her intimate twitches stilled and Louise lay quiet for a moment.

'Better?' Anton asked.

'Positively sedated.'

She lay in sated bliss, pain free for the first time today, and trying to tell herself it was just the sex she wanted as she moved her hand and stroked his thick erection.

'Poor Anton,' she said.

'There have been way too many poor Antons of late,' Anton said. 'I'm going to go and you're going to sleep and—'

'We never discuss this again.' Louise smiled. 'Got it!'

How was she supposed to sleep after that? Louise thought as Anton made his way out.

It took about forty-seven seconds!

CHAPTER SEVEN

LOUISE AWOKE TO the sound of the domestic's floor polisher in the hallway and the even happier sound of no pager, which meant nothing had happened with Emily and so she padded out to the ward.

'How is she?' Louise asked Evie.

'Very good,' Evie said. 'She's slept mostly through and her back ache has eased and the contractions have stopped.' She looked at Louise, who was yawning. 'Why don't you go home?'

'I'm going to have a shower and then I'll see Emily over to her room before I do just that.'

'Well, the royal suite is empty.' Evie smiled as she used the name they all called it. 'I'll go and set it up.'

'I'll do that when I've had my shower,' Louise said, smiling when she heard Anton's voice.

'Morning, Louise,' Anton said, looking all the more handsome for not having shaven. 'How did you sleep?'

'Oh, I went out like a light,' Louise answered. She headed off to the shower and had to wash with the disinfectant soap used for washing hands. Smelling like a bathroom cleaner commercial, she headed out to set up the room for Emily.

It was hardly a royal suite but it had its own loo and

was more spacious than others and there was a trundle bed if Hugh wanted to stay. Louise checked the oxygen and suction and that there were pads and vomit bowels and suchlike.

Anton checked in on Emily and was very happy with her lack of progress and agreed that she could be moved.

'Every day that you don't go into labour is a good day,' Anton said, as Louise helped her onto the bed. 'For now you are on strict bed rest and that means bedpans.'

'Okay.' Emily nodded. She wasn't going to argue if it meant her baby stayed put. 'I feel much more positive today.' She looked over at Louise. 'You can go home now.'

'I am,' Louise said. 'But you're to text me with anything you want me to bring in for you. I can visit tonight or tomorrow. I'm off for two days now but—'

'I'll text you,' Emily interrupted, because Louise lived by her phone and they texted each other most days anyway.

As they headed out—Anton to start his shift, Louise to commence her days off—he asked if he could have a word with her in his office.

'Sure,' Louise said.

She knew what was coming and immediately she broached it. 'Don't worry, I get that last night was an aberration.' She saw him frown. 'A one-off.'

Anton wasn't so sure. He had no regrets about last night and he looked at the woman standing before him and wanted to get to know her some more, but before he did there was something that he first needed to know.

'This referral, are you sure that now is the right time?'

'Very sure,' Louise said. 'I've been thinking about it for close to a year.'

'Okay…' Anton said, because that alone was enough for him to ensure last night remained an *aberration*, although still he would like to give them a chance. 'Why don't you wait a while? Maybe we can—?'

'Anton, I already have waited a while. I'm twenty-nine years old and for twenty-eight of those years I have wanted a baby. I didn't just dress up my dollies and put them in a pram, Anton, I used to put them up my dress…' Anton smiled as she carried on. 'I'm not brilliant at relationships.'

'Why would you say that?'

'Oh, I've gathered quite a list of the reasons over the years.' Louise started to tick off on her fingers. 'I'm high maintenance, vain, obsessed with having a baby, inappropriate at times… I could go on but you get the drift. And, yes, I am all of those things and shall happily continue to be them. But, while relationships may not be my forte, I do know for a fact that I shall be a brilliant mum. So many women do it themselves these days.'

'Even so…'

'It's not a decision I've come to lightly. I've sat on it for close to a year and so, if I could have that referral, it would be completely brilliant.'

He wrote one out for her there and then. 'I'll let his secretary know this morning. When you call ask to speak to her because Richard is very booked up too.'

'Thank you.'

'Louise…'

'Anton.' She turned round. She did not want to hear now how they might stand a chance, and she did not want to be put off her dream. One of the reasons she was attracted to him perhaps was that he had been so unobtainable and she wanted that to remain the same. 'Don't be such a girl!'

Six feet two of testosterone stood there and smiled as she continued.

'It was fun, there can be more fun, just as long as it's conducted well away from work, but I *am* going ahead with this.'

He said nothing as she stepped out and Louise didn't really want him to. She didn't want to hear that maybe they could give it a go. She had fancied him for ever, since the moment she had first laid eyes on him, and now, when the year she had given herself to come to her decision was almost up, when her dream was in sight, Anton was suddenly interested.

Why couldn't he have left it at sex?

That, Louise could deal with.

It was the relationship part that terrified her.

Louise went and visited her family that morning and told them what was going on with Emily. When she got home Emily texted, asking her to go shopping for some nightwear but that there was no rush. And she added...

Something suitable, Louise!!!

Louise killed a couple of happy hours choosing nightwear for a pregnant, soon-to-be breastfeeding woman, while pretending she was shopping for herself. She did her level best to buy not what she'd like but what she guessed Emily would like, and, finally home, she thought about Anton and what had happened.

Not just their kiss and things, more the revelation that he liked her.

She had always been herself with him. Almost, since the day they had met, she had actually *practised* being herself with him. Anton had no idea just how much he had helped her. Not once had he told her to tone it down as she'd gradually returned to the woman she once had been.

She didn't particularly want Anton to know just how bad things had been. In fact, as her fingers traced the scar on her scalp and her tongue slid over the crown on her front tooth, she could not imagine telling him what had happened in her past—it would be a helluva lot to dump on him.

Louise let out a breath as she recalled her family's and friends' reactions.

It had been Emily she had called on Boxing Day and Rory too.

Rory, whose friendship she had dumped, had, when she'd needed him, patched her up enough to go and face her parents at least.

No, she did not even want to think of Anton's reaction to her tale so she pushed all thoughts of that away and pulled out the referral letter and made the call she had been waiting for ever to make.

Anton must have rung ahead as promised because when Louise spoke to the secretary she was told that there had been a cancellation and that she could see Richard the following Wednesday at ten a.m. Louise checked her diary on her phone and saw that she was on a late that day.

Perfect!

Louise put down the phone and did a little happy dance.

Finally, possibly, her baby was on the way!

CHAPTER EIGHT

EVERY QUESTION THAT Louise had, and there were many, was answered.

Susan had come to Louise's appointment with her and Louise was very glad to have her mother by her side. She knew she would probably forget half of what was said later. Also it was easier if her mother understood what was happening first hand.

Richard ordered a full screening, along with a pelvic ultrasound, and did a thorough examination, as well as looking through the app she had on her phone that charted all her dates.

'We have counsellors here and I really suggest that you take up my suggestion and make an appointment. The next step is to await all the blood results and then I'll see you in the new year and we'll look at the ways we can go ahead.'

Louise nodded.

'But you think I'll probably end up having IVF?' Louise said, because that was the impression she had got during the consultation. She was nervous that the fertility drugs might produce too many eggs but with IVF it was more controlled and Louise only wanted one embryo put back. Richard had even discussed egg sharing, which would give Louise one round of IVF free.

'I'm leaning that way, given your irregular cycle and that you want to avoid a multiple pregnancy, but right now I'd suggest you carry on with the iron and folic acid till we get the results back. We might put you on something stronger once they're in. For now, go and have a good Christmas.'

Louise made an appointment for the second week in January, when Richard returned from his Christmas break, and she made an appointment for an ultrasound and then went and had all the bloodwork done as well.

'Aren't you going to book the counsellor?' Susan asked.

'Why would I need to see one?' Louise said. 'You didn't have to see one before you had your three children.'

'True,' Susan responded, 'but before we went in you said that you were going to do *everything* he suggests.'

'And I am,' Louise said, 'apart from that one.'

Louise's cheeks were unusually pink as they walked down the corridor. Her mind was all ajumble because even as little as a couple of weeks ago she'd have happily signed up to talk to someone. She was one hundred per cent sure that she wanted this.

Or make that ninety-nine point nine per cent positive.

'Have you got time for a quick lunch before your shift?' Susan asked.

She did have time but unfortunately that point one per cent, or rather Anton, was already in the canteen and Louise was very conscious of him as they got their meals. Fortunately the table that Susan selected was quite far away from where Anton sat.

'Well, all I can say is that he was a lot better than the GP,' Susan said. 'Do you feel better for having seen him?'

'I do.'

'You're very quiet all of a sudden.'

Louise didn't know whether or not to say anything to her mum.

Actually, she didn't know if there even was anything to discuss. She and Anton had returned to business as usual after the other night. She was being far less flirtatious and Anton was checking up on her work even more than usual, if that was possible.

'I think I like someone, Mum,' Louise admitted. 'I'm a bit confused, to be honest.'

'Does he know that you like him?'

Louise nodded. 'And he also knows I'm doing this but I think if I continue to go ahead then it takes away any chance for us. I don't even know if I want us to have a chance.'

Susan asked what should have been a simple question. 'What's he like?'

'I don't really know.' Louise gave a wry laugh. 'I know what he's like at work and I find him a bit...' She hesitated. 'Well, he's very thorough with his patients and I'm pretty used to doctors dismissing and overriding midwives...' Louise thought for a long moment before continuing. 'I've just fancied him for a long time but nothing ever happened and now, when I've decided to do this, he seems to want to give us a try.'

'How long have you liked him for?' Susan asked.

'About six months.'

'And if he'd tried anything six months ago, what would you have done?'

'Run a mile.'

'If he'd tried anything three months ago, what would you have done?'

'Run a mile,' Louise admitted.

Only now was she truly healing.

'Do you want to give it a try?'

'I think so,' Louise said, 'but I want this so much too.'

She wanted back her one hundred per cent and her unwavering certainty she was finally on the right path. Unthinkingly she looked across the canteen and possibly the cause of her indecision sensed it, because Anton glanced over and briefly met her gaze.

'I don't see a problem.' Susan picked up her knife and fork and brought Louise back to the conversation. 'You don't have an appointment till the second week of January and Richard did say to go and enjoy Christmas. Have some fun, heaven knows, you deserve it. Maybe just try not to think about getting pregnant for a few weeks.'

Louise nodded, though her heart wasn't in it. Her mum tried, she really did, but she simply couldn't get it. Getting pregnant wasn't something Louise could shove in a box and leave in her wardrobe and drag it out in a few weeks and pick up again— it was something she had been building towards for a very long time.

She glanced over and saw that Anton was walking out of the canteen. There had been so little conversation of late between them that Susan could never have guessed the topic of their conversation had just walked past them.

'Think about counselling,' Susan suggested again.

'Why would I when I've got you?' Louise smiled.

'Ah, but since when did you tell me all that's going on?'

Her mother was right, she didn't tell her parents everything. 'Maybe I will,' Louise said, because this year had been one of so many changes. Even as little as a month or so ago she'd have died on the spot had Anton responded to one of her flirts. She was changing, ever changing, and every time she felt certain where she was heading, the road seemed to change direction again.

No.

Louise refused to let go of her dream.

'I need to get to my shift.'

'And I need to hit the shops.' Susan smiled. 'Come over at the weekend, I'll make your favourite.'

'I shall,' Louise said, and gave her mum a kiss goodbye. 'I'll give you a call. Thanks for coming with me today.'

Louise's patient allocation was a mixed bag between Stephanie and Anton's patients and all were prenatal patients, which meant no baby fix for Louise this shift.

'Hi, Carmel, I'm Louise,' she introduced herself to a new patient. Carmel had been admitted via the antenatal clinic where she had been found to have raised blood pressure. 'How are you?'

'Worried,' Carmel said. 'I thought I was just coming for my antenatal appointment and I find out my blood pressure's high and that the baby's still breech. I'm trying to sort out the other children.'

'This is your third?'

Carmel nodded. 'I've got a three- and a five-year-old. My husband really doesn't have any annual leave left and I can't ask my mum.' Carmel started to cry and, having taken her blood pressure, Louise sat on the chair by her bed.

'There's still time for the baby to turn,' Louise said. 'You're not due till January…' she checked her notes '…the seventh.'

'But Stephanie said if it doesn't turn then I'll have a Caesarean before Christmas.'

Louise nodded because, rather than the chance of the mother going into spontaneous labour, Caesareans were performed a couple of weeks before the due date.

'I just can't be here for Christmas. I know the baby might have come then anyway but at least with a natural labour I could have had a chance to be in and out…' Carmel explained what was going on a little better. 'My mum's really ill—it's going to be her last Christmas.'

Poor Carmel had so much going on in her life at the moment that hospital was the last place she wanted to be. Right now, though, it was the place she perhaps needed to be, to concentrate on the baby inside and let go a little. Louise sat with her for ages, listening about Carmel's mum's illness and all the plans they had made for Christmas Day that were now in jeopardy.

Finally, having talked it out, Carmel calmed a bit and Louise pulled the curtains and suggested she sleep. 'I'll put a sign on the door so that you're not disturbed.'

'Unless it's my husband.'

'Of course.' Louise smiled. 'The sign just says to speak to the staff at the desk before coming in.'

She checked in on Felicity, who was one of Anton's high-risk pregnancies, and then she got to Emily.

'How's my favourite patient?' Louise asked a rather grumpy Emily.

Emily was very bored, very worried and also extremely uncomfortable after more than a week and a half spent in bed. She was relying heavily on Louise's chatter and humour to keep her from the dark hole that her mind kept slipping into. 'I'm dying to hear how you got on at your appointment.'

'It went really well,' Louise said, as she took Emily's blood pressure.

'Tell me.'

'He was really positive,' Louise explained, 'though not in a false hope sort of way, just really practical. I'm going to be seeing him in the new year, when all my results are in, to see the best direction to take, but I think it will be IVF.'

'Really!'

'I think so.' Louise nodded. 'He discussed egg sharing, which would mean I'll get a round of IVF free…'

'You don't feel funny about egg sharing?' Emily asked, just as Anton walked in.

'God, no,' Louise said, happy to chat on. 'I'd love to be able to help another woman to get her baby. It would be a win-win situation. I think egg sharing is a wonderful thing.'

She glanced over as Anton pulled out the BP cuff.

'I've done Emily's blood pressure,' Louise said.

'I'm just checking it for myself.'

Louise gritted her jaw. He did this all the time, *all the time*, even more so than before, and though it infuriated Louise she said nothing.

Here wasn't the place.

'Everything looks good,' Anton said to Emily. 'Twenty-nine weeks and four days now. You are doing really well.'

'I'm so glad,' Emily said, 'but I'm also so…' Emily didn't finish. 'I hate that I'm complaining when I'm so glad that I'm still pregnant.'

'Of course you are bored and fed up.' Anton shrugged. 'Would a shower cheer you up?'

'Oh, yes.'

'Just a short one,' Anton said, 'sitting on a chair.'

'Thank you,' Emily said, but when Anton had gone she looked at Louise. 'What's going on with you two?'

'Nothing,' Louise said.

'Nothing?' Emily checked. 'Come on, Louise, it's me. I'm losing my mind here. At least you can tell me what's going on in the real world.'

'Maybe a teeny tiny thing *has* gone on,' Louise said, 'but we're back to him sulking at me now and double-checking everything that I do.'

'Please, Louise, tell me what has happened between you.'

'Nope,' Louise said, but then relented a touch. 'We got off with each other a smudge but I think the big chill is from my getting IVF.'

'Well, it wouldn't be the biggest turn-on.'

'I guess.'

'Can you put it off?'

'I don't want to put it off,' Louise said. 'Then again, I sort of do.' She was truly confused. 'God, could you imagine being in a relationship with Anton? He'd be coming home and checking I'd done hospital corners on the bed and things…'

'He's nothing like that,' Emily said.

'Ah, but you get his hospital bedside manner.'

'Why not just try?'

'Because I've sworn off relationships, they never

work out… I don't know,' Louise sighed, and then she looked at her friend and told her the truth. 'I'm scared to even try.'

'When's the maternity do?' Emily asked.

'Friday, but I'm on a late shift, so I'll only catch the end.'

'If you get changed at work I want to see you before you go.'

'You will.' Louise gave a wicked smile. 'Let's see if he can rustle up another supermodel.'

'Or?'

Louise didn't answer the question because she didn't know the answer herself. 'I'll go and set up the shower for you,' Louise said instead, and opened Emily's locker and started to get her toiletries out. 'What do you want to wear?'

'Whatever makes me look least like a prostitute,' Emily said, because, after all, it was Louise who had shopped for her!

'But you look gorgeous in all of them,' Louise said, 'and I promise that you're going to feel gorgeous too once you've had a shower.'

Emily actually did. After more than a week of washing from a bowl, a brief shower and a hair wash had her feeling so refreshed that she actually put on some make-up and her smile matched the scarlet nightdress that Louise had bought her.

'Wrong room!' Hugh joked, when he dropped in during a lull between patients, please to see how much brighter Emily looked.

In fact, Emily had quite a lot of visitors and Anton glanced into her room as he walked past.

'Is she resting?' Anton asked Louise.

'I'm going to shoo them out soon,' Louise said. 'She's had her sister and mum and now Hugh's boss and his wife have dropped in.'

Alex and Jennifer were lovely, just lovely, but Emily really did need her rest and so, after checking in on Carmel, who seemed much calmer since her sleep and a visit from her husband and children, Louise popped in on Emily, dragging the CTG monitor with her.

'How are you?' Louise asked.

'Fine!' Emily said, but she had that slightly exhausted look in her eyes as she smiled brightly.

'That's good.' Louise turned to the visitors. She knew Alex very well from the five years she had worked in Theatre and she knew Jennifer a little too. 'I'm sorry to be a pain, but I've got to pop Louise on the monitor.'

'Of course,' Jennifer said. 'We were just leaving.'

'Don't rush,' Louise said, while meaning the opposite. 'I'm just going to get some gel.'

That would give them time to say goodbye.

Of course Emily was grateful for visitors but even a shower, after all this time in bed, was draining, and Louise would do everything and anything she had to do to make sure Emily got her rest. By the time she returned with the gel Alex and Jennifer had said their goodbyes and were in the corridor.

'How are you, Louise?' Alex asked. 'Missing Theatre?'

'A bit,' Louise admitted, 'although I simply love it here.'

'Well, we miss you,' Alex said kindly, and then glanced over to the nurses' station, where Anton was writing his notes. 'Oh, there's Anton. Jennifer, I must introduce you—'

'Not now, darling,' Jennifer said. 'We really do have to get home for Josie.'

'It will just take two minutes.' Alex was insistent but as he went to walk over, Jennifer caught his arm.

'Alex, I really am tired.'

'Of course.' Alex changed his mind and they wished Louise goodnight before heading off the ward.

Louise looked at Anton, remembering the night of the theatre do and Anton's stilted response when Alex had said he hadn't yet met his wife. Even if she and Anton were trying to keep their distance a touch, Louise couldn't resist meddling.

'She's gone,' Louise said, as he carried on writing.

'Who?'

'Jennifer.'

'That's good.'

'She's nice, isn't she?' Louise said, and watched his pen pause for a second.

'So I've heard,' Anton responded, and carried on writing.

'Have you met her?'

Anton looked up and met Louise's eyes, which were sparkling with mischief. 'Should I have?'

'I don't know.' Louise smiled, all the more curious, but, looking at him, properly looking at him for the first time since he had handed her the referral, she was curious now for different reasons. 'Why aren't we talking, Anton?'

'We're talking now.'

'Why are you checking everything I do?'

'I'm not.'

'Believe me, you are. I might just as well give you

the obs trolley and follow you around and simply write your findings down.'

'Louise, I like to check my patients myself. It has nothing to do with you.'

'Okay.' She went to go but changed her mind. 'We're not talking, though, are we?'

He glanced at the sticking plaster on her arm from where she had had blood tests. 'How was your appointment?'

'He was very informative,' Louise said.

'You're seeing him again?'

'In January.' Louise nodded.

'May I ask…?' Anton said, and Louise closed her eyes.

'Please don't.'

'So I just sit here and say nothing?' Anton checked. He glanced down the corridor. 'Come to my office.'

Louise did as she wanted to hear what he had to say.

'I want to see if we can have a chance and I don't think we'll get one with you about to go on IVF.'

'Oh, so I'm to put all my plans on hold because you now think we might have a chance.'

'I don't think that's unreasonable.'

'I do,' Louise said. 'I very much do. I've liked you for months,' she said, 'months and months, and now, when I'm just getting it together, when I'm going ahead with what I've decided to do, you suddenly decide, oh, okay, maybe I'll give her a try.'

'Come off it, Louise…'

'No, you come off it,' Louise snapped back. A part of her knew he was right but the other part of her knew that she was. She'd cancelled her dreams for a man once before and had sworn never to do it again and so she went to walk off.

'You won't even discuss it?'

'I need to think,' Louise said.

'Think with me, then.'

'No.'

She was scared to, scared that he might make up her mind, and she was so past being that person. Instead, she gave him a cheeky smile. 'Richard told me to have a *very* nice Christmas.'

Her smile wasn't returned.

'I'm not into Christmas.'

'I meant—'

'I know what you meant, Louise,' Anton said. 'You want some gun for hire.'

'Ooh, Anton!' Louise smiled again and then thought for a moment. 'Actually, I do.'

'Tough.'

Anton stood in his office for a few moments as she walked off.

Maybe he'd been a bit terse there, he conceded.

But it was hearing Louise talk about egg sharing with Emily that had had him on edge. From the little Louise had told him about her fertility issues he had guessed IVF would be her best option if she wanted to get pregnant. Often women changed their minds after the first visit. He had hoped it might be the case with Louise while deep down knowing that it wouldn't be.

He had seen her sitting in the canteen with her mother today—and it had to have been her mum as Anton could see where Louise had got her looks from— but even that had caused disquiet.

Louise had talked this through with her family. It was clearly not a whim.

It just left no room for them.

Anton wanted more than just sex for a few weeks.

Then he changed his mind because a few weeks of straight sex sounded pretty ideal right now.

Perhaps they should try pushing things aside and just seeing how the next few weeks unfolded.

He walked out of his office and there was Louise, walking with a woman in labour. She caught his eye and gave him a wink.

Anton smiled in return.

The tease was back on.

CHAPTER NINE

'I AM SO, so jealous!' Emily said, as Louise teetered in on high heels on Friday night, having finished her shift and got changed into her Christmas party clothes.

'It's fine that you're jealous,' Louise said to Emily, 'because I am so, so jealous of you. I'd love to be in bed now, nursing my bump.'

'You look stunning,' Hugh said.

Louise was dressed in a willow-green dress that clung to her lack of curves and she had her Mistletoe range stockings on, which came with matching panties, bra and suspenders. As they chatted Louise topped her outfit off with a very red coat that looked more like a cape and was a piece of art in itself.

'God help Anton,' Hugh said openly to Louise.

'Sadly, he's stuck on the ward.' Louise rolled her eyes. 'So that was a waste of six pounds.'

As she headed out Hugh turned to Emily, who was trying not to laugh at Hugh's reaction.

'Was she talking about condoms?' Hugh asked.

'She was.'

Oh, Louise was!

As she approached the elevator, there was Anton and his patient must have been sorted because he had changed out of scrubs and was wearing black jeans and a black jumper and looked as festive as one might expect for Anton. He smelt divine, though, Louise thought as she stood beside him, waiting for the lift. 'You've escaped for the weekend,' Louise said.

'I have.'

'Me too!'

She looked at the clothes he was wearing. Black trousers, a black shirt and a very dark grey coat. He looked fantastic rather than festive. 'I didn't know they did out-of-hours funerals,' Louise said as they stepped into the elevator and her eyes ran over his attire.

'You would have me in a reindeer jumper.'

'With a glow stick round your neck,' Louise said as she selected the ground floor. 'It will be fun tonight.'

'Well, I'm just going to put my head in to be polite,' Anton said. 'I don't want to stay long.'

'Yawn, yawn,' Louise said. 'You really are a misery at Christmas, Anton. Well, I'm staying right to the end. I missed out on far too many parties last year.'

She leant against the wall and gave him a smile when she saw he was looking at her.

'You look very nice,' Anton said.

'Thank you,' Louise responded, and she felt a little rush as his eyes raked over her body and this time Anton did look down, all the way to her toes and then back up to her eyes.

She resented that the lift jolted and that the doors opened and someone came in. They all stood in silence but this was no socially awkward nightmare. His delicious, slow perusal continued all the way to the ground floor.

'Do you want a lift to the party?' Anton offered.

'It's a five-minute walk,' Louise said. 'Come back later for your car.'

They stepped out and it was snowing, just a little. It was too damp and not cold enough for it to settle but there in the light of the streetlamps she could see the flakes floating in the night and he saw her smile and chose to walk the short distance.

It was cold, though, and Louise hated the cold.

'I should have worn a more sensible coat,' Louise said through chattering teeth because her coat, though divine, was a bit flimsy. It was the perfect red, though, and squishy and soft, and she dragged it out every December and she explained that to Anton. 'But this is my Christmas party coat. It wasn't the most thought-out purchase of my life.'

'You have a Christmas coat?'

'I have a Christmas wardrobe,' Louise corrected. 'So, you're just staying for a little while.'

'No,' Anton said.

'Oh, I thought you said—'

'You ruined my line. I was going to suggest that you leave five minutes after me but then you said that you were looking forward to it.'

'Oh!'

'I think you are right and that we should enjoy Christmas, perhaps together, and stop concerning ourselves with other things.' He stopped walking and so did she and they faced each other in the night and he pulled her into his lovely warm coat. 'Can you be discreet?'

'Not really,' Louise said with a smile, 'but I am discreet about important things.'

'I know.'

'And having a nice Christmas is a very important thing,' she went on, 'so, yes, I'll be discreet.'

Pressed together, her hands under his coat and around his waist there was nothing discreet about Anton's erection.

'I would kiss you but...' He looked down at her perfectly painted lips for about half a second because he didn't care if it ruined her make-up and neither did she. It had been a very long December, all made worth it by this.

After close to two weeks of deprivation Louise returned to his mouth. His kiss was warm and his lips tender. It was a gentle kiss but it delivered such promise. His tongue was hers again to enjoy. His hands moved under her coat and stroked her back and waist so lightly it was almost a tickle, and when their lips parted their faces barely broke contact and Louise's short breaths blew white in the night. She was ridiculously turned on in his arms.

'We need get there,' Anton said.

'Should we arrive together?' Louise asked. 'If we're going to be discreet?'

'Of course,' Anton said, 'we left work at the same time.'

She went into her bag, which was as well organised as her pockets at work, and did a quick repair job on her face and handed Anton a baby wipe.

'Actually, have the packet,' Louise said, and Anton pocketed it with a smile.

He might rather be needing them.

It was everything a Christmas party should be.

The theme was fun and midwives knew how to have it.

All the Christmas music was playing and Louise was the happiest she had been in a very, very long time amongst her colleagues and friends. Anton was there in the background, making her toes curl in her strappy stilettoes as she danced and had fun and made merry with friends while he suitably ignored her. Now and then, though, they caught the other's eye and had a little smile.

It was far less formal than the theatre do and everyone let off a little seasonal steam, well, everyone but Anton.

He stood chatting with Stephanie and Rory, holding his sparkling water, even though he was off duty now until Monday.

'Louise,' Rory called to her near the end of the evening, 'what are you doing for Emily at Christmas?'

'I don't know,' Louise said. 'I've been racking my brains. She's got everything she needs really but I'm going Christmas shopping tomorrow. I might think of something then.'

'Well, let me know if you want to go halves,' Rory said. 'Or if you see something I could get, then could you get it for me?'

'I shall.'

'I'm going to take Stephanie home,' Rory said, and as Stephanie went to get her coat, even though Anton was there, Louise couldn't resist, once Stephanie had gone, asking Rory a question.

'Is it Stephanie?'

'Who?'

'The woman you like.'

'God.' Rory rolled his eyes. 'Why did I ever say anything?'

'Because we're friends.'

'Just drop it,' Rory said. 'And, no, it's not Stephanie.' He let out a laugh at Louise's suggestion. 'She's married with two children.'

'Maybe that's why you have to keep it so quiet.'

'Louise, it's not Stephanie and you are to leave this alone.' He looked at Anton. 'She's relentless.'

'She is.'

Louise pulled a face at Rory's departing back and then turned and it was just she and Anton.

'Do you want a drink?' Anton asked.

'No, thanks,' Louise said. 'I've had one snowball too many.'

'What *are* you drinking?' Anton asked, because he had seen the pale yellow concoction she had been drinking all night.

'Snowballs—Advocaat, lemonade and lime juice,' she pulled a face.

'You don't like them?'

'I like the *idea* of them,' Louise said, and then her attention was shot as a song came on. 'Ooh, I love this one...'

'Of course you do.'

'No, seriously, it's my favourite.'

It was dance with her or watch her dance alone.

'I thought we were being discreet?' Louise said.

'It's just a dance,' Anton said, as she draped her arms round his neck. 'But Rory's right—you are relentless.'

'I know I am.' Louise smiled.

They were as discreet as two bodies on fire could be, just swaying and looking at each other and talking.

'I want to kiss you under the mistletoe,' Anton said.

'I assume we're not talking about the sad bunch hanging at the bar.'

'No.'

'Did you know these stockings come with matching underwear?'

'I do,' Anton said, 'I saw your work in the magazine.'

'Did you like?'

'I like.' Anton nodded. 'As I said, I want to kiss you under the mistletoe.'

'I am so turned on.' She stated the obvious because he could feel every breath that blew from her lips, he could see her pulse galloping in her neck as well as the arousal in her eyes.

'Good.'

'We need to leave,' Louise said.

'I'm going to go and speak to Brenda and then leave, and you're going to hang around for a little while and then we meet at my car.'

'I live a two-minute walk from here,' Louise said.

'Okay…'

She loved his slow smile as she gave him her address. 'I'll slip the key into your coat pocket,' Louise said. 'You can go and put the kettle on.'

'I shall.'

'Please don't,' Louise said. 'I meant—'

'Oh, I get what you meant.'

Anton said his goodbyes and chatted with Brenda for an aching ten minutes, though on the periphery of his vision he could see Louise near the coats but then off she went, back to the dance floor.

Anton headed out into the night and found her home very easily. Louise had left the heating on. She loathed coming home to a cold house and a furnace of heat hit

Anton as he opened the door as well as the dazzle of decorations, which were about as subtle as Louise.

And as for the bedroom!

Anton couldn't help but smile as he stepped inside Madame Louise's chamber. He looked at the crushed velvet bed that matched the crushed velvet chair by the dressing table and he looked at the array of bottles and make-up on it.

Anton undressed and got into her lovely bed. He had never met someone so unabashed and he liked that about her, liked that she was who she was.

Louise had never been more in demand than in the ten minutes at the end of the party. Everyone, *everyone* wanted her to stop for a chat, and just as she finally got her coat on and was leaving, Brenda suggested they drop over to Louise's as some work dos often ended up there.

'I can't tonight,' Louise said. 'Mum's over.'

'Your mum?'

'I think she and Dad had a row,' Louise lied, but she had to, as her mind danced with a sudden vision of a naked Anton in the hallway greeting half of the maternity staff. 'It's a bit of a sensitive point.'

Louise texted him as she walked out.

I just told the biggest lie

Should I be worried that there is a crib in your bedroom? Anton texted back.

She laughed because she had already told him it was for Emily's baby and it was wrapped in Cellophane too, so she continued the tease.

Aren't we making a baby tonight? Louise fired back.

Get here!!!

She waved as a car carrying her friends tooted, trying not to run on shaky, want-filled legs, and almost breaking her ankle as she walked far too fast for her stilettoes.

She could barely get the key in the door, just so delighted by the turn of events—that they were going to put other things on hold and simply enjoy. Her coat dropped to the floor as she stepped into the bedroom and there he was, naked in her bed and a Christmas wish came true.

'Who's been sleeping in my bed?' Louise smiled.

'No sleeping tonight,' Anton said. 'Come here.'

Louise was not shy; she went straight over, kneeling on her bed and kissing him without restraint.

It was urgent.

Anton was at the tie of her dress as their mouths bruised each other's. He tried to peel it off over arms that were bent because she was holding his head, tonguing him, wanting him, but there was something she first had to do.

'I have to take my make-up off.'

'I'll lick it off.'

'Seriously.' She could hardly breathe, she was somehow straddling him, her dress gaped open and it would be so much easier not to reach for the cold cream. 'It's not vanity, it's work ethic—I'll look like a pizza for my photo shoot otherwise…'

She climbed off the bed and shed her dress and Anton got the full effect of her stunning underwear, and as beautiful as the pictures had been he far preferred the un-airbrushed version.

Louise sat on her chair and slathered her face in cold cream, quickly wiping it off and wishing she hadn't worn so much mascara. Just as she had finished she felt the chair turn and she was face to groin with a naked Anton.

'Poor Anton,' Louise said.

'Not any more,' Anton said, as she started to stroke him. She went to lower her head but he was starting to kneel.

'Stay…' Louise said, because she wanted to taste him.

'You can have it later.'

He caressed the insides of her thighs through her stockings then the white naked flesh so slowly that she was twitching. He stroked her through her damp panties till he moved them aside and explored her again with his fingers till she could almost stand it no more. Her thighs were shaking and finally his hands went for her mistletoe panties and slid them down so slowly that Louise was squirming. Anton pulled her bottom right to the edge of the chair and then took one stockinged leg and put it over his shoulder and then slowly did the same with the other. Such was the greed in his eyes she was almost coming as finally he did kiss what had been under the silken mistletoe.

Louise looked down but his eyes were closed in concentration and her knees started to bend to the skill of his mouth but hands came up and clamped her legs down, so there was nowhere to go but ecstasy.

She felt the cool blowing of his breath and then the warm suction of his mouth and then another soft blow that did nothing to put the fire out. In fact, her hips were lifting, but his mouth would not allow them to.

'Anton...' She didn't need to tell him she was coming, he was lost in it too, moaning, as her thighs clamped his head and she pulsed in his mouth. Anton reached for his cock on instinct. He was close to coming too. He raised himself up, and was stroking himself at her entrance. They were in the most dangerous of places, two people who definitely should know better.

Louise was frantically patting the dressing table behind her, trying to find a drawer, while watching the silver bead at his tip swelling and drizzling.

'Here...' She pulled out a foil packet and ripped it open. She slid it onto his thick length and there was no way they could make it to the bed, but Anton took a turn in the lucky chair and she leapt on his lap. His mouth sucked her breast through her bra as she wriggled into position.

She hovered provocatively over his erection, revelling for a brief moment in the sensation of his mouth and the anticipation of lowering herself. Anton had worked the fabric down and was now at her nipple, her small breast consumed by his mouth, and then his patience expired. His hands pulled her hips down and in one rapid motion Louise was filled by him, a delicious searing but, better still, his hands did not leave her. Her bedroom was like a sauna and the sheen on her body had her a little slippery but his hands gripped her and did not relent, for she would match his needs.

It had her feeling dizzy—the sensation of being on top while being taken. Louise rested her arms on his shoulders as he pulled her down over and over, and then his mouth lost contact with her breast as he swelled that final time. Her hands went to his head and she ground down, coming with him, squealing in pleasure as they hit a giddy peak. They shared a decadent, wet kiss as he shot inside her, a kiss of possession as she pulsed around his length and her head collapsed onto his shoulder.

Louise kissed his salty shoulder as her breathing finally slowed down.

She could feel him soften inside her and she lifted her head and smiled into his eyes.

'Ready for bed?'

CHAPTER TEN

AFTER ONE HOUR and about seven minutes of sleep they woke to Louise's phone at six.

'I thought you were off today,' Anton groaned.

'I am, but I'm going Christmas shopping.'

'At six a.m.?'

'I want to get a book signed for Mum so I have to line up,' Louise said. 'Stay,' she said, kissing his mouth .'Get up when you're ready, or you can come shopping with me.'

'I'll give it a miss, thanks.'

'Have you done your Christmas shopping?'

'I'll do it online. The shops will be crazy.'

'That's half the fun.' She gave him a nudge. 'Come on.'

She went into the shower and Anton lay there, looking up at the ceiling. He had a couple of things to get. Something for the nurses and his secretary and, yes, he might just as well get it over and done with.

'We'll stop by my place and I can get changed,' Anton said, as she came out of the shower.

'Sure.' Naked, she smiled down at him and lifted her hair. 'Check me for bruises,' she said, while craning her neck and looking down at her buttocks where his fingers had dug in, but, no, they were peachy cream too.

'No need to check,' Anton said, for he had been careful, knowing that she had her photo shoot coming up.

Neither could wait till it was over!

Louise dressed while Anton showered. She pulled on jeans and boots and a massive cream jumper and then she tied up her hair and added a coat.

Anton put on the clothes he had worn last night, though they were stopping by his place so he could get changed.

'Ready to do battle?' she asked, thrilled that Anton had agreed to come along with her. She was determined to Christmas him up, especially when they arrived at his apartment.

'You really are a misery,' Louise said, stepping in. She didn't care about the view or the gorgeous furnishings in his apartment—what she cared about was that there wasn't a single decoration. There were a few Christmas cards stacked with his mail on the kitchen bench but, apart from that, it might just as well have been October, instead of just over a week before Christmas.

'Aren't you even going to get a tree?' Louise asked.

'No.'

'Don't you have Christmas trees in Italy?'

'Some,' Anton said, 'but we go more for nativity scenes and lights.'

'You have to do something.'

'I'm hardly ever here, Louise,' Anton said.

'It's not the point. When you come home—'

'I don't like Christmas,' Anton said, but then amended, 'Although I am starting to really enjoy this one.'

'What do you have to get today?'

'I need to get something for my secretary,' Anton said. 'Perfume?'

'Maybe,' Louise said. 'What sort of things does she like?'

Anton spread out his hands—he really had no idea what Shirley liked.

'What sort of things does she talk about?'

'My diary.'

'God, you're so antisocial,' Louise said.

'Oh, she likes cooking,' Anton recalled. 'She's always bringing in things that she's made.'

'Then I have the perfect present,' Louise said, 'because I'm getting it for my mum. That's what we're going to line up for.'

It wasn't just a book. The first twenty people had the option to purchase a morning's cooking lesson with a celebrity chef. It was fabulous and expensive and with it all going to charity it was well worth it.

Celebrating their success at getting the signed books and cookery lessons, at ten a.m., having coffee and cake in an already crowded department store, they chatted.

'If your mother can't cook, why would you spend all that money? Surely it will be wasted?'

'Oh, no.' Louise shook her head. 'If she learns even one thing and gets it right, my dad will be grateful for ever—the poor thing,' she added. 'He has to eat it night after night after night. I usually wriggle out of it when I go and visit. I'll go over tomorrow and say I've just eaten, but you can't do that on Christmas Day.'

'How bad is it?'

'It's terrible. I don't know how she does it. It always looks okay and she thinks it tastes amazing but I swear it's like she's put it in a blender with water added, burnt it and then put it back together to look like a dinner again...' She took out her list. 'Come on, off we go.'

Louise was a brilliant shopper, not that Anton easily fathomed her methods.

'I adore this colour,' Louise said, trying lipstick on the back of her hand. 'Oh, but this one is even better.'

'I thought we were here for your sisters.'

'Oh, they're so easy to buy for,' Louise said. 'Anything I love they want to pinch, so anything I love I know they'll like.'

Make-up, perfume, a pair of boots... 'I'm the same size as Chloe,' she explained, as she tried them on. 'It's so good you're here, I'd have had to make two trips otherwise.'

Bag after bag was loaded with gifts. 'I want to go here,' Louise said, and they got off the escalator at the baby section. 'I'm going to get something for Emily and Hugh's baby,' Louise said. 'Hopefully it will be a waste of money and I can give it to NICU.' She looked at Anton. 'Do you think she'll get to Christmas?'

'I hope so,' Anton said. 'I'm aiming for thirty-three weeks.'

Louise heard the unvoiced *but* and for now chose to ignore it.

They went to the premature baby section and found some tiny outfits and there was one perk to being the obstetrician and midwife shopping for a pregnant friend, they knew what colour to get! Louise said yes to gift-wrapping and they waited as it was beautifully wrapped and then topped with a bow.

'I'll keep it in my locker at work,' Louise said.

It was a lovely, lovely, lovely day of shopping, punctuated with kisses. Neither cared about the grumbles they caused as they blocked the pavement or the escalators when they simply had to kiss the other and by the end Louise was seriously, happily worn out.

'You want to get dinner?' Anton offered.

'Take-out?' Louise suggested. 'But we'll have it at my place. I'm not going to your miserable apartment.'

'I have to go back,' Anton said. 'I have to do an hour's work at least.'

'Fine,' Louise conceded, 'but we'll drop these back at my place first and I'll get some clothes.'

'You won't need them,' Anton said, but Louise was insistent.

All her presents she put in the bedroom. 'I can't wait to wrap them,' Louise said. 'I'll just grab a change of clothes and things, you go and make a drink.'

Louise grabbed more than a change of clothes. In fact, she went into her wardrobe and pulled out some leftover Christmas decorations and stuffed them all into a not so small overnight bag. She also took the tiny silver tree that she'd been meaning to put up at the nurses' station but kept forgetting to take.

'How long are you staying for?' Anton asked, when she came out and he saw the size of her overnight bag.

'Till you kick me out.' Louise gave him a kiss. 'I like to be prepared.'

Anton really did have work to do.

A couple of blood tests were in and he went through them, and there was a patient at thirteen weeks' gestation who was bleeding. Anton went into his study and rang her to check how things were.

Louise could hear him safely talking and quickly set to work.

The little tree she put on his coffee table and she draped some tinsel on the window ledges and put up some stars, a touch worried she might leave some marks on his walls but he'd just have to get over it, Louise decided.

She took out her can and sprayed snow on his gleaming windows, and oh, it looked lovely.

'What the hell have you done?' Anton said, as he came into the lounge, but he was smiling.

'I need nice things around me,' Louise said, 'happy things.'

'It would seem,' Anton said, looking not at her handiwork now but the woman in his arms, 'that so do I.'

CHAPTER ELEVEN

'WHAT HAPPENED LAST Christmas?' Anton asked, late, late on Sunday night. They'd started on the sofa and had watched half a movie and now they lay naked on the floor bathed by the light from the television. 'You said it was tinsel-starved.'

She really would prefer not to talk about it. They had had such a lovely weekend but there were so many parts of so many conversations that they were avoiding, like IVF and Anton's loathing of Christmas, that when he finally broached one of them, Louise answered carefully. There was no way she could tell him all but she told him some.

'I broke up with my boyfriend on Christmas Eve.'

'You said it was tinsel-starved before then, that you didn't go to many parties.'

'It wasn't worth it.'

'In what way?'

'I know you think I'm a flirt…'

'I like that about you.'

'But I'm only really like that with you,' Louise said. 'I mean that. I used to be a shocking flirt and then when I started going out with Wesley…well, I got told off a lot.'

'For flirting with other men?'

'No!' Louise said, shuddering at the memory. 'He decided that if I flirted like that with him, then what was I like when he wasn't there? I don't want to go into it all, but I changed and I hate myself for it. I changed into this one eighth of a person and somehow I got out—on Christmas Eve last year. It took months, just months to even start feeling like myself again.'

'Okay.'

'Do you know the day I did?' Louise asked, smiling as she turned to face him.

'No.'

'We were going to Emily's leaving do and I saw you in the corridor and I asked you to come along…'

'You were wearing red,' Anton easily recalled. 'You were with Emily.'

'That's right, it was for her leaving do. Well, even when I asked if you wanted to come along, I deep down knew that you wouldn't. I was just…' She couldn't really explain. 'I was just flirting again…sort of safe in the knowledge that it wouldn't go anywhere.'

'But it has,' Anton said.

'I guess.' Louise smiled. 'Have you ever been married?' Louise asked.

'Why do you ask?'

'I just wondered.'

'No,' Anton said. 'Have you?'

'God, no,' Louise said.

'Have you ever come close?'

'No,' Louise admitted.

'You and Rory?'

Louise laughed and shook her head. 'We were only together a few weeks. Just when we started going out I found that it was likely that I was going to have issues getting pregnant. It was terrible timing because it was all I could think about. Poor Rory, he started going out with a happy person and when the doctor broke the news I just plunged into despair. It wasn't his baby I wanted, just the thought I might never have one. It was just all too much for him…' She looked at Anton. 'I think I was just low at that time and that's why I must have taken my bastard alert glasses off. I've made a few poor choices with men since then.' She closed her eyes. 'None worse than Wesley, though.'

'How bad did it get?' Anton asked, but Louise couldn't go there and she shook her head.

'What about you?' Louise asked. 'Have you been serious with anyone?'

'Not really, well, there was one who came close…' It was Anton who stopped talking then.

Anton who shook his head.

He simply couldn't go there with someone who might just want him for a matter of weeks.

CHAPTER TWELVE

'CAN YOU KEEP a close eye on Felicity in seven?' Anton asked. 'She's upset because her husband has been unable to get a flight back till later this evening.'

Felicity was one of Anton's high-risk pregnancies and finally the day had arrived where she would meet her baby, but her husband was in Germany with work.

'How is she doing?' Louise asked.

'Very slowly,' Anton said. 'Hopefully he'll get here in time.' He picked up a parcel, beautifully wrapped by Louise. 'I'm going to give this to Shirley now. She's only in this morning to sort out my diary before she takes three weeks off. Then I will be in the antenatal clinic. Call me if you have any concerns.'

'Yes, Anton,' Louise sighed.

Anton heard her sigh but it did not bother him.

Things were not going to change at work. In fact, he was more overbearing if anything, just because he didn't want a mistake to come between them.

'This is for you,' Anton said, as he went into Shirley's office. 'I just wanted to thank you for all your hard work this year and to say merry Christmas.'

'Thank you, Anton.' Shirley smiled.

'I hope you have a lovely break.'

He went to go, even as she opened it, but her cry of surprise had him turn around.

'How?'

Anton stared. His usually calm secretary was shaking as she spoke.

'How did you manage to get this—there were only twenty places.'

'I got there early.'

'You lined up to get me this! Oh, my…'

Anton felt a little guilt at her obvious delight. It really had been far from a hardship to be huddled in a queue with Louise, but it was Shirley's utter shock too that caused more than a little disquiet.

'I never thought…' Shirley started and then stopped. She could hardly say she'd been expecting some bland present from her miserable boss. 'It's wonderful,' she said instead.

God, Anton thought, was he that bad that a simple nice gesture could reduce a staff member to tears?

Yes.

He nodded to Helen, the antenatal nurse who would be working alongside him, and he saw that she gave a slightly strained one back.

Things had to change, Anton realised.

He had to learn to let go a little.

But how?

'How are things?' Louise asked, as she walked into Felicity's room with the CTG machine.

'They're just uncomfortable,' Felicity said. She was determined to have a natural birth and had refused an epidural or anything for pain. 'I'm going to try and have a sleep.'

'Do,' Louise said. 'Do you want me to close the curtains?'

Felicity nodded.

Brenda popped her head in the door. 'Are you going to lunch, Louise?'

'In a minute,' Louise said. 'I'm just doing some obs.' Both Felicity and the baby seemed fine. 'I'll leave this on while I have my lunch,' Louise said about the CTG machine, and Felicity nodded. 'Then later we might have a little walk around, but for now just try and get some rest.'

She closed the curtains and moved a blanket over Felicity, who was half-asleep, and left her to the sound of her baby's heartbeat. Louise would check the tracing when she came back from her break and see the pattern of the contractions.

'Press the bell if you need anything and I'll be here.'

'But you're going to lunch.'

'Yep, but that buzzer is set for me, so just you press it if you need to.'

'Thanks, Louise,' Felicity said. 'What time are you here till?'

Louise thought before answering. 'I'm not sure.'

Louise left the door just a little open so that her colleagues could easily pop in and out and could hear the CTG, then headed to the fridge and got out her lunch.

'Fancy company?' Louise asked Emily as she knocked on her open door.

'Oh, yes!' Emily sat up in the bed. 'How was the party?'

'Excellent.'

'Why didn't you text me all weekend?'

'I did!' Louise said.

'Five-thirty on a Sunday evening suggests to me you were otherwise engaged.'

'I was busy,' Louise said, 'Christmas shopping!'

'You lie,' Emily said.

'Actually, I need to charge my phone,' Louise said, because she hadn't been back home since being at Anton's. 'Can I borrow your charger?'

'Sure.' Emily smiled. 'That's not like you.'

Louise said nothing. She certainly wasn't going to admit to Emily her three-night fest with Anton. As she plugged in her phone and sat down, the background noise of Felicity's baby's heartbeat slowed. Louise was so tuned into that noise, as all midwives were, and she didn't like what she had just heard.

'Are you okay?' Emily asked.

'I think I've got restless leg syndrome.' Louise gave a light response. 'I'm just going to check on someone and then I'll be back.'

She went quietly into Felicity's room. Felicity was dozing and Louise warmed her hand and then slipped it on Felicity's stomach, watching the monitor and patiently waiting for a contraction to come.

'It's just me,' Louise whispered, as Felicity woke up as a contraction deepened and Emily watched as the baby's heart rate dipped. She checked Felicity's pulse to make sure the slower heart rate that the monitor was picking up wasn't Felicity's.

'Turn onto your other side for me,' Louise said to the sleepy woman, and helped Felicity to get on her left side and looked up as Brenda, alerted by the sound of the dip in the baby's heart rate, looked in.

'Page Anton,' Louise said.

Even on her left side the baby's heart rate was dipping during contractions and Louise put some oxygen on Felicity. 'We'll move her over to Delivery,' Brenda said.

'Have you heard from Anton?'

'I've paged him but he hasn't answered,' Brenda said. 'I'll see if he's in the staffroom.'

Louise raced around to check but Anton wasn't there.

She paged him again and then they moved Felicity through to the delivery ward. They were about to move her onto the delivery bed but Louise decided to wait for Anton before doing that as she listened to the baby's heart rate. The way this baby was behaving, they might be running to Theatre any time soon.

She typed in an urgent page for Anton but when there was still no response Louise remembered her phone was in Emily's room. 'Text him,' Louise said to Brenda, and, ripping off a tracing, Louise left Felicity with Brenda and swiftly went to a phone out of earshot.

'Are the pagers working?' she asked the switchboard operator. 'I need Anton Rossi paged and, in case he's busy, I need the second on paged too, urgently.'

She then rang Theatre and, because she had worked there for more than five years, when she rang and explained they might need a theatre very soon, she knew she was being taken seriously and that they would immediately be setting up for a Caesarean.

'I can't get hold of Anton,' Louise said, but then she saw him, his phone in hand, racing towards them. 'Anton! Felicity's having late decelerations. Foetal heart rate is dropping to sixty.'

'How long has this been going on?'

'About fifteen minutes.'

'And you didn't think to tell me sooner! Hell! If Brenda hadn't texted me…' Anton hissed, taking the tracing and looking at it in horror, because time was of the essence. With pretty much one look at the tracing the decision to operate was made. For Anton it was a done deal.

It was like some horrific replay of what had happened two years ago.

'I paged you when it first happened,' Louise said, but there wasn't time for explanations now. As Anton went into the delivery room the overhead speakers crackled into life.

'System error. Professor Hadfield, can you make your way straight to Emergency? Mr Rossi, Delivery Ward, room two.'

Anton briefly closed his eyes.

'Mr Rossi, urgently make your way to Delivery, room two. System error—pagers are down.'

And so it repeated.

'Is that for me?' Felicity cried, terrified by the urgency of the calls overhead.

'Hey…' Louise gave Felicity a cuddle as Anton examined her. 'It's just that the pagers are down and so I had to use my whip a bit on Switchboard to get Anton here.'

'Felicity.' Anton came up to the head-end of the bed. 'Your baby is struggling…' Everything had been done. She was on her side, oxygen was on and she was still on the bed so they could simply speed her to Theatre. 'We're going to take you to Theatre now and do a Caesarean section.'

'Can I be awake at least?'

'We really do need to get your baby out now.'

'I'll be there with you,' Louise said, as the porter arrived. 'I am not leaving your side, I promise you. I can take some pictures of your baby if you like,' Louise offered, and Felicity gave her her phone.

'Can you let Theatre know?' Anton said, before he raced ahead to scrub.

It took everything she could muster to keep the bitterness from her voice. 'I already have, Anton.'

Louise and the porter whisked the bed down the corridor. There was no consent form to be signed—that had been taken care of at the antenatal stage.

'I'm so scared,' Felicity said, as they wheeled her into Theatre.

'I know,' Louise said, cleaning down her shoes and popping on shoe covers, then she put on a theatre hat and gown. 'You've got the best obstetrician,' Louise said. 'I've seen him do many Caesareans and he's brilliant.'

'I know.'

The bed was wheeled through and Louise's old colleagues were waiting. Connor and Miriam helped Louise to get Felicity onto the theatre table and she smiled when she saw Rory arrive. He was a bit breathless and as he caught his breath Louise spoke on. 'You've got an amazing anaesthetist too. Hi, Rory, this is Felicity.'

Rory was lovely with Felicity and went through any allergies and previous anaesthetics and things. 'I'm going to be by your side every minute,' he said to Felicity. 'Till you're awake again, here is where I'll be.'

'I'll be here too,' Louise said.

Theatre was filling. The paediatric team was arriving as Rory slipped the first drug into Felicity's IV.

'Think baby thoughts,' Louise said with a smile as Felicity went under.

Louise was completely supernumerary at this point. She was simply here on love watch for one of her mums. And so, once Felicity had been intubated, Louise simply closed her mind to everything, even bastard Anton. She just sat on a stool and thought lovely baby thoughts.

She heard the swirl of suction and a few curses from Anton as he tried to get one very flat baby out as quickly as possible.

Then there was silence and she looked up as a rather floppy baby was whisked away and she kept thinking baby thoughts as they rubbed it very vigorously and flicked at its little feet. She glanced at Rory as another anaesthetist started to bag him.

But then Rory smiled and Louise looked round and watched as the baby shuddered and she watched as his little legs started to kick and his hands started to fight. His cries of protest were muffled by the oxygen mask but were the most beautiful sounds in the world.

Louise didn't look at Anton, she just told Felicity that her baby was beautiful, wonderful, that he was crying and could she hear him, even though Felicity was still under anaesthetic.

Anton did look at Louise.

She did that, Anton thought.

She made all his patients relax and laugh, and though Felicity could not know what was being said, still Louise said it.

He could have honestly kicked himself for his reaction but, God, it had been almost a replica of what had happened back in Italy.

'He's beautiful,' Louise said over and over.

So too was Louise, Anton thought, knowing he'd just blown any chance for them.

Louise *was* beautiful, even when she was raging.

Not an hour later she marched into the male changing room and slammed the door shut.

'Hey, Louise,' called Rory, who was just getting changed. 'You're in the wrong room.'

'Oh, I'm in the right room,' Louise said. 'Could you excuse us, Rory, please?'

'We will do this in my office,' Anton said. Wet from the shower, a towel around his loins, he did not want to do this now, but Louise had no intention of waiting till he got dressed. She was far, far beyond furious.

'Oh, no, this won't keep.'

'Good luck,' Rory called to Anton as he left them to it.

And then it was just Louise and Anton but even as he went to apologise for what had happened earlier, or to even explain, Louise got in first.

'You can question my morals, you can think what you like about me, but don't you ever, ever—'

'Question your morals?' Anton checked. 'Where the hell did that come from?'

'Don't interrupt me,' Louise raged. 'I've had it with you. What you accused me of today—'

'Louise.'

'No!' She would not hear it.

'I apologise. I did not realise the pagers were down.'

'I did,' Louise said instantly. 'When you didn't come, or make contact, it was the first thing I thought—not that you were negligent and simply couldn't be bothered to get here...'

Her lips were white she was so angry. 'I'm going to speak to Brenda and put in an incident report about the pagers today, and while I'm there I'm going to tell her I don't want to work with you any more.'

'That's a bit extreme.'

'It's isn't extreme. I've thought about doing it before.' She saw him blink in surprise. 'Everything I do you check again—'

'Louise…' Anton wasn't about to deny it. He checked on her more than the other midwives, he was aware of that. In trying to protect her, to protect *them*, from what had happened to him and Dahnya, he had gone over the top. 'If I can explain—'

But Louise was beyond hearing him. She lost her temper then and Louise hadn't lost her temper since that terrible day. 'You don't want a midwife,' Louise shouted, 'you want a doula, rubbing the mums' backs and offering support. Well, I'm over it, Anton. Have you any idea how demoralising it is?' she raged, though possibly she was talking more to Wesley than Anton. 'Have you any idea how humiliating it is…?'

Anton took a step forward, to speak, to calm her down, and then stood frozen as he heard the fear in her voice.

'Get off me!' She put her hands up in defence and there was a shocked moment of silence when she realised what she had said, what she had done, but then came his calm voice.

'I'm not touching you, Louise.'

She pressed her hands to her face and her fingers to her eyes. 'I'm sorry,' Louise said, 'not for what I said before but—'

'It's okay.' Anton was breathless too, as if her unleashed fear had somehow attached to him. 'We'll talk when you've calmed down.'

'No.' Louise shook her head, embarrassed at her outburst but still cross. 'We won't talk because I don't want to hear it, Anton.' And then turned and left.

She was done.

CHAPTER THIRTEEN

'WHAT HAPPENED?' EMILY asked, when Louise returned a couple of hours later to the ward.

'Sorry, I just got waylaid.'

'Louise?'

'I'm fine.'

'You've been crying.'

'There's nothing wrong.'

'Louise?' Emily frowned when she saw Louise's smile was wavering as she took Emily's blood pressure. 'What's going on? Look, I'm bored out of my mind. I mean, I am so seriously bored and I'm fed up with people thinking I can't have a normal conversation, or that they only tell me nice things.' Emily was truly concerned because she hadn't seen red eyes on Louise in a very long time. 'Wesley isn't contacting you again?'

'No, no.' Louise sat down on the bed, even though Brenda might tell her off.

'Tell me.' Emily took her hand.

'Anton.' Louise gulped. Certainly she wasn't going to scare Emily and tell her all that had gone on with Felicity's baby but they really were speaking as friends.

'Okay.'

'Personal or professional?'

'Both,' Louise admitted. 'He checks and double-checks everything, you know what he's like...'

'I do,' Emily said.

'It's like he doesn't trust any of the staff but he does it more with me.'

'Louise.' Emily didn't know whether she should say anything but it was pretty much common knowledge what had happened a few months ago. 'Remember when Gina had her meltdown and went into rehab?'

'Yep, I know, Hugh reported her...' Louise looked at Emily, remembering that there had been more than one complaint, or so the rumours went. 'Did Anton report her as well?'

'I'm saying nothing.'

'Okay.' Louise squeezed her hand in gratitude as Emily spoke on.

'So maybe he feels he has reason to be checking things.'

'Hugh doesn't, though,' Louise pointed out. 'Hugh isn't constantly looking over the nursing staff's shoulders and assuming the worst.'

'I know.' Emily sighed. She adored Anton but had noticed that he was dismissive of the nurses' findings and she could well understand that things might have come to a head. 'So, what's the personal stuff?'

'Do you really need to know that your obstetrician got off with your midwife?'

'Ooh.' Emily gave a delighted smile. 'I think I did really need to know that.'

'Well, it won't be happening again,' Louise said. 'We just had the most terrible row, or rather I did...'

'And what did Anton do?' Emily gently enquired.

'He apologised,' Louise said, and then she frowned

because she wasn't very used to a guy backing down. For too long it had been the other way around. 'Emily…' Louise's eyes filled with tears. 'I shouted for him to get off me and the poor guy was just standing there.'

'Oh, Louise…' Emily rubbed Louise's shoulder. 'It must have been terrifying for you to have a big row. Rows are normal, though. What happened to you wasn't.'

'I know.' Louise blew her nose and recovered herself and gave Emily a smile. 'I really let rip.' Louise let out a small shocked laugh.

'She really did!' Anton was at the door and came over to the bed. 'Your latest ultrasound is back. All looks well, there is a nice amount of fluid.' He had a feel of Emily's stomach.

'Nice size,' Anton said.

'Really?'

'Really.' Anton nodded. 'Now is the time they start to plump up and your baby certainly is.'

They headed out of Emily's room and he turned to Louise. 'What is her blood pressure?'

'Ha-ha,' Louise said. 'Check it yourself.'

Anton gave a wry smile as Louise flounced off but it faded when he saw she went straight up to Brenda.

Louise hadn't been lying when she had said she didn't know when she'd be going home.

Something, something had told her she'd be around for the delivery, which meant she wanted to be around when Felicity was more properly awake, and at four she sat holding a big fat baby who had given everyone a horrible scare.

'Your husband just called and he's at Heathrow and

is on his way,' Louise said. 'And your mum is on her way too.' Felicity smiled. 'And you have the cutest, most gorgeous baby. In fact, he's so cute I don't think I can hand him over...'

Felicity smiled as Louise did just that and placed the baby in her arms.

'He's gorgeous.'

'I was so scared.'

'I know you were but, honestly, he gave us a fright but he's fine.' She stared at the baby, who was gnawing at his wrist. 'He's beautiful and he's also starving,' Louise said.

'Can I feed him?'

'You can,' Louise said, 'because he's trying to find mine and I've told him I've got nothing...' She looked up as Anton came in and then got back to work, helping a very hungry baby latch on.

'Louise, can I have a word before you leave?' Anton asked.

Louise's response was a casual 'Sure', but Anton knew that was for the sake of the patient.

'Felicity,' Anton said. 'Your mother has just arrived...'

'Do you want me to tell her to wait while you feed?' Louise checked, but Felicity shook her head.

'No, let her in.'

Louise stayed for the first feed. She just loved that part and then when finally the baby was fed and content and in his little isolette she gave Felicity a cuddle. 'I'll come by tomorrow and we'll talk more about what happened today, if you want to. I took some photos with your phone, if you want to have a look through them with me.'

'Thank you.'

She popped in to see Emily on her way out, as she always did, but she was just about all smiled out. She just wanted to go home for a good cry, a glass of wine and then bed.

She didn't even pretend to smile when she knocked on Anton's office door and went in.

'Can we talk?'

Louise shook her head. 'I don't want to talk to you, Anton,' Louise said. 'I'm tired. I just want to go home.'

'Louise, what happened today was not about you. I had an incident in Milan...'

'I don't want to hear it, Anton,' Louise said, and then relented. 'Imelda's, then,' Louise said. 'I'm just going to get changed.'

'Sure.'

'I'll meet you over there.'

There was Anton with his sparkling water but there was a glass of wine and some nachos waiting for Louise. Really, she shouldn't because she had the bloody photo shoot in less than a week but Louise shovelled them in her mouth, getting hungrier with each mouthful.

'Do you want to get something else?'

'These are fine,' Louise said, and then looked at him. 'Well?'

'I am so very sorry for today. You did everything right, from ringing Theatre to keeping her on the bed. She was very lucky to have you on duty and I apologise for jumping to the worst conclusion.'

Louise gave a tight shrug. It wasn't just today she was upset about. 'What about the other days?' she challenged. 'I don't think you trust me.'

'No.' Anton shook his head. 'That is not the case.'

'It's very much the case,' Louise said. 'Everything I do you double-check, or you simply dismiss my findings… Aside from the repeated wallops to my ego, it's surely doubling up for the patient.' Louise let out a breath. 'So what happened in Milan?'

'A few years ago, on Christmas morning, I took a handover, and I was told everything was fine, but by lunchtime I had a baby dead—' Louise was about to say something but Anton spoke over her. 'It *was* the hospital's fault,' Anton said. 'Apparently the night midwife had told a junior doctor she had concerns; I took the handover from the registrar and those concerns hadn't been passed on to her. It was just complete miscommunication. I went in to see my patient at ten, and there were many things that I should have been paged about but hadn't been. I took her straight to Theatre and delivered the baby but he only lived for a couple of hours.

'The coroner did not blame me, thank God, but I have never seen friendships fall so rapidly. There was blame, accusations, it was hell. So much so that when the finding came in I no longer trusted anyone I worked with, and I knew I had to make a fresh start, which was why I moved into fertility.'

'But you came back.'

'Yes, I never thought I would but the last months I was there, the parents of Alberto, the baby who had died, came in to try for another baby. It was a shock to us all. I offered to step aside but by then I had quite a good reputation and they asked that I remain. I was very happy when they got pregnant and it was then that I realised how much I had missed obstetrics. I knew I needed a fresh start so I applied to come here. I had always had a good rapport with colleagues until Alberto's death. I wanted to get that back and I tried, but within a few weeks of being here there was an incident...' He looked at Louise and she was glad that Emily had filled her in about Gina because Anton didn't. 'I'm not giving specifics but it shook me and from that point I have been cautious...'

'To the extreme,' Louise said.

'Yes.'

'Terrible things happen, Anton. Terrible, terrible things...'

'I know that. I just wish I had not taken a handover that morning and had checked myself...'

'You can't check everyone, you can't follow everyone around.'

'I'm aware of that.'

'Yet you do.'

'I've spoken to Brenda and I have told her what went on, not just today but in the past. I also told her that I am hoping things will be different in the future.'

'Did you get her "There's no I in team" lecture?' Louise asked, and Anton smiled and nodded.

'I've had it a few times from Brenda already and, yes, I got it again today.'

'Well, I disagree with her,' Louise said. 'There should be an I in team. I am responsible, I am capable, I know I've got this, and if I stuff up then I take responsibility. If we all do that, which we seem to do where I work, then teams do well. We look out for each other,' Louise said. 'We have a buddy system. I don't just glance at CTGs when they're given to me and neither do my colleagues. We take ages discussing them, going over them...'

'I know that.'

'It doesn't feel like it,' Louise said.

'I am hoping things will be different now.'

'Good,' Louise said. 'Is that it?'

'No, I want to know what you meant about me judging you on your morals.'

'This isn't a social get-together, Anton. I'm here to talk about work.'

'Louise.'

'Okay, just because I'm not on a husband hunt, just because I fancied you…'

'Past tense?'

'Oh, it is so past tense,' Louise said. 'So very past tense.'

'Louise,' Anton said, and she must have heard the tentative tone to his voice because immediately her eyes darted away, even before his question was voiced. 'What happened that made you so scared back there?'

'That isn't about work either.' She got up and hoisted up her bag. 'I'm sorry you went through crap and I'm so sorry for the baby and its family.'

'Louise.' He halted her as she went to go. 'The midwife on that morning, I was going out with her. She was busy, meant to go back and check, meant to call, but got waylaid. Can you see why I was very reluctant to get involved with you?'

'I can.' She stood there but didn't give him the answer he was hoping for. 'Well, at least you don't have that problem with me now—we're no longer involved.' She gave him a tight smile. 'Goodnight, Anton.'

Louise got home, closed the door and promptly burst into tears. Despite her tough talk with Anton she could think of nothing worse than losing a baby under those circumstances and at Christmas too.

Then she went into the bath and cried some more. She'd been raging at him and he'd simply stood there.

She was beyond confused and all churned up from her loss of control.

Why couldn't it just be sex? Louise thought. Why did she have to really, really like him?

As she got out of the bath her phone bleeped a text from Emily.

U OK?

Louise gave a rapid reply.

Bloody men! How's baby?

Kick-kicking, or maybe he's waving to you.

Louise sent back a smiley face, knowing what was to come.

Maybe SHE'S waving???? Emily texted, hoping that Louise would give her a clue.

Not telling, came Louise's reply. Ask Hugh.

He won't tell me, Emily replied. Bloody men!

CHAPTER FOURTEEN

ANTON REALLY DID make an effort at work, though Louise wasn't sure if it was temporary. At least he had stopped double-checking everything that she did. Brenda had a word with some of the staff, as Anton had asked her to do. They in turn rang him a little sooner than usual with concerns, and slowly the I in team was working, except Louise was no longer a part of his team.

'Phone for you, Louise,' someone called, and Louise headed out to the desk. It was the IVF clinic, which had been unable to reach her on her mobile or at home, and Louise took out her phone and saw that the battery was flat.

'Are you okay to talk, or do you want to call us back?'

'No, now's fine,' Louise said.

'Richard wanted to let you know that your iron levels are now normal but to keep taking the supplements, especially the folic acid.'

'I shall. Thank you,' Louise said.

'Have a lovely Christmas and we'll see you in the new year.'

Louise's stomach was all aflutter as she ended the call.

'Good news?' Brenda asked, but Louise didn't answer. Her *lovely Christmas* was walking past and this time when he sat down and ignored her it was at Louise's request.

Of course, she still dealt with his patients—after all, Emily was one of them—but the distance she had asked for was there. As far as was reasonable she was allocated other patients and when they spoke it was only about work.

'Can you buddy this?' Beth asked, and Louise nodded and sat down. 'What are you working over Christmas?' Beth asked.

'Tomorrow's my last shift,' Louise said, 'and then I'm off till after New Year.'

'Lucky you!'

'I know.' Louise smiled. 'I can't wait.'

She lied.

They looked at the CTG together and Anton could hear them discussing it, Louise asking a couple of questions before they both signed off on it.

What a mistrusting fool he had been.

He had never worked anywhere better than here. The diligence, the care, was second to none but he'd realised it all too late.

'Do you need anything, Anton?' Beth asked, as Anton signed off on a few prescriptions and then stood.

'Nope, I'm heading home. Goodnight, everyone.'

When Anton stepped into his apartment a little later he felt like ripping the bloody tinsel down, yet he left it.

Louise had been in his apartment for three nights in total yet she was everywhere.

From lipstick on the towels and sheets to long blonde hairs in his comb.

Even the bed smelt of her perfume and Anton woke

to his phone buzzing at three-thirty a.m. and, for a second, so consuming was her scent he actually thought she was in bed beside him.

Instead, it was the ward with news about Emily.

'I'm so sorry...' Emily said, as Anton came into the room at four a.m.

'No apologies,' Anton said, taking off his jacket, and then smiled at Evie, who had set up for Anton to examine Emily.

'I thought I'd wet myself,' Emily said. 'Maybe I did...'

'It is amniotic fluid,' Anton said, taking a swab. 'Your waters are leaking. We will get this swab checked for any signs of infection and keep a close eye on your temperature.'

'How long can I go with a leak?'

'Variable. Do you have any discomfort?'

'My back aches,' Emily said, 'but I'm not sure if that's from being in bed...'

'Have you told Hugh?'

'Not yet,' Emily said. 'He was paged at midnight and he's in Theatre. He'll find out soon enough.'

When Louise came on for her shift she saw Anton sitting at the desk and duly ignored him. She headed around to the kitchen and made herself a cup of tea, trying to ignore the scent and feel of him when he walked into the kitchen behind her.

'Emily's waters are leaking,' Anton said. 'I just thought I'd tell you now, rather than you hear it during handover.'

Louise turned round.

'I've ordered an ultrasound to check the amniotic levels and she is on antibiotics…'

'But?'

'Her back is hurting again. There are no contractions but her uterus is irritable.'

'She's going to have it.'

'You don't know that's the case…'

'I do know that this baby is coming soon,' Louise said, and Anton nodded.

'I don't think she'll hold off for much longer.'

Louise felt her eyes fill up when Anton spoke on.

'I miss working with you, Louise.'

Louise didn't say anything.

'I miss *you*,' Anton said.

She looked at him and, yes, she missed him too.

'Can we start again?' Anton said.

'I don't know.'

'Louise, you seem to have it in your head that I'm controlling. I get that I have been at work, I still will be…' He looked at her. 'Do you know why I've been on water at all the parties over Christmas? It's because I have Hazel who is due to deliver soon and I believe Emily will have that baby any day. I want to be there for them both. Yes, I am fully in control at work, and I get you have seen me at my worst here, but you know why now.'

Louise breathed out and looked at him, the most diligent person she knew, and then he continued speaking.

'You explained you are dieting because you have a photo shoot, that you know what you're doing with your weight, and not once since then have I said anything. I was worried about you because my sister has been there but when you said you knew what you were doing, I accepted that.'

He had.

'My ex…' she didn't want to say it here but it was time to tell him a little, if not all. 'He was so jealous, he didn't get that I could be friends with Rory. He didn't even like Emily…'

'And…?' Anton pushed, but Louise shook her head so he pushed on as best he could, but he was a non-witness after the fact and Louise kept him so.

'I would never come between you and your friends.'

'You weren't exactly friendly towards Rory on the night of the theatre do—you were giving him filthy looks.'

'Oh, that's right,' Anton said. 'And you were so sweet to *Saffron*. I was jealous when I thought you were on together, just as you were with me.'

Louise swallowed, she knew he was right.

'I like your friends. I like it that you can be friendly with an ex. And you can flirt, you can be funny, and I have no issue with it, but what I will not do is go along with the notion that I like you going for IVF so early in our relationship.'

Louise turned to go.

'Wrong word for you, Louise?'

It was.

'I need to think, Anton,' Louise said, and possibly the nicest thing he did then was not to argue his case or demand that they speak. He simply nodded.

'Of course.'

Louise took handover and she was allocated Stephanie's patients, all except for Emily, who was asleep when she went in to her.

'Just rest,' Louise said. 'I'm only doing your blood pressure.'

'When are you going for lunch?' Emily asked sleepily.

'About twelve. Do you want me to have it here with you?'

Emily nodded. 'Unless you need a break from the patients.'

'Don't be daft—of course I'd love to have lunch with you.'

When lunchtime came Louise went and got her salad from the fridge and it was so nice to close the door and sit down with her friend.

'It's going to be strange, not having you around,' Emily admitted.

'I'll be visiting, texting...'

'I know,' Emily said, 'it just won't be the same. Are you excited about your photo shoot tomorrow?'

'I am, though you're to promise you'll text me if anything happens.' Louise went into her pocket and handed Emily a business card. 'This is the hotel I'm at, just in case there's nowhere to put my phone!'

'Louise, you are not leaving your photo shoot,' Emily said, handing her back the card.

'But I want to be here if anything happens.'

'I know you do and I'd love you to be here, but I've got Hugh.'

Louise took back the card and stared at it.

Emily had Hugh.

Yes, Louise could do this alone and she would, but for a moment there she reconsidered. Hugh had been here every day, making Emily laugh, letting her relax, an endless stream of support.

It would be so hard to do this alone.

Louise cleared her throat. She didn't like where her mind was heading. 'Well, if you can hold off tomorrow, Christmas Day would be fine.' Louise gave her friend a wide smile as she teased her. 'At least that would get me out of dinner at Mum's.'

Emily laughed,

'Have you seen what you're wearing for the photo shoot?' Emily asked.

'Oh, it's so nice, all reds and black—Valentine's Day stuff, seriously sexy,' Louise said. 'We've got the presidential suite and I think I'm his girlfriend or wife, the model's Jeremy...' Louise rattled on as, unseen, Anton came in and checked Emily's CTG. 'He's so gorgeous but so gay. Anyway, we wake up and why I'm wearing a bra and panties and shoes at six a.m. I have no idea, but then there are to be photos with me waving him off to work...'

'Still in your undies and shoes?' Emily asked, and Louise nodded.

'Then he comes home with flowers and I'm in my evening stuff then, and I think he takes me over the dining table...'

Emily wished Louise would turn around and see Anton's smile as she spoke.

'Everything is looking good,' Anton said, and Emily watched as Louise jumped, wondering how much he had heard. Emily's heart actually hurt that Louise expected to be told off for being herself, and she watched her friend make herself turn around and smile.

'Hiya,' Louise said. 'I'm just asking Emily to cross her legs tomorrow, but any time after that is fine.'

'How Emily's temperature?'

'All normal. I'm actually on my lunch break.'

'Oh,' Anton said, and left them to it. 'Sorry for interrupting.'

'Why won't you give the two of you a chance?' Emily said. 'Why can't you believe—?'

'Because I stopped believing,' Louise said. 'I want to believe—I want to believe that we might be able to work, that we're as right for each other, as I sometimes feel we are. I just don't know how to start.'

'Have you told him what happened last Christmas?'

'I don't know how to.'

'He needs to know, Louise. If you two are to stand a chance then you have to somehow tell him.'

Louise shook her head. 'I don't want to talk about it ever again.'

'Why don't you ask Anton to come along tomorrow?'

'Good God, no!'

'Think about it—you at your tarty best. What would Wesley have done?'

'I shudder to think,' Louise said. 'Look, I know Anton's not like that. I'm just so scared because I'd have sworn Wesley wasn't like that either.'

'Well, there's one very easy way to find out.'

'I think he's working tomorrow,' Louise said. 'Anyway, don't you want him here?'

'Oh, believe me, if I go into labour I'll be calling him, so you'd know anyway, but please don't leave your photo shoot for me. I know how important it is to you.'

'Okay,' Louise said. 'I still want to know, though.'

'Ask Anton.'

Louise shook her head. 'He's not going to take a day off for that.'

'He's not going to if you don't ask him.'

Louise checked on a patient who was sleeping but in labour and she put her on the CTG machine and took a footstool and climbed up onto the nurses' station where she sat, watching her patient from a distance, listening to the baby's heartbeat.

Anton walked onto the unit and saw Louise sitting up on the bench, back straight, ears trained, like some elongated pixie.

'What are you doing?' Anton asked, as he walked past.

'Watching room seven,' Louise said, and smiled and looked down.

'Are you okay?' Anton said, referring to their conversation in the kitchen that morning.

'I don't know.'

'I know you don't and that's okay.'

'Can you help me down?' Louise asked cheekily, and watched as he glanced at the footstool. 'Whoops!' She kicked away the footstool and Anton smiled and helped her down. The brief contact, the feel of his hands on her waist stirred her senses and made her long to break her self-imposed isolation. She just didn't know how.

'I know we need to talk,' Louise said. 'I just don't know when.'

'That's fine.'

A patient buzzed and he let her go.

'Hello, Carmel,' Louise said, and then saw that Carmel wasn't in bed but in the bathroom, and the noise she was making had Louise instantly push the bell before even going to investigate.

'There's something there,' Carmel said. She was deep-squatting and Emily pulled on gloves with her heart in her mouth. Carmel's baby was breech, and if it was a cord prolapse then it was dire indeed.

Louise pressed the bell in the bathroom in three short bursts as she knelt.

Thankfully it wasn't the cord. Instead two little legs were hanging out. 'Call Stephanie,' Louise said, as Brenda popped her head in the door.

'She's delivering someone,' Brenda said. 'I'll get Anton and the cart.'

'You,' Louise said to Carmel, 'are doing amazingly.' The baby was dangling and it was the hardest thing not to interfere. Instinct meant you wanted traction, to get the head out, but Louise breathed through it, her hands hovering to catch the baby.

She heard or rather sensed that it was Anton who had come in and she went to move aside but he just knelt behind Louise. 'Well done, Carmel,' Anton said.

Louise felt his hand on her shoulder as patiently they waited for Mother Nature to take her course.

It was just so lovely and quiet. Brenda came in with the cart and stood back. There was a baby about to be born and everyone just let it happen.

Patience was a necessary virtue here.

'That's it,' Louise said. 'Put your hands down and feel your baby,' she said, as the baby simply dropped, and Carmel let out a moan as her baby was delivered into her own and Louise's hands.

'Well done,' Anton said, as Brenda went and got a hot blanket and wrapped it around the mother and infant.

Stephanie arrived then, smiling delightedly.

'Well done, Carmel!'

It had been so nice, so lovely and so much less scary with Anton there—a lovely soft birth. Louise's eyes were glittering with happy tears as finally Carmel was back in bed with her husband beside her and her baby in her arms.

It was lovely to see them all cosy and happy.

'It looks like you might get that Christmas at home after all.' Louise smiled.

'Oh, I'm going home tomorrow,' Carmel said. 'Nothing's going to stop us having the Christmas we want now.'

Later, in the kitchen, pulling a teabag from her scrubs to make Carmel her only fantastic cup of hospital tea, she saw the hotel card that she had brought in to give Emily.

Was it a ridiculous idea to ask him to be there tomorrow? Did she really have to put him through some strange test?

Yet a part of Louise wanted him to see the other side of her also.

She walked out and saw Anton sitting at the desk, writing up his notes.

'Are you working tomorrow?' Louise asked.

'I am.'

She put the card down.

'It's my photo shoot tomorrow from ten till seven— see if you can get away for an hour or so. I'll leave your name at Reception.'

Anton read the address and then looked up but Louise was gone.

CHAPTER FIFTEEN

IT REALLY WAS the best job in the world.

Well, apart from midwifery, which Louise absolutely loved, but this was the absolutely cherry on the cake, Louise thought as she looked in the mirror.

Her hair was all backcombed and coiffed, her eyes were heavy with black eyeliner and she had lashings of red lipstick on.

All her body was buffed and oiled and then she'd had to suffer the hardship of putting on the most beautiful underwear in the world.

It was such a dark red that it was almost black and it emphasised the paleness of her skin.

And she got to keep it!

Louise smiled at herself in the mirror.

'Okay, they're ready for you, Louise.'

Now the hard work started.

She stepped into the presidential suite and took off her robe and there was Jeremy in bed, looking all sexy and rumpled but very bored with it all, and there, in the lounge, was Anton.

Oh! She had thought he might manage an hour, she hadn't been expecting him to be here at the start.

He gave her a smile of encouragement and Louise let out a breath and smiled back.

'On the bed, Louise,' Roxy, the director said.

'Morning, Jeremy.' Louise smiled. She had worked with him many times.

'Good morning, Louise.'

It was fun, though it was actually very hard work. There were loads of costume changes and not just for Louise—Jeremy kept having to have his shirt changed as Louise's lipstick wiped off. Cold cream too was Jeremy's friend as her lips left their mark on his stomach.

And not once did Anton frown or make her feel awkward.

As evening fell, the drapes were opened to show London at its dark best, though the Christmas lights would be edited out. This was for Valentine's Day after all.

'He's just home from work,' Roxy said. 'Flowers in hand but there's no time to even give them…'

'Okay.'

Jeremy lifted her up and she wrapped her legs around his hips and crossed her ankles as Roxy gave Jeremy a huge bouquet of dark red roses to hold.

'A bit lower, Louise.'

Louise obliged and as she wiggled her hips to get comfortable on Jeremy's crotch she made everyone, including Anton, laugh as she alluded to his complete lack of response. 'You are so-o-o gay, Jeremy!'

Anton had stayed the whole day. Louise could not believe he'd swapped shifts for her and, better still, clearly Emily's baby was behaving.

At the end of the shoot she put on her robe, feeling dizzy and elated, clutching a huge bag of goodies and ready to head to a smaller room to get changed. Anton joined her and they shared a kiss in the corridor.

'Do you want me to hang up my G-string?' Louise asked, between hot, wet kisses.

'God, no,' Anton said.

'You really don't mind?'

'Mind?' Anton said, not caring what he did to her lipstick.

They were deep, deep kissing and she loved the feel of his erection pressing into her, and then she pulled back and smiled—they must look like two drunken clowns.

'I've booked a room,' Anton said.

'Thank God!'

They made it just past the door. Her robe dropped, her back to the wall, Louise tore at his top because she wanted his skin. Louise worked his zipper and freed him, still frantically kissing as she kicked her panties off. Anton's impatient hands dealt swiftly with a condom and then he lifted her. Louise wrapped her legs around him and crossed her ankles far more naturally this time. She was on the edge of coming as she lowered herself onto him but he slowed things right down as he thrust into her because what he had to say was important.

'I am crazy for you, Louise, and I don't want to change a single thing.'

'I know,' Louise said, 'and I'm crazy about you too.'

She couldn't say more than that because her mouth gave up on words and gave in to the throb between her legs. The wall took her weight then as Anton bucked into her, a delicious come ensuing for them both. Then afterwards, instead of letting her down, he walked her to the bed and let her down there.

'We're going to sort this out, Louise.'

'I know we will.' Louise nodded, except she didn't want to ruin their day with tales of yesterday and it was Christmas tomorrow and Louise didn't want to ruin that again, so instead she smiled.

'I need carbs.'

They shared a huge bowl of pasta, courtesy of room service, and then Louise, who had been up since dawn, fell asleep in his arms. Better than anything, though, was the man who, when anyone else would have been snoring, lay restless beside her and finally kissed her shoulder.

'I'm going to pop into the hospital,' Anton said. 'I've got two women—'

'Go,' Louise said, knowing how difficult it must have been to swap his shift today. 'Call me if something happens with Emily.'

'You don't mind me going in?'

She'd have minded more if he hadn't.

CHAPTER SIXTEEN

TWO PATIENTS WERE on his mind this Christmas Eve and Anton walked into the ward and chatted with Evie.

'Hazel's asleep,' Evie said, as he went through the charts. 'I'd expect you to be called in any time soon, though.'

'How about Emily?'

'Hugh's in with her, he's on call tonight. Stephanie looked in on her an hour ago and there's been no change.'

'Thanks.'

He let Hazel sleep. Anton knew now he would be called if anything happened but, for more social reasons, he tapped on the open door of the royal suite.

'Hi, Anton,' Hugh said. 'All's quiet here.'

'That's good.'

'How was your day off?' Emily asked.

'Good.'

'I was just going to check on a patient.' Hugh stood and yawned.

'I could say the same,' Anton said, 'but I wanted to check in on Emily too.'

'Is this a friendly visit, Anton?' Emily asked when Hugh had left.

'A bit of both,' Anton said, and sat on the bed. 'How are you?'

'I don't know,' Emily admitted. 'I think I've given up hoping for thirty-three weeks.'

'Thirty-one weeks is considered a moderately premature baby,' Anton said. 'Yours is a nice size. I would guess over three pounds in weight and it's had the steroids.'

'How long would it be in NICU?'

'Depends,' Anton said. 'Five weeks, maybe four if all goes well.' He knew this baby was coming and so Anton prepared Emily as best he could. 'All going well with a thirty-one-weeker means there will be some bumps—jaundice, a few apnoea attacks, runs of bradycardia. All these we expect as your baby learns to regulate its temperature and to feed…' He went through it all with her, and even though Emily had been over and over it herself he still clarified some things.

Not once had she cried, Anton thought.

Not since he had done the scan after her appendectomy had he seen Emily shed a tear.

'You can ask me anything,' Anton offered, because she was so practical he just wanted to be sure there was nothing on her mind that he hadn't covered.

'Anything?' Emily said.

'Of course.'

'How was the photo shoot?'

Anton smiled. 'I walked into that one, didn't I?'

'You did.'

'Louise was amazing.'

'She is.'

'Yet,' Anton ventured, 'for someone who is so open

about everything, and I mean *everything*, she's very private too…'

'Yes.'

'I'm not asking you to tell me anything,' Anton said.

'You just want her to?'

Anton nodded and then said, 'I want her to feel able to.'

CHAPTER SEVENTEEN

LOUISE OPENED HER eyes to a dark hotel room on Christmas morning and glanced at the time. It was four a.m. and no Anton.

She lay there remembering this time last year but even though she was alone it didn't feel like it this time, especially when the door opened gently and Anton came in quietly.

'Happy Christmas,' Louise said.

'Buon Natale,' Anton said, as he undressed.

'How's Emily?'

'Any time now,' Anton said. 'I was just about to come back here when another patient went into labour.'

'Hazel?' Louise sleepily checked.

'A little girl,' Anton said. 'She's in NICU but I'm very pleased with how she is doing.'

'A nice way to start Christmas,' Louise said, as he slid into bed and spooned into her.

His hands were cold and so was his face as he dropped a kiss on her shoulder.

'Scratch my back with your jaw.'

He obliged and then, without asking, scratched the back of her neck too, his tongue wet and probing, his jaw all lovely and stubbly, and his hand stroking her very close to boiling.

'Did you stop for condoms?'

'No,' Anton said. 'We have one left.'

'Use it wisely, then.' Louise smiled, though she didn't want his hand to move for a second and as Anton sheathed himself Louise made the beginning of a choice—she would have to go on the Pill. They were both so into each other that common sense was elusive, but she stopped thinking then as she felt him nudging her entrance. Swollen from last night and then swollen again with want, it was Louise who let out a long moan as he took her slowly from behind. His hand was stroking her breast and she craned her neck for his mouth.

He could almost taste her near orgasm on her tongue as it hungrily slathered his. He was being cruel, the best type of cruelty because she was going to come now and he'd keep going through it. She almost shot out of her skin as it hit, and she wished he would stop but she also wished he wouldn't. It was so deliciously relentless, there was no come down. Anton started thrusting faster, driving her to the next, and then he stilled and she wondered why because they were just about there...

'No way,' Louise said, hearing his phone. 'Quickly...'

Oh, he tried, but it would not stop ringing. 'Sorry...' Anton laughed at her urgency, because sadly it was his special phone that was ringing. The one for his special Anton patients. And a very naked Louise lay there as he took the call.

'Get used to it,' Anton said as he was connected, and then he hesitated, because if he was telling Louise to get used to it, well, it was something he'd never said before. There was no time to dwell on it, though, as he listened to Evie.

'I'll be there in about fifteen minutes. Thank you for letting me know.' He ended the call. 'Are you coming in with me to deliver a Christmas baby?'

'Emily!'

'Waters just fully broke...'

'Oh, my goodness...'

'She's doing well. Hugh's on his way in but things are going to move quite fast.'

They had the quickest shower ever and then Anton drove them through London streets on a wet, pre-dawn Christmas morning and he got another phone call from the ward. He asked for them to page the anaesthetist for an epidural as that could sometimes slow things down and also, despite the pethidine she'd been given, Emily was in a lot of pain.

'She'll be okay,' Louise said, only more for herself. 'I'm so scared, Anton,' Louise admitted. 'I really am.'

'I know, but she's going to be fine and so is the baby.' There was no question for Anton, they *had* to be okay. 'Big breath,' Anton said.

'I'm not the one in labour.'

It had just felt like it for a moment, though.

Oh, she was terrified for her friend but Louise was at her sparkly best as she and Anton walked into the delivery ward.

'Oh!' Emily smiled in delighted surprise because it was only five a.m. after all.

'The mobile obstetric squad has arrived,' Louise teased. 'Aren't you lucky that it's us two on?' She smiled and gave Emily a cuddle. 'Oh, hi, Hugh!' Louise winked and noted he was looking a bit white. 'Merry Christmas!'

'Hi, Louise.' Hugh was relieved to see them both too.

'I want an epidural,' Emily said.

'It's on its way. I've already paged Rory. We want to slow this down a little,' Anton explained while examining her, 'and an epidural might help us to do that. You've got a bit of a way to go but because the baby is small you don't have to be fully dilated.'

'I'm scared,' Emily admitted.

'You're going to meet your baby,' Louise said, and she gave Emily's hand a squeeze. 'Let us worry for you, okay? We're getting paid after all.'

Emily nodded.

'NICU's been notified?' Anton checked, and then gave an apologetic smile when Evie rolled her eyes and nodded, and Anton answered for her. 'Of course they have.'

There was a knock on the door and Emily's soon-to-be-favourite person came in.

'Hi, lovely Emily,' Rory said. 'We meet again.'

'Oh, yes,' Louise recalled. 'Rory knocked you out when you had your appendix.'

'Hopefully this will slow things down enough that I miss Christmas dinner,' Louise joked, though they all knew this baby would be born by dawn.

A little high on pethidine, a little ready to fix the world, very determined not to panic about the baby, Emily decided she had the perfect solution, the perfect one to show Louise how wonderful and not controlling or jealous Anton was.

And the man delivering your premature baby had to be seriously wonderful, Emily decided!

'Tell them about your Christmas dinner last year,' Emily said, as Louise sat her up and put her legs over the edge of the bed and then pulled Emily in for an epidural cuddle.

'Relax,' Hugh said, stroking Emily's hair as she leant on Louise, while Rory located the position on Emily's spine.

But Emily didn't want to relax, she wanted this sorted now!

'Tell them!' Emily shouted, and Louise shared a little 'yikes' look with Hugh.

Never argue with a woman in transition!

'I'm going to have a word with you later,' Louise warned. She knew what Emily was doing.

'Okay!' Louise said, as she cuddled Emily. 'Well, I'd broken up with Wesley and I checked myself into a hotel—the most miserable place on God's earth, as it turned out, and I couldn't face the restaurant and families so I had room service and it was awful. I think it was processed chicken...'

'Stay still, Emily,' Rory said.

'She's having a contraction,' Anton said, and Louise rocked her through it and after Rory got back to work she went on with her story.

'Well, I was so miserable but I cheered myself up by realising I'd finally got out of having Christmas dinner at Mum's.'

'It's seriously awful food,' Rory said casually, threading the cannula in.

'You wouldn't know,' Louise retorted. 'The one time you came for dinner you pretended you'd been paged and had to leave. Anyway, I arrived at Mum's on Boxing Day and she'd *saved* me not one but about five dinners, and had decided I needed a mother's love and cooking...'

Anton laughed. 'That bad?'

'So, so bad,' Louise said, and her little tale had got them through the insertion of the epidural and she'd managed not to reveal all.

She looked at Anton and there wasn't a flicker of a ruffled feather at her mention of Rory once being at her family's home.

He was a good man. She'd always known it, now she felt it.

'You'll start to feel it working in a few minutes, Emily,' Rory said.

'I can feel it working already.' Emily sighed in relief as Louise helped her back onto the delivery bed.

Rory left and Louise told Evie she'd got this and then suggested that Anton grab a coffee as she set about darkening the room.

'Sure,' Anton said, even though he didn't feel like leaving, but, confident that he would be called when needed and not wanting to make this birth too different for Emily, he left.

The epidural brought Emily half an hour of rest and she lay on her side, with Hugh beside her as Louise sat on the couch out of view, a quiet presence as they waited for nature to take its course, but thirty minutes later Louise called Anton in.

The room was still quiet and dark but it was a rather full one—Rory and the paediatric team were present for the baby as the baby began its final descent into the world.

'Do you feel like you need to push?' Anton asked, and Emily shook her head as her baby inched its way down.

'A bit,' she said a moment later.

'Try not to,' Anton said. 'Let's do this as slowly as we can.'

'Head end, Hugh,' Louise said, because he looked a bit green, and she left him at Emily's head and went down to the action end, holding Emily's leg as Anton did his best to slow things down.

'Do you want a mirror?' Louise asked.

'Absolutely not.'

'Black hair and lots of it.' Louise was on delighted tiptoe.

'Louise, can you come up here?' Emily gasped. 'I don't want you seeing me…'

'Oh, stop it.' Louise laughed and then Emily truly didn't care what anyone could see because, even with the epidural, there was the odd sensation of her baby moving down.

'Oh!'

'Don't push,' Anton said.

'I think I have to.'

'Breathe,' Hugh said, and got the F word back, but she did manage to breathe through it as Anton helped this little one get a less rapid entrance into the world. And then out came the head and Louise gently suctioned its tiny mouth as its eyes blinked at the new world.

'Happy Christmas,' Anton said, delivering a very vigorous bundle onto Emily's stomach.

Emily got her hotbox blanket wrapped around her shoulders and then another one was placed over a tiny baby whose mum and dad were starting to get to know it.

Anton glanced over at the paediatrician and all was well enough to allow just a minute for a nice cuddle.

'A girl,' Emily said.

The sweetest, sweetest girl, Louise thought. She stood watching over them, holding oxygen near her little mouth as Emily and Hugh got to cuddle her and Louise cried happy tears, baby-just-been-born tears, but then she did what she had to.

'We need to check her…'

And finally Emily started to cry.

CHAPTER EIGHTEEN

LOUISE TOOK THE baby over to the warmer and she was wrapped and given some oxygen and a tube put down her to give her surfactant that would help with her immature lungs.

'We're going to take her up,' Louise said, as Emily completely broke down.

'Can't I go with her?'

'Not yet,' Anton said, 'but you'll be able to see her soon.'

'I'll go with her,' Hugh assured his wife, but Louise could see how upset Emily was. She had been holding onto her emotions for weeks now, quietly determined not to love her baby too much, though, of course she did.

'Hugh, you stay with Emily and I'll stay with the baby,' Louise suggested. 'She's fine, she's beautiful and you'll see her very soon, Emily. I promise I am not going to leave her side.'

Louise did stay with her, the neonatal staff did their thing and Louise watched, but from a chair, smiling when an hour or so later Hugh came in.

'Hi, Dad,' Louise said, watching as Hugh peered in. 'How's Emily?'

'Upset,' Hugh said. 'She'll be fine once she sees her

but Anton says she needs to have a sleep first and she won't.' He took out his phone and went to film the baby, who was crying and unsettled.

'Why don't you go and get some colostrum from her?' Ellie, the neonatal nurse, suggested to Louise. 'Mum might feel better knowing she's fed her.'

'Great idea.' Louise smiled and headed back to the ward.

Emily was back in her room, the door open so she could be watched, but the curtains were drawn.

'Knock-knock,' Louise said, and there was her friend, teary and missing her baby so much. 'She's fine, Hugh's with her,' Louise went on, and explained her plans.

'You just need to get a tiny bit off,' Louise said, 'but she's hungry and it's so good to get the colostrum into them.'

'Okay.'

Emily managed a few drops, which Louise nursed into a syringe, but Louise reassured her that that was more than enough. 'This is like gold for your baby.' Louise was delighted with her catch.

As Louise headed out she glanced at the time and realised she would have to ring her mum, who was going to be incredibly worried, given what had happened last year.

As Anton walked into the kitchen on the maternity unit it was to the sight of Louise brightly smiley and taking a selfie with her phone.

'Forward it onto me,' Anton said.

Louise smiled. He didn't care a bit that she was vain, though in this instance he was mistaken. 'Actually, this is for Mum. She's all stressed and thinks I've made up

Emily's baby. Well, she didn't say that exactly...' She texted her mum the photo and then picked up the small syringe of colostrum. 'Christmas dinner for Baby Linton. I can't believe she's here.'

'Relieved?' Anton asked.

'So, so relieved. I know she's going to get jaundice and give them a few scares but she is just so lovely and such a nice size...'

'Louise.' Anton caught her arm as she went to go. 'How come you didn't go home last Christmas?'

'I told you, I was pretty miserable.'

'Your family are close.'

'Of course.' She shrugged. 'I just didn't want to upset them...'

'You couldn't put on an act for one day?'

'No...' Her voice trailed off. She hadn't wanted to upset her family on Christmas Day and neither did she want to upset him now. Yet her family had been so hurt by her shutting them out. Louise looked into his eyes and knew that her silence was hurting him too. Everyone in the delivery room except Anton knew what had happened last year and if they were going to have a future, and she was starting to think they might, then it was only fair to tell him.

'I couldn't cover up the bruises. I waited till Boxing Day and called Emily, who came straight away. When I wouldn't go to hospital she called Rory and he came to the hotel and sutured my scalp.'

Louise didn't want to see his expression and neither did she want to go into further details of the day right now. She had told him now and she could feel his struggle to react, to suppress, possibly just to breathe as he fathomed just what the saying meant about having the living daylights knocked out of you. The light in Louise had gone out that day and had stayed out for some months, but it was fully back now. 'I'm going to get this up to the baby.' She kissed his taut cheek. 'You need to shave.'

They had a small, fierce cuddle that said more than words could and then Louise said she was heading up to NICU, still unable to meet his eyes.

Hugh watched and Louise did the filming as Baby Linton was given the precious colostrum and a short while later was asleep.

Have a sleep now, Louise texted. Your daughter is and she attached the film and sent it.

A few moments later Hugh's phone buzzed and he smiled as Emily gave him the go-ahead.

'Thanks,' Hugh said, and then he took out a pen and crossed out the 'Baby' on 'Baby Linton'. He wrote the word 'Louise' in instead.

Louise Linton.

'Two Ls means double the love,' Louise said, trying not to cry. 'Thanks, Hugh, that means an awful lot.'

More than anyone could really know.

When Hugh went back to Maternity to be with Emily, Louise sat there, staring at her namesake, and the thought she had briefly visited that morning returned.

She'd have to go back on the Pill. It wouldn't be fair to Anton if there were any mistakes, however unlikely it was that she might naturally fall pregnant. But that ultimately meant, when she came off the Pill again, another few months of the horrible times she'd just been through simply trying to work out her cycle.

Louise knew she was probably looking at another year at best. Could she do it without sulking? Louise wondered. Just let go of her hopes for a baby and chase the dream of a relationship that actually worked?

She walked over and looked at the little one who had caused so much angst but who had already brought so many smiles.

'How's Louise?' Anton came up a couple of hours later and saw Louise standing and gazing into the incubator.

'Tired,' Louise said, still not able to meet his eyes after her revelation. 'Oh, you mean the baby? She's perfect.' She glanced over to where Rory and several staff were gathered around an incubator. Louise knew that it was Henry, a baby she had delivered in November. He had multiple issues and was a very sick baby indeed. She looked down at little Louise, who was behaving beautifully. 'You're a bit of a fraud really, aren't you?'

'Emily's asleep,' Anton said. 'When she wakes up she can come and visit.'

'I'll stay till then.' Louise smiled. 'Can you just watch Louise while I go to the loo?'

Anton glanced over at the neonatal nurse but that wasn't what Louise meant. 'No, you're to be on love watch,' Louise said.

Anton took a seat when usually he wouldn't have and looked at the very special little girl.

'Thank you!' Louise was back a couple of minutes later. 'I really needed that!'

Anton rolled his eyes as Louise, as usual, gave far too much information. When Anton didn't get up she perched on his knee, with her back to him, watching little Louise asleep. She had nasal cannulas in but she was breathing on her own and though she might need a little help with that in the coming days, for now she was doing very well.

'Emily's here,' Anton said, and Louise jumped up and smiled as Emily was wheeled over.

Yes, Louise was far from the tiniest infant here but the machines and equipment were terrifying and Ellie talked them through it.

'I'm going to go,' Louise said, and gave Emily a kiss. 'I'll come and see you tomorrow. Send me a text tonight. Oh, and here…' She handed over a little pink package. 'Open it later. Just enjoy your time with her now.'

She gave her friend a quick cuddle then she and Anton left them to it.

'Do you want to come to Mum and Dad's?' Louise asked, as they stopped by his office to get his laptop.

'Will it cause a lot of questions for you?'

'Torrents,' Louise said, but then the most delicious smell diverted her and she peeked out the door, to see Alex and Jennifer heading onto the ward with two plates and lots of containers.

'Alex,' Louise called, and they turned round.

'They're up seeing the baby,' Louise explained.

'Oh, we didn't come to see them,' Jennifer said, and Louise jumped in.

'How sweet of you to bring Christmas dinner for the obstetrician and midwife,' Louise teased, watching Jennifer turn purple as Anton stepped out.

'Anton.' Alex smiled warmly. 'Merry Christmas.'

'Merry Christmas,' Anton said.

'You haven't met Jennifer…'

'Jennifer.' Anton smiled. 'Merry Christmas.'

'Merry Christmas,' Jennifer croaked, and then turned frantic eyes to Louise. 'We don't want to disturb Emily and Hugh, we were just going to leave them a dinner for tonight…' She was practically thrusting the plates at Louise. 'We'll leave these with you.'

But Louise refused to be rushed.

'That's so nice of you,' Louise said, but instead of taking the plates she peeked under the foil. 'Jennifer, Emily didn't just give birth to a foal—there's enough here to feed a horse.'

It looked and smelt amazing and Louise was shameless in her want for a taste, not just for her but for Anton too. 'That's what a traditional Christmas dinner looks like, Anton.' Louise smiled sweetly at Jennifer. 'It's Anton's first Christmas in England,' Louise explained, and of course she would get her way. 'What a shame he's never tasted a really nice one.'

'I'm sure there's enough for everyone,' Alex said, oblivious to his wife's tension around Anton, and Jennifer gave in.

'Luckily my husband's good with a scalpel!'

It was a very delicate operation.

They went into the kitchen and got out tea plates.

Louise and Anton got two Brussels sprouts each, one roast potato and two slivers of parsnips in butter as Anton watched, fascinated by the argument taking place.

'I don't think Emily needs six piggies in blankets,' Louise said.

'Piggies in blankets?' Anton checked.

'Sausages wrapped in bacon,' Alex translated.

'Two each, then,' Jennifer said, and Alex added them to the tea plates.

'How much turkey can they have?' Alex asked.

'A slice each,' Jennifer said. 'Emily needs her protein.'

Louise shook her head.

'Okay, one and a half,' Jennifer relented.

Alex duly divided.

They got one Yorkshire pudding each too, as well as home-made cranberry and bread sauce, and finally dinner was served!

'You can go now.' Louise smiled. 'Merry Christmas.'

She put sticky notes on Hugh and Emily's plates, warning everyone to keep their greedy mitts off, then Louise closed the kitchen door.

She found a used birthday candle among the ward's Christmas paraphernalia and stuck it in a stale mince pie as their Christmas dinners rotated in the microwave and then she turned the lights off.

'Do you want to pull a cracker?'

'Bon-bon,' Anton said, but they cracked two and sat in hats and, oh, my, Jennifer's cooking was divine, even if you had to fight her to taste it.

'How do you know Jennifer?' Louise asked, as she smeared bread sauce over her turkey.

'I don't.'

'Anton!' Louise looked at his deadpan face. 'No way was that the first time you two have met. Is she pregnant again?' Louise frowned. 'She must be in her mid-forties...'

'I don't know what you're on about,' Anton said, though his lips were twitching to tell.

'Are you having an affair with Jennifer?' Louise asked, smiling widely.

'Where the hell did you produce that from?' Anton smiled back.

'Anton, Jennifer went purple when she saw you and I just know you've seen each other before.'

'I don't know if I like this bread sauce,' was Anton's response to her probing.

'It's addictive,' Louise said, and gave up fishing.

It was the nicest Christmas dinner ever—perfect food, the best company and a baby named Louise snug and safe nearby. After they had finished their delectable meal Louise went over and sat on his knee. 'Thank you for a lovely Christmas, Anton.'

'Thank you,' Anton said, because what she'd told him, though upsetting, hadn't spoiled his Christmas. Instead, it had drawn them closer.

'We both deserve it, I think.'

She felt his arms on her back, lightly stroking the clasp of her bra and as she rested her head on his shoulder it felt the safest place in the world.

'Do you understand why I'm so wary?'

'Now I do,' Anton said. 'I'm glad you were able to tell me and I am so sorry for what happened to you.'

It was then Louise let her dreams go; well, not for ever, but she put them on hold for a while.

'I'm going to cancel my appointment,' Louise said, and she didn't lift her head, not now because she couldn't look him in the eye but because she didn't want Anton to see her cry. 'Well, I'm going to go and get the test results back but I'm not going to go for the IVF.'

He could hear her thick voice and knew there were tears and he rubbed her back.

'Thank you,' Anton said, and they sat for a moment, Anton glad for the chance for them, Louise grateful for it too but just a bit sad for now, though she soon chirped up.

'When I say cancelling the IVF I meant that I'm postponing it,' Louise amended. 'No pressure or anything but I'm not waiting till I'm forty for you to make up your mind whether you want us to be together.'

'You have to make your mind up too,' Anton pointed out.

'Oh, I did yesterday,' Louise said, and pulled her head back and smiled into his eyes. 'I'm already in.' She gave him a light kiss before standing to head for home.

'You're stuck with me now.'

CHAPTER NINETEEN

As THEY WALKED out they bumped into Rory, who was on his way up to NICU to check in on a six-week-old who was doing his level best to spoil everyone's Christmas.

'You look tired,' Louise said.

'Very,' Rory admitted. 'I'm just off to break some bad news to a family.'

'What time do you finish?' Louise asked.

'Six.'

'Do you want to come for a rubbish dinner at Mum's?' Louise asked.

'God, no.' Rory smiled.

'Honestly, if Anton and you *both* come then Mum will assume I'm just bringing all the strays and foreigners who are lonely...' she pointed her thumb in Anton's direction '...rather than grilling me about him.' She knew Rory's family lived miles away. 'You don't want to be on your own on Christmas night.'

'I won't be on my own,' Rory said. 'Thanks for offering, though. I'm going to Gina's to help her celebrate her first sober Christmas in who knows how long.'

'Gina?' Louise checked. 'Is she the one you're—?'

'She's always been the one,' Rory said. 'It's nearly killed me to watch her self-destruct.' He stood there on the edge of breaking down as Anton's hand came on his shoulder. 'Nothing's ever happened between us,' Rory explained. 'And nothing can.'

'Why?' Louise asked.

'Because she's in treatment and you're not supposed to have a relationship for at least a year.'

'Does she know how you feel?' Louise asked.

'No, because I don't want to confuse her. She's trying to sort her stuff out and I don't want to add to it.'

'She's so lucky to have you,' Louise said, 'even if she doesn't know that she has.' Louise let out a breath. 'Who's going to speak to the parents with you?'

'Just me,' Rory said. 'They're all busy with Henry.'

'I know the parents,' Louise said to Rory. 'You're not doing that on your own. Is there any hope?'

'A smudge,' Rory said, and they headed back to NICU and Anton stood and waited as Louise and Rory went in to see the parents.

Anton loved her love.

How she gave it away and then, when surely there should be nothing left, she still gave more.

How she walked so pale out of a horrible room and cuddled her ex as Anton stood there, the least jealous guy in the world. He was simply glad that Rory had Louise to lean on as Anton remembered that horrible Christmas when he'd been the one breaking bad news.

He would be grateful to Rory for ever for being there for Louise last year.

As they walked out into the grey Christmas afternoon and to Anton's car, Louise spoke.

'Rory's right not to tell Gina how he feels,' Louise said.

'Do you think?'

'I do.' Louise nodded. 'I think you do need a whole year to recover from anything big. Not close to a year, you need every single day of it, you need to go through each milestone, each anniversary and do them differently, and as of today I have.'

It had been a hard year, though the previous one had been harder—estranged from family and friends and losing herself in the process. But now here she was, a little bit older, a whole lot wiser, and certainly Louise was herself.

Yes, she was grateful for those difficult years.

It had brought her here after all.

CHAPTER TWENTY

'Ooh…' Louise reached for her phone as it bleeped. 'We do need to stop on our way to the hotel for condoms because it would seem that I just ovulated.'

'You get an alert when you ovulate?' Anton shook his head in disbelief.

'Well, I put in all my cycles and temperatures and things and it calculates it. It's great…'

'You're going to be one of those old ladies who talks about her bowels, aren't you?'

'God, yes.' Louise laughed at the thought. 'I'll probably have an app for it.'

The thing was, Anton wanted to be the old man to see it.

'Where's a bloody chemist when you need one?' Louise grumbled, going through her phone as Anton drove on and came to the biggest, yet ultimately the easiest decision of his life.

'We could stop at a pub,' Louise suggested. 'Nip in to the loos and raid the machines.'

'We're not stopping, Louise. You need to get to your mum's.'

Louise sulked all the way back to the hotel and even more so when they came out of the elevator and she swiped her entry card to their room. 'I've got the hotel room, a hot Italian and no bloody condoms. Where's the justice, I ask you...'

And then the door opened and she simply stopped speaking. For a moment Louise thought she had the wrong room because it was in darkness save for the twinkling fairly-lights reflecting off the tinsel. She had never seen a room more overly decorated, Louise thought. There was green, silver, red and gold tinsel, there were lights hanging everywhere. It was gaudy, it was loud and so, so beautiful.

'You did this?'

'I don't want you ever to think of a hotel room on Christmas Day and be sad again. I want this to be your memory.'

'How?'

'I rang them,' Anton said. 'They were worried it looked over the top, but I reassured them you can *never* have too much tinsel.'

'It's the nicest thing you could have done.'

'Yet,' Anton said, for he intended many nice things for Louise.

They started to kiss, a lovely long kiss that led them to bed. A kiss that had them peeling off their clothes and Louise stared up at the twinkling lights as slowly he removed her underwear, kissing her everywhere.

'Anton...' She was all hot and could barely breathe as he removed her bra and kissed her breasts. Louise unwrapped her presents with haste; Anton took his time.

'Anton...' she pleaded, touching herself in frustration as he slid down her panties, desperate for the soft warmth of his mouth.

'Your turn next,' Louise said, as, panties off, he

kissed up her thigh. Right now she just wanted to concentrate on the lovely feel of his mouth there, except his mouth now teased her stomach and then went back to her breasts, swirling them with his tongue and then working back up to her mouth.

His erection was there, nudging her entrance, teasing her with small thrusts, and her hands balled in frustration.

'We don't have any—'

'Do you want to try for a baby?' Anton said, throwing caution to a delectable wind that had chased him for, oh, quite a while now.

'Our baby?' Louise checked.

'I would hope so.' Anton smiled.

'You're sure?'

'Very,' Anton said. 'But are you?'

He didn't need to ask twice, but the ever-changing Louise changed again, right there in his arms.

'I'm very sure, but it isn't just a baby I want now. I want to have a baby with you,' Louise said.

'You shall,' Anton said, and it brought tears to her eyes because here was the man she loved, who would do all he could to make sure her dream came true.

The feel of him unsheathed driving into her had Louise let out a sob of pleasure. For Anton, it was heady bliss. Sensations sharpened, and he felt the warm grip and then the kiss of her cervix, welcoming him over and over again, till for Anton that was it.

The final swell of him, the passion that shot into her tipped Louise deep into orgasm. Her legs tight around him, she dragged him in deeper and let out a little scream. Then she held him there for her pleasure, just to feel each and every pulse and twitch from them as his breathing made love to her ear.

She looked up at the twinkling lights and never again would she think of Christmas and not remember this.

'What are you doing?' Anton spoke to the pillow as, still inside her, Louise's hand reached across the bed.

'Taking a photo,' Louise said, aiming her camera at the fairy-lights. And capturing the moment, she knew she'd found love, for ever.

CHAPTER TWENTY-ONE

'WILL IT BE a problem, us working together?' Louise asked. They were back at her home, with Louise grabbing everyone's presents from under her tree. 'Honestly, it's something we need to speak about.'

'We'll be fine,' Anton said. 'Louise, the reason I came down harder on you than anyone is because of what happened in Italy that day when it did all go wrong…but you're an amazing midwife, over and over I've seen it. Aside from personally, I love working with you. I know that the patients get the very best care.'

'Thank you,' Louise said. 'Still, if we get sick of each other…' She stopped then and looked at the amazing man beside her. She could never get tired of looking at him, working alongside him, getting to know him.

'I got you two presents,' Louise said.

He opened the first annoying slowly. It was beautifully wrapped and he took his time then smiled at black and white sweets wrapped in Cellophane.

'Humbugs,' Louise said, and popped one in her mouth and then gave him a very nice kiss.

'Peppermint,' Anton replied, having taken it from her mouth.

He opened the other present a little more quickly, given its strange shape, to find a large pepperoni.

'Reminds me of,' Louise teased, 'my first kiss with the pizza man and I'm also ensuring that if we ever do break up then you will never be able to eat pepperoni, or taste mint, without thinking of me. I've just hexed you orally.'

'You *are* a witch!'

'I am!' Louise smiled.

'Then you would know already that I love you.'

'I do.' Louise's eyes were misty with tears as he confirmed his feelings.

'And, if you are a witch, you would know just *how much* I love you and that I would never, ever hurt you.'

'I do know that,' Louise said. 'And if you're my wizard you'll already know that I love you with all my heart.'

'I do.'

'But I'm about to make you suffer.' She smiled at his slight frown. 'We need to get to Mum's.'

Louise's family were as mad as the woman they had produced.

Anton watched as they tore open their presents.

'A cookery book?' Susan blinked. 'Oh, and a lesson. It's a lovely thought, Louise, but I don't need a cookery lesson…'

'It's for charity, Mum.'

'I could teach her a thing or three,' Susan said, 'but I suppose if it's for charity…' She smiled a bright smile. 'Time for dinner. It's so late, you must all be starving.'

They headed to the dining room, which was decorated with so much tinsel that Anton realised where Louise's little problem stemmed from.

At first Anton had no idea what Louise was talking about when she had moaned about her mother's cooking.

It looked as good as Jennifer's, it even smelt as good as Jennifer's, but, oh, my, the taste.

'That,' Anton said, after an incredibly long twenty minutes, putting down his knife and sweating in relief that he'd cleared his plate, 'was amazing, Susan.'

'There's plenty more.' Susan smiled as she collected up the plates.

Anton looked over at Louise's dad, who gave him a thumbs-up.

'Christmas pudding now,' he said. 'Home-made!'

'If you get through this,' Chloe, Louise's younger sister, whispered to him, 'you're in.'

The lights went down and a flaming pudding was brought in and they all duly sang, except for Anton because he didn't know the words.

It looked amazing, dark and rich and smothered in brandy crème, though had he not had a taste of Jennifer's delectable one then Anton would, there and then, have sworn off Christmas pudding for life.

It was a very small price to pay for love, though.

'Family recipe.' Susan winked, as she sat down to eat hers.

'It's wonderful, Mum,' Louise said.

In its own way it was, so much so that Louise decided to share the smile.

'I'm going to take a photo and send it to my friends,' Louise said, as her mother beamed with pride. 'They don't know what they're missing out on!'

Later they crashed on the sofa and watched a film. Anton sat and Louise lay with her head in his lap. Her sisters were going through the Valentine bras she had left over from the shoot. 'There's your namesake,' Louise said, munching on chocolate as Ebenezer Scrooge appeared on screen. Anton smiled. He had never been happier.

He even smiled as Louise's sister wrinkled her nose. 'What's that smell?'

'Mum's making kedgeree for Boxing Day.' Louise yawned.

'What's kedgeree?' Anton asked.

'Rice, eggs, haddock, curry powder.' Louise looked up and met his gaze.

'How about tomorrow we go shopping for a ring?' Anton said.

'Did you just propose?'

'I did.'

'Louise Rossi...' she mused. 'I like it.'

'Good.'

'And I love you.'

'I love you too.'

'But if you're buying my ring in the Boxing Day sales, I expect a really big one, and if we're engaged, then you can tell me what's going on with you and Jennifer.'

'When I get the ring I'll tell you.'

'Mum,' Louise called, 'Dad, we just got engaged.'

There were smiles and congratulations and after a very dry December Anton enjoyed the champagne as he pulled out his phone. 'I'd better ring my family and tell them the news. They're loud,' he warned.

There were lots of '*complimentes!*' and '*salute!*' on

speaker phone as glasses were raised. Much merriment later they came to the rapid decision they would go over there for the New Year and see them and, yes, it would seem they were officially engaged.

Louise checked her own phone and there was a picture of Hugh and Emily sharing a gorgeous Christmas dinner, courtesy of Jennifer and Alex. There was a text too, thanking them for the little pink outfit and hat, which they were sure Baby Louise would be wearing very soon.

There was also a text from Rory and it made her smile.

'How's that smudge of hope?' Anton asked, referring to little Henry.

'Still smudging.' Louise smiled as she read Rory's text. 'It's sparkling apple juice his end and I've been given strict instructions that we're not to say anything, ever, to anyone, about what he said today.'

'I am very glad that Gina has Rory with her,' Anton said.

'And me,' Louise said, and then looked up at the man she would love for ever. 'You do know that you're going to be sleeping on the sofa tonight?'

'Am I?'

'My parents would freak otherwise.' She smiled again. 'Did you know that I'm a twenty-nine-year-old virgin?'

'Of course you are,' Anton said, and stroked her hair. He'd sleep in the garden if he had to.

Louise lay there, her family nearby, Anton's hands in her hair, and all felt right with the world.

Just so completely right.

'I think that I might already be pregnant,' Louise whispered.

'Don't start.' Anton smiled.

'No, I really think I am. I feel different.'

'Stop it.' Anton laughed.

But, then, Anton thought, knowing Louise, knowing how meant to be they were, she possibly was.

They might just have made their own Christmas baby.

* * * * *

MILLS & BOON®

Want to get more from Mills & Boon?

Here's what's available to you if you join the exclusive **Mills & Boon eBook Club** today:

✦ *Convenience – choose your books each month*
✦ *Exclusive – receive your books a month before anywhere else*
✦ *Flexibility – change your subscription at any time*
✦ *Variety – gain access to eBook-only series*
✦ *Value – subscriptions from just £1.99 a month*

So visit **www.millsandboon.co.uk/esubs** today to be a part of this exclusive eBook Club!